JANE AUSTEN'S FIRST LOVE

Center Point
Large Print

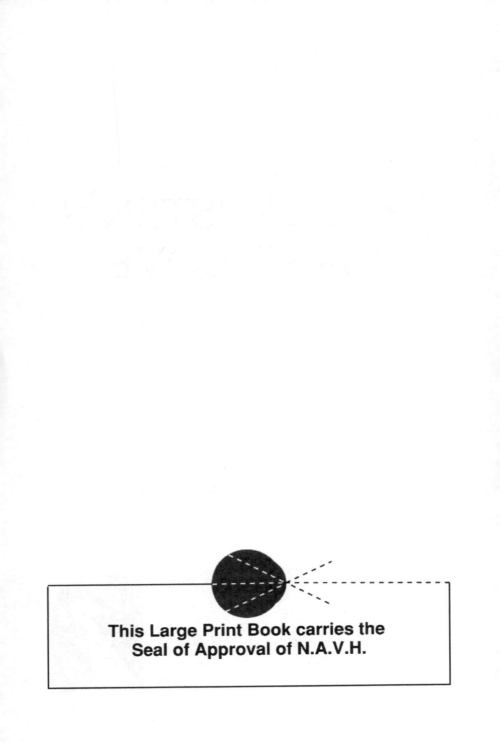

**This Large Print Book carries the
Seal of Approval of N.A.V.H.**

JANE AUSTEN'S FIRST LOVE

Syrie James

CENTER POINT LARGE PRINT
THORNDIKE, MAINE

This Center Point Large Print edition
is published in the year 2015 by arrangement with
The Berkley Publishing Group, a member of Penguin
Group (USA) LLC, a Penguin Random House Company.

Copyright © 2014 by Syrie James.

The text of this Large Print edition is unabridged.
In other aspects, this book may vary
from the original edition.
Printed in the United States of America
on permanent paper.
Set in 16-point Times New Roman type.

ISBN: 978-1-62899-423-0

Library of Congress Cataloging-in-Publication Data

James, Syrie.
  Jane Austen's first love / Syrie James. — Center Point Large Print
edition.
      pages ; cm
  Summary: "Visiting her brother in Kent to celebrate his engagement,
fifteen-year-old Jane Austen meets wealthy, handsome Edward Taylor.
Unsure of her budding relationship, Jane seeks distraction by attempting
to correct the pairings of other prospective couples. But when her
matchmaking aspirations go awry, Jane discovers the danger of relying
on first impressions"—Provided by publisher.
  ISBN 978-1-62899-423-0 (library binding : alk. paper)
  1. Austen, Jane, 1775–1817—Fiction. 2. Large type books. I. Title.
  PS3610.A457J36 2015
  813'.6—dc23
                                                          2014037694

For Laurel Ann Nattress

JANE AUSTEN'S
FIRST LOVE

Chapter the First

The summer of 1791 is so firmly fixed in my memory that I believe I can never forget it; every detail is as fresh and vivid as if it occurred only yesterday, and looking back, there are times when it seems as if my life never really began until that moment—the moment when I first met *him*.

It was a letter which instigated this fond remembrance—a letter I wrote to my sister Cassandra many years past, which she came upon the other day by happenstance. It was a cold morning in late November, and we had recently returned to our Bath apartment following a lovely, all too brief holiday at Lyme. I was setting the table for breakfast, when I observed my sister seated by the window in the drawing-room, deeply engrossed in reading. An open box of old correspondence lay at her feet.

"What are you reading, Cassandra?" inquired I.

"One of your old letters," replied she, smiling. "I came upon this box while I was tidying the wardrobe, and could not prevent myself from taking a look inside."

"My letters? Why do you keep those old things? Re-reading them can hardly prove to make lively entertainment of a morning."

"Oh, but it does. You wrote this one in September 1796 when you were in Kent. Here you speak of a Miss Fletcher: *She wore her purple muslin, which is pretty enough, though it does not become her complexion. There are two traits in her character which are pleasing; namely, she admires Camilla, and drinks no cream in her tea.*" Cassandra laughed softly. "You are a most candid and amusing writer, Jane."

"I am flattered that you think so, but I still say: what is the point of reading my old correspondence? It is full of nothing but useless details which can no longer be of interest to anybody."

"I beg to differ. Reading them is a source of great pleasure for me, dearest." Turning the letter over, she continued, "Look what you write here: *We went by Bifrons and I contemplated with a melancholy pleasure the abode of him, on whom I once fondly doated.*"

I paused, the spoon which I had been holding forgotten in my hand. That single sentence caught at my heart, of a sudden bringing back to mind a person, and a time and place, which I had not thought about in many years—and an attachment which I thought I had long since got over.

Cassandra looked at me, empathy in her eyes. "You are thinking about that summer, are you not?"

I nodded.

"How many years has it been?"

I did the mental calculation. "Twelve and a half years."

She carefully refolded the letter. "They say that memories fade in time—but where particular people and events are concerned, I have not found that to be the case."

I knew that she was thinking of Tom, her own lost love, who had tragically died so many years before. Our eyes caught and held across the room.

"Nor have I."

She came to me, removed the spoon from my hand, and set it on the table; then she took me in her embrace. "You are older and wiser now, Jane. But it is only natural that you should think of him. I know what he meant to you."

So saying, she kissed my cheek, handed me the letter, and left the room.

I sank into the nearest chair, immediately opening and scanning the letter until I found the phrase which was of such interest to me. Then I held the missive to my chest, as a hundred memories came flooding back.

At that point of my life when this history occurs, I had attained my fifteenth year. I was young, I know it; but does age matter? Did Juliet, not fourteen, love her Romeo any less? What of Pyramus and Thisbe's burning passion? Ought we to discount their raw and overpowering feelings, simply because of their youthful age? I think not.

When he was near, at times my heart did not beat to its regular rhythm; in so many ways, I thought he was my perfect match.

To *my* mind, particularly when one took into account my education and the manner in which I was raised, I was, at fifteen, a grown-up person in every way; indeed, I felt as mature and worldly as my sister, who was three years my senior. I was not beautiful, like Cassandra; my hair was far too curly, and neither fashionably light nor dark, but a shade of brown somewhere in between; even so, I received compliments on my hazel eyes and clear complexion, and was often told that I bore a strong resemblance to my father and my six brothers, whom I believed to be handsome.

I lived in the house where I was born, Steventon Rectory, in the county of Hampshire. Although not grand or elegant by any means, it was a dwelling worthy of a scholar and a gentleman and had provided me with all the comforts and joys of a happy childhood. It offered more accommodation than many parsonage houses, making it possible for my father to augment his income as rector by taking in boarding pupils— as such, my sister and I had the benefit of growing up in a house of rowdy boys and being educated at their side. Since Cassandra had finished her studies, and all my brothers were grown and gone except Charles (the youngest, at nearly twelve), the size of the school was much depleted; yet Papa gave it no less attention than before.

We had a lovely garden and a big old barn, where for years my brothers and sister and I had enjoyed holding home theatricals. I had done very little travelling outside of Hampshire, other than two brief intervals away at school, and one family excursion to east Kent to visit my elderly great-uncle at Sevenoaks. I was anxious to see the world.

I had been taking dancing lessons since I was a child and loved nothing more than the idea of a ball; but an *idea* was all it had been, for as much as I perceived myself to be an adult, my mother still forbade me from attending the assemblies at Basingstoke. This was the greatest cross I bore at the time, for I dreamt of three things in life: doing something useful, writing something worthy, and falling in love—and how could I ever fall in love if I had to wait nearly two years before Mamma would allow me to come out?

On Thursday morning, the 18th of March, 1791, I was in my dressing-room, a smallish chamber which communicated with my bedroom and had been especially fitted up for my sister and me. I adored every inch of that room, from the chocolate brown carpet, blue wallpaper, and comforting fireplace, to the painted bookshelves and cheerful striped curtains, for it was a place of quiet and refuge, where I could write in privacy and peace.

I was seated at the small table between the windows, above which hung a looking-glass and our Tonbridge-ware work-boxes, thoroughly engaged in composing a little play I had entitled *The Visit*, and was just considering the next line to be spoken, when I heard the tread of footsteps on the stairs and my mother's voice ringing out:

"Jane! Jane! Come down! You are needed!"

"I am writing, Mamma!" I doubted very much that my reply would hold much weight with her, and sadly this proved to be the case.

My mother entered the room and stopped beside me, shaking her head and clicking her tongue. "Look at you, bent over that table like an interrogation point—do sit up straight, Jane!"

Like myself, my mother was of middle height, and spare and thin; I never understood her personal assertion that she had never been handsome, for with her bright gray eyes, her aristocratic face and nose, and her shiny dark hair (which had retained its colour, although she was two-and-fifty) I thought her attractive. Although at times her behaviour mortified and infuriated me, I loved her dutifully, for she was a clever, honourable woman who worked hard to manage our busy household. However, to my everlasting distress, although she doted on her other children, she seemed to have singled me out as the one with whom to persistently find fault.

"Jane, put down your pen and come downstairs; we have work to do."

"What kind of work?"

"I told you at breakfast! We still have all those shirts to make for Charles, and two new pairs of breeches, and who knows how many handkerchiefs. Cassandra and I have been working all morning, and with only two pairs of hands, it is slow going."

My brother Charles was a cheerful, sweet-tempered, affectionate boy, who had chosen to follow in my brother Frank's footsteps, and was to start at the Naval Academy at Portsmouth a few months hence. We had been sewing his new clothes for months, and although I was very happy to assist in the occupation, I saw no reason to interrupt my writing at that precise moment for such a task.

"Mamma: Charles is not going away until July. We have plenty of time."

"The time will fly by, Jane. Even if we sew every day between now and July, we will be lucky if we finish it all before he leaves."

"May I come down in an hour, Mamma? I am right in the middle of the most amazing scene: eight people are crowded into a tiny drawing-room which only has chairs for six. Two large persons will be obliged to sit on the laps of others—only imagine the hilarity which will ensue!"

"That can wait, Jane; this cannot."

"But, Mamma! I have the whole dialogue in my head. If I stop now, I will forget! Did Shakespeare's mother interrupt *his* efforts with a pen? Did Mozart's father oblige *him* to sew gowns for his sister?"

My mother raised her eyes heavenward. "I know how much you enjoy your writing, Jane. Lord knows, we all love a good laugh now and then, and if anyone understands the pleasures of composition, it is *I*—I flatter myself that my poetry is not entirely unreadable—but it is only a hobby, Jane: an amusement for the family. We are neither of us Mozart nor Shakespeare."

I could not argue with that assessment. The short stories and plays I had written were only fluff and nonsense which I composed to amuse myself and my family. When it came to literary talent, *that* honour belonged to my brothers James and Henry, who had demonstrated their brilliance by editing a newspaper while at Oxford.

"I write because I cannot help it," said I.

"I understand; but that does not make it important. What *is* important is that you improve and perfect your needlework skills, Jane, for they will be of infinite value when you have a family of your own one day."

I turned in my chair to face her. "How do you know I *will* have a family one day?" We had always been allowed—nay, *encouraged*—to speak frankly within the confines of our family; outside the home, it was a different matter. Perhaps this was to my detriment, for I often spoke without sufficient consideration, regardless of the setting; but my mother and father said they wished to know what was on our minds. "*That* will only happen if I *marry,* which requires that I meet an eligible gentleman—which seems highly unlikely given that you will never allow me to attend a real ball!"

She sighed. "We have been over this too many times to count, Jane. You may come out when you are seventeen, just as your sister did. Your father and I do not wish you to enter society or marry at too early an age."

"Dancing does not necessarily lead to matrimony."

"No, but dancing facilitates the means by which one might meet her life's partner, and is one of several, certain steps towards falling in love. I met your father at a ball."

"I know; but Cassandra has been out more than a year already, and she is not in love, nor even close to engaged. No doubt we shall both be required to attend *many* balls before we each find our perfect match. What is the harm in me starting early? Cassandra and I have done everything together since the moment of my birth; our progress in everything we have learnt has always been the same. Cannot you forget our age difference in this one, particular matter?"

"No, I cannot. Now go wash your hands—your fingers are all black—and come downstairs at once." So saying, she quit the room.

With a deep sigh, I returned my aborted manuscript to my writing-box, washed my hands at the basin, and joined my mother and sister in the sitting-room. I threaded my needle and worked beside them in silence, struggling to keep the conversation between the characters in my play alive in my mind; but my mother's and sister's chatter, and the sounds of my father's Latin lesson issuing from the adjoining parlour, forbade it.

After two hours thus employed, I felt I could sit still no longer. Glancing out the rectory window, I observed that the sun had made a bright appearance, and there was nary a cloud in the sky. After a frigid and dreary winter, the last dusting of snow had at last melted away, and the fields beyond, covered in a sparkling frost, beckoned to me. "Mamma, I have finished the long seam on this sleeve, and made good progress on the cuff. May I stop working now and take a walk?"

"You wish to go out in *this* weather?" She was incredulous.

"The post will not deliver itself. *Someone* has to go to Deane and fetch it," replied I lightly, adding to my sister, "Would you like to join me?"

"I would, very much," answered Cassandra, lowering her work. My sister, a prudent, well-judging young woman, was generally less demonstrative of feeling than I—a characteristic which I struggled in vain to emulate. She was also my dearest friend in the world; I valued her advice and counsel above anybody else's, and loved her more than life itself.

"Well! I, too, am ready to do something else for a while," mused my mother, putting her work in her bag, "but to go out? The roads and fields are all covered in frost. You will catch your death of cold!"

"It is nought but a *light* frost, Mamma," countered I.

"There is nothing worse than a light frost, for it will soon melt away, and *then* you are forced to walk over wet ground. I had a childhood friend whose death was occasioned by nothing more— she walked out one morning in April after a hard rain, and her feet got wet through—she never changed her shoes when she came home—and that was the end of her! Have you any notion how many people have died in consequence of catching cold? There is not a disorder in the world except the smallpox which does not spring from it!"

"Mamma," said Cassandra gently, "you are very right to be concerned, but I do not think there is any danger of the frost melting away today. The fields are still quite frozen."

"We have walked for *miles* over fields far

frostier than this," added I. "We have been stuck inside such a long time this winter. I am dying to get out."

My mother stood, and said, "Well, I can see there is no point trying to talk sense into either of *you*. If you catch cold, it will not be *my* fault. But see to it that you put on your boots, change your shoes the minute you get back home, and then it is back to sewing for the three of us."

Cassandra and I donned all the essential accoutrements, and as we were about to leave the house, my mother cried, "Jane! That shawl will never be warm enough! Take it off and fetch your cloak! Why cannot you be more sensible, like your sister?"

Exasperated, I ran back upstairs and did as bidden.

As we stepped outside, I savoured the taste of the crisp, winter air and the refreshing bite of the breeze against my cheeks. "Is not it *glorious* to be outside? It is cold, but not too cold. Sunny, but not too bright."

Cassandra agreed. "It is the perfect day in every way."

"Yes—well—*nearly* perfect." As we struck out along our usual shortcut—the well-travelled path carved across the half-frozen field in the direction of Deane Gate Inn, where the mail was delivered—I could not help but sigh. "Cassandra: why is Mamma so harsh where I am concerned?

She is ever so sweet to you, yet constantly finds imperfection in me."

"I think it is because she admires you more, Jane."

"Admires me more? That makes no sense!"

"It does. You are ever so much brighter than I am, Jane."

"That is not true."

"The point cannot be argued. It is not in *my* nature to invent clever and witty stories, and relate them aloud in such a manner as to have the entire family laughing into stitches. Mamma perceives how very clever you are; so naturally, she expects more from you."

"That is kind of you to say, but I fear it is not so. I know you all indulge me only because you love me. Mamma insists that my writing is not important. It is expert needlework, she said, which is to be the hallmark of my future."

"Every woman needs to be skilled at needlework, Jane; but regardless of what Mamma *says,* she knows you are *capable* of far more than that; I feel certain of it."

"If that is true—what do you think she expects of me?"

"I do not know," replied she, troubled. "It is possible that even *she* does not know."

"How confusing this is! How I wish I could oblige her! How I wish I *could* do *more,* Cassandra; more than darning stockings and making shirts and writing nonsense for no ears other than our own. Nothing of interest ever happens to me. I should dearly love to be useful somehow, to do something which might make a difference in the lives of others—but what that might be is a mystery to me."

"You will discover it in time, Jane. You are still young."

"Young! How that term exasperates me!" My footsteps crunched noisily against the hard, frosty ground. "I am not so very young, Cassandra. And what does age matter, in any case? How often have you said that you consider me your equal in every way? Oh! If only I were seventeen and out like you!"

"Do not wish your life away, Jane."

"I am not wishing it away; I only wish to be *out*. Do you have any idea how hard it is to sit home while you go off to the assembly rooms without me?"

"I understand how you feel, my dearest; and I am sorry for it."

"There are so few real amusements in the world. Dancing is such a glorious activity! It exercises both the body and the mind, all while moving with spirit and elegance to lively music." Holding out my arm as if to an imaginary partner, I curtseyed, then practised my dancing across the field, making several turns.

Cassandra smiled. "You are an excellent dancer,

Jane—so much more elegant and animated than I could ever be."

"You are too modest. I love nothing more than watching *you* dance, dearest; except, perhaps, dancing *myself.* Oh! We know of parents who allowed their daughters to come out at *fourteen,* when accompanied by their mother or an older sister. Why must I be denied the same pleasures? How I wish I could powder my hair and put on a new gown, white gloves, and satin slippers with shoe-roses, and make my debut at the ball at Basingstoke with you tomorrow!"

"It is not all that agreeable to powder one's hair, Jane; I only do it when I absolutely must, and because Mamma insists upon it. And with regard to your debut—you know Mamma will never bend on this matter. I wish you would not continue to let it vex you so."

"How can I do otherwise?" The breeze whipped the strings of my bonnet, and I pulled my cloak more closely about me as we walked along. "It is so unfair. I am tired of dance lessons with Catherine and Alethea, improving my skills for nothing more than children's balls at Manydown, or snug dances in our own parlour with pushed-back furniture and our brothers and neighbours' sons for partners. How I long to converse and dance and flirt openly with gentlemen I have never met!"

With a little laugh, Cassandra said, "What

appeals to you more? The flirting or the dancing?"

"The flirting, absolutely!" We had reached the opposite side of the field now, and holding up the hems of our skirts, we made our way up the mud-encrusted lane, past the tiny village and the church of St. Nicholas, over which my father presided. "Oh, Cassandra! Every night I dream of meeting a worthy young man who incites all my passions—a gentlemanlike, pleasant young man who is intelligent, thoughtful, kind, and accomplished, who shares my enthusiasm for literature and music and nature, with whom I can converse on any topic at length with spirit and debate—if he be good-looking, all the better—"

"Where are you to find this paragon of virtue?"

"I have no idea—but I have conjured him in my imagination. He must exist."

"I fear you expect too much, Jane. No one man can be all these things to you."

"But he must be! For *he* is the only man I shall ever marry. Were I to meet him tomorrow, I should fall instantly and happily in love with him." With a deep sigh, I added, "But *that* can never happen until I am out. Why cannot Mamma and Papa be more liberal-minded on this subject? Can they truly expect me to wait nearly two more years?"

"You reflect a maturity well beyond your years, dearest. Perhaps Mamma will allow you to come out next year, at sixteen. In any case, the time will pass more quickly than you think—and there is much sense in waiting."

"Do you really think so? I cannot agree. I think a girl ought to be introduced into company in a more gradual manner, so as to slowly become accustomed to the alteration of manners required of her. Was not it difficult, Cassandra, for so many years, to be allowed only to smile and be demure, and say barely a word except to friends and relations, and then suddenly at seventeen to be introduced to society with no real preparation?"

Cassandra coloured slightly; it was a moment before she replied. "I suppose it *was* unsettling."

Our discourse was at that moment curtailed by the sight of two friends, Martha and Mary Lloyd, who were just emerging from the Deane Gate Inn with their own daily mail.

Martha and Mary, who resided at Deane parsonage with their widowed mother, had moved to the neighbourhood two years before. Although Mary, at nineteen, was closer in age to me than her sister, it was the kind, intelligent, and sympathetic Martha, ten years my senior, with whom I felt a deep connection, and who had become my own particular friend. Martha had generously finished my new cloak for me the year before, when my fingers had been suffering from chilblains, resulting from a particularly cold winter; and in return, I had dedicated a short story and poem to her.

We exchanged greetings; and upon learning that the Lloyds had no engagements that afternoon, I inquired as to whether they might like to return with us to the rectory.

"We are making clothes for our darling Charles, for the Naval Academy," explained I.

"Oh! I would be happy to help," announced Martha with a smile. "The endeavour will be more enjoyable if we work together, and—" (with a twinkle in her eyes) "I am certain your mother will not mind."

I laughed. My mother, more often than not, embarrassed me by mending clothes and darning stockings when people came to call, insisting that it was an excellent use of her time. Mary also agreed to join us, and while the Lloyd sisters dashed up to the parsonage to get their work-bags, Cassandra and I retrieved our mail. There was only a single letter, addressed to my father, from our brother Edward.

Edward was my second-eldest brother, and he had led a charmed life. At the tender age of twelve, he had so impressed my father's wealthy cousins, Mr. and Mrs. Thomas Knight, with his charm and sunny disposition, that they invited him to accompany them on their wedding trip, and to visit several times at Godmersham Park, their manor home in Kent. When it became clear that they were not to have any children of their own, they expressed their desire to adopt Edward and make him their heir. My father had initially been reticent to the idea, but my mother wisely insisted that Edward should go if he wished it—and wish it he did. The move had elevated Edward's status into a world of wealth and privilege which he could before have only imagined.

"A letter from our Edward! Why, we are starved for news from him!" cried my mother, when we returned to the rectory. "He is so good, so amiable and sweet-tempered. Any letter from him is always a high point in the day for me. Do read it, Mr. Austen, without delay!"

My father, an intelligent and amiable man of nearly sixty years of age, adjusted the fashionable white wig which curled above his ears, and disappeared into his study. Not long after, he came out to the front parlour, where we ladies were at work, and after calling my brother Charles to join us, said,

"This is a most interesting letter. I see no reason why Mary and Martha should not hear it." He gave me the letter, then sat down in his favourite chair. "You may do the honours, Jane."

I opened the letter and read it aloud.

Chapter the Second

Godmersham Park, Kent
11 March, 1791

My dearest father,
I trust you are well. I have news which I
had hoped to share sooner, but Mr. Knight
has kept me much occupied since my
return from the Continent with matters
of business on the estate, with a view
to furthering my education in such
matters—and we have just returned from
a brief trip to town. Both you and my
mother will be pleased to learn, however,
that in my moments of leisure, I have had
the opportunity to involve myself again
in the social activities of the neighbourhood—which brings me to the purpose of
this letter. I have developed a strong
regard for a particular young lady: Miss
Elizabeth Bridges, the third daughter of
Sir Brook William Bridges, 3rd Bt, of
Goodnestone Park. She will soon be
eighteen years of age and was educated
in town. She is an elegant, graceful,
accomplished, beautiful young woman.—
I am honoured and gratified to say that

she returns my affections; for I have asked her to be my wife, and she has accepted.

Here my reading was interrupted by a great cry of thrilled astonishment from my mother. "Engaged! Edward is engaged! Heaven be praised! My first child to be married! I thought it would be James, but no, it is Edward after all, and to the daughter of a baronet!"

"I am so pleased for him," said Cassandra, beaming.

"Did not I tell you all those years ago, Mr. Austen," continued my mother, "that it was for the best that we let him go to your cousins? That it should elevate him beyond any expectations we could ever have for him?"

"You did indeed, Cassy my dear."

"And now I have been proved right! Such a match! It is a great blessing that he is to one day inherit all that property, with Lord knows how many mansions and houses, but to see him happily married, *that* has always been my greatest wish."

"Mine as well, my dearest."

So delighted was I by this news, and so eager was I to read the rest of the letter, that I could yet vouchsafe no comment; but my sister added, "She sounds a most appealing young lady."

Martha and Mary offered their congratulations,

and Charles exclaimed his own excitement; but all were silenced when my father held up a hand and announced in a firm voice, "Let Jane finish the letter, if you please."

All eyes turned to me in expectant silence, and I read on:

Sir Brook and his lady have approved the match, as have Mr. and Mrs. Knight; and my dearest hope now is that you will be as forthcoming with your good wishes. No date has yet been set for the nuptials, but it is Mr. Knight's wish that, (in his words) as we are 'both very young, the event should not take place immediately.' When we do marry, he thinks to give us his small house at Rowling, where we shall be quite content, although our income will be small.

16 March, 1791

Please forgive the interruption in my writing; I received a summons to Goodnestone Park where I spent the past several days, and I have even more good news to impart: Elizabeth's eldest sister, Fanny, is now also engaged! She is to marry a Mr. Lewis Cage, a propertied gentleman thirty years of age of excellent character. It has been decided that both weddings should not take place until the end of the year. However, Lady Bridges feels such happiness at the good fortune of her daughters, that she does not wish to wait so long to celebrate the impending unions. There is talk of a fortnight or more of parties at Goodnestone during the month of June, the details of which are not yet final, but which will almost certainly include an engagement ball, a picnic, a strawberry-picking party, and a Midsummer's Eve bonfire. To these events, a number of relations and neighbours will be invited; and I have been graciously allowed to extend a special invitation to my family at Steventon. I sincerely hope that you, my mother, my sisters, and Charles will be able to attend. Sir Brook generously offers you accommodation at Goodnestone for the length of your stay, and furthermore, invites you all to arrive a few days ahead of the other guests, in order that our families might have time to become acquainted.

Charles, I believe, will particularly enjoy a visit to Goodnestone, as the Bridgeses have three sons still living at home, one of whom is exactly his age; and my sisters will also be in good company with their six amiable daughters. I should mention that Lady Bridges is a woman who, while strictly adhering to the rules of society in general, has somewhat lenient views where her daughters are concerned; as such, and particularly since these festivities are to include only family and close friends, all her children older than ten are to be included in everything (the ball as well); therefore, Jane and Charles are free to do the same.

I could not prevent a little shriek of delight at this last remark; but my mother and father both waved their hands impatiently at me to continue.

Father, I suppose it may be difficult for you to get away in June; indeed, on your account, I would have preferred the festivities to be held in July or August. However the Bridges family leaves for Bath at the end of June, for a stay of many weeks; and I have long been scheduled to take a Scottish tour with Mr. and Mrs. Knight and a few friends, departing 4 July. The timing, however, may prove to be a benefit to you with regard to travel arrangements: for at the end of May, Mr. Knight is obliged to oversee certain matters at his properties at Chawton, and he offers to bring you home with him to

Godmersham, where I trust you will be very comfortable for some days until we remove to Goodnestone. This means that you will only incur travel expenses on your return trip. Should it prove possible for you to come, I will put you in touch with both Mr. Knight and Lady Bridges. Please know that all here would be very pleased to have you join us here in Kent in June for what promises to be a very pleasant and memorable summer.

I look forward to hearing from you. Please give my love to my mother, sisters, and Charles. With every good wish, and the greatest affection, I remain your son,

Edward Austen

My spirits, while reading my brother's letter, can scarcely be described. Two weeks of parties, and an engagement ball—to which I was invited! I would get to see Godmersham Park at last!

"It is a thoughtful invitation," said my father, leaning back in his chair. "What a shame we cannot go."

With those words, it seemed as if all the light and energy had drained from the room.

"What do you mean, Papa?" cried I. "Of course we *must* go. This is an important occasion. Edward is the first person in our family to be engaged."

"And I have six other children to follow. Let us hope that *they* will choose partners who live closer to our neighbourhood."

"Papa," said Cassandra, "if it is the expense of travel which worries you, it cannot be *very* great, as we shall only be obliged to travel post on our return."

"It is not the cost, child. As Edward so astutely points out, I cannot get away in June. School is in session until the first of July. I could never think of leaving a month before my pupils' studies are finished."

My mother looked up from her work and sighed. "If they truly wished for us to come, they would be holding all these parties during our holiday from school, instead of gadding off to Bath and Scotland for their own amusement. It is too bad, for I would have truly liked to go. We have not seen Thomas and Catherine Knight these many years, and we had only those few, short days with Edward when he came back from the Continent. It would be gratifying to be in his company for several weeks on end. If only Kent were not so far away."

"What matters how far away it is?" exclaimed I. "Kent is Edward's *home* now! Are not you keen to see where he has been living all this time? Do not you wish to see the great house and lands that he is to inherit?"

"*I* do," answered Cassandra quietly.

"I have *always* longed to see them," said Charles.

"As do I," admitted my mother, "but may I remind you: duty comes before pleasure."

"My first duty is to the school," insisted Papa, "for those boys' fathers do not pay me to go off on a pleasure trip whenever it suits my fancy."

"But Mamma, Papa!" cried I. "Edward is engaged to be married! How can you give your approval of the match unless you meet Elizabeth Bridges for yourself?"

"That *is* a dilemma, Jane," replied my mother. "But whether or not we approve is of little importance, I fear. *Her* parents have approved *him,* and the Knights have approved *her*. *They* have all the consequence in this matter; our feelings will not make any difference."

"Edward is three-and-twenty now. We must trust his judgement and his choice. And *you* cannot afford to miss a month of school, my boy." Papa patted Charles's knee. "Think of the consequences of so many weeks of idleness; you would fall behind in Latin grammar and all your other studies."

A forlorn look descended on Charles's countenance. "I suppose I shall never see Godmersham now." Asking if he might be permitted to join the other boys outside, and receiving permission, he quit the room.

My heart went out to Charles, and when he had

gone, I said, "Papa, after all these years under your tutelage, Charles must be far ahead of the boys at the Naval Academy where Latin grammar and his other studies are concerned. To miss these last few weeks of school would surely do him no harm." I directed a silent, pleading glance at my sister, who took up my cause and added:

"Think how much it would mean to Charles to go."

"We would be back before he departs for Portsmouth," added I warmly. "It would be a last hurrah for him before he leaves us for so many years. You saw how dearly he wishes to go to Kent! And oh! So do I! Papa, Mamma, we never go *anywhere*. Am I doomed to waste all my days of youth in this humble spot? The Knights live in grand style at Godmersham (or so we are told)! I can only imagine the grace and refinement we should find at Goodnestone Park! It would be thrilling to see their houses and to meet the Bridges family and to live amongst them, *as one of them,* even if only for a short time. I am certain if I were so fortunate as to experience a month in such company and in such surroundings, I should never forget it!"

As I spoke, my mother and father exchanged a discomfited glance. I suddenly felt all the impertinence of my remark; for although it was true that we had rarely travelled, and did not have a great deal of money, we lived comfortably enough.

Before I could voice my remorse, however, my mother said solemnly:

"It *would* be lovely to indulge in that way of life for a little while. We may have given up Edward all those years ago, but he is still our son, and I am still his mother. He has invited us, after all; if I could, I *should* like to see where he lives, and meet the woman he is to marry."

My heart leapt with hope and possibility. My father, reaching out and taking my mother's hand, said:

"Would you, Cassy?"

"I would. But how can I?"

"Just because I am obliged to stay behind, do not let that stop you. If you wish to go, then go; and take the children with you."

"And be gone for a month entire? Mr. Austen, this Mansion of Learning cannot run without me here to manage it! You do not realise all the work which is required to run a household of this size. There are the meals to plan, the bread to bake, the beer to brew, the cows to milk, and the butter to churn—the work in the poultry-yard is never done—and my vegetable garden is at its most productive in June. Were I to leave, who should supervise all that? Who would make sure all those hungry boys are fed, and that they and their linen stay reasonably clean?"

"You are indeed the indisputable leader of this establishment," concurred my father, kissing my mother's hand, "but you would only be gone a month. I feel confident that, for so brief a period, I can find a way to cope. I could perhaps hire a woman from the village to help."

Martha, who (like her sister) had sat in respectful silence throughout this entire conversation, now spoke. "There is no need for you to go to that expense, Mr. Austen. If you wish, I should be happy to take on Mrs. Austen's duties in her absence."

My heart quickened and I sat up on my chair. "Would you truly, Martha?"

"It would be my pleasure—" (adding to my father) "if you and Mrs. Austen are amenable to the notion, sir. I am sure my mother and sister can manage at home without me. I am experienced at supervising a kitchen and poultry-yard. I could stop in every day and do what is needed, and I could look after the boys as well—I do love children, sir—and my sister and I could take care of the vegetable garden—would not you be willing, Mary?"

"I should be glad to oblige," returned Mary with a nod. "Your garden is always ever so much more bountiful than ours, Mrs. Austen."

"Oh!" cried my mother, tears dancing in her eyes. "What a generous offer!"

"You are very good and dear friends," said Cassandra gratefully; and I concurred.

"Martha, Mary, thank you," said my father with

affection and appreciation; and turning to my mother, added, "It seems our friends have made it possible for you to go away after all, Mrs. Austen. What say you? Have you any more reservations?"

"Well—I do not like the idea of being parted from you for so many weeks, Mr. Austen, or travelling all that way without you."

"You will be so occupied every day in Kent, you will not even miss me," replied Papa dismissively, "and as you will be conveyed there in the Knights' own coach, you will be perfectly safe and comfortable."

"How can you vouch for our comfort and safety?" cried she. "We are to have the benefit of a private carriage in one direction only; and *they* are as prone to accident and overturns as any other vehicle. The roads in this country are very bad; the turnpikes—as they have the assurance to call them—are such a disgrace, it is a crime to make one pay for them! Some are full of stones as big as one's horses, and abominable ruts and holes that threaten to swallow one up, particularly at the end of spring, after a hard rain, when they are floating with mud. And there are constant other dangers: highwaymen are everywhere on the long stretches of country-side. Have you forgotten? Did not we read just the other day about a post-chaise which was stopped by a vile criminal, and its passengers robbed of their watches and rings and all their money? Not to mention how prone I am to sickness while travelling—it is such a long journey, I do not know if I should survive it—and the inconvenience of stopping the night at inns which will no doubt be drafty, dirty, have hard beds, and serve bad food."

During this speech, my sister and friends sat with lowered gazes over their work, but the look on their countenances echoed my own silent amusement and impatience.

My father, whose eyes conveyed similar feelings, adopted a grave expression, and said, "My dear, everything you say is true. It sounds to me as if you have talked yourself out of going."

"Oh! But I want to go! My heart is set upon it!"

"Well then, if that is so—I cannot guarantee that your journey will be free of incident or mishap—but these are the risks you must be willing to take."

My mother frowned, then let out a sigh. "All right, then."

Thrilled, I cried, "Do you mean it? We can go? Oh, Mamma! Papa!"

"Jane," interrupted my mother, "do not get too excited. Just because I have agreed to go to Kent, do not imagine that I will allow you or your brother to attend every party they mean to hold, particularly that ball."

A crushing disappointment washed over me. "Not attend the ball? But Mamma—"

"Lady Bridges, it seems to me, has some very

strange notions," continued my mother. "To include *children* at such events—to allow one's daughters such liberties before they are out—I know that *some* people do it, but I cannot approve. Girls should not mix with general company until they are of age."

"Oh! Mamma!" Tears started in my eyes.

Cassandra, glancing at me, and seeming to gather her courage, said:

"You held me back in just such a way, Mamma, and I cannot think that it did me good."

"Whatever can you mean?"

"I mean that—for a young lady to be immediately required on the day of coming out to be accomplished at everything, and to converse openly with strangers, when all the years before she was either kept at home or told never to speak—I found it very difficult, and would not wish the same for Jane."

Silently, I cheered my sister's remarks, and gave her a grateful look.

My mother looked very surprised. "Well, this is an opinion I have not heard from you before, Cassandra."

"I never really questioned it before, Mamma; it is just the way things were. But looking back, I think it was too much to expect."

My mother went quiet for a moment, as she seemed to turn over the matter in her mind. "What do you think, Mr. Austen?"

"Our daughter makes an excellent point," responded he. "Although I still believe that seventeen is a better age to be introduced to society in general, I see no reason why someone of Jane's or Charles's age should not attend the events which Edward described. As for the ball, it is to be held at their house, not an assembly room, and is apparently to include only family and friends; therefore, how is it any different from the dances and parties we hold here at home, with our own family and neighbours?"

After some consideration, my mother nodded. "There is sense in what you say. I suppose we could make an exception, for this one visit to Kent."

"Oh! Thank you!" I was delighted beyond expression.

"Now pick up your needle and thread, Jane," continued my mother with resolution. "Some one ought to tell Charles that he is going on holiday with us in June; and if we are to finish all these clothes, *we* had best stop talking, and apply ourselves to our work."

Chapter the Third

Since the arrival of Edward's letter, hardly anything else was talked of or thought of other than our visit to Kent. Charles spoke so often and with such great excitement of every extraordinary thing which he expected to see and do there (conjuring Kent as a golden land of perfect beauty—a veritable Utopia), that the other schoolboys were soon fed up with him, and threatened to box his ears should he mention another word about it.

The next ten weeks were devoted to a fury of sewing and cleaning such as I had never before experienced in my life, for my mother insisted that if she was to turn over her house to Martha Lloyd to run, it should be nothing less than spotless.

An exchange of letters ensued between my brother Edward, Mr. Knight, Lady Bridges, and my mother and father, confirming all the offers made in Edward's first letter, as well as the travel arrangements. My mother, sister, and I, with kind assistance on numerous occasions from Martha and Mary, completed Charles's new clothes for the Naval Academy with such remarkable speed that when May arrived, we had time to pause and reflect upon our own wardrobes.

"Mamma," said I over breakfast one morning, "what do you imagine the ladies will be wearing at Godmersham and Goodnestone? Will they be splendidly dressed?"

"I suppose they will," replied my mother, as she thickly spread a piece of toast with butter and jam. "I shall never forget the elegance of Mrs. Knight's gown when first I saw her all those years ago, nor her hat, which was the very height of fashion. I have no doubt the Bridges ladies will all be similarly attired."

"What should we wear?" asked Cassandra, visibly concerned.

"Our gowns are all so old and worn." I frowned into my dish of cocoa. "My green one in particular is so washed out as to appear almost gray."

"I have always admired a gray gown," commented my father from behind his newspaper.

"I owned a gray gown myself at your age," said my mother, "a lovely dove gray it was, and very becoming."

"Mamma!" I set down my cup in its saucer with a violent clink. "Papa! How can we attend all those parties and a ball, wearing our old gowns? We will be looked down on as the poor relations! At least my slippers are in good order, but I have mended my gloves so many times that the fingertips are merely strings."

"Do not fret, Jane," returned my mother. "I have given thought to the matter, and although we cannot afford new clothes, if we add some new ornaments to our present apparel, it will freshen them up. Your blue satin gown is still very pretty, and if we add a gold sash, it will do very well for this occasion. I have a piece of white lace from an old gown that will smarten it up even further—and there is a bit of satin ribbon in my work-bag which will be just the thing for your pink gown, Cassandra. We can trim up our best hats and bonnets as well."

"That sounds lovely, Mamma," responded my sister.

I nodded, for her ideas pleased me. "What about our hair?"

"Edward wrote that the Bridges ladies will powder theirs for the ball, so we must remember to bring pomatum and powder, Cassandra—we do not want to offend our hosts by appearing less than genteel."

"Might I powder my hair for the ball as well?" said I hopefully.

"Jane!" My mother frowned at me. "You know better than to ask such a question. Hair powdering is a practice in which you may indulge only *after* you come out, and not one day before."

I sighed. For nearly a month entire I should be in a circle of very fashionable people, many of whom were only a few years older than myself, but at the most formal event, I should appear like the merest child. Oh well, thought I with resignation, at least we were *going* to Kent, and *that* would be an adventure!

We followed my mother's suggestions, adding such embellishments to our gowns as we could devise, so that in due order we all felt some semblance of pride in our wardrobe. A week before our departure, my father returned from

Basingstoke with a surprise: he had purchased for each of us a new pair of gloves.

"You think to spoil us, Mr. Austen," cried my mother, kissing him soundly.

Cassandra and I were profuse with our gratitude. He smiled and kissed me on the head, saying, "I could not think of you going with holes in your gloves, Jane."

As we made the final preparations for our departure, my mother was in a panic, striving, for my father's sake, to ensure that all would go smoothly in the household while we were gone; but after spending several days with Martha going over all the particulars, and witnessing that good woman's skill, experience, and good-humoured attitude in managing such affairs, my mother's anxieties were soon tamed.

The last days of busy activity passed away. On an evening in late May, Mr. Knight arrived as promised in his handsome coach, which was sizeable enough to accommodate all our party, and attended by several liveried servants. I had not seen Mr. Knight in many years, but he lived up to my remembrance as a well-dressed man of fifty-six with a kind smile who, although a bit stooped in stature, yet held himself with a regal bearing. According to the fashion, he wore a gracefully-styled, white powdered wig, like my father's.

"Such a pleasure to see you, cousin. You are

46

looking very well!" cried he, heartily shaking my father's hand. After warmly greeting my mother and Charles, he turned to me and Cassandra, saying, "Who are these bewitching young ladies? How you have grown since last we met!" He proclaimed us both to be beauties, an utterance which, had it been made by a youthful rattle, I would have taken as disingenuous; but the look in his eyes was so sincere that I could only blush and laugh.

We were all delighted with Mr. Knight and passed a pleasant evening in his company, during which he and my parents were engrossed in conversation, going over all the minutiae of our lives during the past several years.

"From the moment my Catherine saw your son Edward," said he to my mother and father, "age eleven I think he was, she fell in love with him, and insisted she must have him. I cannot express my gratitude to you both, for your generosity in allowing him to come to us. Since the very first day, he has been the sunshine in our lives." Here Mr. Knight's voice broke, and he wiped away a tear. "We count ourselves blessed by his presence."

My parents' eyes welled up as well; and for some time we all were too choked up to speak.

When my mother and I pressed Mr. Knight for information about Miss Elizabeth Bridges and her family, he only smiled and said she was a lovely young lady, and as for the rest of the Bridgeses, they were so numerous, and he felt so unequal to the task of describing them, that he would leave that information to his wife to impart, once we got to Kent.

The next morning, we all rose early to make ready for our departure. With great anticipation I watched our trunks being loaded on board the coach, and then climbed within to take my place beside Charles and Cassandra.

"We shall miss you, George," Mr. Knight called out the window, "but I promise to take care of your wife and family as if they were my own."

"I know you will," agreed my father, "for you have done just so with our Edward; and we could not be happier or more grateful."

As the vehicle pulled away, and we all waved at Papa one last time, my mother whispered tearfully, "Oh! This is very hard. I do not know what I was thinking, agreeing to go to Kent without your father! I dare say I shall miss him too much to enjoy a single minute of this holiday."

For the sake of my mother, Mr. Knight planned a three-day journey, so as to spend fewer hours each day upon the road. Even so, the rigors of travel did not agree with her. Although the first day of our crossing was uneventful, the weather pleasantly cool, and the roads dry, Mamma felt unwell almost the whole way, and was obliged to eat some bread to settle her stomach, and to take bitters whenever we changed horses. The motion of the coach had a very different effect on my other companions, who fell promptly asleep. *I* was too excited to slumber, my mind occupied both with the prospects we passed by and all the delights which were before us.

On the second day, a heavy shower made the roads dirty and heavy. The rattle of the chaise caused my mother a violent headache and increased the sickness to which she was prone. Upon arrival at the Bull and George at Dartford, she went immediately to bed. Mr. Knight saw to it that the rest of us were well-fed with beef-steaks and boiled fowl; we slept reasonably well, and set off again early in the morning.

Although rain continued intermittently throughout the following day, we were fitted with a famous set of horses who took us speedily from Rochester to Sittingbourne. The final leg of our journey was accomplished with ease, and even my mother's spirits seemed to revive as we traversed the green Kentish country-side, everyone eager to see those places towards which we were moving. We left the road, and soon crossed a bridge over a slow-moving river suffused with reeds and other vegetation, the length of which was gracefully lined with trees whose leafy limbs bent almost to the water's edge. Moments later as we rounded a bend, I gained my first sight of Godmersham Park through the drizzle.

"Oh! Mr. Knight!" cried I. "Your house and park are very grand."

My mother, sister, and Charles were equally enchanted. Green lawns spread in every direction as far as the eye could see, comprising an immense park studded with grazing sheep. Just as impressive was the house itself, a very large and handsome Palladian brick mansion which fronted a rise of wooded downland. The centre block of the building was flanked by two-storeyed wings on either side, and there were all the requisite windows, ornaments, and chimneys one could wish for, to provide a most pleasing aspect to the whole. Mr. Knight spoke with relish regarding the finer points of the house's construction, including details about the masonry and ashlar window dressings, of which he was particularly fond.

"Is Edward really to inherit *all this?*" said Charles softly in my ear.

I nodded, and replied in a quiet voice, "This is just one of the many properties in Kent which belong to Mr. Knight. And you know he also owns another great house and an entire village not far from us, at Chawton."

"I cannot imagine being so rich," whispered Charles reverently.

Nor could I; but my heart beat with pride and pleasure for Edward and his good fortune. Soon after, we drove up to the house; as if by providence, the rain stopped, the front door opened, and a parade of servants emerged and lined up on the gravel sweep to greet us. The step of the coach was unfolded, the door opened, and when it came my turn to climb down, I caught sight of Edward and Mrs. Knight taking their place at the head of the line. My brother—with his slim but sturdy figure, dressed as he was in a dark, well-tailored coat, satin breeches, perfectly tied white cravat, and shiny black, buckled shoes— looked every bit the charming, aristocratic young gentleman.

"Welcome, Mamma." Smiling broadly, he came forward to embrace her, and then greeted Mr. Knight and the rest of us in turn. "I cannot tell you how glad I am to see you all."

Mrs. Knight was equally welcoming. A well-bred gentlewoman who still retained the beauty of her youth, her eyes were quick and intelligent, and her manners composed, friendly, and sincere. "We have so longed for you to visit," said she, after we exchanged the appropriate courtesies. "I hope your journey was pleasant and free of incident?"

"The only pleasure it afforded me was its object," said my mother wearily. "I have survived it as best I could, thanks in great part to the solicitous care of your good husband, and I confess I have never been more delighted to arrive anywhere."

We were all glad, after such a journey, to be released from the confinement of a carriage, and ready to enjoy all the comforts that the house could provide.

Charles, Cassandra, and I looked on in speechless amazement as we entered the mansion. The high ceilings of the hall and drawing-room were splendidly decorated with intricate, white-painted plasterwork and carvings; white columns and other lavish embellishments surrounded the main doorways; and there were superb marble chimney-pieces. There was an excellent library in the east wing, which I looked forward to investigating further. My mother, who tended to find fault more often than to praise, was visibly moved by all she saw and keen to speak of it. We were all warm in our admiration, and I felt all of my brother Edward's consequence; to be master of Godmersham, I thought, would be truly something!

"It is all so lovely," said I to my sister when we were left on our own in our bedchamber, the yellow room, appropriately named for the warm colour of its paper and furnishings. "A week hardly seems long enough to explore the pleasures of this place."

"True," agreed she, "but the Bridgeses expect us soon at Goodnestone Park—which gives us something else to look forward to. I am sure their house will be very grand as well."

・ ・ ・

The next day, I determined to satisfy my curiosity on particular points with regard to my brother's intended bride. As we all sat down to an early dinner after church, with the butler and two footmen standing at the ready, I said:

"Edward, how did you meet Miss Elizabeth Bridges?"

"We have been acquainted with her family for many years."

"It is only very recently, however," put in Mrs. Knight, as she helped herself to a serving of roast goose from the proffered silver platter, "after Edward came home from his Grand Tour, that he and Miss Elizabeth became attached."

"When I left for the Continent, Elizabeth was just a girl. When I saw her again, at an assembly at Canterbury last November—well." A gleam came into Edward's eyes, and his features softened. "Four years had changed her a great deal." His affection for his fiancée shone plainly on his countenance; it made me smile.

My mother was more vociferous in her reaction, exclaiming in a scolding tone,

"Well! You might have written us something about her, Edward, before announcing your engagement so unexpectedly! But we are ever so pleased for you!" To the table at large, she said brightly, "It is plain to see that he is out of his head in love with her! And that is a good thing, for when you consider all the difficulties which can arise between a couple on the path of life, they ought to at least *begin* by being truly in love."

This remark elicited a laugh from everyone at the table, and a blush from Edward, who lowered his eyes and concentrated on eating his meal.

"What can you tell us about the other members of the Bridges family?" said I to Mrs. Knight.

"Oh! I can tell you our house is dull and quiet compared to Goodnestone Park," replied she. "*There* you will find young people of all ages running up and down the halls, and their parents have a right to be very proud of every single one."

"Do I understand correctly that they have eleven children?" inquired my mother.

"They do. They have five sons all called Brook, and six daughters."

"Five sons called Brook?" repeated I, aghast. "You are joking!"

"It is no joke," replied Edward. "It is a fact."

"But how amusing! Five sons called Brook, when tradition calls for only one! What a testament to the vanity of the father, to name every son after himself!"

"Jane!" admonished my mother with a reprimanding glare. "Think about what you are going to say before it comes out of your mouth!" (adding to the Knights) "Please forgive my daughter, she constantly embarrasses me, she speaks far too freely."

I wanted to sink into the floor.

"You need not apologise, Mrs. Austen. I like a girl who speaks her mind. I find it refreshing." Mrs. Knight's eyes found mine as she sipped her wine, and her look was so kind and affable, I knew from that moment that I had found a friend. "I *do* comprehend why it would seem a mark of vanity for a man to name every son after himself. But there is a long family history behind the name Brook Bridges, dating back to well before the reign of Queen Elizabeth."

"Sir Brook wanted to ensure that whoever inherited the estate," explained Mr. Knight, "whether it be the eldest son or, in the great passage of time, any of his younger brothers, would always be called Brook Bridges. It turned out to be an excellent strategy, for they lost their first son young—he died ten years ago in a schoolyard accident at Eton—and one of their other boys died in infancy as well."

"Oh. I see." My cheeks grew crimson; I was truly mortified now by my outburst, and vowed to *try* to be more careful about what I said in future. "Does not it cause great confusion, though, to have every son named the same?"

"They are called by their middle names to distinguish them," answered my brother Edward. "Brook Henry is called *Henry,* Brook John is called *John,* and so forth."

"Will we meet them all when we go to

Goodnestone on Saturday?" asked Cassandra.

"Not all," replied Mr. Knight, "for their eldest son is away on the Grand Tour at present, and Henry, who was recently ordained, is obliged to begin his duties at his benefice at Danbury, Essex, this very month."

"Sir Brook and Lady Bridges have no love for Eton after what happened to their first-born son," added Mrs. Knight, "so the youngest three are being educated at home."

"What are the daughters like?" asked I.

"They are all graceful, brown-haired beauties," answered Mrs. Knight, "the eldest of whom were educated in town at a prestigious school in Queen Square, and came away very elegantly accomplished."

"How long a drive is it to Goodnestone Park?" inquired my mother.

"About sixteen miles," replied Mr. Knight.

"Sixteen miles!" cried my mother in dismay. "Well! That is a very long way indeed. I had no idea it was so far! And them expecting us in a week's time! I am afraid we shall have to put off going a while longer, Mr. Knight, for after three days on the road, I have done with travelling and need to rest my stomach. I could not bear to see the inside of a conveyance for another fortnight at the very least."

This idea was met with great disappointment and protest from Charles, my sister, and myself.

As I pointed out to my mother, we had come all this way to meet the Bridgeses, and Elizabeth in particular; to put off our visit for another two weeks would nearly cut in half the length of our stay at Goodnestone.

"Besides, they are expecting us for dinner on Saturday," I reminded her, "their annual strawberry-picking party is on Monday next, and the engagement ball is two nights later!"

"I am sorry Jane, but there is nothing for it. You know how ill I have been. While on the road, I could scarcely eat. Even now, I am afraid to take anything stronger than tea and toast, despite the many fine foods on offer at this table. With the state of the roads in this weather, sixteen miles could take three hours—and I assure you, another hour in a carriage would kill me."

Mr. Knight, having only just returned from a long and tiring trip himself, was perfectly content to remain at home another ten days; his lady, however, seemed to read my distress, for she smiled softly, and said to her husband, "Certainly *we* cannot think of going anywhere until Mrs. Austen is well enough to travel—but surely Edward *must* go as scheduled. And as for the other young people—might we send them ahead on their own as well? We have entertained the Bridges girls here at Godmersham several times, without their parents being present. Lady Bridges said her children in particular are looking forward to meeting the young Austens in advance of the other guests, to have the opportunity to become acquainted."

"A sensible notion, dearest," replied Mr. Knight.

"Yes! Yes!" remarked my mother. "It is indeed an excellent solution, Mrs. Knight. Pray, write to Lady Bridges at once, and if she approves of the scheme, let us send the young people on before us."

The described message was sent by post, and a few days later, we were all gathered in the parlour, when a servant brought in a letter for Mrs. Knight. It was from Lady Bridges, expressing her approbation of the proposed plan, and her expectation of our arrival on Saturday at noon, with my mother and the Knights to follow on the morning of the ball. I was thrilled by this turn of events, and looked forward eagerly to our visit.

The week at Godmersham passed quickly and quietly, as if in a dream. Everywhere one looked, there was something beautiful to meet the eye, from the house and furnishings to the prospects from every window. The food and wine were plentiful and excellent in quality, and there was ice with every meal—a real delicacy which we never got at home, and which I knew only the very rich could afford in summer. The weather was not cooperative, with several days of thunder-showers preventing us from making an excursion to Canterbury to visit the renowned cathedral, but I did not mind, for I found a good book in the library and a warm place by the hearth, where I passed many long and happy hours. Whenever the sun made an appearance, my sister, Charles, and I took lovely long walks, exploring the park, the river, and the Greek Temple on a distant eminence, all of which we found delightful.

On our last day the skies opened up again, the rain continuing long into the night, drumming against the window-panes with such ferocity that it awakened me several times. I worried that our trip would be delayed after all; but to my relief, we awakened to clearing skies and the singing of birds. Mrs. Knight was concerned that the roads might be too dirty to travel, but her husband assured her that his chaise was a sturdy vehicle, and the horses were so familiar with every turning of the route, as to be able to traverse it safely and expeditiously.

Edward was so anxious to see his lady love that Mr. Knight gave him leave to ride off with his servant an hour ahead of us, insisting that his postillion would take very proper care of the three of us.

To Goodnestone, therefore, we were to go.

Cassandra and I admired the picturesque country-side as we drove along, while Charles was more enthralled by the manner in which the liveried postillion, rising so regularly in his stirrups, handled the pair of horses.

It was very muddy in spots, yet we made good progress. We had been on our way about two hours when we came to a long and lovely stretch of luxuriant woods, in which the tall, leafy trees at the road-side met overhead, forming a kind of tunnel. After some time passing through this pretty and secluded section, we suddenly burst out into a pleasant, open country dotted with grazing sheep. I immediately observed a lane leading across a vast field towards a distant grove, through which I could perceive the upper story and gabled roof-top of an immense, modern mansion house with a white stone façade, two elegant wings, and many chimneys.

"Sir!" cried I to the postillion through the open window, over the soft plodding of the horses' hooves and the gentle jangle of their harnesses, "what house is that?"

"That be Bifrons, miss," said he loudly in return, "the residence of Edward Taylor, Esquire; been in the Taylor family for generations, Bifrons has."

"For generations?" commented Cassandra to me in surprise. "From what little I can perceive, it appears to be very new."

"It looks very new!" echoed I to the postillion.

"It is, miss! The first house stood here since

Elizabethan times, and all red brick it was, and grown very old. The Reverend Mr. Taylor had it all rebuilt in the newer style some fifteen years past, and very grand it is. The manor house is let out to tenants at present, as the reverend and most of his family be out of the country."

"Did you say the *Reverend* Edward Taylor?" inquired I.

"Yes, miss. It seems he succeeded to Bifrons upon the death of his brother."

"The house looks even bigger than Godmersham," remarked Charles in awe.

"If only there were not so many trees blocking the way," murmured I. "I long for a better view of the place."

Here ended this conversation, for our journey was abruptly interrupted by events of an unexpected and catastrophic nature.

We were proceeding down a small incline, the horses moving at a round trot, when I felt a queer jarring, as if one of the animals had stumbled. The vehicle began shaking dramatically to and fro, and then to our consternation it pitched to one side, sank with a heavy jolt, and came to rest at an alarming angle, leaving all within in a state of extreme unbalance.

"What happened?" exclaimed Charles, as we all struggled to remain upright in the injured vehicle.

Looking out the window, I replied: "It appears

as though we have fallen into a deep and muddy rut."

"Oh dear," said Cassandra, very worried.

The postillion dismounted and glanced in at us. "Is anybody hurt?"

My brother and sister shook their heads.

"No, sir," said I.

With a grunt, he returned to the fore, where he stood in silence, surveying the situation and frowning deeply.

"Should we get out?" asked Charles.

"I think not," replied Cassandra. "It is so dirty. We had best wait and see what he wishes for us to do."

Still on foot, the postillion picked up the reins and spoke sharply to the horses, urging them forward; but although they strained and pulled, the chaise did not move. A few minutes passed thus engaged, with no more promising outlook. I was feeling very discouraged, and wondering how we should ever be liberated from the mire, when I heard the sound of horses approaching.

Through the window of the chaise, I caught sight of two riders coming towards us across the empty fields. As they drew nearer, I became aware of their distinguishing features. They were young men, perhaps sixteen or seventeen years of age, and from the quality of their clothes, hats, and tall leather boots, and the way they held themselves in the saddle, I knew them to be the sons of gentlemen. The first had a ruddy countenance which, although pleasing, was not regular enough to be called handsome.

My full attention, however, was directed at the young man riding beside him, who was so good-looking as to make it difficult to look away.

Chapter the Fourth

"Good morning," said he (his voice deep and commanding) to the postillion, drawing up beside our disabled carriage. "My cousin and I could not help but see your predicament. I hope no one is injured?"

"They are not, sir," responded the postillion.

The young man had a long, oval face; dark eyes flashed beneath arched brows; his nose was perfectly straight; his lips were full and well shaped above a determined chin. His complexion was clear and a shade or two darker than my own, suggesting that he had recently spent time in sunnier, foreign climes, or spent a great deal of time out of doors. His hunter green coat and dark brown breeches were so perfectly tailored as to shew off his fine figure to great advantage; and contrary to fashion, he sported no wig or powder; rather his hair, which fell in a haphazard manner to just below his ears, was as sleek and silky as the mane of his magnificent horse, and in precisely the same shade of deep auburn.

Nimbly dismounting, and unheedful of the mud (his tall, sturdy boots giving him some protection), the young man walked around the vehicle, and bent to study the half-submerged wheels. "From what I can determine, the wheels are not broken, but only stuck in this quagmire. I have already sent a servant to fetch two dray-horses. They should be here momentarily, and can pull you out."

"Why thank ye, Mr. Taylor, sir. We'd be most grateful, for surely otherwise we'll be stuck here till nightfall and beyond."

The young man appeared very surprised at being addressed by name. He looked at the side of our chaise as if seeking proof of its owner, but the coat of arms was obscured by splattered mud. Returning his glance to the servant, he paused, and said, "Are you Thomas Knight's man, of Godmersham Park?"

"I am, sir, and I am honoured that you should recall it; for it has been a good two years I believe since I last saw ye, and even then I was never formally made known to you." Removing his hat, and bowing respectfully, the postillion added: "May I further say: welcome back to England, Mr. Taylor, sir."

"Thank you."

I darted Cassandra a look of surprise. From this exchange, and the age of the young gentleman, I deduced him to be the son of the afore-mentioned

Reverend Edward Taylor, who owned the nearby manor house.

While his companion sat silently upon his steed, young Mr. Taylor asked, "What is your name, sir?"

"Sam, sir."

"Where are you going, Sam? Are Mr. and Mrs. Knight within the coach?"

"They are not, sir. I am taking Mr. Knight's house guests to Goodnestone for a visit, sir."

"Ah! I see. How many passengers are on board?"

"Three, sir. Two young ladies, sisters as they are, and a lad."

"Well, let us get them out. Even with our dray-horses, it will be a piece of work to pull this chaise from the mire, and harder still with three people weighing it down."

Sam pulled down the steps and threw open the chaise door. "You'd best all step down."

Charles moved dexterously to the opening and hesitated, frowning. I perceived the difficulty: the chaise was positioned at such an angle that the doorway partly faced the sky, and the steps led more to the side than down, complicating one's descent; moreover, the road was deep in mud.

"I have got you," said Mr. Taylor; without further ado, he picked up my little brother and carried him to the safety of the road-side.

Cassandra was next.

"Take my hand, miss," said the postillion.

Mr. Taylor's as yet nameless companion (whom I believe he had called his cousin) leapt from his horse and crossed to the carriage's open door, silently offering his own assistance—an action no doubt prompted, I deduced, by my sister's beauty.

Both men held out their gloved hands to Cassandra and helped her out, although so awkwardly as to result in her landing in a deep pocket of mud, which engulfed her feet to the ankles.

"Oh!" cried she in dismay, raising her skirts as she was assisted through the mud to the firmer bank immediately adjacent. In the process, she lost one of her slippers, which the postillion adroitly rescued from the mire and held aloft as if a dead thing. "Oh, Jane, do be careful; I am afraid I have ruined my shoes."

While Cassandra's rescuers quietly apologised at the road-side, and made what efforts they could to wipe her shoes clean on the grass before she put them on again, I attempted to determine my best means of exit; but before I could proceed, Mr. Taylor walked back to the open doorway of the chaise and stopped before me. With an accent and inflection on the final appellation so flawless as to resemble (at least in my imagination) a native Italian speaker, he said, "May I help you down, *signorina*?"

I froze; I could not avert my gaze; Mr. Taylor's handsome countenance was but a foot or two from mine, and his arrival, like a knight in shining armour, had been so unexpected, his eyes were so dark and sparkling, and the overall effect was so appealing, that for the space of a breath, I forgot where I was or that any action was required of me.

"Miss? Are you quite well?"

I nodded.

"May I help you descend?"

"Yes." I cleared my throat. "Thank you."

"I ought to carry you. Otherwise, you will ruin your shoes, as did your sister."

"Carry me?" A picture formed in my mind, as I envisioned his proposal: my arms were wrapped around his neck, and my face was against his silken hair, as he swept me into his arms and brought me to the embankment. The notion caused my heart to beat with more rapidity than usual and a warmth to rise to my cheeks. Such familiarity would be *most* inappropriate—an action reserved for only the most dire of circumstances—which this decidedly was not. "I think," replied I quickly, "I had rather climb down myself."

He looked dubious. "Well then, if you want to avoid the mud, I only see one option. You must climb out past the back wheel and over the rear platform. From there I can jump you down to the bank."

I stared at him in quiet disbelief. "A daring proposal, sir, and one which I imagine *you* could execute with ease. But it will be rather difficult to accomplish, wearing a gown."

"I imagine you can find a way, *mademoiselle*. But it is up to you, and whether or not you wish to sacrifice your shoes."

I paused, considering. His suggestion involved some risk, as the vehicle lay at a very marked pitch; but it *was* admittedly preferable to walking through the mire. Moreover, his tone, and the look on his countenance, seemed to me akin to the throwing of a gauntlet. "Very well. I shall try it."

"Jane!" cried Cassandra from the embankment where she waited with Charles and the other gentleman. "Do not attempt it. You might fall."

"I will not fall," answered I, with more confidence than I truly felt.

Not wanting to soil my new gloves, I removed them and stowed them in my reticule; then, holding up my skirts, I placed my hands on either side of the carriage door, and propelled myself up and out. It was a precarious business; by supporting myself on the large, very muddy wheel, I managed to scramble onto the rear platform and over the trunks, but so precipitous was it, that I nearly slid off. Throughout my exertion, Mr. Taylor stood close by (I suppose to catch me if required); but with the greatest of efforts I was able to right myself, and from there to jump down as directed, onto the bank into his waiting hands.

I was vaguely sensible of a cheer (from Charles)

and applause from Mr. Taylor's cousin; but these sounds melted away, so overpowered was I by the circumstance in which, for an instant, I found myself. My hands were pressed against the soft wool of Mr. Taylor's coat, and his large hands were firmly clasping my upper arms as he looked down at me. There was a fluttering in my heart and stomach such as I had never before felt or imagined, and my cheeks burned—from fear or exertion, I knew not which. Did he feel a similar emotion? I could not say; but during the brief interval in which he held me thus, as his dark eyes gazed down into mine, I imagined that they held a look of deep interest which matched my own.

Releasing me, he said, "There. That was not so hard, was it?"

"Not at all," lied I, relieved that the exercise was completed, that I was safely on the ground, and that there was again some physical distance between us, so that I might regain some semblance of composure. It was ridiculous, a voice in my head cried, to swoon so over a total stranger, no matter *how* handsome he might be; but at the same time, another inner voice exulted over this unexpected meeting—for was it not exactly the sort of circumstance of which I had been dreaming for many years? These inner musings were instantly terminated when Cassandra, shaking her head, said:

"Thank goodness Mamma was not here to see *that*."

Mr. Taylor now turned to her and Charles. "And how are *you,* miss? I trust you both have suffered nothing worse in this misadventure than a pair of muddy—" (glancing down at Cassandra's shoes with mock alarm) "*very muddy*—slippers?"

"We are quite well, sir. Thank you for stopping to assist us."

"Yes! Thank you!" cried Charles, regarding our rescuer with undisguised gratitude, wonder, and veneration.

Mr. Taylor only shrugged his shoulders. "It was my duty. You broke down on the road passing my family's estate. I could not ride by and do nothing. It is just lucky it occurred today, while I happened to be at Bifrons—I am not living here at present, but with my cousins at Ileden, a few miles distant—and a fortnight ago, I would have been out of the country."

"From whence have you returned?" inquired Cassandra.

"From Italy. My family is still abroad." He paused then, and with a smile, removed his hat. "Forgive me, here we are chatting away without a proper introduction. It is very awkward—but I trust that the necessity of the case will plead my excuse—it seems we have no choice but to circumvent convention. This fellow here—" (waving his hat towards his companion) "is my cousin Thomas Watkinson Payler, Esquire."

Mr. Payler bowed, with a particular smile for

my sister. "A pleasure to meet you," said he quietly but elegantly.

With a bow of his own, our rescuer added: "I am Edward Taylor."

I smiled to myself, for Edward was, and always had been, one of my favourite names.

Cassandra curtseyed and introduced herself, myself, and my brother, and when all of us had paid our respects, I asked,

"Do you have brothers, Mr. Taylor?"

"Four of them."

"Are they all called Edward?"

"What? Of course not." His eyes narrowed as he studied me. "What a strange question; why do you ask?"

I felt my cheeks redden. It was not only a strange question, but an impertinent one; what would he think of me? But having started down that road, I was obliged to continue. "The Bridgeses have five sons called Brook," responded I with an impish, nervous shrug. "I thought it might be a tradition in this part of the country to name every son the same."

Taking in my teasing manner, he laughed—a look and sound so congenial, it lit up his whole face, removed all my discomfort, and made me laugh in response. "It is a *tradition,* I believe, only where the Bridgeses are concerned. We have two Edwards in my family, my father and myself— and that is quite enough."

"We seem to run into Edwards everywhere we go," remarked Charles. "We have a brother called Edward."

"Ah yes—so you do!" replied Edward Taylor. "I had the honour to make Mr. Austen's acquaintance only last week—he was not in the country the last time I was here. He is lately engaged to Miss Elizabeth Bridges, is that not so?"

"It is, sir."

"He mentioned that his family was to be visiting from Hampshire—and here you are."

All subjects suddenly ceased, as two servants arrived with a pair of large dray-horses. Edward Taylor ordered the postillion and a groom to unhitch the horses from the chaise and replace them with the sturdier beasts. Under his direction, our trunks were then unfastened from the carriage to lighten the load. At length, the vehicle was successfully pulled from the mire, deemed to be in sound condition, our own horses returned to their former positions, and everything made ready for us to proceed.

Once more we thanked our rescuer, and he and Mr. Payler helped us to climb aboard the vehicle again. I fully expected them to mount their horses and ride away (an idea which caused me a great pang of disappointment); but instead Mr. Taylor gazed ahead with a frown, and said, "It is still a good five miles to Goodnestone; I travelled that way the other day, and the road is fairly floating in places. There are some deep, hidden pockets that may cause grave difficulties to anyone not intimately familiar with them. Thomas: we ought to accompany the Austens on their way to Goodnestone, so that I might point out all the low spots to Sam and prevent further catastrophe. What say you?"

"I have no objection," returned Thomas Payler.

"It is settled, then. We shall be your escort. *Adieu.*" So saying, Edward Taylor shut the chaise door. He and Mr. Payler went directly to their horses, mounted, and we were soon all on our way.

Chapter the Fifth

The remaining five miles of the journey were given over to a minute discussion of the accident in all its particulars, the manner in which we had been rescued—so quickly and with such a minimum of discomfort!—and our good fortune in the acquisition of the two gallant riders who now accompanied us.

"It was very good of them to stop and help us," said Cassandra, "and particularly thoughtful of them to accompany us in this manner."

I agreed. Through the window, as I observed Mr. Taylor on horseback, his hat tilted back, his lips curved in an easy smile, the sight unaccountably made my skin tingle. "I wonder how long Mr. Taylor lived on the Continent?"

"He spoke a few words of French *and* Italian," noted Cassandra.

"He must have many fascinating experiences to relate."

"I wonder what occasioned his family to go abroad?"

"I wonder what occasioned *him* to return on his own?"

"Well *I* am glad he is back," cried Charles with enthusiasm. "I think Edward Taylor the best young man I ever met in my entire life. Did you see how he rescued me?"

"And what of Mr. Payler?" teased Cassandra, nudging my brother. "Do not forget him. Was not it kind of him to help me down from the carriage?"

"Yes, but he *should* have carried you." Charles made a face. "Your shoes are a terrible mess."

"They are indeed. Jane took the better route; and I do think she enjoyed every minute of it."

I felt colour rise to my face.

"Generally you are rather shy with strangers," added my sister, "yet you chatted very easily with Mr. Taylor."

"Did I? I suppose it was the excitement of the accident. I—I was not myself."

"There is nothing to be ashamed of, Jane. Mr.

Taylor is a dashing young man—many a girl would feel as you did if she jumped down into his arms."

My cheeks now burned, recalling the rush of feeling which had enveloped me at that particular moment, feelings which I was not equal to revealing aloud, particularly in the presence of my little brother. I turned to the window and for the rest of the way remained silent, attempting to redirect my thoughts to the object before us: it would be my first glimpse of the family into which my brother was marrying, and I was eager and curious to meet the young lady who was to be his wife. Yet my attention continued to be drawn to the young man riding beside us. Edward Taylor presented a fine figure on horseback; watching him now, as he directed the postillion to avoid unseen hazards along the muddy lane, my stomach was again all in a flutter. What would happen when we reached Goodnestone? I wondered. Would Mr. Taylor and his cousin immediately take their leave? It seemed likely, for what business could they have at the Bridgeses' house? Yet I hoped it would *not* be so—for I wished very much for our acquaintance to continue.

We travelled through fine and level open country, and reached our destination with no further mishap. The property was set in a beautiful situation adjoining the small but charming village of Goodnestone. We passed the church, the farm, and what appeared to be the dower house, then turned onto a narrow lane curving upwards towards the manor house, which sat majestically on a high rise of ground. A handsome, rectangular, brick Palladian mansion standing three stories high, Goodnestone was very grand. I gazed up in awe at the roof, where a massive, central stone pediment was situated between two chimneys. Beneath it were arranged three symmetrical rows of innumerable windows and a handsome front doorway flanked by apertures topped by elegant half-moons. On the other side of the gravel sweep, a flight of stone steps led down to a circular parterre with an imposing central column; beyond that lay an immense, open park bordered by distant, verdant woods.

Our noisy and deliberate approach brought us to the attention of the household, and by the time we halted in front of the door, a large and impressive assemblage of servants, dogs, and family members (including our brother Edward) had produced and arranged themselves for a formal greeting. As we disembarked, I observed that the Bridgeses were as numerous as promised, the six daughters and three young sons all richly attired. I did not yet perceive a woman who might fit with Lady Bridges's description, but the young ladies bore a great family resemblance: all were pretty, possessing the same long, angular noses, rose-bud mouths, and smooth, pale complexions; and their heads were each a mass of long, embellished curls.

The man who could only be the formidable Sir Brook William Bridges came forward. A fat, amiable gentleman of fifty-seven years of age with a florid, jowled face, he walked slowly, his breathing was laboured, and his speech was accompanied by a deep, periodic cough; but rising above these infirmities, he met us with a smile as he shook our hands.

"Hello, young Austens! I am Sir Brook; how lovely to meet you all. You must be Cassandra—Jane—and Charles. Welcome; you are very welcome here." As we bowed and curtseyed, he turned to our companions, and cried, "What ho, cousin Edward. Good day, Mr. Payler. What brings you hither, did you meet up with the Austens on the road?"

This remark was interesting indeed, for it elucidated a relationship I had not anticipated: just as Edward Taylor was a cousin of Mr. Payler's, it seemed he was a cousin of the Bridges family as well!

"We did, sir," replied Edward Taylor. "Their carriage half toppled over just passing Bifrons, from an unfortunate encounter with a quagmire. We pulled them out and shepherded them here to avoid any further calamities."

"A quagmire, eh? Well, that explains why this

poor vehicle, the animals, and your boots are all over in mud!" Before he could comment further, a pale, graceful, extravagantly attired woman strolled through the front door, remarking elegantly:

"Ah! Here you are at last. I was beginning to worry."

Sir Brook sighed. "Please forgive my wife's belated appearance. Lady Bridges is too fashion-able—or fancies herself to be so—to be punctual."

Lady Bridges was, I recalled, forty-four years of age; she still retained the handsome features which had made her a beauty in her youth. "Punctuality, I find, is a highly overrated quality in an individual," said she, as she patted the fashionable white cap which adorned her long, dark curls. "I had much rather be calm and tardy, Sir Brook, than rush about madly as you do, to please a clock. Our guests' arrival was delayed in any case." Glancing at us (with a quick review of our dress, which she seemed to find wanting), she added, "Is everyone all right?"

"They are. They suffered a mishap on the road," said Sir Brook. "Their chaise was rescued by my cousin Edward here, and thankfully all survived with heads and limbs intact."

"Thank goodness for that." As Lady Bridges's glance touched on Edward Taylor, she briefly frowned—a reaction which puzzled me.

"Edward!" cried Sir Brook, "Now that you are here, you and Mr. Payler must stay for dinner."

With dignity, Edward Taylor replied: "Thank you for the kind invitation, sir, but we are not dressed for dinner, and our boots are in no condition to enter your hall."

"Nonsense! Your coats are easily brushed and pressed, boys, and Andrew will shine your boots while we play a game of billiards—I believe you owe me a chance to win back my half-crown."

Mr. Taylor hesitated; but upon observing Lady Bridges's silent acquiescence and Mr. Payler's unspoken assent, he said, "Thank you, sir. We should be happy to stay."

The riders dismounted and waved off the groom, insisting that they would stable their horses themselves; they then walked off deliberately, clearly familiar with the place.

I watched them go, unable to contain my smile.

To perceive that Edward Taylor was so well known to Sir Brook and Lady Bridges—indeed, was *related* to them, and apparently very well liked by him—was agreeable indeed; but most importantly: he was staying to dinner! If I was lucky, I might have a chance to converse with him again!

Further contemplations of Mr. Taylor were cut short when my brother Edward stepped forward to make the formal introductions, beginning with Lady Bridges.

"It is a pleasure to meet the sisters of our Elizabeth's fiancé," said Lady Bridges, holding out her hand to Cassandra and me. "It is a shame that your mother and Mr. and Mrs. Knight were obliged to put off their appearance; but I am thankful that *you* were able to arrive before the main festivities begin, and the neighbours descend on us."

"We are grateful to you for your kind hospitality," said Cassandra, a sentiment I echoed, and to which Lady Bridges replied:

"Sir Brook was not *quite* truthful when he said you suffered no casualties on the road, my dear. Your slippers and stockings are a sight."

"Sadly," returned Cassandra, colouring, "the only other pair I brought are my dancing shoes."

"A good pair of shoes will be procured for you—surely one of my daughters' feet will be your size." Turning to Charles, Lady Bridges said, "How do *you* do, little man? There is no doubt that *you* are Edward's brother, for you greatly favour him. I have a son almost exactly your age, who has been anxious to meet you." She called to her own boy, a well-behaved but grave little fellow who was introduced as "Edward," to which Charles replied with a laugh,

"Not another Edward! My *brother* is Edward; *Mr. Taylor* is Edward; I shall never be able to keep all of you straight!"

"Well, I have two names," responded the lad.

"You may call me Brook Edward, if you like."

"Thank you, sir," said Charles. "That will do very nicely."

From that moment on, and for several years after, I could think of Brook Edward Bridges with no other appellation.

Our trunks by now had been unfastened from the chaise, and as the vehicle was driven away to the stables, Lady Bridges glanced at it in some perplexity. "Where is your maid? Has not she come with you?"

"No, ma'am," replied my sister. "We have no lady's maid. We dress ourselves."

"Indeed? Well, that will not do at *Goodnestone*." (Her hand on her chest in dismay.) "Not in the home of the heiress to the title *Baron Fitzwalter*. But we have more than enough maids to go around, and will be happy to share."

My brother Edward now introduced the daughters of the family. Fanny, the eldest at twenty, offered her hand to us with a faint smile. "I am flattered that you came all this way— from Hampshire, is it?—to honour me and my betrothal." (An afterthought:) "And my sister's. It is going to be quite a summer! I do hope our festivities will exceed all your expectations, and that you will go home with happy memories of your visit."

This speech was extraordinary to me, as it was so self-satisfied, and so neatly encapsulated the entirety of our stay, while already anticipating our departure.

It was apparent, even before her name was pronounced, that the next young lady brought forward was my brother's intended; for his broad smile, the deep affection in his gaze, and the manner in which he held her hand, proclaimed his adoration. It was not difficult to understand why Elizabeth had bewitched my brother. Although she was no prettier than her sisters, there was an air of elegance and confidence about her, which revealed her *self-awareness* of her own beauty, femininity, and charms, as well as the effect of those charms on others. That charm did not appear to reach great depths, however; for her soft voice appeared more to convey a discharge of a duty to *appear* welcoming, rather than a sincere reflection of the emotion.

The remaining Bridges daughters were very different from the first two, and all most amiable. Sophia was nineteen, and Marianne sixteen. Both possessed pleasant and cheerful dispositions, and an openness of manner which drew me to them immediately.

"Since we are soon to be sisters," said Sophia with enthusiasm, "shall we dispense with the formalities and go by our Christian names?"

"That would be wonderful," agreed I. "Surely it will make us *feel* like sisters ever so much sooner."

We admired Louisa, age thirteen, and Harriot, ten, who looked very sweet. The lively dispositions of the youngest boys, John and George (who were eight and six) were betrayed by the great difficulty they had in standing still. The introductions being at an end, it was time to move within.

"Have you been told anything of Goodnestone's history?" inquired Sir Brook as my sister and I followed the others into the house.

"We have not yet had that pleasure," replied Cassandra.

"Oh! Do not bore these children with a tedious history!" warned Lady Bridges. "They have only just arrived, and are in need of refreshment."

"I will be brief," asserted Sir Brook with a smile. "Goodnestone has been occupied since Tudor times. During the reign of Queen Anne, the estate was sold to Brook Bridges, the first baronet, who demolished the Elizabethan structure and built this new Palladian house."

"The date of its erection, 1705, is etched onto a brick just over there," added Lady Bridges.

"Not 1705," corrected Sir Brook, "*1704*. Since I took possession, I have enlarged and improved the house rather dramatically. Come, let us show you."

We issued into an ante-room designed in an unusual oval shape and beautifully embellished with detailed crown moulding, a carved white marble fireplace, and a series of large niches beneath gracefully carved arches, wherein works of art were displayed. The walls were adorned with delicate, colourful paintings featuring floral patterns, cherubs, and scroll-work—designs which I had heretofore only seen in books.

"Oh!" exclaimed Cassandra in wonder.

"What an enchanting room," remarked I. "And these paintings—are they Italianate in nature?"

"They are indeed, Miss Jane. As a young man, I travelled extensively on the Continent and spent a great deal of time in Italy, where I became enamoured of its architecture and art. This chamber is a small tribute to the Florentine masters."

The ante-room was further distinguished by three mahogany-panelled doors leading to other parts of the house. Through the middle door, I perceived a central hall and a grand staircase; to the right, a formal dining-room; to the left, the drawing-room, into which we now progressed, to join the family who awaited us. The chamber was large, airy, and exquisitely furnished, with stunningly carved moulding crowning the high ceiling and doorway, and tall windows framed by shutters and heavy draperies. The walls were adorned with paintings, including a set of four views of Venice, a portrait of a young Lady Bridges, and two of Sir Brook as a young man, which (he proudly explained) had been painted by the celebrated, rival Italian artists Mengs and Bartoni.

"Robert Mylne himself designed and furnished this chamber," proclaimed her ladyship with pride, as she arranged herself on a sofa. "It was a great *coup* on our part to retain him, for he has won a great many architectural awards, and designed a number of country-houses and city buildings, as well as bridges."

Although I had never heard of Mengs, Bartoni, nor Mr. Mylne in all my life, I could not deny that the portraits were of superior quality, and the proportions of the room were very elegant indeed. "I presume," said I teasingly, as I accepted a glass of lemonade from a footman's silver tray, "that Mr. Mylne designed actual *bridges,* and not people by the *name* of Bridges?"

Lady Bridges, Fanny, and Elizabeth appeared to be either puzzled or taken aback by my comment, but everyone else laughed.

"Well well, you are a witty young thing, Miss Jane!" cried Sir Brook. "But surely you have heard of Mr. Mylne? He is from a remarkable Scots dynasty of architects and master-masons, famous for his beautiful interiors at Inveraray Castle, and of course the Blackfriars Bridge in town."

Thankfully, I was not obliged to reveal my ignorance, for a general discussion now broke out concerning our mishap on the road, which seemed to be of great interest to everybody. In Charles's retelling of it, the level of danger in the event, and the heroic efforts of our rescuers, rose to such great proportions, that when Edward Taylor and Thomas Payler at last entered the room (their boots freshly polished), they were treated like a pair of conquerors returning from battle.

Mr. Taylor laughed. "We are neither of us Sir Galahad, nor any other knight of the round table; far too much fuss is being made over a trivial incident."

"Let us make a hero out of you, cousin," cried Sir Brook, patting him on the back, "what is the harm in it? Lord knows we have little else to talk about."

A tour of the gardens was proposed; but before the examination could begin, Lady Bridges insisted that my sister change her shoes and stockings.

"What do you say to that game of billiards in the meantime?" suggested Sir Brook to Mr. Taylor and Mr. Payler. As he led them away, Charles, declining the tour, dashed upstairs with Brook Edward and Louisa, with whom he seemed to have formed an immediate friendship.

I accompanied the ladies into the central hall, whose primary feature was the grand staircase, an elaborately carved affair of dark oak which made two turns in its upwards sweep towards the open first-floor landing. I felt like a princess as we issued up the wide steps, past the open string, paired balusters, swept and ramped hand-rails, and ornate panelling.

My sister and I were put in possession of a comfortable apartment, conveniently located near the chambers shared by the Bridges daughters. Cassandra conducted her toilette; several pairs of shoes and silk stockings were produced (in a style and quality superior to any my sister and I had ever possessed); a nearly perfect fit was attained; and the dirty articles taken away. Fanny and Marianne excused themselves, explaining that they would like to lie down before dinner. Her ladyship, Elizabeth, and Sophia alone now remained in our company; and retrieving our bonnets, we issued downstairs.

The distinctive sounds of a game of billiards in progress issued from a room just off the central hall. Lady Bridges remarked with a sniff,

"Sir Brook seems to spend all his time in the gun-room now, ever since he had that billiard-table installed. I really do not understand the appeal of—"

Although her ladyship continued speaking, the balance of her declaration was lost to me, for my full attention was captured by the sight of Edward Taylor within the chamber in question. As he leaned over the billiard-table with his cue, with his gleaming auburn hair casually falling over his forehead, and his dark eyes scrutinizing his shot, the picture he presented was so visually arresting, that I could not prevent myself from pausing in the doorway to watch. With a mighty crack, he struck one of the balls with his cue. Although I was unfamiliar with the rules of the game, from the enthusiastic reactions of the others, I deduced him to be skilled at the sport.

"Sir Brook!" commanded Lady Bridges. "You promised these children a tour of the gardens."

"Forgive me, boys." Sir Brook reluctantly put down his cue. "I trust you can find a way to play on without me."

Edward Taylor bowed; as he glanced in my direction, I perceived a smile. Was it meant for me? As I turned to follow my group across the hall, the memory of that smile and those beautiful dark eyes made my heart beat like a drum, and I looked forward to the time, later that evening, when I knew I should see him again.

Chapter the Sixth

The park that you see before you *used* to be formal gardens, in that old, traditional style," said Lady Bridges as we crossed the great lawn behind the house. "I insisted that Sir Brook tear it out as soon as we took possession."

"It was a pretty thing," said Sir Brook with a regretful sigh. "It put one in the mind of Versailles."

"Precisely why we were obliged to do away with it! It was *so* out of fashion," cried Lady

Bridges. "I could not bear all those paths which crossed back and forth, or the tightly manicured flower-beds, with the trees and shrubs sculpted into unnatural shapes."

"Our re-landscaped park is ever so much more stylish and picturesque," agreed Elizabeth.

"I am sure it is a pleasant place to walk on a fine morning," enthused I, appreciating the natural look of the landscape, which I favoured; yet I could not help but feel a pang for the poor, departed, formal gardens, which had no doubt required great effort and expense to design and install, and whose inhabitants, due to the whims of a changing taste, had met with such an untimely end.

As we followed a curving path to another part of the grounds, Lady Bridges described with pride every plant and shrub along the way. We passed through a wooden gate in an ivy-covered wall, and to my delight emerged into a large, enclosed garden, in which a verdant lawn was bordered by a riot of colourful flowers. Through a distant opening in the high brick walls I perceived the entrance to another garden, and beyond that, yet another; farther on stood the graceful stone tower of the church.

"This is the first of three walled gardens, each of which leads into the other," explained Lady Bridges. "We have an excellent fruit orchard— quite the best fruit-trees in the country!—and our strawberry beds are superior to anybody's in the kingdom, and celebrated for their variety and quality. The flower garden dates back to Elizabethan times, and the wisteria and roses are remarkable, for they are imported from the Far East."

I wondered what made roses from the Far East particularly remarkable; did they emit a more potent fragrance than roses native to our country, or did they come in a different size or hue? I was saved from posing any such impertinent questions by Sir Brook's experiencing a sudden coughing fit. Lady Bridges insisted that we retrace our steps in the direction of the house, where our hosts said they would rest before dinner. As they disappeared within, Marianne made a reappearance, and we ladies decided to take a turn in the park.

"We are so glad to have this interval to speak to you on our own," remarked Sophia, as we crossed the expanse of lawn towards the woods, "for soon the house will be full of people."

"We heard that your mother has a great many events planned," said I.

"She does, indeed," responded Marianne. "Monday is our annual strawberry-picking party, which will include an *al-fresco* luncheon and lawn games. All the Paylers will be here for that and everything else, as well as our neighbours the Fieldings, and Mr. Cage—Fanny's intended—is due to arrive that morning with a friend."

"After that," added Elizabeth, "is our engage-ment ball. Edward is to wear his blue coat—he looks so handsome in it—and my new gown is so becoming, just wait until you see it!"

"There is to be a sketching and painting contest," said Sophia, "a cricket match, horse-races, carriage rides, a dinner-party at a neighbour's house, a concert—there is something else, I have forgotten what—and a Midsummer's Eve bonfire."

To have all these thrilling events before me, was a truly wonderful prospect. "It all sounds tremendous."

"I only hope that in between, we can find a moment to ourselves," said Sophia. "You must tell us what you particularly like to do."

"Do you ride?" asked Elizabeth.

"We did when we were younger," admitted I, "but Cassandra and I never became very adept."

"What about drawing and painting?" asked Marianne.

"*My* previous attempts at art were dreadful," responded I, "but that is Cassandra's area of expertise. Her water-colour portraits are quite true to life."

Cassandra blushed. "If you are such a proponent of my art, Jane, why do you never allow me to draw *your* portrait?"

"It is no mark against your skill, dearest; it is only that I cannot abide the thought of looking at myself hanging on a wall."

"I hope you win the drawing and painting contest, Cassandra," cried Sophia, smiling. "It will throw my mother's plans into complete disarray."

"Mamma considers all her children to be prodigies," added Marianne. "It is why she is holding the contest, we are certain—because she feels one of us will take the prize. So please do your best work and shew her what you are made of."

We all laughed congenially.

"What are your interests and occupations, Jane?" inquired Sophia as we walked on, enjoying the open expanse of the pleasure grounds.

I thought for a moment. I had many interests; it was hard to know where to begin. "Well," answered I hesitantly, "although I know that *some* consider it to be the lowest and most coarse form of behaviour—I love to read—novels."

Sophia gave a little gasp. "Marianne and I both love to read, and novels most especially!"

"Do you?" said I, delighted.

"My father has an excellent library, and we borrow what we cannot buy," said Cassandra.

We began going over the titles of our favourite novels. After some minutes thus engaged, Elizabeth said:

"Forgive me, but I know nothing of books. I do not wish to take away from your conversation, so

I will leave you and return to the house. Please enjoy the rest of your walk."

We curtseyed, and Elizabeth departed.

"No one else in our family shares our enthusiasm for literature." Sophia sighed. "It is delightful to be able to converse on this topic with *you*."

As we continued our stroll, our shared admiration of the works of Henry Fielding (*Tom Jones*), Jonathan Swift (*Gulliver's Travels*), Goethe (*The Sorrows of Young Werther*), and Fanny Burney was brought to light.

"*Evelina* is one of my favourites," said Sophia, to which Cassandra and I offered our assent.

"I believe *Cecilia* is the best book I have ever read," said I. "Fanny Burney is a genius. I am captivated by her depiction of characters like Mrs. Delville, who are not perfect, but neither are they wholly good nor evil—they possess both noble qualities *and* incurable defects—as such, they seem to me more true to life than any I have read in novels elsewhere."

Sophia's eyes widened. "What a fine assessment of Miss Burney's literature. I never thought of that before."

I wanted to add that it was my dearest hope to write something equally fine one day; but my own efforts were so unworthy, and the dream so unattainable, that I could not voice it aloud.

• • •

Marianne soon grew weary (I recalled Mrs. Knight describing her as being something of an invalid), so we returned to the house. As we approached the grand edifice, Cassandra asked, "Should we change our gowns for dinner to-night?"

"No; you are to be our only guests," replied Sophia. "That is—you and Edward Taylor and his cousin Thomas."

"Is it true that Edward Taylor is *your* cousin?" said I.

"He is. His father is a very distant cousin of our father's," answered Sophia. "We are told the connection goes back a hundred and fifty years, to the time of King Charles I."

"That is a very *distant* cousin indeed!" laughed Cassandra.

"How old is Mr. Taylor?" asked I.

"He is sixteen," answered Marianne, "although he will turn seventeen later this month."

I could not stop my smile. Edward Taylor was exactly eighteen months my senior—the perfect age, I thought, for *me*.

"We have not had much opportunity to get to know each other," added Sophia. "We used to play together as children—he was the sweetest little boy—but when he and his brothers and sisters were very small, his family emigrated to the Continent. They have been gone ever since,

94

other than one annum about two years past, when they returned to Bifrons to check on their property."

"The Taylors have lived abroad all that time?" said I, astonished.

"Yes, and there the family still remains; it is only Edward who has come home for good."

I wanted to ask why it was only Edward who had come home, but the opportunity was lost, for we had reached the house now, and as Sophia led the way up the main staircase, she went on:

"As far as we—and Papa—are concerned, Edward Taylor is a member of our family. Papa insisted that he and the Paylers, with whom he is residing, be included in all our festivities this month, and we are so glad."

Boldly, I asked: "Does your mother share his enthusiasm for Mr. Taylor?"

Sophia hesitated; then, catching some understanding in my tone and expression, she replied in a lowered tone: "I think you have guessed that she does not."

"Why not? He seems very amiable to me."

"Oh! He is," replied Marianne. "We *love* Edward Taylor. But Mamma disapproves of the way he was brought up, travelling all over the Continent as he has done since he was five years old. She considers him a little too wild, a great deal too foreign, and worst of all (and I do not agree), pompous and overly-educated."

"Mamma's favourite saying," added Sophia

with a sigh, "is: *a little bit of learning goes a long way at Goodnestone*. I think she fears that, with Edward's wealth of knowledge, experience of the world, and many accomplishments, her own children will somehow appear to disadvantage—and of course *we* do not care a fig about that!"

We were now arrived upstairs, and all separated to our respective chambers to get ready for the evening—an event which I eagerly anticipated, as it meant I would have the opportunity to see more of Edward Taylor, who grew more fascinating with every moment.

Chapter the Seventh

From the moment of our arrival at Goodnestone, Charles and Brook Edward had become inseparable, and it did my heart good to see my brother so happily engaged. After seeing to it that my brother was comfortably settled in the room he shared with his new friend, Cassandra and I removed to our own chamber to unpack our trunks and prepare our toilette for dinner.

Lady Bridges offered to send one of her daughters' maids to assist us, an indulgence we gracefully declined, preferring to spend a few moments alone together; and we got ready as we usually did.

"The Bridgeses seem to me a delightful family,"

said Cassandra as she sat at the dressing-table while I helped re-arrange her hair.

"I prefer Sophia, Marianne, and Sir Bridges to anyone else in the household."

"It is too early to pass such a judgement, Jane. We have only just arrived."

"Three weeks more will make no difference in my impressions of them. It was plain to see who and what they all were upon our first introduction. Sophia and Marianne are bright and compassionate. Sir Bridges is a congenial, admirable man in failing health, who finds his wife extremely irritating. Lady Bridges is a proud woman who places too much emphasis on appearances and social standing—"

"Jane!"

"Fanny seems to be a self-centered snob. Elizabeth is only one step removed from such self-importance by her love of our brother—"

"Jane, enough! You are too harsh. All the Bridgeses have very interesting qualities."

Having finished with my sister's hair, we changed places, and she set to work tidying mine. *"Interesting,"* said I, "is a term I reserve to describe people or things so dull or ordinary, that I can find no more promising attribution."

"*I* use it to describe things I like; and I like them all very much."

"You like everybody, dearest; it is perhaps your finest quality, and one which I can never hope to emulate." I sighed. "If only I could be as good as you, I would be truly content."

"You *are* very good, Jane; a better person than you know, and I am proud to call you sister."

Our gazes caught in the looking-glass. I repeated the sentiment, and we exchanged a smile of deep affection.

"I hope," said Cassandra, "at dinner, you will be a *bit* more gracious to Lady Bridges, with no more ironic inquiries about bridges. I fear she does not possess our sense of humour."

"I fear you are right," replied I with a laugh. "Hereafter, I shall endeavour to follow Mamma's advice, and *think* before I speak."

The house was alive with the laughter of children as the family gathered for dinner. The moment we entered the drawing-room, my brother Edward moved to Elizabeth's side, and the two fell into the quiet, affectionate tête-à-tête peculiar to lovers. Fanny and Sophia were apprehended by their mother, whose opinions she sought with regard to changes in the menu for the *al-fresco* party to be held a few days hence.

My heart leapt when Edward Taylor's dark eyes caught mine, and beat even faster when, after exchanging a few words with his cousin, the two crossed the room to where Cassandra, Marianne, and I stood together.

"How have you fared since your arrival, ladies?"

"I hope you enjoyed a lovely afternoon?" added Mr. Payler, with a shy glance at Cassandra.

"We did, thank you," answered she.

"My only regret is that I never had the opportunity to thank you both again for your assistance this morning," replied I. "Had you not appeared so fortuitously and been so obliging, our unfortunate incident on the road might have had a more disastrous result."

"I am truly sorry for the inconvenience and distress this morning's events must have caused you," replied Edward sincerely; continuing, with a twinkle in his eyes, "however, I must admit, for *my part,* I cannot consider it to be an unfortunate incident."

"No?"

"No; for it provided me a chance to—" He paused, as if rethinking what he was about to say. "—a chance to do something very rare, which is essential to my happiness."

"Pray tell, what is that, Mr. Taylor?"

"It allowed me the opportunity to prove *useful.*"

I smiled. "To prove useful is, indeed, something to which *I* daily aspire; but it so often eludes me."

"Well then, you understand how I feel. The circumstance also provided another benefit, Miss Jane. It concluded with an invitation to dinner at Goodnestone, which is always a delightful prospect."

Our conversation was interrupted by the announcement that dinner was served, and we all progressed into the very sizeable dining-room, which Sophia explained was the room they used for dancing, when the furniture was removed. I was astonished by how elegantly the long table was draped and set, and the quantity of plate on view, considering that it was only a family dinner. A great many footmen assisted us as the family took their seats by rote, leaving open seats only on the side of the table opposite Mr. Taylor, which (to my disappointment) prevented any meaningful continuation of a discussion I had only just begun to enjoy.

Sir Brook made a toast of welcome to his visitors, noting his delight that we had come all the way from Hampshire to celebrate his daughters' engagements. To my brother Edward he added, "It is no secret how pleased Lady Bridges and I are by our Elizabeth's choice of husband; and as for Fanny's intended, Mr. Lewis Cage—he, too, is a most amiable man, and we look forward to his joining us for what I believe will be a remarkable month."

As the soup was served, I said to Sophia beside me, "What is Mr. Cage like? Do you know him well?"

"Not really," answered she quietly. "Their betrothal was very sudden, and just a fortnight after Elizabeth and Edward announced *their* engagement. We have only met a few times. I know that he is very fond of books."

Marianne added in a low voice, "I dare say Fanny has never read but one book in her entire life—and I cannot be certain she even finished it."

"She and Mr. Cage must have found other interests in common," said I, smiling, "other than reading."

Sophia did not immediately reply, and Marianne said with gravity,

"Of course you are right, Jane."

As the dinner continued, light conversation was heard from the top of the table, and congenial laughter from the children at the bottom. I made a point of complimenting all the dishes that I tried, which seemed to please Lady Bridges when she overheard it. At one point, I found Edward Taylor looking at me, and our glances converged in a brief but mutual smile.

After the desserts were consumed, we left the men and withdrew to the drawing-room, where Charles and Brook Edward engaged in a game of chess, the younger boys played on the floor, and Lady Bridges held court on a sofa, with Fanny and Sophia on either side, Elizabeth and Marianne seated beside them, and Louisa and Harriot at their feet, in a tableau which looked to be a family habit of long standing. Cassandra and I procured two unoccupied chairs close by, and I said to Lady Bridges:

"I believe you mentioned in your letter, ma'am, that both your daughters' weddings will take place at the end of the year?"

"Yes." Lady Bridges's smile reflected her genuine enthusiasm with regard to the subject matter. "It was Mr. Knight's wish at the first, that Edward and Elizabeth not be married immediately, as they are both so young, and Sir Brook and I could not agree more. We think to have a double wedding in December."

"Mamma," said Fanny with a calculated sweetness, "I have told you before: my wedding day must be all my *own*. And I still do not understand why *I* must wait until December. *I* am not so very young, and neither is Mr. Cage. Surely *our* nuptials should not be governed by the cautious thinking of Mr. Knight!"

"You and Mr. Cage have not been very long acquainted, my dear," said Lady Bridges. "Your father and I were engaged for more than two years, and I believe that an engagement of some length is a healthy thing. Besides, when I think of all the linen and wedding clothes which I must have made up for your trousseaus—and on top of *that,* all the festivities I am obliged to arrange *this* month—it is enough to make one's head spin."

"I still say it is not fair," protested Fanny with a frown. "I am the eldest; I should be able to marry whenever I choose. Mr. Cage lives so far away;

a lengthy engagement is really not convenient, Mamma."

"It is not such a hardship for Mr. Cage to come hither to see you, Fanny," replied Lady Bridges. "Remember, he can always stay with his friend Mr. Deedes in Canterbury."

"Where does Mr. Cage live?" inquired I.

"He is the owner of the manor of West Langdon in Milgate, Bearsted, devised to him many years past," answered Fanny proudly. "He has told me all about it, and I so long to live there! It is by all accounts a large and magnificent estate, with ever so many grand parlours and chambers and extensive pleasure-grounds."

"Where is Bearsted?" asked Cassandra.

"It is some thirty-eight miles to the west," answered Elizabeth, "near Maidstone."

"Fanny will be very happy with Mr. Cage," noted Louisa with an envious sigh, from where she sat on the carpet, "for he has a fine house *and* three thousand a year."

"I hope Mr. Cage possesses other fine qualities, apart from his house and income," said I, laughing.

"Oh that he does, my dear," replied Lady Bridges. "He is a most amiable man of unexceptionable good character."

"I will have a new carriage and four, and ever so many gowns, and family jewels which are worth a fortune," said Fanny. "We will have ever so much more to live on than Elizabeth and Edward.

As it does not suit Mr. Knight to give up much at present, *their* income will be small."

Elizabeth blushed at this declaration and cried defensively,

"Edward is heir to numerous properties at Godmersham *and* Chawton, and will one day be far richer than Mr. Cage could ever hope to be!"

"Perhaps so, but in the meantime, you must be content to live at Rowling."

"Rowling is an excellent house. Papa is fitting it up very nicely for us."

"I am sure you will be happy there, even if it *is* small and dark. Sadly, the parlour does not have a good exposure, the windows face full west, and I hope you will not find the fireplace too drafty; the last tenants made complaints of that nature."

"I am sure the house will be charming and suit all our needs," insisted Elizabeth, her eyes flashing. "At least it is within walking distance of Goodnestone, so I may see Mamma and Papa whenever I wish! Whereas *you* will be a full thirty-eight miles away, and may only see them at Christmas!"

"Girls! Girls!" cried Lady Bridges. "I will hear no more of this! We have much to celebrate to-night. If you cannot be civil to each other, you had better not speak at all."

I, too, was weary of this discourse, and troubled to see that such contention existed between the sisters; Cassandra's countenance reflected her equal disenchantment. At that moment the door opened, and the tea and coffee were brought in.

As the beverage service was set up, to my surprise, I noticed Edward Taylor and Thomas Payler standing in the open doorway, beckoning to my sister and me. From their silent gestures, they made known to us that they wished to go without—and wanted us to join them. The other ladies in the room appeared too engrossed to perceive their presence.

Cassandra shook her head slightly at me. I was dismayed; Edward Taylor wished for me to join him for a walk! How could I refuse? It was not at all inappropriate if we both went, for we would have two escorts. To my sister, I whispered:

"You *cannot* deny me this." Standing, I said to Lady Bridges: "Forgive me, madam. I have a slight headache; I am sorry to miss tea, but I think I require some fresh air. Might my sister and I be allowed to take a walk in your gardens?"

"You may," replied she, adding, "I wonder where the gentlemen are? They should have arrived by now." Her attention was then diverted to the business of serving the tea and coffee.

I gave Cassandra a meaningful, imploring glance; she hesitated with slight confusion, but at last, sighing, rose and accompanied me as I crossed the room and slipped out the doorway.

Holding a finger to his lips, Edward Taylor led us through the oval ante-room into the central hall, where he quietly closed the connecting door. I could not help but smile.

"What is the meaning of this intriguing removal, Mr. Taylor?" stated I softly. "Were you not enjoying a glass of port with the other gentlemen?"

"We were," replied he, keeping his voice equally low so as not to be overheard, "and I enjoy a good port as much as the next man; but Sir Brook and your brother have spent the past twenty-five minutes discussing the difficulties of rent collection from recalcitrant farmers, and have now embarked on the price of hay. It seemed the ideal time to make our exit."

"I should think these subjects to be of interest to you," said Thomas Payler, "as you and I shall one day be in charge of tenant farmers ourselves, and will have regular dealings with the sale of hay."

"That day, thank God, is very far off. It is hard enough that I was sent home to learn about such things from my father's steward, while my brothers and sisters enjoy the delights of southern Italy for another year; I prefer to talk of something else of an evening—and a very fine evening it is, ladies. Would you fancy a walk out of doors? It would be our pleasure to escort you."

My sister and I answered in the affirmative; and after running upstairs to fetch our shawls, in short order we were all bounding out the back door of the house.

Chapter the Eighth

It was still very light out, with only a slight chill in the evening air.

"We have made good our escape!" Edward Taylor spun in a circle with delight as we headed down the path in the direction of the walled gardens. "I like nothing better than a long stroll on a summer evening."

"My sister and I are also partial to long walks," remarked Cassandra, to which I added,

"Although *we* are equally as fond of morning as evening."

"Of what else are you fond, Miss Jane?" said Mr. Taylor, smiling.

"Oh, so many things: music, dancing, reading."

"Music is one of my greatest passions as well. Do you play an instrument?"

"The pianoforte—I have only been studying a few years, but I am determined to improve. And you?"

"I play the violin a bit."

"A bit?" cried Thomas Payler. "You are too modest, cousin. Edward's musical skills—those of his whole family, in fact—put everyone in *my* family to shame. He is quite the virtuoso."

Edward Taylor coloured slightly, and as if determined to change the subject, inquired of me,

"You said you enjoy reading?"

"I do."

"That is something else we have in common. Give me a good history book, particularly military history or memoir, or a work about mythology or travel, and I will happily disappear within its pages for hours. Have you read *Quintus Tertius* or *Plutarch's Lives*?"

"I have not. Your catalogue is somewhat different from my own," admitted I. "I have read many of the classics, and studied history and geography and some mythology; but I have read very little travel literature, and I have never read a military history in my life." When I told him, after some hesitation, that I preferred novels, he smiled deeply and said:

"My father never allowed us to read novels—but as I understand it, there is a growing taste for such works."

"I cannot understand *why*," commented Mr. Payler. "You will get more practical information out of an hour with a newspaper or a journal, than from a hundred hours with a novel."

"We come from a family of great novel readers," said Cassandra. "Reading aloud often makes up our evening entertainment."

Mr. Payler blushed and appeared disconcerted. "Oh! Do forgive me, Miss Austen. I meant no disrespect. But—what do you *see* in novels? From what I hear, they embody only the poorest form of writing."

"From what you *hear?*" repeated I. "I take it, Mr. Payler, that you have never read a novel?"

"Never. It is said that they are designed to entertain the weak of mind."

"Sir," said I with animation, "that could not be further from the truth. *Some* novels might be poorly written, but in the main, I believe the opposite to be the case. A *good* novel—a well-written novel—not only entertains the reader with effusions of wit and humour, it touches the emotions and conveys a comprehensive understanding of human nature—all via the simple and remarkable act of trans-mitting words on a page—while at the same time displaying, in the best-chosen language, the greatest powers of the human mind."

Edward Taylor's eyebrows lifted; my remark seemed to have made a favourable impression. "What do you say to *that,* Thomas?"

"I say: Miss Jane is such a persuasive young lady, that should I spend much more time in her company, I shall be in danger of becoming a novel reader myself." Mr. Payler uttered the reply with such good humour, that we all could not help but laugh.

We had traversed the first walled garden by now, and reached the tall brick pillars which marked the opening into the middle enclosed garden, which I had not yet visited. We entered; and I smiled in wonder.

It was immense; and it was truly lovely.

Bordering a central lawn, gravel pathways wound past well-clipped hedges and beneath pergolas entwined with flowering vines. The flower-beds held Lady Bridges's promised (imported?) roses, as well as dahlias, petunias, and numerous other varieties of flowers, many of which were in glorious bloom, and the air was redolent with their perfume. Like the first garden, the entire enclosure was surrounded by very high brick walls covered in ivy and creeping vines. As the paths were only wide enough for two, Mr. Payler moved ahead with Cassandra. Suddenly, a perfect pink rose was held before my nose, as Edward Taylor said with a slight bow:

"*Für Sie, junge Fräulein*: *eine Rose so schoen wie Sie.*"

Accepting the bloom, I replied with a laugh, "Thank you, sir; but you have me at a disadvantage. If that was German you spoke, I know not a single word of it; only a bit of French."

"Forgive me. I spent so many years in Germany, the language is as natural to me as breathing; but I will speak it no more. I said: for you, miss: a rose as beautiful as yourself."

I blushed, my heart fluttering both from his comment and from his approving smile as he regarded me. "You seem to know a great many languages besides German," said I, as we walked side by side, our footsteps lightly resounding against the pleasant crush of gravel.

He shrugged. "I speak French and Italian fluently as well."

"Fluently!" I was astonished.

"I can also read and speak Spanish, but my knowledge is rudimentary in comparison with the others, so I do not count it. Of Latin and Greek, I have acquired only so much as served the purposes of my studies; I can make translations when a gun is put to my head, but I do not consider myself a proficient, so I do not count them, either."

I shook my head in wonder. "I have studied a bit of Latin and Greek myself, but am not so proficient yet as to make translations. You speak of these accomplishments as if they are routine; but they are not, for a young man only sixteen years of age."

"I will be seventeen in three weeks, on Midsummer's Day. Speaking of which, my aunt Payler has decided to throw me a birthday party at Ileden. The Bridges family are all invited. I hope you and your family will come as well?"

"I am sure we should be delighted to attend, and appreciate the invitation. But do not try to change the subject, Mr. Taylor! To be fluent in four languages, and able to read or converse in three others, at almost seventeen—it is quite extraordinary."

"All my brothers and sisters are equally adept. When you live in the country where a language is native, and see it written and hear it spoken every day, it is not so difficult to pick up."

His modesty was charming.

"Perhaps not. It must have been thrilling to reside on the Continent as you did, where language is a living and breathing thing. I have never had that pleasure. What little French I have learned came from a book, or from one of my brief intervals at school."

"When and where did you attend school?"

"The first time, I was seven. My sister, a cousin, and I were sent to a Mrs. Cawley's in Oxford, but she soon moved us to Southampton, where—I still recall the stink of fish—we nearly died from typhus fever. Tragically, my aunt Cooper, who fetched us home, did catch the fever and died."

"Oh no. I am so sorry."

"We were all very sad. It was two years before my father dared to try a school again; but when I was nine, we went to The Abbey House School in Reading—a quaint academy for young ladies, run by a stout woman of middle age who had a cork leg, and who went by the name Mrs. La Tournelle."

"*Went by* the name?"

"Her real name was Sarah Hackitt. She could not speak a word of French. Apparently she thought a foreign name made her sound ever so much more exotic, accomplished, and important."

Edward Taylor laughed.

"Mrs. La Tournelle loved to speak of plays, acting, and the private life of actors—but unfortunately her talents were limited to making tea and ordering dinner. The teaching duties were relegated to her partner, Miss Pitts, and three schoolmistresses, from whom we learned several accomplishments expected of young ladies, the basic subjects, and a few words of French."

"Did you like it there?"

"I did, very much. I could have happily stayed much longer, but my father could not afford it, and after a year he brought us home. He runs a boarding-school, and my sister and I have studied under his guidance ever since, along with my brothers and the boys who came and went." Ahead of us, I observed Mr. Payler quietly say something to Cassandra which made her laugh. "What about you, Mr. Taylor? Tell me about your schooldays."

"I have never had any."

"None?" I stared at him, confounded.

"An attempt was made by my father to send me and my brother Herbert to a day-school in Brussels when I was six years old, and he was five, but our pockets were picked by our school-fellows on the first day, and the visit was not repeated. Instead, we were taught at home, like you, by my father, who is a scholarly man himself—and we have had masters in particular subjects. That, in fact, was one of my father's two purposes in emigrating."

"Two purposes?"

"My father rebuilt Bifrons in the modern style around the time I was born, and in the process overextended himself and was obliged to retrench. He let out Bifrons for a great deal of money, whilst it was relatively inexpensive to live abroad. Excellent masters in languages and the arts could also be procured abroad very cheaply, which satisfied his desire to promote the education of his children."

"How large is your family?"

"My mother had seven children in as many years, including a set of twins. Sadly, she died soon after we arrived in Brussels, after the last one—my sister Margaret—was born."

"Oh! I did not know your mother had passed away—and so long ago. I am so very, very sorry."

"Thank you." He frowned, his eyes flashing with perturbation. "My father insists that it was just her time; but I remember how weary she looked, even before we left England. I believe that the strain of carrying so many children, and giving birth in such rapid succession, simply wore her out." The pain and resentment in his voice were unmistakable.

My heart went out to him. "I can only imagine how difficult it must have been to lose your mother—and at such a young age! Your brothers and sisters must not remember her at all."

"Most of them do not. I am fortunate to have a few memories. I recall that she had soft, pale skin, and a sweet voice." He paused, gazing at the blooming garden around us. "I remember sitting beside her on a bench in one of the gardens at Bifrons—there was always a baby in her lap—she used to read to me and my brothers. She loved Bifrons. She often told me how lucky I was, to be the eldest; that the entire estate would be mine one day." He sighed deeply and shook his head. "I would give up Bifrons and every penny my family possesses to have her back."

"I imagine you would," said I quietly; and glancing up at his distressed countenance, I felt tears of sympathy threaten behind my eyes.

He looked at me, paused, and then said, "That all happened long ago, Miss Jane. As my father says, there is no use looking back, only forward. We managed, somehow, to go on without her. I am home now, all these years later, with a view to learning all I can about Bifrons and its admin-istration, and I must make the best of it."

I nodded. I had many more questions I wished to ask him, concerning his life and education abroad and his return hither; but the information regarding his mother's death had so changed the mood of our conversation, that somehow further inquiry did not seem appropriate. We walked in silence for a little while, catching up to Cassandra and Thomas Payler, who had made the full circuit of the middle garden now, and were waiting not far from the portal where we had entered. As we approached, Edward Taylor found his smile again and looking round, said,

"This a lovely garden."

"It is."

Studying the ancient, mossy, ivy- and vine-covered brick wall surrounding us, he added: "I particularly admire these walls."

"The walls?" repeated I, amused.

"These walls, according to Lady Bridges, have stood here for more than a hundred years—and will no doubt still be standing two hundred years hence. Fascinating, is it not, to think of all the people who will see them and walk within their confines, long after we have all stopped breathing?"

Mr. Payler laughed and shook his head. "You have read too many history books, cousin."

"We are a living part of history!" cried Edward Taylor. "We are making history this very moment." Without further preamble, he leapt up onto a sturdy wooden bench which was situated along the partition, caught hold of the ancient bricks and vines, and began climbing up the wall itself.

"Edward!" cried Mr. Payler. "What are you doing?"

My heart beat in my throat; the wall at that

juncture was more than eight feet high! Farther on, and for the greater part of the enclosure, the walls were even higher yet, towering an alarming eleven feet above the ground—and they did not appear to be very wide. "Come down, Mr. Taylor!" cried I.

He ignored me, and with some effort, managed to reach the top of the brick wall, where he cautiously rose to his feet, turning to look down at us.

"My brothers and I used to dare each other to walk the length of walls such as this, in every European village and town we visited or lived in. A sum of money was always involved. What do you say, cousin? Are you game?"

"Do not be a fool," said Mr. Payler. "You could fall and kill yourself."

"Therein lies the challenge. Where would be the interest, if the wall were but two feet high?"

"Mr. Taylor," cautioned Cassandra, "please come down. You need not risk your life for our entertainment."

"I am not risking my life, I promise you. I only propose to walk the length of this one section of the wall which is lower than the rest, from here to that bench over there. Should it be required, there are plenty of shrubs on both sides to cushion my fall. Thomas? Are you in? How much will you put up to see if I can do it?"

Mr. Payler sighed. "Fine. A half-crown says you cannot make it all that way."

"Done!" Edward Taylor smiled and, spreading his arms wide, and putting one foot before the other, he began to make his way along the wall's upper ledge.

"Do be careful, Mr. Taylor," said I, worried.

"I am always careful."

We shadowed him as he progressed, our eyes riveted to his every step atop the wall. He did not seem concerned at all—indeed, he moved dexterously and gracefully, with barely a pause, displaying an athleticism which was truly remarkable—yet I watched with mild alarm, hardly daring to breathe. He only faltered slightly at one point, where I thought he seemed in danger of falling into a bed of roses; but by bending his knees slightly, he regained his balance and continued. Thankfully, he arrived unscathed at the appointed spot, where he hopped down handily from wall to bench to ground, and turned to Mr. Payler with a victorious smile.

"A half-crown, was it?"

"You devil; this is akin to highway robbery. You accomplished that far too easily." Mr. Payler retrieved the promised coin from his pocket and gave it to Edward Taylor, who flipped it several times in the air with pride.

"Do you want to win back what you lost, Thomas?" Mr. Taylor smiled playfully. "I will double your money if you walk the wall back to where I started."

"No thank you. You have clearly done this sort of thing plenty of times. I have not."

"It is not difficult, nor as high as it looks. You cannot play it safe every moment, cousin. Every now and then you must take a chance—step outside your customary sphere."

"This is a *sphere* I do not wish to exit. I have a higher regard for my own life and limb than you do."

"Perhaps. But what are you *really* afraid of? That you might break a bone? Are you afraid of death? Or—are you afraid of something far worse than either of these—that you might not *live?*"

The cousins regarded each other in tense silence for several moments. Mr. Payler lowered his gaze but vouchsafed no answer. Suddenly, I heard myself cry:

"I will do it!" The words escaped my lips before I could stop them, astonishing me, I think, as much as my companions.

Edward Taylor paused. "Miss Jane—no. The wager was meant only to challenge my cousin, not you."

"I have no interest in the wager; only the *challenge.*" I had grown up in a house full of boys. I had accepted dares, and had climbed up, over, and along any number of stiles, walls, and fences with them ever since I could remember. Although sometimes afraid, I had usually enjoyed the effort—but admittedly, I had never climbed anything nearly so high as this. For some inexplicable reason, however, I felt the sudden need to prove to both Edward Taylor and myself that I could walk this wall. "If you could do it, then so can I."

"Jane!" admonished Cassandra. "Do not be foolish. It is unsafe."

"Therein lies the challenge," quoted I, with what I hoped was a confident smile (in truth, I was quaking inside).

Mr. Taylor laughed. "Very well, Miss Jane. Show my cousin Thomas how it is done."

I walked up to the bench beside the wall and, gathering up my skirts and petticoat, tied a portion of them into a sizeable knot, which raised them a foot or two above my ankles.

"Jane!" cried Cassandra again, her cheeks growing very pink.

"We both have done the same many times," I reminded her, "whenever we crossed a muddy road or shallow creek." I knew full well that what I was doing was shocking; on the occasions mentioned, we had been alone or in the company of our brothers.

Edward Taylor held out his hand to me. I took it, and as he helped me to climb up onto the bench, I was momentarily distracted by the sensation of his firm grip against my own—a feeling which was not at all *brotherly*. I reminded myself to let go, and to study the wall before me.

"There is a nice chink in the brick right there to get you started," advised he. "Rest your foot on it. The vines are old and sturdy; they will take your weight as you hoist yourself up."

I followed his instructions and carefully accomplished my climb, my feet finding purchase at the top of the wall, where I slowly raised myself to a stand. Once there, however, I froze, my heart seeming to lodge in my throat, for the top was higher and the upper edge more contracted than I had anticipated. I slowly turned, holding out my arms for balance, awkwardly keeping one foot in front of the other, the lawn and shrubbery looming far below me on the opposite side of the wall, and the bench and flower-beds on the other.

"Jane! Come down. Please!" cried Cassandra.

I dared not look at her—I dared not look at anything except my feet and the narrow ledge before me—for if I fell, I might be seriously injured.

"She will be all right," said Edward Taylor reassuringly. To me, he added: "I shall walk beside you. Should you feel unsteady, you have only to bend your knees, take a breath, and move on."

I took a step; then another; and another. I began to waver slightly. I heard Cassandra's worried exclamation.

"Bend your knees," Edward Taylor reminded me. "Take a breath."

I did so, and immediately recovered. Encouraged, I slowly proceeded, with Mr. Taylor as my shadow. Being up so high was both thrilling and terrifying, but I willed myself to remain calm. When I passed the rose-beds, I took particular care, not wanting to taste their sharp thorns. I concentrated on each step, one at a time, rather than the goal; and before I knew it, I had reached the end of the wall around the corner from the garden entrance, where Edward Taylor had begun his own walk. I dared to look down now, flush with triumph. Thomas Payler appeared less than enthused by my achievement, but Mr. Taylor, beaming, cried:

"Well done, Miss Jane!"

As I sat down atop the wall, he stepped up on the bench and raised his hands to help me descend. I allowed him to assist me, bracing myself on his shoulders as he lifted me down from the wall to the bench, and from there to the gravel path. It was but the work of an instant, but in that instant, every sense seemed heightened: my heart pounded more violently in my ears; I was aware of his breath upon my cheek, and the warmth of his hands at my waist; my vision was filled with the beauty of his shining dark eyes. I dare say, in that instant, I felt more aware of my every feeling, and of being alive, than I had ever yet experienced; and I did not wish for it to end.

"You are a natural," murmured he softly, "an

athlete worthy of competition with the ancient Greeks themselves."

My cheeks were burning; I could not reply.

He released me and took a step back. As I unknotted my skirts and smoothed them out, I smiled at my sister, hoping that she would be proud of me; instead I saw vivid disapproval on her countenance, and unaccountably, thought I detected a trace of tears. Before I could discover what this was about, another young lady's voice rang out:

"Jane! Jane!" It was Sophia; she, Marianne, and Louisa appeared and hurried in to us, all astonishment. "Was that you up on the wall?"

I found myself blushing. "It was."

"Oh! You are quite mad!" exclaimed Marianne.

"What were you doing up there?" asked Sophia.

"I was enjoying the night air," answered I casually.

"What if you had fallen?" cried Louisa.

"I suppose it is a good thing that I did not."

The young ladies laughed. Sophia cautioned her sisters and our male companions: "Promise me that none of you will tell Mamma about this. I fear she might be appalled."

Everyone nodded conspiratorially except for my sister, who was frowning and would not look at me, which made me cross.

"Mamma is already in quite the mood," teased Marianne good-naturedly. "How dare you leave us alone with her so long? She wanted to play quadrille, but with you two gone, cousin Edward and Mr. Payler mysteriously vanished, and only five people interested, she could not make up a table without leaving someone out."

"I will apologise to her before I go," said Edward Taylor, with a hint of mischief in his eyes, "but I am very glad we left when we did, for I cannot abide quadrille."

"Speaking of which," commented Mr. Payler to his cousin, "it is getting rather late."

"So it is. Pray, forgive us, ladies; I regret to put an end to such a lovely evening, but we had best take our leave if we are to get back to Ileden before dark."

We all headed back to the manor house, where he and Mr. Payler said their farewells to Sir Brook and Lady Bridges, and then the others. They seemed on the point of departure for the stables; I felt a stab of deep disappointment. Would he not say good-night to me? But all at once, Edward Taylor stopped before me in the drawing-room with a parting bow. "It has been a pleasure."

His guileless expression caused a fluttering in my stomach. "Good-bye," I managed, my voice unsteady.

"Not *good-bye,* Miss Jane; only *good-night. Buonanotte. Bonne nuit. Gute Nacht. Buenas noches.*"

I could not help but smile. "I shall see you soon, then?"

He returned my smile as he issued through the door, calling over his shoulder: "I shall look forward to it."

Chapter the Ninth

When my sister and I later said our good-nights to the rest of the household, and climbed the stairs to retire, I was still floating on a wave of euphoria, smiling at the memory of the many unforgettable, exhilarating experiences which I had undergone in the past day: our unexpected meeting with Edward Taylor at the road-side; stealing away from the house together in early evening; the depth of our conversation in the garden; the sight of him nimbly walking the wall; the thrill of completing that walk myself; the memory of what it had felt to be held briefly in his arms; the smile in his dark eyes as he bid me good-night.

It was incredible that, only eleven hours before, I had not even been aware that such a person as Edward Taylor existed in the world. It seemed to me that I would, forever after, view my life as having two distinct divisions: that portion which occurred before I met Edward Taylor, and everything that followed.

These happy musings were instantly suspended the moment Cassandra and I reached the privacy of our chamber, for she shut the door and cried,

"What were you thinking, Jane? How could you even conceive of performing such a stunt as that?"

I stared at her, shocked to be the recipient of such hurt and anger from my sister, who was generally so loving, tranquil, and unruffled. "It was just an impulse, Cassandra. I—"

"What you did was reckless and very selfish."

"Selfish? How?"

"Did it not even occur to you to think how *I* might feel, to see you engaged in such dangerous activity?"

I flushed, unwilling to admit that I had not considered her feelings at all. "It was not so *very* dangerous."

"It was! That wall was eight feet high! You could have broken your neck!" Tears welled in her eyes. "What if something had happened to you? Can you imagine how it would have affected me, Mamma, Papa, all our family—not to mention the Bridges family, who are so kindly hosting us? Had you been hurt, all should have suffered—but me most particularly, Jane. You are a treasure to me, my dearest sister, my closest friend—I cannot imagine my life without you in it! To see you up there in so precarious a position, in danger (or so it seemed to me) of falling at any moment—I believe I aged a year in those few minutes!"

To see my beloved sister so distressed, and all on my account, invoked similar emotions in me, compounded by a sudden, overwhelming sense of guilt. "Oh! Dearest; forgive me. I am so sorry!" Tears spilled from my eyes as I wrapped my arms around her. "I did not think of any of that. I did not mean to worry you. I saw the challenge in Edward Taylor's eyes, and I merely acted upon it."

"He was not challenging *you*."

I felt her tears against my cheek as she returned my hug. "No; I suppose I wanted to challenge myself."

"Was that truly your motivation? Or were you, perchance, hoping to gain his good opinion by shewing him how daring you could be?"

My face grew warm. "I was doing no such thing."

Cassandra drew back from our embrace and looked at me. "You were. *He* was showing off to impress you; and you did the same."

If there was truth in my sister's assertion, I could not—or did not—wish to see it. "He was not showing off. Edward Taylor is an enthusiastic, energetic young man; I think he was just having a bit of fun."

"I do not approve of his idea of fun." As we undressed and prepared for bed, Cassandra went on, "This must be what Lady Bridges meant when she said he was *a little too wild*. What he did was imprudent and unsafe. He did not consider how his actions might affect or worry us, any more than you did; nor did he seem to care about the consequences, had he fallen and injured himself. And then to encourage *you* to follow in his footsteps! This is wild and irresponsible behaviour indeed, Jane."

"I cannot agree. He did *not* encourage me; he *tried* to stop me from attempting it, you will recall, but I was very determined, and he did not think to worry us, and had no concern for his own safety, because he *knew* he could do it—he had done so many times before. Did you see with what ease he traversed the wall?"

"Nevertheless: you both behaved very irresponsibly."

I sighed. "Fine. Perhaps *I* did, I regret the pain I have caused you, and I promise to be more circumspect in future; but I refuse to allow Edward Taylor to share the blame. Be angry with *me,* Cassandra, but pray, do not be angry with *him*. I spoke with him at length during our walk in the garden, and have seen a side to him that you have not."

"What side is that?"

"Oh! He is so unlike anyone I have ever met! He is charming, accomplished, and so intelligent—and he has had the most fascinating life."

Cassandra sat down beside me on the bed, and as she brushed my hair, I shared with her the many things that Edward Taylor had told me about himself, his family, all the languages he spoke, and that his mother had died when he was just five years old.

"How tragic for her; and how sad to think of all those little children growing up without their mother."

"I think he feels her loss very deeply. And yet, look how well he has turned out, despite it."

"He *is* a very attractive young man, Jane," admitted my sister reluctantly, "and indeed very charming."

"Oh, Cassandra; he is more than charming. I like him so very much!"

"I know you do, dearest. But—I cannot help but feel that you behave very differently when in his company. You said so yourself this morning after you met: *I was not myself.* Why, in this one day alone, you have been leaping out of carriages and climbing up on walls in a manner far more rash and exertive than you have ever exhibited on your own."

"Yes; but it has been so exciting, Cassandra! *He* is so exciting!" We exchanged positions on the bed, and I returned the favour and brushed my sister's hair. "I cannot forget what he said before I walked the wall: *Should you feel unsteady, you have only to bend your knees, take a breath, and move on*. The more I think about it, there is great wisdom in those words. Should I ever find myself wavering in the attempt of something—should I feel stuck in some way or afraid to take action—I shall remember that maxim, and take it to heart."

"I suppose it is a good saying, which can apply to a great many things."

When our preparations for the night were complete, we drew back the white cotton counterpane and climbed into the bed we were to share. Cassandra blew out the candle, plunging the room into semi-darkness. After a moment, I turned to her on the adjacent feather pillow, and said quietly:

"Do you think Edward Taylor likes me?"

She did not immediately answer. "Well: he sought you out particularly, Jane, for our walk in the garden."

"He and Mr. Payler sought out us both."

"They did; but Mr. Taylor gave all his attention to you."

"That does not mean he likes me. He is heir to a great house and fortune—do you think it is too much to hope for, that he might be interested in a girl like me?" Before she could reply, a sudden thought occurred to me. "Oh! How thoughtless I have been. All this time, I have been thinking only of myself! How was *your* walk with Thomas Payler? I am sure he likes *you,* Cassandra! From the moment we first met on the road, he has had

130

eyes only for you. Did you find him amiable?"

Even in the dim light, I could discern her blush. Carefully, she said, "He is rather quiet, but he is an affable young man."

"Well then! The next few weeks are going to be very interesting! When do you think we shall see them again?"

"As Sophia claims they will be invited to all the same festivities that we are, I should think it will be very soon."

I rolled over, smiling into my pillow in anticipation.

The next morning after church, the house was all in a flutter with a visit from two dress-makers. Bolts of cloth in a multitude of colours were laid out on the tables and sofas in the drawing-room, where the Bridges ladies were to choose their frocks to be constructed for the Midsummer's Eve bonfire. At the same time, the dress-makers took final fittings upstairs for the new gowns which were to be worn at the engagement ball on Wednesday. Lady Bridges and Fanny had gone up first, and while the rest of us perused the silks and satins on display, I made the following worried observation to Sophia:

"It is only three days until Wednesday. That is not much time to finish new gowns for all the ladies in your family."

"I know. I try to get Mamma to think ahead, but

it is a lost cause. She always leaves everything to the last minute."

"Our gowns will be ready in time," said Elizabeth with a shrug. "They always are."

"How, I cannot tell you," added Marianne. "In truth, I feel sorry for our dress-makers."

"They must have a bevy of elves helping them," said I impishly, "who work day and night in a workshop in the woods."

Cassandra laughed.

"What a fanciful idea." Sophia smiled.

Louisa's and Harriot's eyes widened, and they began whispering amongst themselves.

Elizabeth took no notice of my comment. Unrolling a bolt of embellished green silk and holding it up before her, she asked, "Does this colour suit me?"

"It is beautiful," replied I, struggling to contain a pang of envy, for I had never owned a gown made of anything nearly so fine.

"It goes perfectly with your complexion," agreed Cassandra, "and I am sure Edward will love you in it."

Louisa and Harriot now came over to me, their countenances alive with curiosity. "Tell us about the elves' workshop, Jane," said Louisa softly.

"We have never heard of one," added Harriot quietly. "Is there really such a thing?"

I smiled and, leading them to an unoccupied sofa, encouraged them to sit beside me. In a low tone, I said: "There are many such places all across England."

"Truly?" Louisa's eyes widened, but she appeared sceptical.

"Have you considered how many ladies there are, ordering new gowns every day, often at the drop of a hat, which frequently require hours and hours of detailed embroidery and trimmings? How do you imagine all the dress-makers complete their work in time?"

"Oh! I never thought of that!" cried Harriot breathlessly.

"If they really exist," said Louisa dubiously, "why have I never seen one?"

"The elves must remain out of sight—that is rather the point, do not you see? A dress-maker would never wish to admit that she requires so much help; so the elves work in secret, in cottages hidden in the very deepest part of the woods, and it is only the result of their progress that you perceive."

"Oh!" responded Louisa, nodding in wonder.

"I should love to see one of their workshops," exclaimed Harriot wistfully.

"So should I," remarked Sophia, joining us.

"Well, only the dress-makers know where the elves reside, and I doubt very much that they would reveal their whereabouts, lest great ladies like your mother should find out—no, that would be scandalous! But I have *heard* that one such cottage exists in the woods but a few miles off from Goodnestone Park; by all accounts it is a very charming cottage, with white roses trailing round the door, but so covered over with ivy and other vegetation that it is almost impossible to detect unless you know precisely where to look."

"Oh! How I should like to find it!" cried Harriot.

Marianne, smiling at me, said to her younger sisters: "We ought to take a long walk in the woods sometime and search for it."

Elizabeth, who had apparently also overheard our conversation, looked our way and said calmly,

"Do not be ridiculous, all of you. Such ideas as you are giving Louisa and Harriot! There are no such things as elves, nor any secret workshops in the woods. Our dress-makers do all the work themselves."

This pronouncement served to eradicate the delightful air of fancy which had, for some moments, permeated the room. In the brief silence which followed, the girls looked to me and their other sisters to refute this charge; but as no one could bring themselves to do so, they could only be disappointed.

"I told you Jane was just making it up," cried Louisa to her little sister.

"Were you?" Harriot demanded of me.

I nodded, feeling guilty now. "I do hope you will forgive me. At times, I let my imagination run away with me."

Harriot shrugged. "That is quite all right." She urged me to bend lower, and whispered in my ear: "I liked what you said. It was a nice little story. And *I* still believe that elves might exist."

"I entirely agree with you," whispered I in return, as we exchanged a conspiratorial smile.

A strawberry-picking party had been an annual occurrence at Goodnestone for nearly two decades, always taking place during the second week of June. Thankfully the weather co-operated, and the next day was very fine, with a bright sun and scattered clouds—ideal for a party to be held out of doors.

Anticipation of the affair was very great, and as everyone wanted to reserve his appetite for the cold, *al-fresco* collation to be served that morning after the fruit was picked, breakfast was a lighter meal and served an hour earlier than usual.

"Goodnestone is famous for its strawberry beds," said her ladyship at the breakfast-table, while adding cream to her tea. "We have the best fruit in Kent; nay, I dare say the best fruit in the country; would not you agree, Sir Brook?"

Sir Brook, his nose buried in his newspaper, responded with a simple and distracted, "Yes, dear."

"Our beds are the finest, and we have all the finest sorts," continued Lady Bridges. "Hautboys which are very scarce elsewhere, we have in abundance; our beds of chilis are good as well, and some space is given to the white wood, which although small, has the finest flavour of all."

"Such delicious fruit!" agreed Sophia. "Strawberries are everybody's favourite."

"The neighbours talk of nothing else all year but our party," her ladyship went on, "how much they enjoy it, and how much they look forward to it. To receive an invitation is always the highest compliment; but of course we must be very select as to whom we include, for it would not do to have *too* many people descend on one's garden at the very same moment."

It was a day which I had looked forward to as well, but for reasons very different from the neighbours: the foremost being that Edward Taylor was to join in the festivities. On another note, I knew that it heralded the arrival of Fanny's fiancé, Mr. Lewis Cage, a man whom I was most curious to meet.

As we later gathered in the drawing-room to await the arrival of the guests (the ladies dressed for a garden outing, wearing our largest bonnets and carrying our parasols), Sophia mentioned to Cassandra and me:

"Mr. Lewis Cage is bringing his particular friend, Mr. William Deedes of Canterbury, with whom he is residing during his stay in the neighbourhood."

"What do you know of Mr. Deedes?" inquired I.

136

"I know that he and Mr. Cage attended Cambridge together. Mr. Deedes has also had a long association with your brother Edward and the Knights."

"Indeed?" said Cassandra. "Have you met Mr. Deedes?"

"I have, at several assemblies in Canterbury." Sophia flushed a little as she added: "Of course we have seen more of Mr. Cage, ever since he and Fanny became betrothed."

My anticipation of the expected visitors was shared by Louisa, Charles, and Brook Edward, who kept running to the window to ascertain if they could perceive a hint of an impending arrival.

At a quarter to eleven, Charles cried, "I hear horsemen! I hear horsemen!"

"Shall we go without?" exclaimed Louisa.

Lady Bridges insisted that, as there was to be a succession of guests, with no idea of anyone's precise arrival time, we ought to remain where we were. Very soon the horses could be seen approaching, their hooves making a pleasant clatter in the sweep. Everyone made ready; Fanny looked less animated than I might have expected, for a young woman about to greet the man she was to wed; while unaccountably, Sophia appeared more glowing than usual, and kept her eyes directed at her lap.

The gentlemen were announced; they entered; greetings were exchanged.

Both were well-dressed, mature, and distinguished-looking, as befitted gentlemen of thirty years of age. Mr. Lewis Cage was a quiet, reserved man of medium height and no great beauty, although he possessed a noble mien: his manners were very fine, and his person graceful. He was gracious to Sir Brook and Lady Bridges, and very civil to the rest of the family, reserving his only display of mild emotion for Fanny, who received a deep bow and a look of fondness. To my sister, Charles, and me, when introductions had been made, Mr. Cage said politely:

"It is a pleasure to meet you. I look forward to getting better acquainted with you all over the next few weeks."

"As do we," replied Cassandra sincerely.

I wanted to reply in kind, but thought better of it and instead curtseyed and smiled demurely, behaviour which I believed my mother would deem more befitting for a young lady of my age upon introduction to a strange gentleman so much my senior.

Mr. Deedes was more lively than his companion. A fine, tall, good-looking man with easy, unaffected manners, Cassandra and I thought him much handsomer than Mr. Cage, and on first meeting, more amiable.

"Mr. Deedes is even more wealthy than his friend," Marianne told us in confidence. "In addition to a residence in Canterbury, he inherited several other properties from his father, including an ancient house near Bromley-green called Claypits Manor, and the adjoining manor of Bishopswood."

While Mr. Cage sat down across from Fanny and lapsed into silence, Mr. Deedes made a point of speaking to all the principal people in the room; after shaking hands with Charles, he made overtures to my brother Edward, my sister, and myself, adding:

"I have heard a great deal about you two young ladies from your brother."

"Have you indeed?" Cassandra smiled. "What is Edward saying about us behind our backs?"

"All good things, I assure you."

My brother laughed. "Deedes and I have had a long association. We used to get into all manner of scrapes before I went on my Grand Tour. Now at last we are to travel together. He is to join me and the Knights and a few other friends on our tour of Scotland next month."

"I cannot tell you how delighted I am to be included, and how much I look forward to the excursion," added Mr. Deedes.

"I am sure it will be very agreeable," responded Cassandra.

"Oh! I wish I were going," cried I. "How I should love to see Scotland!"

"Well, perhaps when you are a bit older, Jane," said my brother kindly.

The sounds of horses and carriages were now heard in the sweep; there was some bustle without; and soon a group of new arrivals entered the drawing-room. The first to appear was Edward Taylor, looking very handsome in a blue coat. He glanced my way; he smiled; and I was all anticipation, my heart beating faster as I imagined the morning ahead.

Chapter the Tenth

I had no opportunity to say hello to Edward Taylor, for at the same moment that he arrived, Thomas Payler made his entrance along with his mother and father and a large parade of children, all of whom were splendidly attired and carried baskets trimmed to match their clothing.

"What a fine-looking family," whispered Cassandra to me.

"Yes, but they are rather overdressed for the occasion," whispered I in return. "Their finery more befits a dinner than a morning in the garden."

"Hush," warned Cassandra sternly, as Lady Bridges came forth and proceeded to introduce us to all the members of the family. Mr. and Mrs. Thomas Watkinson Payler were a handsome, aristocratic-looking, good-humoured, talkative couple in their middle forties, who were very proud of their progeny, and not afraid to say so. They had seven sons (Thomas being the eldest at eighteen) and one daughter, Charlotte, a very pretty, demure young lady who wore an attractive bonnet with pale green ribbons, and who struck me as being the very opposite of her parents, in that she was quiet and reserved.

"The Austens are sisters to Elizabeth's intended, Edward," remarked Lady Bridges when the presentations were complete. "They are from a tiny village in Hampshire, where their father is a clergyman; but of course you know that Edward is heir to a host of properties in that county, as well as Godmersham Park, and when he inherits, he will change his name to Knight."

"Mr. Watkinson Payler, Esquire, has quite an illustrious history," added Sir Brook, "for his ancestor was created a baronet during the reign of Charles I, and he would continue to be so today, had not the lack of surviving issue caused the baronetcy to expire at the start of this century. They have a delightful coat of arms—three lions and three mullets of six points each—truly delightful."

"What do these girls care about coats of arms?" cried Lady Bridges, adding, "You *will* be interested to know, however, that Mr. and Mrs. Watkinson Payler both had their portraits painted at the time of their marriage, by Joshua Reynolds himself!"

"Oh! You need not mention that," said Mr. Thomas Watkinson Payler (Esquire), with a dismissive wave of his hand, immediately continuing, in a voice deep with pride, "It was a small indulgence, we paid but seventy guineas for the honour."

"We were fortunate that he made himself available," said Mrs. Watkinson Payler, "for Joshua Reynolds had just then been appointed the first president of the Royal Academy. He enjoyed *then,* even as he does now, a reputation as the foremost portraitist of our age. The portraits are on view at Ileden Manor, and should you wish to see them, we should be only too happy to oblige you. We live only four miles distant."

"I am sure we should love to see them," said Cassandra graciously, "should the opportunity arise."

"Let us try to arrange something while you are in the neighbourhood, Miss Austen and Miss Jane," said Mrs. Watkinson Payler. "Perhaps a dinner for our three families?" She and Lady Bridges discussed the possibility, and settled on a date for the event the following week.

"Jane," said Lady Bridges, nodding towards the Paylers' daughter who stood silently nearby, "it just occurred to me that Charlotte is *exactly* the same age as you—you are fifteen, is that not so?"

I nodded.

"Well! You are the only two young ladies

present who can make that claim, and I am sure you shall both get along famously."

I smiled at Miss Payler, who sweetly returned the gesture; but we were unable to investigate this prophecy, as some minutes were immediately given over to a discussion of how the Paylers were related to Edward Taylor, the facts being these: that Edward's dear departed mother Margaret, whom everyone remembered as the loveliest of women, was the sister of Mr. Thomas Watkinson Payler, present owner of Ileden; and thus Edward Taylor was his nephew, and first cousin to all his children. As the connection was through Edward Taylor's mother, and not his father, it meant the Paylers were in no way related by blood to the Bridgeses, a fact which was greatly lamented by everybody.

The final guests to round out the party were the family currently leasing Bifrons Park: Admiral and Mrs. Fielding and their son. The admiral was a small, quiet, thoughtful, weathered man, recently retired, who had opted to lease the estate for three years to determine whether or not he wished to settle permanently in the area. He had married late, had spent most of his life at sea, and seemed to have very little in common with his wife. Mrs. Fielding was a fat, red-faced woman whose clothing and accessories reflected a sense of too much money and too little taste. Although civil and well-meaning, she was prosing and pompous, and from the moment of our first acquaintance, I ascertained that she thought or said nothing of consequence, except as it related to her own and her son's concerns. Indeed, her life seemed entirely devoted to promoting the happiness of their son Frederic, an equally heavy-looking, shy lad of seventeen, who took a full minute to formulate even the simplest sentence before he spoke it.

With everybody assembled (a group of more than thirty people), Lady Bridges directed a servant to hand out baskets to all those who had come without, and issued the following directive: that although we were welcome to eat as many berries as we liked during the picking, we were expected to fill our baskets, and to deliver them to one of the tables in the garden, where cold meats, bread, cheese, cream, and other refreshments were to be served at half-past two. Following this, there would be lawn games.

All soon issued outside, our object: the walled garden enclosing the strawberry beds, which lay just beyond the garden where I had walked with Edward Taylor two days previously.

During this progression, everyone instinctively separated into parties according to age, interests, or familiarity. The youngest boys and girls, a very sizeable crowd, all led the charge, determined to find (and no doubt eat) the best strawberries for themselves. The older gentlemen—Sir Brook,

Admiral Fielding, and Mr. Thomas Watkinson Payler—made up the next grouping; Lady Bridges and Mrs. Fielding walked just behind; the lovers—Fanny and Mr. Cage, and my brother Edward and Elizabeth, walked in pairs, quietly conversing; Frederic Fielding gravitated to Edward Taylor, Thomas Payler, and his two eldest brothers; Mrs. Watkinson Payler and her daughter Charlotte chatted beneath their parasols; and Mr. Deedes took charge of Sophia, Marianne, Cassandra, and myself.

All of this occurred in the most natural manner; but as we made our way across the lawn, I could not help but glance aside at Edward Taylor, hoping that he would choose to pick strawberries with me.

Mr. Deedes, with a good-natured smile, said, "Miss Austen, Miss Jane: did I hear that you are from Hampshire?" At Cassandra's affirmative reply, he added, "Regrettably I have never visited that part of England, but I understand you have a marvellous cathedral."

"Yes, at Winchester," answered Cassandra.

This conversation continued, but I could not attend; my thoughts were all of Edward Taylor, who was walking so close by. As we approached the wooden door leading into the first of the three walled gardens, he caught my eye, and my pulse quickened; I thought I perceived an expression intimating that he was on the verge of quitting his present company to join ours; but Mrs. Watkinson Payler, pausing until we caught up to her and her daughter, turned to me with an eager smile, and said,

"Miss Jane! It seems that Lady Bridges has singled out you and my daughter Charlotte to be companions! Shall we walk together so that you can become acquainted?"

"That would be very nice indeed, Mrs. Payler," said I, striving to shew more enthusiasm than I felt, for she and her daughter did seem to be affable ladies. As the three of us separated from my party, with a sinking feeling, I observed Edward Taylor pass through the opening with the other young gentlemen. I soon followed in the company of Mrs. Watkinson Payler and her daughter, who walked quietly at her mother's side.

As we crossed through the first walled garden, where servants were preparing for the collation to be held later that day, Mrs. Watkinson Payler said: "Tell us all about yourself, Miss Jane. Are you out yet?"

"No, ma'am."

"Neither is Charlotte. But her father and I are allowing her and all of our sons to participate in all the events at Goodnestone this summer, nevertheless. We saw no reason not to, as this is a celebration for family and friends, and so many other children are to be included. Is your mother extending you the same consideration?"

"She is, ma'am."

"I am glad to hear it, for then you and Charlotte will see a great deal of each other! What fun you will have!"

I darted a smile at Charlotte, and in an attempt to include her in the conversation, said: "I hope that proves to be the case, Miss Payler."

Charlotte seemed to be on the point of replying; but her mother cried,

"Oh! Is not it a lovely day for an *al-fresco* party? It is just the same as last year! What a long row of tables and chairs they have set up here, and all decorated so prettily with flowers! And as always, it is situated beneath a canvas shelter and a good shade tree—so thoughtful! Wait until you see all the food and beverages they will be bringing out! We have been honoured to attend the Bridgeses' strawberry-picking party three years in a row now, and I must say, it is always the highest compliment to be invited! The last two years were not nearly as nice as the summer of 1788, for *that* summer the Taylors were in residence at Bifrons, which occasioned our inclusion—and oh! What a delightful family they are! The Reverend Edward Taylor is so very learned, and all my nieces and nephews are so handsome and amiable, particularly the eldest! The last time we had seen them they were so very small, I could form no opinion of them— Charlotte was but a little child when they emigrated abroad, and my nephew Edward only five years old himself—but now only look at him, nearly seventeen and every bit the gentleman! Have you heard him play the violin?"

"I have not had that pleasure."

"Oh! It is a pleasure indeed. Have you met his brothers and sisters?"

"No. This is my first visit to this neighbour-hood."

"Every one of them is proficient in the arts, but where music is concerned, Edward is the most gifted. He is so charming, so accomplished, and he has travelled the world!" Leaning in towards me, and lowering her voice briefly, Mrs. Watkinson Payler continued: "Lady Bridges does not much care for him, which I say only reflects her lack of good judgement, for he is one of the finest young men I have ever had the pleasure of knowing, and I am very proud to be his aunt."

I smiled with pleasure, for these assessments of Edward Taylor's character met with my own perceptions; it was very agreeable to know that his aunt thought so highly of him.

We were making our way through the second walled garden, and my thoughts reverted to that recent evening when Mr. Taylor and I had walked atop the wall. What, I wondered, would Mrs. Watkinson Payler think of him (and of me!), were she to be made aware of our (shocking and) dreadful behaviour? Thankfully unaware of my musings, the lady nodded towards the young man in question (who was walking ahead of us, chatting with his friend and cousins), and added, "Charlotte! Is not your cousin Edward handsome and charming?" Without waiting for a reply, she went on, "When he and his family were last at Bifrons, he spent a great deal of time with Charlotte, you know."

A slight blush overcame Charlotte's features, and she glanced away. An unexpected feeling of dread descended on me; I had presentiment of what Mrs. Watkinson Payler might be about to say next. I hoped I was wrong. "Did he?"

"Yes. Edward was ever so sweet to her, even though she was but thirteen at the time. Since he has come back again and is staying at our house, they see each other every day." Lowering her voice again, she added in confidence: "I think he is falling in love with her—and she with him— and nothing could make me happier! It is my dearest hope that he and Charlotte will marry one day."

My stomach clenched and my mouth went dry; I could make no reply. I remained silent until we reached the opening in the high, brick walls leading into the third enclosed garden, which I knew contained the strawberry beds, and through which the greater part of the company had already passed.

"Pray, excuse me," said Mrs. Watkinson Payler,

"I will see you within. Charlotte: stay right there." So saying, she darted up to Edward Taylor, to whom she made a cheerful remark, before venturing through the entrance herself.

My mind was in a daze, distracted and dismayed by Mrs. Watkinson Payler's previous words. Oh! Was it true that Edward Taylor was in love with Charlotte? If so, did she return his feelings? Did that mean I had no chance of ever winning his affections?

From the corner of my eye, I saw Thomas Payler pause and gaze earnestly at my sister, as if he wished to seek out her company—but apparently he lacked the nerve, for with a lowered gaze, he proceeded into the next garden with his brothers. As Cassandra walked on with Sophia and Marianne, Edward Taylor turned back to me with a friendly smile and said:

"Good morning, Miss Jane."

I returned the greeting, my heart pounding with a mixture of hope and anxiety. Many people, I noticed, had paired off by now. Would Edward Taylor choose me or Charlotte as his strawberry-picking companion? If so, who would it be?

"You are in for a treat, Miss Jane," said he. "It has been several years since I picked straw-berries at Goodnestone, but they were the best I had ever tasted." Glancing over his shoulder, he added quietly: "By the way, Mr. Fielding has something he particularly wishes to say to you. I hope he will gather his courage and be successful."

Alarm spread through me. Frederic Fielding, standing nervously a few feet off, blushed a deep red and stared at the ground. Edward Taylor now held out his arm to Charlotte, and said,

"Shall we, cousin?"

Charlotte, with a lovely smile, took his proffered arm, and the two strode away together.

Hot tears threatened behind my eyes. I wanted to run back to the house, to weep in my chamber, but I was too devastated to move. Mrs. Watkinson Payler must be right! He had chosen Charlotte!

Frederic Fielding strode hesitantly forward, twisting his hands nervously. After stammering a few nonsensical syllables, he managed to stutter, "Miss Jane, would you—would you do me the honour of—of consenting to be my companion in the strawberry-picking?"

Disappointment enveloped me; but I gathered my wits, blinked back my tears, and replied as I ought. Mr. Fielding bowed and turned to walk beside me.

Seeing Edward Taylor just ahead of us, speaking quietly and congenially to Charlotte, made my heart ache with hurt and jealousy; but I knew these to be uncharitable emotions, and struggled to contain them. I wanted to hate both Mrs. Watkinson Payler and her daughter, but I could not. It was only right, I told myself, that Mr. Taylor should like his cousin and prefer to pick berries with her. He had known her for several years, after all, whereas he had only just met me.

We entered the last walled garden, which was equally as large as the two which had preceded it, and equally as lovely. I was immediately enveloped by the sweet fragrance of ripe strawberries, and looking around me, my sense of misery began to slowly dissipate. It was a most delightful place, with rows of fruit-trees of several varieties lining the perimeter, beneath which, and taking advantage of their verdant shade, were situated a great many wrought-iron benches; in the centre, enjoying the full effects of the sun, were innumerable beds of strawberries, cloaked with bright green leaves and heavy with ripe, red fruit. Birds twittered in the tree-branches and butterflies danced in the air. Our party, although sizeable in number, were so dispersed as to not make the area feel at all crowded, with the oldest gentlemen seated on shady benches quietly conversing, and everyone else stooped low in pairs or threes here and there, chattering gaily as they filled their baskets.

Mr. Fielding indicated a strawberry bed that had not yet been taken. We immediately proceeded there and bent at our task, searching for and gently retrieving the ripest berries as our prizes. I could not help but taste a few; they were indeed just as delicious as promised. Our intercourse was minimal; now and then he gave me a shy smile, and we exchanged a few remarks about the weather and the state of the roads. Knowing that he and his family were the present tenants of the house which Edward Taylor would one day inherit, I asked:

"How do you enjoy living at Bifrons, Mr. Fielding?"

He hesitated. "It is a very big house."

"I understand it is very grand as well."

"It is very big."

"Where did you live before?"

A great deal of thought seemed to be required before he articulated his reply. "In Hertfordshire, while my father was at sea."

I asked him where he had gone to school, but he gave only the briefest of answers, putting an end to the subject.

Half-an-hour passed in this awkward manner. He never asked me a single question, or made a remark of his own accord. I was trying to think of some thing to say which might be of interest to him, when his mother, across the way, and wiping her brow with a handkerchief, cried:

"Frederic! It is so hot. I can no longer bend and stoop in this manner, but neither can I turn in a basket half-empty. Come, come over here! You must assist me!"

Rising, Mr. Fielding bowed to me and begged my pardon. I nodded cordially in parting, relieved to see him go. I stood, and glancing halfway down the garden, spotted Cassandra, Marianne, and Sophia working happily together in a strawberry bed. I considered joining them; but at that moment, a deep, familiar voice sounded just behind me.

"Have you walked any more walls lately?"

My heart jumped with surprise and pleasure, as I turned and gazed up into the beautiful, dark eyes of Edward Taylor.

Chapter the Eleventh

No, sir; that was a one-time-only event, I am afraid. My sister would not look kindly on me walking atop any more walls," said I, laughing.

"What a shame. I admit, I have never seen a young lady attempt such a thing before. You exhibited remarkable skill at the endeavour."

The expression on Edward Taylor's countenance was so earnest and flattering, it sent a shiver of happiness up my spine. "Thank you. So did you."

He smiled.

I wanted to ask why he was here, and not with Charlotte—and why he was standing before me with an empty basket—but I did not wish to break the spell; fortunately he took charge of the matter himself, by explaining:

"My cousin and I filled our baskets already. She was fatigued and went to sit in the shade. I saw you on your own, and I thought I might join you and start on a second basket—if that is agreeable to you."

"Oh! Yes," I managed. That he had chosen Charlotte *first,* was a source of some little hurt; but I determined not to think about it. He was talking to *me* now. I crouched down and prepared to work; but he said,

"That is an awkward position. Pray, use my coat to sit or kneel upon."

"Oh, I could not—" began I; but he had already removed said garment and was laying it on the ground before me.

"It is too hot to wear it, in any case. This will serve a better purpose."

"Thank you." I arranged myself on the garment as directed; it did indeed promote my comfort. Edward Taylor kneeled down in the dirt beside me, and we returned to berry-picking. With him so near, it was difficult for me to concentrate, or to determine how best to begin a conversation; but once again he performed the service.

"You seem to be an experienced strawberry-picker."

"Apparently not as experienced—or as fast—as you."

"My basket was half the size of yours."

"Ah. Point taken." I picked another berry and gently stowed it. "We have strawberry beds at home, at Steventon. Picking the fruit, and eating it, has long been one of my favourite pursuits."

"Mine as well. We used to have strawberry beds at Bifrons, not so extensive as these. One of my earliest memories—I might have been four years old—is of me and my brother Herbert stuffing ourselves on berries, then returning to the house with our clothes and hands and faces all sticky and stained red, to the amusement of my mother, and the great displeasure of my father."

"I hope you were not punished for it."

"Oh, we were! We were sent to bed without dinner. After a cold bath."

Our eyes met, and we both laughed. I said: "I am sorry. There is nothing funny about a hungry stomach or a cold bath."

"There is nothing funny about *my father*. He has very strict ideas of how his children ought to behave. He also greatly prized his strawberries, perhaps even more than does Lady Bridges— although in *her* case, I believe the gardeners must take all the responsibility for the growing and care of the strawberry plants; whereas my father, however much I may resent him in other ways, is a dedicated agriculturalist, deservedly earning the reputation of being a most excellent farmer."

It was dismaying to learn that he resented his father; I wished to know more on that subject, but was uncertain how to go about the inquiry. "I understand that your father is a clergyman as well?"

"He was a clergyman before he came into

possession of Bifrons, after the passing of his older brother—after which he devoted his time to the farm and scholarly pursuits. When we first went abroad, my father so greatly missed farming, that after two years in Brussels and one year in Heidelberg, when we removed to Carlsruhe—"

"Carlsruhe? Where is that?"

"In Baden-Württemberg, southwest Germany, near the Franco-German border."

"Why did you go there?"

"Carlsruhe offered resources of various kinds, especially masters well versed in all those subjects which my father deemed essential to our education. We lived there very happily for five years, and my father indulged his bent by convincing the Margrave of Baden-Baden—the reigning prince—to let him one of his farms of some seven or eight hundred acres."

"He leased a farm from a prince!"

"He did. Rissing—so the farm was called—was very much out of order during the first period; but my father found an intelligent bailiff who spoke English, and with his help, greatly improved it and increased its productivity."

"An arrangement which, I suppose, proved very satisfactory to the margrave."

He laughed. "Yes."

Edward Taylor's manner was so congenial, and his discourse so captivating, that I found myself once again entirely at ease in his company.

Across the way, I perceived Charlotte Payler seated on a bench beside her mother, both fanning themselves. Mrs. Payler smiled briefly at me, and I thought I perceived slight irritation in her eyes. All at once, I felt a little guilty about the attention which Edward Taylor was paying me. Her desires for her daughter were clearly very important to her. I had no wish to hurt her or Miss Payler; but then, I had no idea if Miss Payler and Mr. Taylor shared those feelings and intentions which her mother had expressed. And what of *my* feelings? Were not they equally important? I reminded myself that Charlotte had the opportunity to see Edward Taylor every single day, for he was now residing at her very house; I had to make the most of what little time I was allowed to spend with him.

I looked away. As Edward Taylor and I proceeded down the row of plants, he helped me move his coat to the new location, and we resumed our conversation. "Did you ever meet the prince who owned the farm?" I asked him.

"We inhabited a house which looked towards the margrave's palace and on the intervening gardens, so we kept company on a regular basis."

"A regular basis?" said I in surprise.

"He was a popular and courteous fellow. He had been in England and spoke English fluently. He patronized literature, art, and science as far as local circumstances and his means admitted. His eldest son, the hereditary prince, had married a princess of Darmstadt, a most delightful *Frau*, and we associated with them and their *kinder*. From every member of this family we experienced, during our stay at Carlsruhe, the greatest kindness and attention."

"What illustrious acquaintances!" cried I in wonderment. "Did you have other such associations while abroad?"

He shrugged, and said indifferently, "We regularly met with all the English travellers of rank."

"Such as?"

"You wish to know their names?"

"I do."

"Well, let me think. In Germany, it was the Lord Chancellor Thurlow and the Lord and Lady Hertford. In Florence, the Duke of Argyll, Lady Charlotte Campbell, and Lord Hervey, to name a few. During our stay in Rome last winter, the Princess Santa Corce, wife of the Spanish ambassador, had balls and dinners frequently. Her house was open to the English, as was, for a time, that of the Cardinal de Bernis, who had been the French ambassador—"

He paused; I suppose I was staring at him in awe, as I tried to imagine attending assemblies and dinners in the Italian capital with lords, princesses, cardinals, and ambassadors; but it was entirely beyond my comprehension. To think that he had experienced all this! It was incredible.

Edward Taylor blushed, and said: "Pray, forgive me; this must all sound very tedious."

"No—no—it is not tedious at all. I am most interested, I assure you. Please go on. Who else have you met?"

He seemed embarrassed now. "Well. There was the Princess Giustiniani, Duchess of Corbara, and her sister; they were the beauties of Rome last season."

"How elegant they must have looked."

"They *were* lovely—but as to meaningful conversation, they had nothing to offer." The look and smile he gave me indicated, without words, that our present discourse was far preferable to him than had been the other.

My cheeks grew warm; I was flattered. *He* seemed to feel he had already said too much, but I was too fascinated to leave the subject. "Tell me more. Who else did you associate with?"

"At Rome, a great many French emigrants passed their evenings at my father's house when we were disengaged and had music. But really, I would rather not—"

"Who?"

"Who?" He laughed lightly. "All right, if you must know: the Prince and Princess of Monaco, the Marquis de Duras (he sang well, and took a third in trios with my sisters), the Abbe Maury, various *artisti* including Canova—" Noting my expression, he stopped again, and coloured more deeply.

Struck dumb, I worked in silence for a moment, adding berries to my basket. I was familiar with the *names* of some of those mentioned, having read about them in the newspapers, or heard them talked about in my father's dialogues with his most worldly friends; but I did not know anyone who had actually *met* such well-known persons. Yet it was clear that to *him,* such acquaintance-ships had been an everyday occurrence. At length I said,

"What a fascinating life you have led, Mr. Taylor. My own life seems very small in comparison."

"I am sure it is not."

"I have never been abroad. I only know of the world's many wonders from reading about them in books and seeing pictures of them. It can never compare with viewing such places in person. I am envious of all that you have seen and experienced—and at so young an age."

"I have had an unusual upbringing, I am aware; I am grateful for it, and I long to see more. I would like to live abroad again some day."

"Would you really?"

"Yes." He sighed, as if the weight of the world were upon his shoulders. "But that is highly unlikely, since—" He did not finish, seeming to think better of his remark. We moved on again along the row of strawberry plants, and instead he said: "We have talked far too long about me, Miss Jane. Pray, tell me more about yourself. Forgive my ignorance; I know you hail from Hampshire, but where exactly is Steventon?"

"It is a small village not far from Winchester."

"How do you like it there?"

"I like it very well. We have many good friends."

"An excellent recommendation for a neighbourhood."

"Our house is comfortable—although nothing like the houses I have seen in Kent, which are so large and magnificent. The way you live here—it is like a dream!"

His smile vanished. "There is more to dream about in life than a large house." He fell briefly silent, pulling a berry from beneath the leaves with such force that juice squeezed onto his hand. He seemed perturbed about something, although I knew not what. Before I could inquire into it, he said, "Do you have other brothers and sisters, besides the ones I have met?"

"Cassandra is my only sister. I have six brothers in all."

"A family of eight children! The same as me."

"Yes."

"Tell me about them." He popped the fruit he had just picked into his mouth and ate it.

I obliged him with details about my other brothers. He seemed particularly interested in the fact that my brother Frank was a sailor, and that Charles was destined for the same profession.

"My brother Bridges is a midshipman, currently serving on the frigate *Acquilon*. He is, I think, about the same age as your brother Charles."

"Is he enjoying his time at sea?"

"Very much."

"You said he is called *Bridges?*"

Edward Taylor nodded, his lips twitching to hold back a smile. "I know; it is remarkable, is it not, how unimaginative is our race, when it comes to choosing names?"

We laughed. "It is remarkable, too, that our families are so alike. My father, like yours, is both a clergyman, a scholar, and an agriculturalist. He is not the sort one might have expected to take to farming, and yet he has, and he is much respected for it. The chief difference, it seems, is that your father was so fortunate as to inherit great wealth and property, while mine scrambles every day to earn his living. This, I believe, motivated his interest in farming: with many sons to educate and a houseful of students to feed, I think he saw in it the potential of both a source of income and a supply of food."

"He sounds like an intelligent and resourceful man."

"He is. I quite admire him."

The sun was past its zenith now, and it had grown quite hot. I wiped the perspiration from my brow, noting that Edward Taylor was in a similar glow. He removed his hat and ran his sunbrowned fingers through his glossy reddish brown hair, then shook his head as if to cool it, an action which made my heart beat to an irregular rhythm. To distract myself, I plucked the stem and leaves off a particularly rosy strawberry and partook of its juicy sweetness. Mr. Taylor did the same.

We ate the berries in silence, kneeling side by side, just inches away from each other, my skirts nearly touching his bent leg. Of a sudden, he said softly:

"You have a bit of strawberry, near your mouth, just there." Reaching up, he gently brushed something from my cheek. That slight pressure of his fingertips caused a tingle to rush through me. Our eyes met and held; the expression on his countenance as he looked at me was very arresting—filled with deep interest and something more, which seemed to indicate a rising esteem. My heart pounded.

He hesitated, then dropped his hand.

I sat down and looked away, my cheeks burning, struggling to recover both my mental and physical equilibrium. We returned to berrypicking. The sweet aroma of sun-ripened berries filled the air. Around me I heard the twitter of birds in the trees, the delicate buzz of bees, the chatter of the other gatherers, the intimate murmurs of my brother Edward and Elizabeth beneath an apple tree, and the hum of conversation from the gentlemen and women who sat in the shade fanning themselves. Edward Taylor seemed to be having as much difficulty resuming our discussion as did I. At length he said, with an unfamiliar trace of awkwardness:

"I believe we were speaking about your father's farm?"

"I believe we were."

"How large is it?"

"My father's farm?"

"Yes. How many hands does he employ? What is he growing this annum?"

In some bemusement, I answered: "I cannot tell you."

"No? It is a secret, then?"

I laughed. "Hardly. I simply do not know. He leases, I believe, about two hundred acres just up the road from our house—it is called Cheesedown Farm—but as for the specifics to which you refer—I have not the vaguest idea!"

"I take it, then, that farming is not one of *your* passions?"

I shook my head. "I have the greatest respect for farmers. We cannot do without them; the food they produce sustains us and the community. I have a deep appreciation of the land—and there is much amusement and many comforts attending a farm in the country. But I admit, on a day-to-day basis, my interests lie elsewhere."

"That is something else we have in common!" Mr. Taylor smiled as he added another berry to his basket.

"Oh? I thought, when you asked such probing questions, that you shared your father's enthusiasm for agriculture."

"Not at all. I was just attempting to be—polite." We both laughed, as he continued, "My brothers and sisters and I spent the bulk of our time studying while in Carlsruhe, but we were also obliged, for health and exercise, to work on the farm several mornings a week. Do not get me wrong; I love to be out of doors. I take pleasure in vigorous activity. I enjoy a morning of berry-picking, like this, or a long walk through the woods; but I would rather hop a fence than mend it, would rather climb a tree than trim it, and would rather ride an ox than feed it."

"How I agree with you! I know this might sound shameless or even sacrilegious—and I do so admire my father's devotion to his farm—but to constantly be worrying about the vagaries of the weather—"

"—and the rise and fall of the market—"

"—to oversee labourers, and till the soil—"

"—plant seeds, and clear weeds—"

"—the work and responsibilities have always seemed to me very tedious."

"Yes!"

We exchanged a smile; I felt the mood ease

again between us, to something fine and comfortable.

Gesturing towards our baskets, which were now filled to the brim, he said, "In that vein: I think we have done our duty where agriculture is concerned today—do you agree? Shall we move into the shade and sit for a little while?"

This idea, while very appealing to me, never materialised; for at that moment Lady Bridges made a general announcement, observing that everyone seemed to have completed their berry-picking, and inquiring as to whether they had enjoyed themselves. Her question was met with enthusiastic replies and applause, after which her ladyship directed everyone to bring their filled baskets back to the tables in the first garden, where refreshments were now being served.

I retrieved Edward Taylor's coat, shook it briskly to remove the dust which had there accrued, and returned it, uttering my thanks. The whole party began to remove *en masse*, and as we moved with it, Mrs. Watkinson Payler appeared abruptly beside us with her daughter in tow, and with a bright smile said,

"Edward! Charlotte has not entirely recovered from the heat, I dare say she would be most appreciative if you would give her your arm."

Mr. Taylor, after the briefest hesitation, smiled handsomely, and hanging his basket over one arm, he offered her an elbow. "It would be my honour, Charlotte."

My heart sank as Charlotte quietly slipped her hand through the bend of Edward Taylor's arm; but my spirits immediately revived when, turning to me, and holding out his other arm, he added,

"Miss Jane? May I escort you both?"

Chapter the Twelfth

A fine-looking repast had been laid out, with pitchers of lemonade as well as wine and wine punch. A great many servants stood at attention, accepting the strawberry baskets and placing them strategically. Mr. Taylor selected a central location immediately across the row of tables from his cousin Thomas, and held out a chair for Charlotte to his left, and for me to his right.

My sister swept in and claimed the chair beside mine, and as all the party arranged themselves in congenial comfort, my sister bent to my ear and said in a low voice,

"You seem to be enjoying yourself this morning."

I could not reply; but she squeezed my hand lovingly, and we exchanged a little smile.

Just then, I heard Elizabeth's affectionate but softly reproving voice, as she whispered to my brother, "Surely, Edward, you would not think of filling my glass *yourself*."

"Ah," replied my brother, colouring slightly, as he set down the wine bottle in his hand. "You are correct as always, my love. Thank you."

A servant rushed in to fulfil the duty. Even so, I winced inwardly at Elizabeth's reproof. At home at Steventon, we would not think twice about filling our own wine-glasses while at table. It was a sharp reminder of how much my brother's life had changed, and would continue to change in the years to come.

There came the sound of a knife tapping against glass; Sir Brook was calling for attention and urging everyone to settle down. When quiet reigned, he cried out in his booming voice,

"It is a great pleasure to see you all at an event which, I am proud to say, for the past twenty-odd years, has been deemed the highlight of the summer. That will surely *not* be the case *this* summer, however—for as you know, Lady Bridges has been busy as a bee planning a great many more festivities to follow this one—the first of which is the ball to be held here at Goodnestone two days hence, this very Wednesday, where I intend to make a formal announcement which you have all been anticipating. However, as I have my family and my dearest and most particular friends all gathered today in one place, I cannot deny myself the gratification of making a little advance, *unofficial* declaration regarding the two happy circumstances which have motivated this month of celebrations: the first of which, is that my daughter Fanny is to wed the esteemed Mr. Lewis Cage, Esquire, of West Langdon, Milgate!"

A hearty ovation followed. Fanny and Mr. Cage stood to be recognised. While he humbly bowed, her countenance gleamed with pride as she looked all around her, seeming to relish the approbation of the assemblage.

"I have not done!" cried Sir Brook, motioning for a reluctant Fanny to sit, and for the crowd to quiet down. "I have yet another proud announcement: my daughter Elizabeth is betrothed to a very fine young man, Mr. Edward Austen, of Godmersham Park!" More applause, as Elizabeth and my brother Edward happily stood, to receive the party's adulation. "It is certainly a very singular instance of good fortune in one family, that two girls, almost unknown, should have attached to themselves two young men of such unexceptionable characters," continued Sir Brook, "and I pray to God that their future conduct will ever do credit to their choice. The date of the weddings has not yet been fixed, but will almost certainly take place in December. In the meantime, let us enjoy the celebrations of these engagements, which begin on Wednesday and continue through Midsummer's Eve. Ladies and gentlemen: will you please rise and raise your glasses to the affianced couples, and join me in wishing them every happiness?"

All stood; glasses were lifted; words of congratulations were shouted; and everybody drank. Sir Brook then directed us to eat and be merry, which we accordingly did, enjoying the many offerings on the table from the cold meats, bread, cheeses, and cakes, to the salad and cucumber, and of course the strawberries and cream.

The meal, while delicious, would have been more agreeable from *my* point of view, had not Edward Taylor spent the preponderance of the time making observations to Charlotte, and engaging in conversation with his cousin Thomas across the table. My time with him in the strawberry garden had been so thoroughly engaging; we had experienced a connection which I should not soon forget. How could he now, not half-an-hour later, say nary a word to me, and act as if I did not exist? Meanwhile, Charlotte merely nodded and smiled sweetly at his every word.

Cassandra and I were limited as to conversation, for I could not speak openly about what—or *who*—was on my mind, with the very object seated immediately beside me.

We had all nearly consumed our fill, when Mrs. Fielding reminded everyone that the following week, in honour of the betrothed couples, she and the admiral were to host a concert at Bifrons, for which they had engaged professional musicians.

"It promises to be a truly delightful affair," said she, waving one fat, white arm in the air. "I have a very great appreciation for music, and an excellent ear for it as well. I should have been very skilled at the art had I ever had the opportunity to learn, for my own brother played the oboe, and the apple does not far fall from the tree, for," (nudging her son seated beside her) "my Frederic is a true prodigy on the oboe, which he has studied since he was nine years old, when he had learnt all he could on the clarinet and the flute; and I dare say he has such a musical ear, that he can hear particular notes in a sonata or concerto in a way that no one else can."

Frederic blushed a deep red and kept his eyes on his food.

Determined to engage Edward Taylor in some fashion, I whispered to him,

"What an interesting remark with regard to Mr. Fielding's musical ear, in that it sounds very clever, yet there is no way to prove it."

Edward Taylor laughed.

"My girls are also very accomplished on the pianoforte," exclaimed Lady Bridges with a sniff. "They have all studied with the best music-masters, and were trained especially at an elite academy in town."

"My nephew Edward is a great proficient on the violin," remarked Mrs. Watkinson Payler proudly.

"His entire family has performed concerts in Europe."

"Is that so?" inquired Mr. Cage with interest.

"I do play the violin, sir," replied Mr. Taylor modestly. "Music has always been my father's hobby, and his partiality to it was gradually imparted to all his children; but I would not wish my abilities to be overstated."

"My brother-in-law—this young man's father—told me," said Mr. Watkinson Payler, "that his children performed a sort of travelling concert at least once a week, wherever they happened to be living, and the locals often came to listen. Some months ago, he wrote of a particular evening in Verona, when their family was invited to join a group of professional musicians, and they held a magnificent concert before a vast audience including all the grandees of the town."

"How delightful!" cried Mr. Deedes.

Edward Taylor's blush deepened. "It was an unexpected but very pleasant introduction to the society of Verona, yes."

"I have never heard anyone play the violin as well as my nephew!" cried Mrs. Watkinson Payler. "Edward: you must play for everyone sometime, perhaps next week, after the concert at Bifrons? Lady Bridges, your daughters might delight us with their talents on the same occasion."

Lady Bridges coloured violently at this, and

said, "There will be no time for personal demonstrations on that evening, I believe. Mrs. Fielding, have you not engaged musicians for two full hours?"

"I have," replied Mrs. Fielding.

"Well!" cried Lady Bridges. "We would not wish to tire our audience with *too* much of a good thing." She quickly changed the subject, and the conversation at the table turned to other things.

I glanced at Edward Taylor with wonder; there seemed to be no end to the extent of his accomplishments. It was both sad and amusing to think that Lady Bridges (apparently) found his abilities such a threat to her own progeny, that she would not allow him to display them. "I hope to hear you play one day myself, Mr. Taylor," murmured I, "although, while I confess to a love of music, I dare say I will hear the notes in the same manner as everyone else."

He laughed again and seemed about to reply, when our attention was captured by a commotion at the far end of the table. Fanny was speaking in urgent tones with Mr. Cage, and the tenor of their discussion, which was escalating into a real argument, could be heard:

"But I *must* have a chariot," cried Fanny heatedly. "I cannot abide a chaise."

"A chaise is an excellent vehicle, my dear," countered Mr. Cage. "I have owned one these past ten years, and never had a moment's trouble with it."

"But *everybody* has a chaise. They are so common."

"I myself have never admired a chaise," agreed Lady Bridges. "Why, every hack is a chaise."

"Precisely," exclaimed Fanny. "It is very confined, barely half the size of a coach, and has that horrid seat which pulls out. I cannot ride facing backwards; it makes me very ill."

"You shall never be required to ride backwards, my dearest; I promise."

"You are entirely missing the point. A chaise is driven by a *postillion,* whereas a chariot, with its coach-box and driver, four horses, and seating for four passengers, with both seats facing *forward,* is ever so much more elegant!"

"Well," replied Mr. Cage, looking troubled, "I will give the matter some consideration, my dear."

"See that you do," insisted Fanny.

Sir Brook looked mortified by this exchange; he quickly stood and invited all the ladies and gentlemen who wished to escape the heat, to retreat back to the house. The younger people, he announced, or indeed all those who were so inclined, were free to enjoy shuttlecock and bilbocatch on the rear lawn, and archery in the park at the front of the house.

The party then broke up into two distinct parts, with the elders retreating with Sir Brook and

Lady Bridges to the mansion. As all the young people began to merrily advance towards the exit from the walled gardens, Mr. Taylor turned to Charlotte, and said:

"Have you ever shot a bow and arrow, cousin?"

Miss Payler shook her head.

"I have practised archery with my brothers ever since I was small," said I, feeling rather smug. "Mr. Taylor, may I challenge you to a round?"

"I would love to," returned he sincerely, "but I promised Charlotte the first game of shuttlecock."

He whisked Charlotte away. Deflated, I walked on with my sister.

"Charlotte is a very pretty and demure young lady," observed Cassandra.

"She is *demure,* indeed. Does she ever speak? I do not believe I have yet heard her utter a single word!"

"I am sure she speaks, dearest. She is merely quiet and modest, two very becoming attributes for a young lady."

"Well then, she is the very opposite of me! Oh! She dresses so perfectly, and nods so sweetly—do you think she is the sort of girl whom Mr. Taylor prefers?"

"I could not say."

"Mrs. Watkinson Payler certainly thinks so. She is convinced that he and her daughter are in love with each other. She is determined that they will wed some day."

"How does Edward Taylor feel about that?"

"I have no idea." I could not prevent a frown, for as much as I hated to admit it, Edward Taylor and Charlotte Payler *did* make a lovely couple. I averted my glance, as it pained me to see them together.

As we approached the rear lawn, I told Cassandra bits and pieces of what I could remember from my conversation with him that morning.

"Edward Taylor's childhood has been truly extraordinary," remarked my sister.

"It has! I have never met anyone else half so fascinating. Oh, Cassandra! When we were together earlier, picking strawberries, it seemed almost as if time had stopped, as if no one else in the world existed but just us two. It felt so *right* to be with him."

Cassandra hesitated, then gently said, "However right it felt to *you,* dearest—you must know that a match between you and Edward Taylor is extremely unlikely."

"Unlikely? Why?" responded I, nettled. "Because his family is so wealthy? Because he is the heir to Bifrons, and has consorted with princes and princesses?"

"Yes. We have nothing, Jane, but our father's good name. No property, no dowries. Edward Taylor will no doubt—certainly his father will expect him to—marry someone like Charlotte Payler, who comes from money and property."

I knew in my heart that she was right, but was not ready to accept it. "Our brother Edward was born of the same parents as ourselves, yet *he* is considered perfectly eligible for the rich Elizabeth Bridges."

"Yes, but only because he was adopted by an even wealthier family."

I sighed. "It is not fair."

"Nobody said that life was fair, dearest."

"Did you see the way Elizabeth spoke to him about the wine? I think her a dictatorial, self-centered snob, with no sense of humour and not a shred of imagination. They are very ill suited to each other."

"I disagree. I believe it to be a most promising match."

"You do? Why?"

"Because there is true love on both sides; it is very evident. I think our brother, coming from our comparatively humble beginning, must feel he requires a strong, aristocratic wife to help him fit into the society he now keeps. We have observed Elizabeth, on several occasions—including the incident with the wine—prove herself very adept at doing just that."

I nodded slowly, conceding her point. "They do seem to be very much in love; and perhaps she *is* good for him. Therefore, I will try to think better of her. But this brings me back to my earlier point: why should not Edward Taylor marry for

178

the same reason? Is it inconceivable that he should ever love someone like me?"

"It not inconceivable at all, my dearest. I believe that any young man of taste and sense, once making your acquaintance, should fall madly in love with you." She spoke with such deep and genuine affection, as to make me smile.

"May I repeat the compliment with regard to *you?* Cassandra, I observed Thomas Payler looking at you earlier this morning with the most earnest and yearning expression! It was clear to me that he wished to pick strawberries with you, but lacked sufficient courage to make the overture."

Cassandra coloured slightly. "Please, do not joke about such things."

"I am not joking. He likes you, I know it. Were he to follow his inclination and seek out your company—"

"Jane: I insist—for all the reasons previously described—that it is highly unlikely Mr. Payler would ever be interested in me. And I—" She seemed unable to go on.

"You are wiser than I in many things, Cassandra; but I think you are wrong about *this*. I cannot believe that wealth, class, and status are *irrevocable* impediments to love. Where true love reigns, I believe anything is possible."

"That is a fine belief, dearest; but it is not really practical."

We had arrived at the rear lawn, where several nets had been set up for shuttlecock. Edward Taylor and Charlotte Payler were already engaged in playing a game. Shuttlecock was a sport in which I had very little experience, and I watched with a pang of envy as they bandied the feathered shuttle to and fro, each of them playing with enjoyment and expertise.

"We are only here for three weeks," continued Cassandra. "We may not return for many years. Even if you should form an attachment with Edward Taylor, you must know it would have to be of very brief duration."

With an aching heart, I replied:

"Then it will be brief. And who can say what the future might hold?"

Chapter the Thirteenth

Goodnestone Park
Tuesday 7 June, 1791

My Dearest Martha,
Thank you for your letter, which found its way to me here this morning. It is refreshing to hear news of home, particularly to learn that you are faring so well as mistress of the rectory, and more to the point, enjoying said duties. As for my last

letter, wherein I gave a description of Goodnestone Park and all its inhabitants, although it might seem to be a shame to destroy anything written by my own hand (and I am flattered that you think the epistle contains several clever turns of phrase), I insist that you burn it (along with all the rest of mine) when you have finished reading it for the seventeenth or eighteenth time. I would not wish its contents ever to be made known to those few whom I so good-naturedly abused, even if they were all accurately depicted!

I have scarcely had a moment to myself since our arrival. The house is so full of people that there is hardly a quiet corner to be found anywhere; and you know how much I love quiet corners. My mother and the Knights are to come tomorrow. The strawberry-picking party proved to be particularly diverting. I was so fortunate as to spend time conversing again with Edward Taylor, the young gentleman who so obligingly retrieved us from the road upon our journey hither. He is truly the most engaging, well-travelled, and accomplished young man I have ever met in my life. I must tell you more when next I see you, for there is not room enough in this missive to do him justice. I wish I could scold you for your implication; but indeed, the Bard's line, "Who ever loved that loved not at first sight?" does apply, at least to me; I am already in a fair way towards falling in love with him! Should he ever return the sentiment, it will be a great disappointment to his aunt, Mrs. Watkinson Payler, who has designs on him for her daughter Charlotte (a pretty, rich young lady whom Mr. Taylor seems to dote on, but who is far too reserved for my taste). Yesterday, I hoped to capture his attention by displaying my considerable skills on the archery range, but as I am already proficient at the sport, he spent all his time teaching Charlotte how to shoot a bow and arrow. How irritating it was to see him standing over her for such a lengthy period, and in such an intimate posture! How I wish he had been instructing me! It seems that a young lady, if she has the misfortune of knowing anything, should conceal it as well as she can.

Now I have something truly unexpected to tell you. This morning I rose early and, before breakfast, I removed to the drawing-room, which was as yet uninhabited, hoping for a rare, quiet moment to practise on the pianoforte. I had just sat down at the instrument when my brother Edward suddenly appeared, hastened within, and shut the door. "Jane," said he, in great distress and perturbation, "I need your help." "My help? Why?" said I. He explained that he and Elizabeth had quarrelled last night. He had made a thoughtless remark, his fiancée was furious with him, and he wanted to write her a note of apology. "However," said he, "I think something more than a standard letter is required— a poem perhaps, or something in the romantic vein—but I am hopeless at that sort of thing. You are a clever writer, Jane. Would you do me a great favour and draft a note to Elizabeth with pretty words of apology, which I can then transcribe in my own hand? It will have to be our secret, of course; it must seem as if I wrote it myself."

You can only imagine how surprised I was by this request! At the same time, I was delighted by his faith in my abilities. Of course I told him that I would be only too happy to help. (I break no vows of secrecy in this disclosure, for he said I might tell you and Cassandra, but no one else.) He required my services imme- diately, in the hopes that the breach could be mended by this evening at the latest (for the engagement ball is tomorrow). I spent a good two hours labouring over the endeavour. It was rather a trial to compose, as he did not wish to share the particulars for which he was apologising, requiring the admission of guilt to be constructed in the most general terms. At length I found inspiration in Shakespeare (three copies of his complete works, which appear to have never been read, adorn the library shelves here). My brother proclaimed the finished work to be brilliant. He is recopying it now; we must wait to see its effects, which I hope will prove fruitful!

I expect I shall hardly sleep a wink to-night, for the ball is tomorrow—my first real ball! Although it will not be held at an assembly room filled with handsome strangers, as you and I so often imagined, there will be one tall, handsome young gentleman with whom I hope to dance (his identity I leave you to guess); after that, I will have nothing else to wish for. From the bustle which has been going on all day in preparation for the event, I predict it will be very grand; my only regret is that my mother steadfastly refuses to allow me to powder my hair. I can only hope, when she arrives tomorrow, that I can succeed in changing her mind. I must close now, for

Sophia, Marianne, and Cassandra are calling me to join them for a walk into the village. Fare you well.—Please give my greatest love to my father when you speak to him, and a handshake to all the boys.

With best love, &c.,
I am affectionately yours,
Jane Austen

How ill I have written. Your hand is so much more delicate than mine. I begin to hate myself.

Here is the note of apology which I wrote for my brother Edward:

My Dearest, Loveliest Elizabeth,
Words cannot express my chagrin over the words I so errantly spoke last night; and yet I must appeal to you in words, for they are my only ally. I spoke in haste, without thought or consideration for your feelings; I was self-serving and thoughtless. To know I have hurt you pains me so deeply, that I can never forgive myself; I only hope that you can forgive me.

Do you have any idea how much you mean to me? My heart has been yours from the very instant I first beheld you. When I look to the future, our future, I know that we are meant to be together. To thee I belong, and always will. Pray, allow me to quote the words of the world's most celebrated poet:

> Hear my soul speak; my heart beats
>   for none but thee . . .
> One half of me is yours, the other half
>   yours . . .
> And so all yours . . .
> My bounty is as boundless as the sea,
> My love as deep; the more I give to
>   thee,
> The more I have, for both are infinite.

My dearest Elizabeth, I admire you; I honour you; I look up to you; I adore and love you. Indeed, thy sweet love such wealth brings, that I do scorn to change my state with kings. Pray, forgive me, say you will, this moment, else my heart will be torn asunder, and I shall never recover, for without you at my side, I am nothing.

With greatest love,
Your Edward

In reviewing the note, I thought that *some* might consider it overly dramatic, but I deemed it appropriate for the circumstance and for the individuals involved. My theory proved to be correct, for when I descended for dinner that evening, Edward drew me aside, glowing, and said that Elizabeth had cried when she read it. The intent was achieved; they had made up their quarrel.

"I cannot thank you enough, Jane, or tell you what I owe you. You are truly a genius." My brother hugged and kissed me, beaming with happiness; then, spying Elizabeth coming down the stairs, he spoke softly in my ear: "Remember: this is our secret."

Elizabeth's eyes were lit with affection for her fiancé, a sight which did my *own* heart good. I could see that she and my brother truly cared for each other, and to know that I had been of some small service in this matter—that my own words had brought them back together, and helped to rekindle her love for him—was a source of great satisfaction. I had truly proved *useful* at last!

That night, as predicted, my mind was so filled with anticipation for the next day's ball, and the enjoyment I expected to receive from it, that I tossed and turned in bed for hours, driving my sister to distraction. At last, well into the wee hours, I fell into a fitful slumber, only to awaken just as the first rays of dawn were lighting the sky.

Lying in bed, I heard the house coming awake as servants scurried down the hallways, going about their duties. I rose, dressed, and went downstairs to find preparations for the evening's entertainment already in progress: immense flower arrangements were being placed on stands in the foyer and central hall, chandeliers were being fixed with fresh wax candles, and all the furniture and the carpet in the dining-room were in the process of being removed, to transform it into a ball-room. At the same time, the furniture in the library was being re-arranged, and some of it taken out, to temporarily accommodate the dining-room table and chairs, for both the day's meals and the supper that evening.

Wishing to remain out of the way, I walked for an hour in the park, an exercise which did my spirits a great deal of good. Not long after breakfast the Knights' carriage arrived, bringing with it my mother and Mr. and Mrs. Knight. I had so enjoyed the past few days at Goodnestone (wherein I had experienced a unique and pleasing sense of freedom from my mother's constant supervision), that I was surprised by how very glad I was to see her. I was happy to see the Knights as well, and the morning was given over to a lengthy discussion regarding everything which had happened to each during our separation, with my mother particularly interested in the details of the strawberry-picking party, how large were the beds, what variety of berries were cultivated there, how the weather conditions in Kent had affected their growth, &c. Lady Bridges was delighted by this line of inquiry, which might have gone on for a full hour uninterrupted, had not Mr. Knight proclaimed his need to stretch his legs after the confinement of the carriage, at which point he, Mrs. Knight, Sir Brook, and Lady Bridges took my mother without to view the gardens.

All morning, the young ladies were in a fever of worry and anticipation, for their new gowns had not yet been delivered. I could not imagine waiting in such suspense for a garment to arrive, which was to be worn that very evening! Elizabeth assured me that this was the general state of things in their household, and that all would be well. Indeed, at three o'clock another carriage drew up, bringing the dress-maker with all the new garments which were required.

Although it was yet early, all the ladies immediately rushed upstairs to dress, so that any final adjustments to their gowns could be made. My sister and I took advantage of this respite to practise our steps out on the back lawn, after which we retreated to our chamber to begin our toilette. I was filled with excitement. To think that to-night, I would dance at my very first real ball!

We put on our best gowns, which—although perfectly acceptable for a Basingstoke assembly— were nowhere as nice as those being worn by the Bridgeses. However, they were presentable: Cassandra's was the rose-coloured silk she had worn upon coming out, adorned with new trimmings, and she looked quite beautiful. Although mine had been made over from one of Cassandra's old gowns, the satin was still in good shape and free of stains, and it was a shade of dusky blue of which I was particularly fond. The sleeves were trimmed with gold braid, and I thought my new sash of gold silk looked quite stylish. My only regret remained unaltered: that even though the preponderance of the company would be powdering their hair to-night, my mother would not permit me to do so.

We had just finished dressing when there came a knock at the door; it was one of Lady Bridges's housemaids, promoted for the moment to assist us with our hair.

As Cassandra sat down at the dressing-table, the maid (who introduced herself as Sally) said, "Do ye have any hair pieces, miss?"

"We do not," answered I.

"Well, never mind, ye both have such lovely long hair, it will do just fine without."

Sally set about brushing Cassandra's hair, pinning part of it up, while leaving another part long and curly. When she finished, she said that she would prefer to do my hair next, and then apply pomatum and powder to us both afterwards.

I sat down before the looking-glass, unable to prevent a deep sigh. "There is no need for pomatum or powder in my case, Sally. I am not to share in that particular ritual of beauty to-night."

"What do ye mean, miss?" said Sally to me in surprise, as she brushed my hair. "No powder? Why ever not? This be a grand ball, ain't it?"

"Yes, it is," responded I tightly, "but my mother thinks me too young for powder."

"Too young?" The maid shook her head. "Ye're never too young in *this* house, miss. Why, all the Bridges boys and young ladies have been powderin' their hair for every formal occasion since they were ten years old."

"Since age ten?" cried I. "Do you mean to say that—even little Harriot Bridges is going to have powdered hair to-night?"

"Yes, miss. It don't seem right for you to be the only one with natural hair."

Ire spread through me. I met Cassandra's eye in the looking-glass; she returned a sympathetic glance.

"I am sorry, Jane; it is Mamma's rule, not mine."

I sat in stony silence until the maid finished my hair, and had wound around it a blue satin ribbon which complemented my gown. On any other night, I would have thought I looked quite nice; but to-night was different. I thanked her; she nodded graciously, then beckoned to my sister to sit down again at the dressing-table, where she draped a long cloth around her shoulders in preparation for the application of pomatum and powder.

Having no desire to observe a ritual in which I could not take part, I left the chamber. As I emerged into the passage, Louisa and Harriot appeared, attired in their new gowns, their hair elegantly styled with supplementary hair pieces, and fully powdered in bluish gray—the very image of all the fashionable ladies of the age whom I had so long admired.

I had never seen girls so young attired in such a manner except in old paintings, and the picture they presented was very striking; it made an unexpected impression, which I could not quite identify. As, at that moment, I was feeling rather sorry for myself, I deduced the emotion to be envy.

The young girls skipped up to me.

"Do not we look magnificent?" cried Harriot, beaming, as she paused to twirl in all her finery.

"You both look fit to be presented to the queen," replied I sincerely, to which the girls broke out into giggles and ran off.

I stood still for half a minute, steeped in misery, listening to the laughter from behind the closed doors along the passage, wherein the other young ladies were dressing. Lining the corridor were various ancestral pictures of regal men and ladies, all of them wearing wigs or with powdered hair. I yearned with all my heart to look just like them. My melancholy and despair grew to such a height, that I could no longer bear it. Tears started in my eyes; and, sobbing, I ran down the hall to the bedroom which I knew to be newly occupied by my mother. I rapped urgently on the door, identifying myself; she bid me to come in.

"What is the matter, Jane?" exclaimed my mother from the chair where she was reading. She was fully dressed in her best russet gown and white fichu, her curly hair already powdered beneath her white cap. "What do these tears signify?"

"Oh! Mamma! You cannot mean to humiliate me like this!" I flew to her side and kneeled before her, taking one of her hands in mine, as my tears flowed.

She set down her book. "How have I humiliated you?"

In between sobs, I told her about Louisa and Harriot. My mother looked surprised.

"I have wanted this for such a long time, Mamma. It is my only opportunity to feel what it is to be truly grown-up. Will not you consider and relent? Otherwise, I am to be the only person at the ball to-night with natural hair! I will be laughed at!"

My mother was silent for a moment; then she patted my back distractedly. "Well, well, we cannot have *that,* can we? We are not at Steventon now. If those are the rules of *this* house—if little Harriot Bridges, at age ten, is to have powdered hair—well!"

I glanced up at her, hope rising. "Do you mean—"

"I have been here but a few hours, Jane, but already I have sized up Lady Bridges. That woman has her nose so high up in the air, it is a wonder she can take a step without falling on her face! We cannot have *her* looking down on us! Why, her daughters are all so beautiful and accomplished, nobody else's daughters can hope to hold a candle to *them!* Even her strawberries are the best in the land, or so *she* claims, and her precious roses won a prize at some fair or other; well! My own roses are equally as fine, I assure you, for all that they have not been judged and won ribbons! You are a young lady now, Jane! Even if you are not yet *out,* we cannot have Lady Bridges or any of her ilk looking at you like a child!"

"Oh! Thank you, Mamma!" I threw my arms around her, so filled with relief and happiness that I thought I might burst.

"There, there, Jane," said my mother, "you will ruin my *ensemble.* Now dry your tears, and go get your hair powdered. Mind you, this indulgence will apply this one night only."

"I understand."

"One thing further: remember what I said, you are not to dance to-night with any strange men, only your brothers or your cousins."

"Only brothers and cousins?" cried I, distressed

once again. "But Mamma, there are but a handful of young men who meet that description! I have been here some days already. I have become good friends with some of the Bridgeses's friends, and in particular with their cousin, Edward Taylor. He is a remarkable young man, Mamma. I would give anything to dance with him."

"Edward Taylor?" She pursed her lips. "Is he the young man just come back from abroad, who is heir to that big house down the road, what is it called?"

"Bifrons. Yes. That is he."

"Well, Lady Bridges has her cap in a twist about *that* young gentleman; she seems to perceive anyone who is musical, well-educated, or well-travelled as a threat to her own precious progeny. Let us give her something else to fret about, Jane! He is, in any case, soon to be our cousin through marriage, is not he? You have my permission, my dear; you may dance with him—and I suppose with anyone else you call a *friend*. But I still say: no strangers."

"Thank you!" cried I again, kissing her cheek with relief; and I flew from the chamber.

I returned to my own room, where the scent of lavender hung heavy in the air, and I found that my sister had been transformed into a regal beauty.

"You look stunning," cried I, and without pausing added, "and you will never guess what has happened! Mamma has just given her consent for me to powder my hair! And to dance with any friends I like!"

"Has she?" replied Cassandra. "I am happy for you, Jane."

"Well done, miss," said Sally, beaming.

I resumed my seat at the dressing-table, my heart drumming with anticipation, as Sally covered my shoulders and upper body with a protective drape; she then applied pomatum to my hair, and liberally added the fragrant, bluish gray starch with a puff. Very quickly, powder filled the air and got up my nose and into my mouth, causing me to choke and sneeze. When she had finished and removed the drape, I was so enveloped by the flowery aroma, I felt slightly ill.

Cassandra, who had been watching from a chair by the hearth, said:

"There, you have achieved your goal. Are you content?"

"I am not sure." Coughing and brushing off the excess powder from my gown, I added, "I did not realise it was such a messy business."

"I tried to tell you." She smiled. "You look very elegant, Jane."

"Do I?" Turning and glancing in the mirror again, I viewed my reflection with a start. "I hope so. For in truth, I do not recognise myself."

Chapter the Fourteenth

Fanny and Elizabeth waited until the last moment to make their entrances before dinner. When at last they came down the stairs—Fanny stunning in violet satin, and Elizabeth very striking in a yellow silk gown with white lace trimmings, each adorned with a ribbon of matching silk tied round her powdered curly head, each beaming with supreme self-confidence as if certain she deserved all attention to be focused on herself—everyone turned as one to smile and comment with admiration. Mr. Cage looked proud; my brother Edward stood absolutely riveted; and when Elizabeth took his arm to enter the dining-room, he could look at nothing else.

Dinner was a hurried affair, as everyone's spirits were too high to eat more than a few morsels. Fanny and Elizabeth were particularly animated, for their engagements were to be officially announced that evening, and they were to lead the first two sets. All the ladies were resplendent in their gaily-coloured gowns, with their hair stylishly dressed; the boys and the gentlemen looked equally well in their finery. Gazing about me at all the powdered heads—and catching my mother's private, gently approving smile—I felt a part of something very grand.

In the half-hour that followed I was in a fever of anticipation, knowing that Edward Taylor would soon arrive; thinking about him, going over our previous conversations in my mind, and anticipating the evening's events to come, made me flush with pleasure. I knew that Charlotte Payler would be in attendance, as well as many other young ladies from the neighbourhood whom I had not met; but even with so many partners to choose from—considering the manner in which he had deliberately sought me out at the strawberry-picking party—surely on this special evening, he would ask me to dance.

The gentlemen soon joined us in the drawing-room, where we awaited the arrival of the guests. Mr. Cage stood by the door, conversing with Mr. Deedes. I sat down upon a sofa beside Fanny and told her how well she looked; she matter-of-factly returned the compliment. Wishing to get to know her better, I commented:

"How elegant Mr. Cage appears to-night. His jacket and waistcoat are beautifully embellished."

She glanced briefly at him, as if noticing him for the first time. "They are indeed."

"It must be thrilling to be engaged to such a fine man, and to know that you have found your one, true love."

My statement had been well-meant; I had expected it to encourage from her a modest smile, or perhaps a yearning sigh; to my dismay it induced instead a heavy exhalation, accompanied by a frown. "What makes you think that Mr. Cage is my one true love?"

I stared at her. "But—is not he? You are to marry him! Surely you must love him?"

She leaned towards me and lowered her voice. "If I share something with you in confidence, do you promise you will not repeat it?"

"I promise."

"Mr. Cage loves *me,* of that I am certain; but how could I love *him?* He is thirty years old!"

So surprised was I by her remark that I had no ready or proper response; indeed, I was completely at a loss, for thirty *did* seem rather ancient to me, and I knew Mr. Cage to be ten years older than Fanny. At length I replied with some hesitation, "Is not your father many years your mother's senior?"

"Yes; and you see how happy *they* are," replied she sarcastically. "A day does not go by when my father does not bite my mother's head off, or vice versa."

I floundered: "That may be so; yet I am sure they love each other. Many other such matches, although unequal in age, are also happy. As I understand it, Mr. Cage comes from a good family, and he seems a most amiable man."

"His lineage is excellent: there I have no complaints. As to amiability, at times, he is so accommodating that he is tiresome. He does go *on and on* about books; sometimes I have no idea what he is talking about." In an even more hushed tone she added, "And he is very plain."

Her attitude astonished me. "Mr. Cage may not be handsome in the classical sense, but he has a genteel figure and a sensible-looking face."

"How cleverly you speak. I will agree with you: he has a *sensible*-looking face. But what beauty wishes to be paired with a sensible-looking man, when she could have a handsome one? For I am a beauty, everyone says so."

"Fanny," said I, aghast, "if you do not like Mr. Cage, and do not even like to look at him, why are you marrying him?"

"I did not say that I do not *like* him. I like him well enough; I just do not *love* him."

"But to marry without affection!" I could think of nothing worse.

"You are very young, Jane; but one day you will find out: there are many reasons for marrying, and love does not always enter into it." With eyebrows raised, Fanny added softly: "Do you know how rich he is?"

I could formulate no reply.

"Do not look so shocked, Jane. Money is the best reason I know for marrying, and one of the best recipes for happiness. I could not let Elizabeth marry before *me,* and I could not let anyone *else* get him, could I? I will have my own coach, all the hats and gowns I could wish for, the family jewels—which I understand are quite sensational—and an estate every bit as grand as Goodnestone. I promise you, I will be very happy."

I felt such disgust, that I could stomach the conversation no longer.

"I do hope that you achieve the happiness that you deserve, Fanny," was my reply, as I stood and crossed the room. To conceive of living forever with a person one could neither respect nor admire! It seemed to me a crime against morality and humanity. I shuddered to think of the misery Mr. Cage should endure, by chaining himself for life to a woman who could not even pretend to care for him. I felt sorry for him. At the same time, although I had never truly *liked* Fanny (and liked her *now* even less than before), I found that I felt sorry for her as well. She appeared to me misguided; perhaps her upbringing, with a mother whose primary concerns were societal and centered on appearances, had prepared her very ill for making the most important decision in her life. Despite her protests, surely she could never be content in such a marriage.

I wished that I could talk to Cassandra about all this, to hear her opinions and vent my feelings; but I had been sworn to secrecy. Just then, to my relief, I heard a carriage drawing up in the sweep, signalling the arrival of the first guests; and the matter was, for the time being, swept from my mind.

In short order, the room was full of people. Those whom I had already met at the strawberry-picking party comprised but a modest proportion of the guests, and the sight of so many strangers filled me with a sense of disquiet. Where was Edward Taylor? The first circle were grave and formal, their manners matched by Sir Brook and Lady Bridges, as they accepted congratulations on behalf of the engaged couples, and discussed the advantages of the unions. Our hosts were too busy with their acquaintances to remember the presence of any guests who were unknown to the general company; but through the thoughtful perceptiveness of Sophia and Marianne, my sister and I were introduced to various persons who feigned an interest in us, and whose names I would not remember the next morning.

Mr. Deedes secured Sophia for the first two dances, and Marianne accepted an offer from one of the Paylers' sons, a sixteen-year-old called Harry. To my dismay, I noticed Frederic Fielding gazing at me in a penetrating manner, which seemed to convey his desire for a similar connection; I quickly moved away so as not to encourage him. Observing my brother Edward and Elizabeth, who stood intimately conversing beside a nearby window, brought back to mind my recent success in repairing that relationship. How agreeable it was, I thought, that a love-letter I had written had made such a contribution to their happiness! If only I could prove of such use to another couple—how delightful that would be!

In my cursory glance around the crowded drawing-room, I saw Charlotte Payler standing silently with her brothers Christopher (a handsome lad of eighteen) and Thomas. She looked beautiful in an absolutely elegant gown, which I thought put my own to shame. Thomas Payler kept darting intermittent, longing glances at Cassandra. Clearly he wished to be with her—perhaps was considering asking her to dance at this very moment—but he seemed to lack the courage to bring it about. Cassandra liked *him;* I felt certain of it. Oh! Why did he not simply cross the room and ask her?

Impatience rose within me, and with it, a solution to this romantic dilemma. Here, I realised, was the very opportunity I had been hoping for! Deciding that simplicity was best, I strode up to him and his brother deliberately.

"Good evening, Mr. Payler, Mr. Payler."

They both bowed and returned the greeting. Thomas Payler said, "I almost did not recognise you, Miss Jane, with your hair all done up."

"Oh? Is that why you have not yet spoken to my sister? Perhaps you did not recognise her, either?"

"No; I saw her." He coloured, his eyes finding Cassandra across the room.

"Well, I was not supposed to tell you this, but—"

Confidentially, I added, "She is very much hoping that you will ask her to dance with you."

"Is she?" He seemed astonished.

"She told me so herself."

"Oh! I see—thank you." He blushed even more violently.

Christopher Payler punched his older brother in the arm. "You have talked of nothing else for three days, Thomas! Go on, ask her! What are you waiting for?"

Still, Thomas Payler gave no indication of impending action.

"You had better hurry," insisted I, "before somebody else engages her for the first dance. I will take you to her!"

I gestured for him to accompany me. Hesitantly he took a step, then two more, and soon was threading his way through the crowd with me, until we reached Cassandra's side. She turned and seemed about to ask me something, when she noticed Mr. Payler and paused.

He stood before her, tongue-tied. Fearing that in another moment he might lose his nerve, I gave him a silent, vigorously encouraging look, filled with meaning.

He immediately blurted—the words issuing from his mouth as if shot from a cannon—

"Miss Austen, would you do me the honour of dancing the first set with me?"

Cassandra curtseyed. "I would be delighted, sir."

To say that Mr. Payler was overjoyed by her response would be an understatement. With a curious look in my direction, my sister took Mr. Payler's gloved hand, and they joined the procession which was just then removing into the entry hall, and from there into the ball-room beyond. I watched them go with absolute delight. It was only a set of dances to be sure, but it was a step in the right direction—and I had helped to bring it about! What might not be the end of it?

It was only when the drawing-room had partially emptied, that it began to dawn on me that I did not have a partner for the first dance myself; worse yet, the one person whom I most wished to see had not yet made his appearance. I waited with some anxiety, feeling entirely alone although in a room still filled with people. Was I truly to sit out the first two dances? How mortifying that would be! And where, oh where, was Edward Taylor?

Just then I saw him, walking confidently into the room, in the opposite direction of all those who were withdrawing. He looked very handsome in his green coat and embroidered waistcoat, which shewed his fine figure to great advantage. His shoes were adorned with gleaming buckles, his white neckcloth was perfectly tied, and his hair— *his hair!* With a cold shock I saw that he wore his hair as usual, the gleaming natural chestnut waves brushed back from his face.

Edward Taylor, alone of all the people in the house, had not even a hint of powder in his hair! I could not account for it. My first thought was: how very odd. Could it be that he had forgotten this was a formal ball? If so, he should be mortified! Indeed, several people looked at him askance as they walked by, and I observed two ladies exchanging remarks behind their fans. But Edward Taylor took no notice, greeting people and shaking hands with his customary self-assurance.

Soon he looked my way, and I saw his eyes widen—with what emotion, I could not determine—then he moved through the thinning crowd to meet me, and we bid each other good evening.

I could not help glancing at his hair; should I mention it? I did not wish to offend him. "Good evening, sir. What a pleasure to see you again." With a sweeping gesture, I made a dramatic curtsey, which I deemed appropriate to the occasion and my style of dress.

"It is a great pleasure to see you, Miss Jane." He bowed, and seemed to weigh his words as he added: "What a pretty gown. You look very— *noble*—to-night."

"Noble?" There was something in his tone and expression when he pronounced the word, which—although delivered with good humour, a raised eyebrow, and a smile—indicated a hint of something like mild disgust. Greatly puzzled, I wished to pursue the subject further, but at that moment Mrs. Watkinson Payler rushed up behind him and cried:

"Edward! There you are!" Taking him by the arm, she continued, "I *know* you would not wish Charlotte to be without a partner for the first set. Now come! She is waiting for you, and Sir Brook is about to speak!"

With a bow to me, Edward Taylor declared: "Forgive me. I shall see you inside?"

"Yes," faltered I; and with a heavy heart, I followed them into the ball-room.

The entire company squeezed into the former dining-room, which was emptied of furniture except for a row of chairs along one wall. When all had assembled within, Sir Brook issued a welcoming address in his deep, congenial voice, then announced the engagements of his daughters in a manner and verbiage similar to that which had been expressed at the strawberry-picking party. Applause followed.

The chamber, although sizeable, could accommodate no more than two dozen people at most for dancing; as such, many of the older set now progressed back to the library or the drawing-room to play cards, while others stood or sat along the perimeter. Fanny and Mr. Cage, given precedence, moved to the top of the room, as the other dancers began to take their places.

I waited in a fever of anticipation; although my hopes of having Edward Taylor as my partner had been dashed, yet I still wished to dance. Was it too late? What if no one asked me? Even Louisa Bridges, I noted, was taking to the floor with one of the younger Payler boys! It was painful to see Edward Taylor standing opposite his cousin Charlotte, him smiling so cheerfully, her looking all loveliness. I was embarrassed to think that my own gown had been made over, while hers was clearly new, expensive, and constructed especially for the occasion. We were so different; she behaved so perfectly and modestly, whereas I (at times) could not hold my tongue, and was anything but demure. To whom was Edward Taylor more attracted? What if he preferred Charlotte over me? The idea made me miserable.

No gentleman stepped in my direction or spoke to me. Mortified, I retreated to the side, not far from where my mother was situated in conversation with Mrs. Fielding, two elderly women, and several unattached ladies. My cheeks burned. It was my first ball, yet here I stood, ignored and slighted, with the older ladies and spinsters! To further my discomfort, my head began to itch slightly. I discreetly attempted to scratch behind my ear, where (having forgotten my elaborate *coiffure*) I came into contact with hair which felt stiff, heavy, and foreign to the touch. This effort went no further, for my mother hit me with her fan and whispered harshly,

"Jane! Stop that! You will ruin your new gloves!"

I lowered my hand, which came away dusted with powder. Suddenly, Frederic Fielding stood before me, blushing furiously as he uttered a nervous invitation to dance. *Now,* I had no wish to refuse; indeed, how grateful was I for the offer! His countenance lit up as I nodded, curtseyed, and followed him onto the floor.

The musicians played; the dancing began; and my thoughts were put into another channel. As Edward Taylor and Charlotte were in a different line and moving in a different direction, I lost sight of them as we worked our way down the row, and I gave all my attention to the endeavour. Everything that I had learned from dancing-masters at home and with the Bigg sisters at Manydown House, all the children's balls which I had attended, and all the hours I had practised diligently on the lawn, now came to my aid. My partner was clumsy and silent, but his flawed moves were made up for by his visible eagerness to please; and I was in a mood to be pleased. The music filled me and surrounded me, lifting my spirits; the exercise was so vigorous that I forgot my discomforts and disappointments, and I danced with real enjoyment.

Upon completing our two dances, Mr. Fielding

and I exchanged courtesies and expressed our mutual thanks. I began to search the crowd for Mr. Taylor, but before I knew it, to my surprise, I was engaged by Thomas Payler for the next two dances.

"Thank you, Miss Jane," said he with a significant look, as we lined up in formation, before Elizabeth and my brother Edward led the second set. "Your sister is a very fine dancer."

"I am pleased that you found her so."

Mr. Payler proved to be a very fine dancer himself, although his conversation was minimal, and when he did speak, it was only to ask questions about my sister's interests and pursuits. Did she like riding? What sort of books did she read? I was only too pleased to answer his inquiries, and to know that my little intervention had proved such a success!

As we moved down the line, I observed that Fanny was not dancing with her fiancé, but rather with Mr. Deedes, and Sophia, in very good looks, was dancing with Mr. Cage. An odd notion struck me: how well Sophia and Mr. Cage looked together! But I shook my head, knowing that could never be. I danced a set with my brother Charles, and after that with Brook Edward, who both proved to be charming partners.

Marianne, grown weary, retired for the evening. I sat down to supper in the drawing-room with Sophia and Cassandra. We were having a merry time going over all that each had experienced so far that evening, and comparing notes with regard to our partners, when I perceived Edward Taylor sitting across the room, supping at a small table with Charlotte and her brothers Thomas and Christopher. The sight of them laughing in such an amiable, confidential manner made my heart suddenly ache, so I turned my full attention to my own partners.

"Mr. Deedes is truly an elegant dancer," observed Sophia, smiling.

"I thought you looked far more comfortable with Mr. Cage," noted I, a remark which made Sophia blush.

"Jane, you are incorrigible!" protested she. "Mr. Cage is marrying my sister."

I probed Cassandra for information about Mr. Payler, but she would only say that he had found his voice at last, and they had enjoyed a pleasant conversation during one of the intervals.

When the music began again in the ball-room, I was quickly engaged by my brother Edward.

I had not had the opportunity to dance with my brother Edward in many long years, and as he was very accomplished at the art, I took great pleasure in it. The ball-room was grown very hot now, and as we moved down the line I was all in a glow; the air was close as well, from the exertion of so many dancers. Even so, by the next set, I was so enjoying myself, that I believe I could have partnered with anybody and been content; and it was that moment that Edward Taylor materialised at my elbow with a smile, and said:

"May I have the honour of the next dance, Miss Jane?"

With his gleaming natural hair, he stood apart from everyone else in the room, an effect which was startling but not at all displeasing; indeed, I could not deny that he looked very handsome.

"You may, Mr. Taylor," replied I, adding in my mind: *I thought you would never ask.*

Chapter the Fifteenth

I happily took Edward Taylor's arm, we moved into line, the music started up, and the set began. From the very first moment—the graceful manner in which he danced and held his arms, and the commanding way his eyes held contact with mine through every step and rotation—it became clear that he was a far more skilful and experienced partner than anyone else with whom I had engaged that evening.

As the formations permitted, we engaged in the following conversation:

"I have been hoping to dance with you all evening, *mademoiselle*," commented he.

"Oh?"

"Every time I looked, you were already engaged."

"I did not avoid you by design."

"I am glad to hear it. Do I understand correctly that this is your first ball?"

"*Oui.*"

"You surprise me. I would have thought you a veteran."

"I have had a lesson or two, sir. As have you, I would wager?"

"One or two."

"No doubt your father engaged dancing-masters for you since you were very small?"

"He did."

"And I suppose you have spent many years dancing in the ball-rooms of Europe?"

"Guilty as charged.—But none were more pleasant than this one—and no partner was ever more skilled or becoming."

"You are a great flatterer, sir."

"I speak only the truth."

"Indeed? You said something earlier which puzzled me."

"Pray, what was that?"

"You remarked that I look very *noble.*"

"And indeed you do."

"I cannot tell if that is a compliment or a criticism."

"Cannot you?"

"No. Ordinarily, *noble* implies—"

I was unable to complete my statement, for the dance ended with the usual courtesies, and a second dance immediately followed, its movements involving a group of six people, and so complex as to prevent further conversation. When we had finished the set (which afforded me more pleasure than I could have imagined), the musicians took an interval, and Edward Taylor inquired as to whether I would like a glass of punch. Having acquired same from a table in the central hall, we were lingering in a corner to sip the beverage, when I returned to the question which I had put to him earlier.

"With regard to our previous discussion—I cannot decide if I like being called *noble*."

"Why not? I should think it flattering to be compared to an aristocrat or patrician."

"Had someone else uttered the remark, or had you made it in a different way, perhaps it might have been flattering; but not the way *you* said it."

"Oh?" He looked at me directly, but did not reply; he seemed to be attempting to take a measure of my thoughts, before formulating his own response. I continued:

"Pray forgive me, for I do not mean to seem impertinent; I know you are acquainted with, perhaps good friends with, many people from the noble class, as well as from the royal families of Europe—"

He nodded silently, waiting to hear what I had to say.

I rushed on. "Although I have had less exposure to such persons myself, I have been taught all my life to have the greatest respect for them. And yet, certain things I have read and heard have led me to *imagine* that class to be filled with many self-important people, who believe themselves to be far above the rest of us, although in truth the only thing which sets them apart is the accident of their birth."

My comment seemed to take Edward Taylor by surprise; he laughed. "You are a bold young lady, Miss Jane."

"Am I? Why? Have I shocked you?"

"On the contrary; you have put into words my own thoughts exactly; feelings which certain of my brothers and I have shared for a great many years, but have never been allowed to express openly with anyone else, other than each other."

"Then you *do* have an antipathy towards the noble class?"

"Not an antipathy, no; not at all." Noting that my glass was empty, he inquired as to whether I wished more, and upon receiving a negative reply, he graciously relieved me of it, and returned both empty vessels to the table. "I have found many people of rank and title to be very amiable," continued he, "but I have met enough of them, and known them well enough, to understand their weaknesses and see through their pretences. I cannot look up to them as a sort of divine presence, as *some* do. At heart I feel their equal, just as you do."

It was pleasing to learn that we shared this point of view, yet it still did not answer my primary question. "Did you truly mean to flatter me, then, when you called me *noble?* Or, as I suspect, was there some other, less than charitable intent behind the word?"

He regarded me with a deep and thoughtful expression, and at length said:

"Perhaps, although I was unconscious of it at the time, there is something in what you say; for although I would never deliberately wish to give offence to you or anyone else, there are certain *practices* of the noble set which I find less than appealing—and *one* practice in particular, which is very much in evidence to-night."

I thought I could guess the practice to which he referred; and the particular direction of his next, brief glance confirmed it. "I take it you mean—hair powdering?"

He nodded.

"Then—you did not powder your hair to-night as some kind of—protest?"

"You could call it that. I prefer to think of it as the expression of a personal conviction."

"A conviction? Please explain yourself. What is wrong with hair powdering?"

"What is right with it?"

"It is beautiful."

"Beauty is a matter of taste."

"But—everyone does it."

"Not everyone; only those who can afford it. Hair-powder is expensive. It is an affectation of the upper classes."

"You call it an affectation; others call it fashion."

"And what is fashion, but mannerisms, styles, and clothing which are generally determined by royalty or the wealthy, and imitated by everyone who has the means?"

His comment surprised me; I had never heard anyone express a similar view. "If people imitate, I think, it is due to admiration and a desire to feel that they belong."

"That seems to be so; but is it not sad, Miss Jane, the lengths to which some people will go, simply to feel a sense of belonging, or to chase a perception of beauty? In other cultures, people engage in practices which they think beautiful, but which I consider hideous or ridiculous—for example in China, where they bind feet."

"I have read about that. Those poor young girls—to have their feet broken and forever bound—and never to be able to stand for more than a few minutes at a time—it is barbaric!"

"In some African cultures, long necks are so prized that women wear brass coil rings around their necks to stretch them out, increasing the number of rings as a woman ages, making it impossible to support their own head unaided.

In other countries, their lips are pierced and stretched out with a plate or plugs. Head binding was popular in the ancient world, to permanently modify a newborn infant's skull into a shape thought to exude intelligence."

"Oh! But these procedures are truly horrible! They modify the very shape of the body itself. How can you compare them to the simple act of hair powdering?"

"It is the *intent* behind the practice which offends me: to alter one's *appearance* in a manner which is considered, at that point in time, to be more aesthetically pleasing. Look at all the heads around us, Jane. Everyone looks exactly the same! God gave us hair in such a range of exquisite, natural shades and textures; why cover up that beauty with a wig, or defile it with powder? Particularly *white* or *gray* powder, which makes everyone look so incredibly ancient."

"I never thought about that before."

"The whole thing has always seemed rather silly to me."

"Perhaps it *is* silly." I shrugged. "But—silly things do not appear quite so silly, when they are done by a sizeable number of rational-seeming people all at the very same time."

He laughed. "An admirable defense of many harebrained customs; although, I admit, hair powdering was not entirely foolish when it first came into being."

"Oh? When and why did the custom start? And how do you know?"

"I have read a great deal on the subject. It is an ancient practice. It began in the sixteenth century with the wearing of wigs—" He stopped himself, glancing at the people milling and chatting around us. Coloured slightly, he added, "Forgive me, but it occurs to me—this is not a subject suitable to discuss with a lady, and certainly not at a ball."

My curiosity was now piqued. "Mr. Taylor, you must tell me. Why did people begin wearing wigs?"

He shook his head.

"I can only suppose it was to improve their personal appearance?"

Reluctantly, he said, "That was one of the reasons."

"And the other reasons?"

"Are you certain you wish to know?"

"I do."

He hesitated; then glancing meaningfully towards the back of the house, he gestured for me to follow him. We made our way together to the small vestibule at the rear, and from there stepped outside into the evening air, where I sighed with relief, grateful to be enveloped by its invigorating coolness. Another couple stood nearby conversing; or rather, I should say they were quarrelling: it was Fanny and Mr. Cage, and she appeared to be in quite a fit of temper. I caught the phrases *not what you promised me* and *I can never be happy unless*—; but heard no more, as Edward Taylor deliberately continued out to the lawn, putting some distance between us and the arguing lovers.

I accompanied him. It was that hour of twilight which I have always thought very pleasing: not yet dark, yet no longer day; the sun lay below the horizon, diffusing the sky with its soft light. The muted sounds of the musicians starting up again could be heard from within the house.

"There; now we may safely talk in private," said he, taking a seat on a stone bench, and inviting me to sit beside him.

Fanny and Mr. Cage, I noticed, had retreated into the house. "I cannot think why such privacy was required to explain why people began wearing wigs in the sixteenth century."

"I warned you: it is not a conversation to be holding with a lady."

"You cannot frighten me off with such a declaration."

"Then listen at your peril: I read that it was first employed to compensate for a certain illness incurred by men—" Colouring deeply, he went on: "—an illness which promoted baldness."

I did not comprehend his allusion, but had no wish to betray my ignorance. "And?"

"Wigs also became preferable when certain unwholesome conditions occurred in the natural hair." Raising his hand to his head, he made a scratching motion.

I understood *this* reference and made a face, for it was still a common problem.

"The wealthy often shaved their natural hair," continued he, "and wore a wig, which could be more easily cleaned. But even though the wearing of wigs rose in popularity for these reasons among the upper classes, it was apparently royal patronage which sealed its success."

"Oh! Queen Elizabeth lost some of her hair to small-pox—and ever after wore a red wig!"

"Yes. And later, in the early 1600s, King Louis XIII of France went prematurely bald, and took to wig-wearing. The practice soon spread to all the European countries and became *de rigueur* for men and women of social rank."

"I see. But what of powdering?"

He paused. "Have you ever worn a wig?"

"Never."

"Nor have I. But apparently, when worn for any length of time, a wig becomes—shall we say—less pleasant. So they were coated with powder because—"

"—it carried the scent of orange or lavender," I interrupted, comprehending.

He nodded in affirmation.

"Fascinating." As I contemplated what I had just learned, I added: "Lately, I have noticed only men wearing wigs; the tendency among women and young men is to simply powder their hair. Why is that?"

"I think wigs grew too expensive, and so the style changed. I hope it is going to change again, and soon. Hair powdering is still all the rage among the upper crust in France, but dying out in other parts of Europe—and for good reason. It is not a good time to be emulating the fashions of the French aristocracy."

Again, his statement took me by surprise; it was something I had never considered before. "I am, of course, well aware of what is happening in France," said I slowly. I had read about it in the newspapers, and heard my mother, father, and brothers talk about the crisis amongst themselves and with visiting friends. "The people are poor; many are starving. They feel their king is indifferent and incompetent. Two years ago, they rose up, stormed the Bastille, and formed an assembly to draft a new constitution. They think to govern themselves. But—"

"It is anarchy! The army is in considerable disarray; commoners have formed militias and armed themselves. To think that a monarchy could collapse so easily—it is terrifying. The king and his family have long since been evicted from Versailles, and now their very lives are in peril."

"Surely the people would never harm the royal family."

"The people are so angry, there is no telling

what they might do. And it is not just the royals who are in danger. Soldiers drawn from the lower classes are turning against and attacking their officers, simply because they are of noble birth; if this continues, every noble could be in jeopardy. The other monarchies of Europe are looking at what is happening in France with grave concern, and considering whether they ought to intervene to support Louis XVI, or to prevent the spread of revolution. I think there will be all-out war soon."

"So I hear; but not with England, I hope?"

"Yes, with England; and no doubt Austria, the Netherlands, Germany—it is coming, Miss Jane. Nothing can stop it, I fear."

"Oh!" The idea was very distressing. "I hope you are wrong."

Edward Taylor looked at me, softening. "Forgive me; living in Europe, I have perhaps been more privy to this information than have you, and thus more aware of the dire possibilities. How did we get off on this disagreeable subject, in any case?"

"I believe you brought it up in some connection with powdered hair."

"Ah! So I did. I only meant to say that, in the current political climate, considering that Louis XVI and Marie Antoinette powder their hair as a mark of rank and privilege—I should think no one else in his right mind would want any part of it— no matter how popular the custom."

"You make an excellent point. But that is not

why *you* refuse to follow the fashion. You thought it foolish long before that."

"Foolish and old-fashioned." He stood and suggested we return to the house. As we slowly made our way thither, I said,

"You have given me a lot to think about, Mr. Taylor. I am intrigued by your notions; but I admit, I still think it very brave of you to shew up here to-night with natural hair. Is not it rather awkward, being the only person present who looks different from the rest?"

"A bit. But were I to follow a fashion merely to copy others, I should be no better than the sheep out on that lawn, who will follow their flock blindly wherever they are led—if it came to it, off a cliff to their death. But pray, allow me to better explain my way of thinking, by way of a small illustration. Will you indulge me?"

"How?"

"I shall pose three questions for you to answer— three questions which *appear* deceptively easy, yet not one in a hundred people answer them all correctly. At the end, I will reveal the answers."

Mystified, and ever ready to meet an intellectual challenge, I replied, "I will."

"Question one. True or false: Queen Elizabeth ascended to the throne on 17 November 1558."

I hesitated. It did indeed seem to be a simple question; every educated child in England was obliged to memorise that date. Yet he had said the questions would *appear* easy. Perhaps, I thought, I had got the date wrong? The *year* I was certain of; but as to the month, or the day of the month— could it be that I remembered (or had been taught) it incorrectly? Not wishing to be foolish or deceived, I said boldly: "False."

"Question two. True or false: King Henry VIII had six wives."

Again, I paused. Everyone knew that Henry VIII had six wives! How could ninety-nine out of a hundred people get that answer wrong? I considered the possibilities. I remembered that his marriage to his fourth wife, Anne of Cleves, had never been consummated, and was very quickly annulled. Perhaps this annulment meant that the marriage was not legitimate, and therefore in actuality, Henry VIII had only had five wives? "False," said I.

"Question three. True or false: Shakespeare was baptised with the first name William."

I sighed in frustration. Did the Bard have a different Christian name at birth? It was entirely possible. Was this another trick question? For some reason, however, I could not bring myself to say false this time; so very reluctantly I said, "True?"

"Very good on the last question. It is indeed true."

"And the others?"

"To all three questions, the answer is true."

"All three are true!" cried I, aghast. "You said they were deceptively easy—but that nearly everyone gets them wrong!"

"And so they do." He struggled to hold back a smile. "Do not hate me, Miss Jane: it was not your *knowledge* which was being tested, but your *conviction*—your ability to remain *true* to what you believe is true."

"Oh!" I gasped, blushed, and could not help but laugh as I playfully nudged his arm. "How diabolical you are! A child could have answered those questions. How easily I talked myself out of the proper responses!"

"Now you understand, I hope, what I was trying to say."

I paused and considered. "I think I do. You believe that one should not, *must* not, be swayed by popular opinion or the ideas of others, to think or act against his or her own convictions."

He nodded. "It is not always easy, particularly at our age, when we are still subject to the dictates of our parents; but if possible, we must be true to ourselves, for I believe the only route to happiness is to follow our own hearts."

Chapter the Sixteenth

What a difference an hour or two of conversation can make, with an intelligent, deep-thinking person! I had entered the ball-room that night with one set of ideas, and after my dialogue with Edward Taylor, returned to it with quite another. How strange did the dancers, their every head either encumbered by a wig or doused in powder, all now appear to me! A practice to which I had long aspired, and had considered to be the height of fashion, I now observed in a very different light. I was mortified to think that I had been happy—nay, anxious—to indulge in such behaviour.

Edward Taylor and I had no sooner entered the ball-room, than he said, "Would you care to dance again, Miss Jane?"

I shook my head, presuming him to be teasing. "We cannot, Mr. Taylor. We already completed one set. We are not supposed to dance another."

"Ah yes, I had forgotten—that *is* the custom in this country—but I do not see the sense in it. If we enjoy each other's company and wish to dance together again, who could it hurt? Would you *like* to dance with me again?"

"I would, sir. But—I fear Lady Bridges would not approve. And what would my mother think? It would not be proper!"

"We have already erred against propriety, I believe, in talking outside together unescorted for a considerable period. Why should you worry now about such an insubstantial thing as dancing together in a room full of people?"

"Oh!" I had not considered that what we did before was wrong. "But sir, having offended against decorum once is no reason to do so a second time."

"On the contrary, it is the perfect excuse, since you cannot possibly offend for the first time again."

I laughed. "Your arguments divert me; but I repeat, to dance again would be scandalous."

"Let us be scandalous, then!" He offered me his arm, a laughing challenge in his eyes.

I tried to resist, but could no more do so than I could stop breathing. Again, he led me to the floor and we danced another set—and following that, yet another! He made such a pleasing partner, that for this delightful interval, I took no notice of anyone or anything else around me, other than that which related to the exercise itself.

When this last dance was finished, and I was so winded as to require a brief respite, I felt a sharp tug on my arm as my mother drew me forcibly away from Mr. Taylor, marched me out of the room to a quiet spot in the central hall, and whirled on me with wrath.

"Jane! How dare you! Have I taught you nothing?

Did not you see the other young ladies standing around the room, waiting and hoping for a partner, while *you* danced half the evening away with that young rogue! One set only per partner, *that* is the rule!"

"I am sorry, Mamma. He asked me, and I felt it would be rude to refuse—"

"Sorry! A lot of good *that* does now, with the ball nearly over! And where did you disappear to for an hour or more? I looked all over the house for you but you were nowhere to be seen."

I blushed. "I was only sitting outside and talking with Edward Taylor. We did nothing improper, I assure you."

"Nothing improper! Nothing improper! Sitting outside together! Unchaperoned! I am shocked, shocked, I tell you, by your behaviour, and by the behaviour of modern young men! A great alteration has taken place in them since *my* time, when a sense of decorum and modesty marked their characters! All that is gone now, entirely gone. Sitting down and talking together for hours on end! The very idea! You both have set a very bad example. I said you could dance with him, but not *six* dances in the same evening! What will Lady Bridges and Sir Brook say? Do not think that *they* have not noticed!"

"I thought you did not care what Lady Bridges thinks."

"What? Such impertinence, I never witnessed

before in such a girl!" (lowering her voice to a fierce whisper) "No; I do not care to have her *approval,* for she is a vain and snobbish woman— but neither do I wish to be turned out of this house as a result of your impudence! And I *do* care what Sir Brook thinks, for he is a fine and honest man and very honourable!" (resuming her previous tone) "Oh! All I wished for was to breed you up virtuously; I hoped to see you respectable, modest, and good. But I might have spared myself the trouble! Jane, if everyone acted as you did, everything would go to sixes and sevens, and all order would soon be at an end throughout the kingdom!"

"Upon my honour, Mamma," said I, "I have done nothing this evening that can contribute to the overthrow of the kingdom."

"You are mistaken, child, for the welfare of every nation depends upon the virtue of its individuals, and anyone who offends in so gross a manner against decorum and propriety as *you* have done is certainly hastening its ruin. You will not dance with Mr. Taylor again to-night; and I forbid you from being alone with him at any time during the remainder of our stay at Goodnestone. Is that clear?"

Tears started in my eyes. "Yes, Mamma."

Prodding me with her fan, my mother angrily escorted me back to the ball-room, where upon entering she cried in a low voice: "Here comes

Mr. Knight. He has been asking after you all night, and you must dance with him. And do not do anything else to shame me!"

Across the way, I glimpsed Edward Taylor regarding me with a concerned expression, but I was immediately engaged by the kindly Mr. Knight, and returned to the dance floor. He made an attentive and congenial partner, as did Sir Brook, who asked me to dance directly afterwards. So distracted was I, however, by thoughts of my mother's stern disapproval, and her promised punitive measures with regard to Edward Taylor, that I could hardly enjoy the activity, and no longer had any appetite for the ball itself.

I was glad when at half-past two in the morning the ball-room began to clear out, as the weary but happy crowd said their good-byes. I moved with the assemblage, looking for my sister. I had not yet found her when Edward Taylor appeared at my side, and said,

"Miss Jane. I saw your mother speaking with you earlier. Was she angry because of me?"

"She was."

"I am very sorry."

"I am the sorrier, for she has forbade me from having any contact with you in future which is not strictly chaperoned."

"Well: that is not so very dire a punishment. There will be so many people at all the events Lady Bridges has planned over the coming fortnight, I believe we will be chaperoned every-where we go, whether or not we like it."

His attitude so charmed me out of my mental anguish that I laughed. "You may be right."

He glanced at the dispersing crowd around us. "I wanted to tell you something, but I must speak quickly, lest we incur your mother's further wrath by inadvertently ending up *sans chaperon* at this very moment."

I laughed again, all attention. "Yes?"

Bracing one hand on the wall beside me, he leaned in closely, and said: "Do you remember after we met on Saturday, I gave you several reasons why I could not be sorry your carriage had met with an unhappy fate that day?"

"I do. You said you were glad because it provided you with an opportunity to be useful, and concluded with an invitation to dinner at Goodnestone."

"All of which was true; but I was not entirely honest. I neglected to include the most important reason of all."

"Which was?"

"It afforded me the opportunity," said he softly, "to meet *you* some days earlier than might have occurred otherwise."

I could not reply; nay, I could hardly breathe.

"I shall see you Friday," added he with a smile in his eyes as he walked away.

I believe I stood at the door a full five minutes

after he left, my limbs trembling, unable to remember when Friday was, or what might be happening that day. Cassandra at length rescued me, insisting that it was time to go to bed. So filled with energy, awe, and wonder was I, however, that I doubted if I should be able to close my eyes.

My sister, aware that my mother had already reproved me for my indiscretion at the ball, only mentioned it in passing with a heavy sigh. Although she professed herself to be too exhausted to take down her hair, I was determined to return mine to its natural state as soon as we reached our chamber. Immediately, I spread a cloth upon the floor, unpinned my hair, and vigorously brushed it until the last remnants of the starchy substance had been removed.

As Cassandra slept, I lay in bed thinking about *him* for a long, long while—about all the new ideas and feelings which had been simmering within me ever since our discussion that evening, about the six dances we had shared, and most particularly about what he had said at the last.

It all implied that he liked me! It did not discount the possibility that he also liked someone else; I sensed in my bones that he *did* have affection for Charlotte Payler; but it now seemed incontrovertible that he liked *me* as well— perhaps liked me as much as I liked him!

But oh! If I was honest with myself, my feelings

had long since gone past that particular emotion, to something deeper and far more potent.

"Cassandra," whispered I.

"Mmmmmmm?" returned she drowsily, before drifting back to sleep.

"I *love* him," murmured I, hugging my pillow, aware that my words were audible to no one but myself. "I *love* Edward Taylor."

The household slept in late the next morning. My sister and I entered the dining-room at noon to find the furniture all back in its rightful place, the previous night's ball nothing but a memory or a topic of languid conversation. The chamber was only half-full; the sleepy-eyed diners therein assembled still had their hair styled as it had been the night before, a little the worse for having been slept on; the younger boys and I were the only creatures present with natural hair.

"I apologised to Lady Bridges and Sir Brook last night for your behaviour at the ball, Jane," remarked my mother sternly when I sat down. "I expect you to apologise to them yourself this morning."

"Yes, ma'am." I was too happy to let her reprobation or her directive bother me. I would apologise; I did not care. I would not have traded that conversation with Edward Taylor, nor those six dances, for anything in the world.

"What happened to your hair, Jane? You were so

anxious to powder it, I expected that you should be begging me to keep it in that style for a week at least; yet here you are with your own brown curls again already."

"I have changed my mind about the style, Mamma," replied I as I sipped my tea. "I do not find it to be quite so fashionable as I thought."

My mother shook her head and raised her eyes heavenward. "I declare, you are a very strange girl, Jane. I shall never understand you."

Fanny and Mr. Cage were seated at opposite ends of the table; both were silent and seemed to be in a foul mood. Mr. Cage, after consuming very little, left the house to go riding.

"Thank goodness, I thought he should never leave," said Fanny, throwing down her napkin.

"Is there something wrong, Miss Bridges?" inquired Mr. Deedes.

"There is, Mr. Deedes, but I do not wish to speak of it."

"You are only tired, I fear," said Mr. Deedes soothingly, "after being up so late last night. You will feel differently when you are more rested."

Fanny met his friendly gaze, and was charmed; her features softened. "Perhaps you are right, sir. I shall go upstairs and take a nap. But if you see Mr. Cage, pray tell him that I am not speaking to him unless *he* apologises."

No sooner had Fanny exited, than Lady Bridges entered.

Marianne said in some distress, "Have Fanny and Mr. Cage quarrelled?"

"They have," responded Lady Bridges with a shrug, "but over *what* Fanny will not tell me."

"I am so sorry," said Cassandra. "I do hope they make up soon."

"Do not worry, they shall," answered her ladyship, as she took a seat. "When people are young and in love, these little quarrels are always to be expected. It will sort itself out."

I was not as confident of that outcome as she, for I could not forget what Fanny had told me the night before with regard to her *true* feelings for Mr. Cage, and her purpose in marrying him. However, as the admission had been made in confidence, I could not share it; and so I remained silent.

Chapter the Seventeenth

A more animated group met for breakfast on Friday morning, than had inhabited the room the day before. Fanny's quarrel with Mr. Cage seemed to be forgotten; but as I could still perceive no genuine warmth or affection from *her* towards her fiancé, I still found the situation troubling.

"Thank goodness we have sunny skies," cried Sophia, clasping her hands with delight as she glanced out the window. "It is a perfect day to go to the windmill."

It was the day of the sketching and painting contest, an activity which was to include only the young people, and as Frederic Fielding did not draw, the only guests other than those in residence at Goodnestone were Charlotte Payler, her eldest brothers, and Edward Taylor. My heart leapt when *he* entered the hall. He bid me a friendly good morning, and said,

"Are you going to paint or draw today?"

"Neither. I could not paint or sketch under any motivation other than to save my life. I will be happy to watch. And you?"

"I am no proficient, either; my art-masters despaired of me, but I shall risk embarrassing myself by dabbling a bit in water-colours."

Our object was Chillenden Mill, only a mile and a half away by road, and less on foot across the fields, where an ancient windmill was said to be set in very picturesque environs. The wagons had been sent ahead earlier that morning carrying all the art supplies, chairs, easels, &c. which would be required by those who chose to paint or draw, as well as the refreshments and other necessities peculiar to a picnic. Lady Bridges, Mrs. Knight, and my mother were to be the only senior members of the party, and they chose to be driven thither; the artists were to walk.

I fully anticipated that Edward Taylor would ask

Charlotte to accompany him, but to my delight, he invited me to be his walking companion—an excursion which, he said smiling, was entirely within the approved confines of my mother's directive, as there were so many other people going with us. I thought I detected quiet disappointment in Charlotte's eyes as Mr. Taylor and I walked off together, and I felt a strange mix of emotions, encompassing both empathy and happiness; I chose to concentrate only on the latter.

A very pretty walk it was, as we climbed over stiles and traversed meadows alive with the waving heads of brilliant yellow and white blooms, and dotted with cows and sheep. Edward Taylor and I talked en route upon a multitude of subjects, and we were soon engaged in a lively historical dispute. He had much to say in defense of Queen Elizabeth and her ministers, whom he saw as deserving, experienced, and able, but whom I truly hated.

"How can you persist in such opinions?" cried I. "Elizabeth was truly wicked, and encouraged in her crimes by vile and abandoned men. They assisted her in confining a good, amiable woman, nay a *queen,* for nineteen years—and then brought her to an untimely, unmerited, and scandalous death!"

"It *is* a sad blot on history, what they did to Mary Stuart," agreed he. "*There* was a family who were always ill-used, betrayed, or neglected, and whose virtues are seldom allowed, while their errors are never forgotten."

We discussed Goldsmith's popular four-volume *History of England*, which Edward Taylor proclaimed to be a heavily biased abridgment of David Hume's far superior six-volume work. "As if that was not bad enough," commented he, "Goldsmith went on to publish a *one-volume* abridgment of his *own abridgment*."

"It makes one wonder just how brief a *History of England* can be, before it loses any meaning entirely!"

At length we made our way up an ascent to a wide, grassy area of high, exposed ground, where was situated the post-mill, which was just as old and charming as promised. The day was so fine, and the skies so remarkably clear and blue, that lovely pastoral prospects could be seen stretching in every direction, with Knowlton Court to the east, and beyond it Deal; Canterbury to the west; and Ramsgate to the north. The supplies were soon unloaded, and as the artists claimed their easels, chairs, boards, paints, and pencils, I heard Fanny say with disappointment to Mr. Cage:

"Do you really mean not to join in the fun?"

Mr. Cage replied: "Pray forgive me, but I have absolutely no artistic bent. I cannot even draw a stick figure."

Charles and I were the only other young people

present who admitted to the same lack of talent; we were equally happy to admire the endeavours of the artists and take in the views, until the interval when the refreshments were served, and that moment when our services would be required to join in the voting.

The army of artists scattered and established themselves either alone, in pairs, or in groups before particular prospects, and after setting up their materials, began. To my satisfaction, Thomas Payler deliberately sought out my sister and helped her situate herself; they were now painting alongside each other. I was less delighted to see Edward Taylor helping Charlotte to set up her easel, and then take the spot next to her. They were part of a larger conclave who had assembled in a position overlooking the windmill and an expanse of scenic woods and farmlands.

I felt an unexpected twinge of regret that I had not chosen to paint or sketch as well, for then it might have been *me* seated at Edward Taylor's side. I had acknowledged my own feelings for him to *myself* the night before, but although I sensed that he liked me, I had no proof that the depth of my affection was returned. And yet, at the ball, and during our many other stirring conversations, I had felt such a powerful connection to him! Who, I wondered with a pang, did he prefer—Charlotte or me? Or did he have no preference? Was he like a butterfly, happy to flit from one flower to another, with no strong attachment to any? But he had said how glad he was to meet me! He had called me remarkable! Perhaps he gave out such compliments easily. For all I knew, he might be saying something equally as endearing to Charlotte at that very moment. Oh! It was all such a muddle, so difficult and confusing! How was a girl ever to know what a young man was thinking or feeling?

I turned away, determined to redirect my thoughts, and ventured towards a group of three artists comprised of Sophia, Fanny, and Mr. Deedes, who had all made very promising beginnings on their pictures. Sophia's work in particular I thought excellent. Fanny commented on Mr. Deedes's talent, and inquired as to how he had achieved his perspective; Sophia wondered how he had made up a particular colour. Mr. Deedes answered their questions and offered his humble suggestions, as to how they might improve their own paintings.

For a while longer, I strolled amongst the artists. Cassandra's painting was truly beautiful, and I told her so. At last, I allowed my wandering to take me back to the place and the person whom I most wished to see. As I approached, I observed the pictures which Mr. Taylor and Miss Payler were engaged in painting. His was of only moderate quality; as he had earlier admitted, *he* was no proficient; but Charlotte's reflected a real talent. Oh! To observe that she, at fifteen, was so accomplished at an art in which I possessed no skills whatsoever! It was very disconcerting.

Charlotte, upon noticing me, smiled, and said in a gentle voice,

"What a shame that you do not paint, Miss Jane, for I wish you could join us. I find it a most enjoyable activity."

It was the first time that Miss Payler had ever addressed me—the first time I had ever heard her speak aloud. And oh, such a remark! Although her expression and tone were sweetness itself, her words made a very different impression: they seemed to imply what I already knew—that I was deficient in having never gained this particular accomplishment, which was expected of all young ladies. Self-doubt and jealousy rose within me, and a stinging response came to my mind; but I bit my tongue, not wishing to appear anything less than proper and *demure* before Mr. Taylor, and instead said with as much earnestness as I could muster:

"I admire art and artists, Miss Payler, and wish most sincerely that I had your talent."

Charlotte blushed and lowered her eyes. "It is kind of you to say so."

"Miss Jane," said Edward Taylor, indicating his work in progress with his brush, "I would appreciate your opinion of *my* painting. Does this in any way resemble a windmill?"

Tactfully I replied, "It is a commendable effort, Mr. Taylor."

"You lie through your teeth. It is horrible. I know my strengths, and this is not one of them."

"Well," admitted I, "it is perhaps not the *best* I have seen."

He laughed.

"You have made the full circuit, Miss Jane," commented Christopher Payler, who was working at an easel nearby. "Who, in your opinion, *is* the best artist among us?"

"I cannot answer that! Even if I *had* made my mind up, which I have not—it is to be a secret ballot."

"My sister is too smart for you." My brother Edward glanced up at me with a wink from where he sat over his own drawing. "She never gives away her *secrets*."

We shared a conspiratorial smile. At that moment, Lady Bridges announced that the picnic was ready, and all should take a respite from their artistic endeavours, to enjoy some refreshment. In short order, everyone progressed to the blankets which had been laid across the ground, and sat down in an attitude of relaxed contentment, while helping themselves to the assorted cold foods and beverages which had been provided. The animated conversation soon turned to the cricket match which was to take place the following day, in which all the young men were eager to participate, and which all the ladies looked forward to watching.

"Cousin Edward ought to be one of the team captains," said Thomas Payler. "He is a capital player."

Edward Taylor modestly took issue with this assessment, but accepted the assignment. A discussion ensued as to who should be the other team captain, whether the section of the Goodnestone lawn designated by Sir Brook would truly make the best playing field, who ought to make up each team, who should be wicket keeper, batsmen, &c., and if indeed there were enough cricketers. Upon determining that they were a few men short, speculation began as to whether they ought to ask some of the servants to participate.

As my sister and I had, since we were little girls, been playing cricket with my brothers and the boys at my father's school, I whispered to her: "Do you think we ought to offer to play?"

Cassandra shook her head. "We are too old for such things now. Mamma would surely deem such conduct very immodest and unbefitting a young lady."

I did not press the point. The discussion was soon put to an end, when Lady Bridges reminded everyone that the judging of the artists' work was to begin in one hour's time. At this pronouncement, the company scattered anxiously back to their former positions to take up their brushes and pencils. In due course, the contest reached its conclusion, and all the artists were obliged to step away from their creations. Slips of paper and pencils were handed round, with the instructions that everyone was to vote for the work they considered the most superior in each of the two categories.

"Are we allowed to vote for ourselves?" asked Brook Edward.

"You may," answered his mother, "for I have no way to prevent you, you rascal—" (instigating hearty laughter from everyone); "—but I urge you *all* to follow your conscience, and vote for the *best*."

Lady Bridges maintained that, as she was the mother of so many contestants, she ought not to count the votes herself, and she coerced Mr. Cage into taking on the task. Not long after, he solemnly delivered the verdicts: the winner in the drawing category was Marianne, and in the painting competition, it was a three-way tie between Sophia, Fanny, and Cassandra.

This announcement was met with cheers and applause, everyone seemingly delighted by, and agreeing with, the outcome, with the exception of Lady Bridges herself; for although happy with the *former,* she was clearly displeased by the *latter,* apparently having counted on all the honours going solely to her own children, rather than being shared by anyone else.

By the time we left the windmill, a thick cloud cover had gathered, turning the sky a dusky white. New pairings were formed as we all progressed back to the house. Edward Taylor walked with Charles, and as they passed by, I heard them engaged in a debate filled with nautical terms. I strolled with my mother, who, upon observing Cassandra walking with Thomas Payler, commented with delight,

"How lovely it is to see your sister with such a pleasant, good-looking, and *propertied* young gentleman, as Thomas Payler! *He* observes the rules of propriety, I observe, and so does she! Why cannot you be more like your sister, Jane? Oh! Have you noticed the way he looks at her? He is clearly falling in love with her."

"Is he?" responded I lightly, hoping my tone did not give away my deep interest in the matter.

"Why, I am surprised you did not perceive it; anyone with eyes could hardly miss it! And why should he *not* fall in love with her? Cassandra is so sweet and beautiful, she is a fine catch for any young man, for all that she has no money. Oh! I knew how it would be, were we to come to Kent! Love is indeed in the air, Jane; if my hopes take flight, your sister might well receive an offer before we go home."

"I hope you are right, Mamma."

I smiled to myself, having no wish to tell her what little I had done to encourage the match; but to see that my plans for them were taking root in such a discernible way, was agreeable indeed. I began to realise how uniquely gifted I was when it came to fostering romance. Why, had not the love note I wrote on my brother Edward's behalf only a few days past charmed Elizabeth and rekindled their relationship? Their reconciliation might never have happened had not I intervened. How satisfying it was, to know that, since my arrival at Goodnestone, I had already been of very real help in promoting a connection between *two* couples!

I had longed for a way to be useful; perhaps, I thought, *this* was what I was meant to do. Could I, I wondered, be of further use in a similar manner? Were there any other people who might require my assistance, in fixing or promoting their romantic interests?

Glancing behind me, I caught sight of Sophia, smiling as she walked and chatted with Mr. Cage. Just ahead of me strolled Fanny and Mr. Deedes; from the bits and pieces of their conversation which drifted back to me, they seemed to be discussing their shared passion for art. A memory recurred of the same two pairs dancing at the ball. Of a sudden, a strange feeling came over me, as if a divine voice had spoken in my mind:

"What a fine-looking couple Sophia and Mr. Cage made! How much more natural did *they* appear together, than did Fanny with her own fiancé! And how very *right* Fanny looked, when paired with Mr. Deedes!"

A wild association of new, unexpected notions began to infiltrate my brain, filling me with such excitement that I could scarcely breathe.

Ever since Fanny's secret admission that she did not love Mr. Cage, but was only marrying him for his money, my heart had bled for Mr. Cage. To see on a daily basis so incongruous a match, had filled me with disgust and despair. From what I could tell, Fanny and Mr. Cage had done nothing but argue since he arrived—a sign that both were unhappy. They had nothing in common. Surely they should never be getting married!

On the other hand, the connection which Fanny and Mr. Deedes had shared in the ball-room, and at the breakfast-table, and as they now chatted so amiably before me, was too obvious to ignore. They were sweet to each other; they shared a talent and appreciation for art; they were meant to be together.

Fanny ought to be with Mr. Deedes!

I felt absolutely certain that, under the right circumstances—given the opportunity to know each other better—Fanny and Mr. Deedes would discover their true affinity. *She* would come to realise that a match *ought* to be based on love, not material prospects; that she had made a mistake in accepting Mr. Cage; and that she ought to break off her engagement. The blow would be

softened by *his* coming to the very same conclusion.

In time, Fanny and Mr. Deedes could announce
their own attachment.

By then, Mr. Cage would have found a partner
more suitable to *his* character.

There was no doubt in my mind as to who that
other partner should be: Sophia Bridges. Mr. Cage
was a pleasant gentleman, and so much admired;
Sophia was one of the most intelligent, affable
young ladies whom I had ever met. He was a great
reader; so was she. And had I not seen her melt at
the sight of him? Given the gentlest of pushes in
the proper direction, they should surely find in
each other their ideal match!

I felt certain that something very unusual was at
work here; that I had been given insight into a
matter of great importance, which I was compelled
to act upon. Such a correction to the pairings
would be in everyone's best interests, and would
promote the greater happiness of all parties.

I saw that I must take action, yet I must be sly
about it. I could not confide in Cassandra, without
breaking my vow to Fanny. Nor did I wish any of
the people involved to know that any scheming
had been done on their behalf; no, it must all
come about as naturally as if they had thought of
it themselves.

I had very little time, I realised, to accomplish
my goals. In a fortnight, I would be leaving Kent,

and everybody else was to disperse shortly there-
after—the Bridgeses to Bath, and Mr. Deedes
to Scotland with the Knights and my brother
Edward. I must act quickly. But how to go about
giving all four parties that little, necessary push?
That was the dilemma which stayed on my mind
all evening, and kept me awake far into the night.

Chapter the Eighteenth

The following morning dawned gray and cold,
with very threatening skies. Nevertheless, the
same group gathered early on the Goodnestone
grounds for the planned cricket match, which was
to be held on a wide, grassy field at the front of
the house, beyond the steps leading down to the
parterre.

I had been, up until now, too preoccupied by my
own thoughts to notice the weather. Despite many
long hours of pondering, I had yet to come up
with a satisfying means by which to promote the
romantic pairings I desired. However, a sharp east
wind which nearly blew off my bonnet, brought
the matter to my attention.

"I do not like the look of those clouds,"
remarked Elizabeth with a worried expression.

"I would not worry," responded Sophia optimis-
tically. "Many a cricket game has been played on
a cloudy day."

"*Gray* clouds are one thing," commented Mr. Cage, "but *those* clouds are black. It looks as if we are due for a shower."

"Mr. Cage, do not be so gloomy!" cried Fanny. "Yesterday was fine; surely it will brighten soon."

As I shivered and wrapped my cloak more tightly about me, an animated discussion ensued amongst the party, involving predictions as to the state of the weather, half of those assembled absolutely certain that the clouds would burn off by noon, and the other half predicting rain.

The Paylers arrived late, the sons rushing to join their teams, who had begun forming on the cricket field. As Mrs. Watkinson Payler and Charlotte hurried up to the benches where the ladies were gathered, they brought bad news: there had been a kitchen fire at Ileden the preceding evening, which had nearly destroyed the entire outbuilding. The winds were such that the manor house itself had been in grave danger for a good long hour; but thankfully the offices were set at such a distance from the house, that a shift of wind prevented any further calamity.

"I cannot guess how long it may take to rebuild the kitchen," said Mrs. Watkinson Payler despondently. "We are in a terrible mess at present."

"I am so sorry," cried Lady Bridges, "for the inconvenience you are suffering. I cannot imagine how we should get on without a kitchen. Shall I have Cook make up dishes for your family, and send them thither?"

"Oh! Do not trouble yourself, Lady Bridges," replied Mrs. Watkinson Payler, "for we have a neighbour not half a mile distant, a very good woman who has offered to help us out in a similar manner. But, however," added she in disappointment, "I regret to say that we will be unable to host the dinner at Ileden next week, as we had promised."

"Do not give the dinner another thought," answered Lady Bridges. "We can find something else to do. And if there is any way in which we can help you, please do not hesitate to ask."

Mrs. Fielding, who had been very silent ever since her arrival, now abruptly said, in a tone of great anguish: "There is something I must tell you, Lady Bridges; it concerns the concert we hoped to hold at Bifrons on Tuesday."

"Oh?"

"I have just received a letter from the musicians. It seems that several of their party have fallen ill, and they have withdrawn from the engagement."

"Oh dear!" said Elizabeth.

"I am quite distressed," went on Mrs. Fielding. "I do not know what to do, for I cannot get anybody else to perform at *this* late date."

"The concert need not be cancelled," suggested I. "I am sure there are many talented musicians amongst our own company who could give a performance. Edward Taylor plays the violin; and did not you say, Mrs. Fielding, that your son is a fine musician?"

Mrs. Fielding went very red. "He is indeed most accomplished; and although it would be a very great responsibility for one so young, had he several weeks to prepare, I am sure he could give a splendid performance which would delight you all; but there is no time, Miss Jane. I would not wish to throw something together."

"Yes, yes, I understand you completely," replied Lady Bridges hastily. "If there is to be a concert at Bifrons, you would prefer it to be the kind of *sophisticated* evening which you had anticipated, with professional performers, and nothing less."

"Precisely," said Mrs. Fielding, looking very much relieved.

"But what are we to do instead, Mamma?" cried Elizabeth, disappointed. "That is two events now cancelled."

Lady Bridges was unable to make a response; for at that very instant there came a great crack of thunder, the heavens opened up, and a heavy shower began, sending cricketers and spectators alike running, screaming, and laughing, back to the safety of the house.

After drying off as best we could, all gathered in the drawing-room, where we stood warming ourselves by the fire, or staring out the windows at the downpour, while Lady Bridges ordered tea and coffee to be brought round.

"If it is a brief shower," remarked Mr. Deedes, "we might still play when the clouds pass over."

"Indeed we might," agreed Edward Taylor. "I once played a match on the Prato in Florence during a light rain, and last autumn in Rome, immediately after a shower, we played cricket in the Villa Borghese, where the Prince Borghese had constructed a circus for us in his grounds."

"This is not Italy," remarked Thomas Payler disconsolately. "Those clouds are not going anywhere."

"Indeed, it looks to be a very bad storm," observed his father.

Everyone made such conversation as they could, attempting to put on cheerful faces; but when an hour had passed with no let-up in the rain, except for an increase in its severity, and an amplification of the sharp, rushing wind, Lady Bridges arranged for the collation, which had been intended to be eaten during the interval in the cricket match, to be served in the dining-room.

The food was consumed, but without as much enjoyment as might have been wished, for every face continued to turn to the windows, contemplating aloud upon the weather in a very despondent state of mind.

"Oh! It was so unlucky.—How the gods did

tease!—Such bad luck!—It was hard to believe the day before had been so very fair.—June was supposed to be fair and mild.—The weather must not always be judged by the calendar.—We may sometimes have finer days in November, than June.—There was nothing worse than a wet day in the country.—If only the rain would let up, they could play on the morrow.—At this rate, the field should be flooded for days."

As the meal concluded with no break in the rain, everyone agreed, with great disappointment, that the cricket match certainly could not go forward that day, nor on the morrow, and should probably have to be postponed for a week at the very least.

"It is a shame," said Mr. Deedes, "but there is no reason to be gloomy; it can be held another time. We are to be together for a fortnight, after all."

"I hope that is long enough," remarked Sir Brook. "The last time we had clouds this black, and a rain this hard, was in early spring; it continued for ten days entire, and it took a fortnight after *that* for the roads to dry."

"Oh! Do not say such a thing!" cried Lady Bridges, very distressed. "Already, on top of the cricket match, we have had two other events cancelled: a dinner and a concert. If this bad weather continues for many days, then *all* my planning shall be in vain."

"Mamma is right!" cried Fanny. "If it rains like

this, there can be no horse-racing, nor any walks in the woods next week."

"If the roads *are* very dirty or flooded," added Elizabeth dismally, "we can never do the carriage ride to Canterbury, either."

"And what of the Midsummer's Eve bonfire?" said Sophia, sighing. "It *cannot* rain on Midsummer's Eve."

"Blasted weather," said my brother Edward. "It is going to ruin everything."

Conversation drew to a halt. Everyone was in low spirits, every face wearing a miserable expression. The youngest three Bridges children, growing restless, were collected by the nursemaid and taken upstairs; at which point Sir Brook stood and said:

"Lady Bridges: I have had enough of this gloom and doom. Here we are, all assembled with our dearest friends and relations. If we are not to play cricket today, let us play something else. Let us set up the card tables in the library, and allow the young people to join us, or if they prefer, to engage in parlour games of their choice."

This suggestion was met with enthusiasm by all around; and as those we looked up to removed to the library, the young people progressed back to the drawing-room, and suggestions for parlour games were exchanged.

"It is such a dark and gloomy day, we ought to play Snapdragon," suggested Edward Taylor.

"That is a Christmas game," argued Mr. Cage, "and too dangerous."

"It is perfectly safe," insisted Edward Taylor.

I could not agree; I had played Snapdragon before, and although it had proved rather thrilling, I had nearly always burned myself.

The group, however, was overwhelmingly eager to play it, regardless of the dangers or the season; and a servant was dispatched to procure the necessary *accoutrements*. The drapes were closed, and in short order, a wide, shallow bowl was set up in the centre of a table; brandy was poured within; and a quantity of raisins was added, more than enough to accommodate all the party.

"According to one tradition," said Edward Taylor, "the person who snatches the most fruit out of the brandy will marry their true love within a year."

"Indeed?" said Mr. Deedes, with great interest. "I had not heard that."

As our party was so large, it was determined that we ought to split into two halves: one group would play, while the other half recited the accompanying chant, and then we should switch. I was part of the chanting group at the first. We gathered round the table as Mr. Deedes set the brandy alight. In the dim light of the room, the blue flames playing across the liquor created an eerie and quite spectacular effect. Everyone looked rather demonic as they all pressed forward, attempting to pluck raisins out of the burning brandy and extinguish them by eating them, at the risk of burning their fingers and mouths.

At the same time, my group chanted:

> Here he comes with flaming bowl, Don't he mean to take his toll, Snip! Snap! Dragon!
> Take care you don't take too much, Be not greedy in your clutch, Snip! Snap! Dragon!
> With his blue and lapping tongue, Many of you will be stung, Snip! Snap! Dragon!
> For he snaps at all that comes, Snatching at his feast of plums, Snip! Snap! Dragon!

The game proved both hilarious, and as usual, slightly perilous. At one point the bowl nearly turned over, threatening to send burning brandy spilling to the ground. I burned my fingers and tongue on some of the raisins, as did several of the others, but we intrepidly kept on playing. Towards the end of the game, however, when Charlotte cried out upon plucking out a burning raisin, Edward Taylor came to her aid; taking her hand, he examined the red marks found there, then called for a servant to bring ice and salve, and removed himself from the game to attend to her.

With so much commotion, it was difficult to observe everything that was going on, or to keep track of how many raisins everybody ate, so the scoring was on the honour system. Sophia and Mr. Deedes were both particularly avid players; but although they did very well, it was determined that my brother Edward had won by a small margin.

"I simply had to win," cried he when the game concluded, "as my wedding is in December. I want there to be no doubt that I am marrying my one, true love."

This statement was met by a sweet clamour from the assemblage, and a look of surpassing affection from Elizabeth. I was happy for my brother, and their loving display made me smile with pleasure; but another such display produced a very different effect. Sitting on a sofa across from me, Charlotte's valiant knight still hovered over her with concern, and she was all blushing gratitude. Observing these familiarities made me warm with envy and confusion. How unfair it was that *she,* as his cousin, could accept such attentions with impunity, in a manner which I could never hope to do!

Cassandra came over and sat beside me. "You are sulking, Jane," whispered she with both sympathy and reproval.

I averted my gaze and sat in silence, reminding myself that such behaviour on *my* part was unattractive and unworthy. But oh! At that moment, how dearly I wished that *I* was Edward Taylor's cousin!

All the players seated themselves on the chairs and sofas around the room, and various conversations erupted. My mind continued in a fog, barely conscious of what anybody was saying; but in time, I became aware that Sophia was commenting to Edward Taylor,

"How lucky you are, to think that you have visited Rome and so many other extraordinary places, and seen so many ancient wonders."

"*I* have been to Rome as well," interjected my brother Edward, "and it is indeed a marvel of antiquity, but some day I should dearly love to see Athens."

"As would I!" cried Edward Taylor. "The closest I have got to *that* venerable city however is what I have read in books, and a few rehearsals for *A Midsummer Night's Dream.*"

"Rehearsals?" repeated Cassandra with interest. "Have you participated in theatricals, Mr. Taylor?"

"Only home theatricals, strictly amateur proceedings." Leaping up from his seat, Edward Taylor arranged himself apart from his cousin, on the floor. "My father, in addition to a fondness for music, has always had a decided taste for theatre; he encouraged it in us as children, and we came to enjoy it as well. I cannot tell you how many times my brothers and sisters and I have mourned over the dead body of Julius Caesar, and *to be'd* and *not to be'd*, for my father's amusement—or our own."

"We did the same thing," said Cassandra. "We put on a great many plays in our barn at Steventon."

"I was there for many of them in the early years," added my brother Edward, "and what fun it was! I shall never forget our first play: *Matilda* by Dr. Francklin, a tragedy complete with passionate threats of murder and suicide. My brother James always directed, and wrote the most amusing prologues and epilogues in verse; I spoke the former on that occasion."

I sat up, invigorated by this conversation. "After that we turned to comedy—Sheridan's *The Rivals*. The scenery we painted for it is still in the barn."

"We all played parts," added Cassandra, smiling, "but—I can never forget it—the best of the company, the standout was you, Jane. How old were you then?"

"Eight years old."

"Jane played the pert maidservant Lucy, and we all thought it a remarkable performance in one so young."

"That was just the first of many," said my brother Edward. "Jane is quite an accomplished actress."

Their compliments, so sweet but undeserved, made me blush.

As the two Edwards and my sister shared additional anecdotes with regard to home theatrical experiences, I happened to catch sight of Fanny and Mr. Cage, who were seated nearby on the same couch, yet in an attitude so distant as to suggest that they hardly knew each other. They had, as far as I could tell, barely spoken a word to each other all day; it was almost impossible to believe that they were engaged, or that they felt anything more for each other than antipathy.

As the theatrical discussion continued around me, a thrilling notion suddenly came to my mind—an answer, nay, *the* answer—to the dilemmas which I had been previously pondering.

"Oh!" cried I, an exclamation so startling that it caused everyone in the room to cease speaking abruptly and look at me.

"Jane—what is it?" said Marianne.

"I have just had the most wonderful idea!" said I. "We ought to put on a play."

Chapter the Nineteenth

W ho should put on a play?" said Sophia.
"Why, *we* should. All the young people here," answered I.

The rehearsing and performing of a play, I

knew, required many long hours spent together in a confined setting. It was the perfect activity in which to engage, in order to promote the romantic conclusions to which I aspired. Were my prospective lovers to be so occupied, I thought, it would surely give me the opportunity to do that *small* amount of directing which might be required to throw them in each other's way, and propel them onto the desired course—particularly if the *right* play was chosen (I already had one in mind), and appropriately cast.

I had an additional reason for desiring such an enterprise; a reason which I knew was not *quite* proper, yet I could not help but think of it: were Edward Taylor to agree to be in the play—and should we each be assigned the roles which I was imagining—a certain amount of *cousinly* interplay might be required. The idea filled me with excitement and anticipation, and made me blush.

"We are to be together for nearly a fortnight more, until Midsummer's Day," continued I matter-of-factly, determined to give no hint of my secret aspirations. "Several events which Lady Bridges went to such trouble to arrange have already been cancelled; if this rain continues as we fear, it will mean the abandonment of a great many more activities in which we had all hoped to engage. But if we are to be cooped up inside all week or even longer, we need not be idle. Let us make the best of it! How better could we spend our time than in an endeavour so infinitely enjoyable as rehearsing for, and acting in, a home theatrical?"

Mr. Taylor, who had been lying casually on the floor, now sat up at attention. "I think it a capital idea. I have not done anything theatrical in a while, and any obligation that keeps me *here,* and out from under my father's steward's thumb, would be very welcome."

"I have always wanted to be in a play!" said Sophia with enthusiasm.

"So have I," admitted Mr. Deedes, "but I never had the opportunity."

"Could I be in it?" exclaimed Brook Edward and Charles simultaneously.

"And me!" cried Louisa.

"If we are particular about the play we choose," remarked I carefully, "and ensure that it has a great many characters, then everyone who wishes to can be in it."

"A play *could* prove very diverting," agreed my brother Edward. To his intended, he added: "What do *you* think, my love?"

Elizabeth brightened. "We used to put on short sketches as children in the nursery with our older brothers, and my sisters and I did one or two readings at school. I believe I proved myself *then* to be quite an accomplished actress; *now* I should surely be even more capable."

"All you *proved* then," cried Fanny sourly, "is that you can read lines from a book while standing on a stage." Elizabeth looked put out by this remark; but Fanny, taking no notice, added to the company at large: "I, on the other hand, have a genuine flair for drama; no one in my family is more theatrical than I, and I dare say, had I ever been in a real production, I should have been given the leading part every time."

"Whenever we thought of putting on an *actual* play," said Sophia, laughing, "we were never sure how or where to go about it, and it seemed like such a monumental effort, we never made any headway beyond the preliminary idea."

"A home theatrical does require a lot of effort," returned my brother Edward, "but it is doable; and between Mr. Taylor, myself, and my sisters, it seems we have enough people of experience here to direct and manage it—if everyone is interested."

"I feel up for performing any role that was ever written," said Edward Taylor, "although I would prefer to do something humorous; I am in no mood for a tale of woe."

Excellent, thought I; for the part I had in mind for him was very much comedic.

"I agree! We simply cannot do a *tragedy,*" cried Mr. Deedes. "This is a summer to be happy."

"Only a comedy will do," agreed Sophia with a smile.

I was delighted by the direction the conversation was taking. Frederic said:

"I was in a play once. I had six speeches, and I wore a red coat and a green hat. My mother said I performed just as I should have done, for I received a great deal of laughter and applause from the audience."

"Who would be *our* audience?" inquired Charlotte softly.

Her remark surprised me, not only because she had actually spoken *aloud,* but due to her emphasis on the word *our,* which implied that she wished to participate in the endeavour as well. I could not even imagine Charlotte Payler on the stage. She was so quiet and introspective, I had presumed she would decline to be involved.

"An audience is not required," replied I. "We *could* do it only for our own amusement."

"Oh, no! If we do a play, then we *must* have an audience," insisted Elizabeth. "What is the point of going to all that effort, if no one is to see it?"

"I agree," said my brother Edward. "We ought to have all our parents attend the performance at the very least, and the servants as well."

This idea met with general approval; but Thomas Payler in a grave tone said,

"I have acted myself a bit at school, and nobody is fonder of such an exercise than I; but a fortnight is not very long to rehearse and put on an entire play."

"It is long enough," insisted I, "if everyone makes a strong effort."

Cassandra nodded. "We put together full-length productions at Christmas and during the summer holidays in the barn at Steventon, in a briefer span than that."

"So did we," agreed Edward Taylor. "It really depends on which play you do—and how and where you produce it."

"Where would we perform the play?" asked Elizabeth. "We have nothing like a theatre at Goodnestone; and our barn is part of our working farm."

"We do not need a theatre *or* a barn," answered I. "Any room in this house would suffice, provided that your mother and father do not mind a little shifting of the furniture."

"Oh! I am sure they would not mind," said Marianne. "Papa loves a play!"

"Which play do you think we ought to choose?" asked Mr. Deedes eagerly.

"Wait." Mr. Cage rose from his chair with a frown. "You cannot all be serious about this idea. Fanny, do you truly mean to act?"

The disapproval in Mr. Cage's voice was so marked as to cause me some little alarm. Thankfully, the others shared my own enthusiasm for the project. Fanny replied warmly:

"If there is to be a play, I must be included, and I will accept nothing less than the very best part."

Mr. Cage shook his head. "I am not certain that a private theatrical is a proper endeavour for gentlemen and ladies."

"That is very old-fashioned thinking," said my brother Edward. "It is not as though we were going to act five nights a week in a theatre and be paid for it, or have our names splashed across a wealth of advertisements! No one but us need ever know a thing about it."

"We think only of a very respectable private production at home," added I, "with no audience other than our own most intimate friends and relations—just as *my* family, and the Taylors, have been doing for years on end."

"I understand," said Mr. Cage, "yet I fear Sir Brook and Lady Bridges would not approve; and I am not sure *I* approve of the idea of my future wife *acting*."

Fanny turned to him with imploring eyes and a sudden, sweet smile. "What is the harm in a little acting, Mr. Cage? Many women of the first consideration are so employed every day of their lives. My father was our biggest proponent in such activities when we were young, and you said yourself that you have often gone up to London expressly to see a play."

Mr. Cage softened somewhat. "That is different, dear; in town, I went to see acting by hardened professionals. Although a few of you may have *some* experience, you have not been bred to the trade. Any efforts you should make would be raw and amateurish."

"And what of that?" Sophia smiled. "It is summer, Mr. Cage! Let us be raw and amateurish! Let us have our fun. It would be so amusing!"

Mr. Cage shrugged, now visibly uncomfortable at pursuing a direction which was clearly so different from the popular opinion. "Well; perhaps it *could* be considered—if the right play were chosen—it must be something perfectly unexceptionable—and Sir Brook and her ladyship must be applied to before any decision can be made."

"It occurs to me," said Elizabeth with sudden worry, "even if Mamma does agree to the idea of a play in *general,* she might complain that it would be pulling too much attention away from what is *supposed* to be a celebration in honour of our engagements."

"As it happens," replied I hastily, "I have a play in mind which I *think*—I *hope*—your mother would consider to fit in perfectly with the theme of the occasion."

"Oh? Of what play are you thinking?" inquired Edward Taylor.

I paused and took a breath, barely able to contain my excitement. "Midsummer's Eve is twelve days hence, on the 23rd of June. In honour of *that* occasion, and in keeping with the subject of love, which is the very *foundation* of the two betrothals we are honouring—" (with a smile to the engaged couples) "I suggest we present our production on Midsummer's Eve, before the bonfire; and that the play ought to be *A Midsummer Night's Dream*."

A pause succeeded. Everyone looked surprised. They seemed to be considering my proposal; and then there came a general, approving uproar as opinions were expressed and exchanged.

"To perform *A Midsummer Night's Dream* on Midsummer's Eve itself!" exclaimed my brother Edward. "What an inspired notion."

"The 23rd is my birthday!" cried Charles.

"Is it?" replied Edward Taylor. "We have nearly the same birthday, Charles; for I was born on the 24th."

"Would not a home theatrical be a fine way to celebrate both of your special days?" said I.

"It would," agreed Edward Taylor; and Charles nodded with enthusiasm.

"It is the perfect play," remarked Cassandra, smiling, "at the perfect time of year."

Fanny appeared bewildered. "I am all for doing a play, but what is *A Midsummer Night's Dream*?"

"It is a play by Shakespeare," answered Sophia, "a romantic adventure involving fairies and magic and couples who are comically re-arranged, before a happy ending reunites them with their own true loves."

"Fairies? Oh! It sounds delightful," cried

Elizabeth; and at the same moment, her voice joined with Fanny's as they both inquired, "Is there a good part for me?"

"There are good parts for everyone," said I.

In a very brief time, it became apparent that there exists in many people a powerful ambition for acting, for everyone began to talk at once upon the subject with unabated eagerness. Not everyone was familiar with the play, but many had either read it or seen it on the stage (an experience I could only dream about). It was one of *my* favourite works by Shakespeare; I had perused it with pleasure many times. After issuing the further elucidation that it had a large number of major characters for both male and female performers which were nearly equal in importance, and a great many smaller parts which were excellent in and of themselves, it was almost universally agreed that *A Midsummer Night's Dream* would be the ideal vehicle for our company and purpose. Everybody loved the idea; everybody wanted to participate.

Only one person made an objection: Mr. Cage. Very calmly, he said,

"I can see that you are all determined to do a play; but are you certain you are up to taking on a work as complex as Shakespeare? He is not for amateurs. He wrote in a language and style very different from the way we speak today."

"I *do* find his plays hard to comprehend,"

agreed Thomas Payler, "and they are all so incredibly *long!*"

"*A Midsummer Night's Dream* is one of Shakespeare's shortest plays," responded I. "I believe the entire thing can be done in under two hours; less, if we make a few judicious trims."

"I have not looked at a volume of Shakespeare since I was nineteen," cried Mr. Deedes, "but I have *seen* several of his plays acted since then. I feel certain we can rise to the challenge!"

"It is a fairly simple play," agreed Sophia, "and extremely charming."

Edward Taylor said: "At first, *some* of Shakespeare's dialogue might seem difficult to understand, but one somehow falls into the flow of its meaning. Believe me, Thomas, with practice, the rhythm of the words will become second nature to you, and you will find it thrilling to enunciate it as it rolls off your tongue."

"Well; I suppose—if everyone else agrees," said Thomas doubtfully.

Mr. Cage shrugged. "If the rest of you wish to proceed with this folly, I shall not stand in your way; but I shall be content to watch from the side-lines, or to assist, if I can be useful in some other occupation—but I should never feel comfortable on a stage."

This declaration was very worrying to me, for if my plan was to succeed, Mr. Cage *must* participate and play a particular role.

"If we are all agreed on the play," pointed out Edward Taylor, "we will require someone to manage the production."

"I hope you will not consider me impertinent, or too forward," said I quickly, "but I should dearly love to be considered for the position."

"*You,* Jane?" Fanny shook her head. "You are too young to manage a play."

"I am not *so* young," returned I boldly. "I will be sixteen in December; and I have been observing, or participating in, home theatricals ever since I was seven years old. The last few years, my brother James allowed me to assist him in managing the productions."

"That is true," said Cassandra. "Jane may have been young at the time, but her interest in and contributions to our Steventon theatricals cannot be overstated."

"This *was* Jane's idea in the first place," pointed out Edward Taylor. "She chose the play; I say, let her manage it if she feels equal to the task."

His vote of confidence thrilled me. But Fanny countered:

"Jane is too young to take on so great and important a task. We had better let Mr. Deedes do it, for he is the eldest."

"Oh, no!" cried Mr. Deedes with a laugh. "Give me a small part, whatever you think I am capable of, and I will do my best not to let you down; but any more than that, I would not think of."

"I think the honour of managing the play ought to go to my Edward," said Elizabeth, gazing up at her fiancé proudly. "He is the next eldest among us, and has all the experience required."

"Yes! Edward! Edward Austen! Edward Austen!" cried a chorus of voices with enthusiasm.

"That sounds fairly unanimous to me," said Mr. Deedes. "Will you do it, Austen?"

My own spirits now plummeted, for if I did not manage the play, how should I have any control over the casting? My brother Edward, observing my expression, hesitated before answering:

"I am honoured by your confidence in me, and I should be glad to accept the challenge; however, I cannot do it on my own. Fanny, you think Jane too young—and perhaps you will say that as her brother, I am prejudiced—but I believe my sister to be a most imaginative young lady. Her sensibilities will prove invaluable in general, and her skill with a pen in particular is very great; should any speeches require trimming, she is the one for the job. As has been pointed out, this enterprise was entirely Jane's idea, and I could not in good conscience go forward without her assisting me at the helm. What say you all? Have I your approval?"

"Hear hear!" cried Mr. Deedes.

"Yes! Jane!" exclaimed Marianne.

The company broke out into cheerful applause, and even Fanny, looking round, and not wanting to behave in a manner dissimilar to the others, eventually joined in indifferently.

Filled with happiness, I smiled gratefully at my brother Edward, who winked at me affectionately in return.

"I could do with one other assistant, as well," added he. "I have had little experience with Shakespeare, whereas that is apparently Mr. Taylor's area of expertise. Will you help us, sir?"

"I should be happy to," replied Edward Taylor.

Now I was immeasurably pleased! Edward Taylor and I would be helping to manage the play together! I had very little time to savour the moment, however; for at that instant, all the card-players, having heard the commotion, returned to the drawing-room, and Lady Bridges said:

"What are you young people talking about with such enthusiasm?"

"And who or what are you applauding?" inquired my mother.

Everyone rose and made room for the elders of our party to be seated.

Sophia said with excitement, "We are applauding your son and daughter, Mrs. Austen, who have agreed to lead us in a most delightful activity—that is, if you agree, Papa and Mamma."

"What activity is that?" said Sir Brook.

With grace and passion, my brother Edward presented our plan, and explained why it was the perfect antidote to the rain. To my immense disappointment, Lady Bridges listened with growing horror, and finally cried:

"A home theatrical? What on earth put *that* idea into your head? I would not hear of such a thing!"

Chapter the Twentieth

O h!" cried Fanny, very let down, upon hearing her mother's pronouncement.

"Why not, Mamma?" said Elizabeth, equally distressed.

"You and your sisters are not children anymore!" cried Lady Bridges. "You are not living in the nursery. You are grown women now. I will not have you behaving like the members of some common travelling company. It would be ill-advised and imprudent to attempt anything of the kind, *particularly* now, with regard to your situation. We have just announced your betrothals! You both must conduct yourselves, going forward, with a certain caution and decorum."

"I understand your concern, Lady Bridges," said my brother Edward soothingly, "and indeed, I should never wish Elizabeth to be involved in anything indecorous." He went on to make the same thoughtful arguments and rejoinders which he had made earlier, on behalf of the respectability of the production. Augmenting this were sensible observations by Edward Taylor, Fanny, Sophia, and Elizabeth; all of which sadly combined to produce a far less successful effect on our hostess, than they had had on Mr. Cage.

My heart began to fail me, for it seemed that Lady Bridges would not budge from her position, even when the timeliness of the play and the value of the topic we had chosen were pointed out.

"Of all plays," cried she, "I can think of nothing more abhorrent than *A Midsummer Night's Dream*!"

"But why? It is an enchanting and romantic play, Mamma," said Sophia.

"It is a very *silly* play! I saw it once in town, years ago. It was full of fairies and magic and nonsense and I know not what else—it is not a respectable play at all!"

"I beg to differ with you, my dear," countered Sir Brook. "I think it a most respectable play, and I should be delighted to see it performed at Goodnestone."

"Sir?" responded Lady Bridges in stunned surprise.

"Nobody is fonder of the exercise of talent in our youth than I," persisted he. "I still remember the sketches our children did for us when they were young—my God, that does seems ages ago! You have been worrying yourself half to death, my dear, as to how to keep the young people occupied over the coming fortnight, what with so many of your plans being cancelled, and the threat of more rain; well here is your answer. Let them stay home and rehearse indoors, and let them entertain us. It should make a very good ending to our celebrations this summer."

Lady Bridges, greatly vexed, said to her husband: "You cannot mean what you say! At the very time that we are supposed to be, as a family, behaving with utmost respectability, and promoting the sanctity of marriage, you would have our children turn our house into a *theatre?*"

"Surely the whole house will not be affected," replied Sir Brook.

"Not at all!" interjected my brother Edward. "One room only will serve; and the choice of that chamber will be entirely at your discretion."

"But—" (with an apologetic look at her friends) "What should our *neighbours* think of us were we to do such a thing, as to put on a play at Goodnestone!"

"I should think it very entertaining," replied Mrs. Knight.

"Indeed it would be," agreed Mr. Payler. "When we visited my brother's family in Surrey last autumn, home theatricals were all the rage."

"All the most respectable families were putting on one play or another," added Mrs. Payler.

Lady Bridges stared at them. "Were they really?"

"We have certainly been doing so in *my*

household for a great many years," said my mother, "and young people from the best houses in the neighbourhood often took part, to the great pleasure of all their families."

"It was the same in Hertfordshire, before we removed here," said Mrs. Fielding. "My Frederic, when he was just fifteen, played—I have forgotten the name of his character—it was some play or other, a tragedy as I recall—at Linchfield Hall at Christmas; he was absolutely lovely in it."

Taking in these opinions, Lady Bridges responded uncertainly, "Well, I suppose if *you* do not find the idea objectionable—"

"Oh! Not objectionable at all!" cried my mother. "Quite the reverse!"

"My children *would* be allowed to participate, would they not?" said Mrs. Payler.

"Yes, yes; there would be a part for Frederic, would not there?" Mrs. Fielding's red face shone hopefully.

"If we do *A Midsummer Night's Dream*," said my brother Edward, "there will be parts enough for everyone."

The approbation of her friends was apparently all the reassurance which Lady Bridges required to validate the project; and in short order, she gave her permission, saying only:

"You may have your play, then; *where,* is yet to be determined; but know that, if good weather should return, and the roads are passable, I would like to go forward with as many of the events which I had *earlier* planned, as may be possible."

All agreed that this sounded perfectly reasonable. My brother Edward suddenly said:

"Do you know, the dining-room seems to me the ideal setting in which to put on the play. The niche at the far end of the room, where the musicians played last night, looks very Grecian with its faux columns, and would make an excellent area for the stage; and the door at that end—it communicates with the gun and billiard room, does it not?"

Sir Brook answered that it did indeed; to which Edward Taylor pointed out that said chamber would make the perfect green-room for the actors, and an excellent venue from which to make entrances and exits.

"We could not wish for anything better," agreed I. To Sir Brook and Lady Bridges, I added with great concern, "However, we should be obliged to once again shift the furniture in the dining-room (as you did for the ball) in order to create a space to perform, and to set up the chairs for the audience—and this inconvenience would last not a day, but nearly a fortnight."

Sir Brook and Lady Bridges, in grave tones, now discussed the prospect amongst themselves, and after some consideration, and the rejection of several proposed alternatives, concluded that the dining-room was indeed the best location for the theatre, even though it would require the family to dine in the drawing-room for the duration, and greatly limit the use of that room for anything else; but that the library could serve instead as the parlour during the interim.

Their offer was met with universal gratitude and alacrity.

"Will we have an actual stage?" inquired Marianne softly. "Do you truly mean to build one?"

"My sons built a sort of a stage in the barn at Steventon," replied my mother with a loud laugh, "but the materials cost a pretty penny, I can tell you."

"Mamma!" said I, mortified by her remark, as it placed such emphasis on the cost involved. Indeed, Lady Bridges retorted with a sniff:

"The expense would be trifling and nothing to worry about, I am sure; but why go to all the *trouble* of building something which will only be used for one performance, and immediately taken down?"

"I agree with you entirely, Lady Bridges," said Sir Brook. "The financial outlay of the enterprise cannot be of any great importance; but whatever you young people do or create, it must not injure our lovely room."

"I promise that no harm will come to any part of your house in this endeavour, sir," replied my brother Edward; to which Edward Taylor added:

"My own family put on our plays in the parlour of whatever house we happened to be living in at the time, and we made the performance our object, without so much as a door in flat or a single piece of scenery. We can easily do the same here, independent of the usual trappings of theatre. All we need is a performance *space,* rather than an actual stage."

"Oh, but you must have *some* scenery," said Mr. Knight, "or it will not look and feel like a real play."

"You can do very well with a few simple things to suggest the setting," said my mother very practically, "that will cost you nothing. Some small trees in pots from the conservatory to insinuate the forest, for example, and a table and several chairs for the duke's palace."

All those familiar with the play agreed this to be an excellent idea, and Sir Brook gave his approval.

"What about a curtain?" said Elizabeth.

"Oh yes!" cried Louisa. "We must have a curtain!"

"We made our own curtain of green baize at Steventon," mentioned Cassandra, "and hung it from a line draped between two posts."

"A curtain I will allow you," said Sir Brook. "I will have my carpenter put up something temporary from which to hang it. Order as many yards of cloth as you deem necessary."

"I shall have the maids make it up," agreed Lady Bridges.

A great many young voices rang out, thanking Sir Brook and his lady for this concession, and my brother Edward then said:

"We need as many copies of the book as possible. How many of you have the works of Shakespeare in your libraries?"

It turned out that everyone did. Sir Brook knew of several such sets at Goodnestone, and promised to locate the volumes required; Edward Taylor maintained that his father's library, which remained intact at Bifrons during the Fieldings' residence, also contained several copies of the plays; Mr. Payler said he had at least two complete sets of Shakespeare's works on his shelves, and promised to have *A Midsummer Night's Dream* sent over; Mr. Cage and Mr. Deedes both owned the books, but although the former's house was too far away to be of any help, the latter would have his servant fetch the relevant volume from his residence in Canterbury.

Knowing the play as well as I did, I believed there would be books enough for the most principal characters, and that the remaining parts were small enough, that their speeches could be copied out.

A break in the rain now being observed, which promised to be of short duration, the Paylers and Fieldings announced that they ought to go home before the roads got any worse. Mr. and Mrs. Knight also determined that in view of this change of plan, they would go home to Godmersham and return on Midsummer's Eve for the play's performance. Another matter of some consequence now occurred to me, and I said carefully:

"If we are to mount an entire production in less than a fortnight, we will need to rehearse every day. If the rain continues, it might be more convenient if everyone in the cast could stay at Goodnestone, at least part of the time—but—I wonder if that is even possible?"

"Lady Bridges," said my brother Edward, "would you be amenable to such a plan? Would you have room enough for everyone?"

The house was very full already with its infusion of guests, and I worried that we were asking too much. Indeed, Lady Bridges frowned and thought for a moment, but at last said that if the young people did not mind sleeping on a pallet or blanket on the floor, either in a room with her own children, or in one of the few unoccupied chambers on the top floor, she ought to be able to find a place for everybody.

All those people so involved offered their acquiescence and thanks, and were granted their parents' permission; and everyone was delighted.

"I need to familiarise myself with the play again," said my brother Edward, "and will read it over to-night. Everyone who wishes to participate ought to meet here tomorrow at two o'clock after church; at that time, Jane, Mr. Taylor, and I will decide on casting, and we can hold our first table reading."

It was further and universally agreed that all those who *could,* should read the play, and bring their copies with them. The visitors then departed, thanking Sir Brook and Lady Bridges for their hospitality.

I could hardly contain my delight. We were to do a play!

Chapter the Twenty-first

As confident as I now felt that the play would advance, there was one aspect of the production which was of paramount and immediate interest to me: the casting. If the endeavour was to benefit my prospective lovers (and myself) in the way I imagined, we must play very particular parts.

I read the play again that evening. I found to my satisfaction that it had just the right number of roles for everyone who wished to be in our company, down to the youngest child, who could play fairies and attendants. The love scenes and their complications were delightful. Were my actors to be properly paired, who could say where it might lead? In enacting their parts, true feelings might be kindled; a very *real* intimacy might well emerge! *This* was my hope.

I began by making assignments (in my mind) as follows: Fanny ought to play Hermia, and her lover Lysander should be Mr. Deedes. Sophia would make an ideal Helena; her paramour Demetrius must be Mr. Cage. It occurred to me that, in the same vein, two parts existed which were ideal for Thomas Payler and Cassandra: Theseus, the Duke of Athens, and his fiancée Hippolyta—a couple who celebrated their wedding in the final act. With one play, I could promote the future happiness of three prospective couples!

But there was more. It was perhaps indulgent, immodest, even slightly immoral; but I had high hopes for myself as well. Although I had never seen Edward Taylor act, he claimed to have experience performing—and based on what I had seen and heard of his many other talents, I presumed he should be equal to the part of Nick Bottom, which required a comedic actor of consummate skill. If Edward Taylor played Bottom, then I could be happy with no other role than Titania, queen of the fairies. Not only was it a marvellous part with some wondrous speeches, but there was a love scene between Titania and Bottom, which I blushed to think of, and very much looked forward to playing.

The dilemma *now* became: how was I to persuade my brother Edward and Mr. Taylor that my ideas were not only sound, but imperative—without appearing too assertive nor overly ambitious—and without betraying any indication of my underlying motives, however benevolent they might be? And even more important: how was I to get Mr. Cage to agree to take part?

I concluded that the best course of action was to begin with the proposed actors themselves, and see what influence I might have which could advance the scheme.

After the ladies and I had all removed for the night, I ventured down the hall, knocked at Fanny's door, and announced myself. She bid me come in. I entered to find Fanny at her dressing-table, her lady's maid in the process of taking down her mistress's hair.

"Jane," said Fanny, "I was just thinking about you." She directed me to a nearby chair. "What is that play called again? A Midsummer Dream?"

"*A Midsummer Night's Dream.*"

"Yes, well, I think it quite brilliant to perform it on Midsummer's Eve itself."

Before I could respond, the door burst open and Elizabeth marched in, crying out: "Fanny! Where is my best hairbrush?" Upon observing me, she blushed slightly, but her eyes still flashed angrily as they fixed upon the gilded object in the maid's hand. "Ah ha! I see you have taken it again! You have no respect for the property of others!"

Holding out her hand to the lady's maid, she added, "I do not blame you, Barrett—I know my sister is the thief—but give it to me please. It is mine."

The maid, upon receiving an almost imperceptible shrug from Fanny, returned the article to its owner, then began fishing in a drawer for a replacement.

"I only borrowed it for a moment," said Fanny. "There is no need to act so peevishly about it."

Elizabeth, as she turned to go, darted a questioning look in my direction, prompting Fanny to add:

"I was just talking to Jane about the play. Jane: which character do you think is best for me?"

Elizabeth now stopped to listen.

"I do not like to say," replied I carefully, "without first talking to my brother and Edward Taylor."

"But you are so familiar with the play!" cried Fanny, pausing to reprimand her maid for pulling too hard with the newly-found hairbrush. "You must have some thoughts about it."

"I should like to know which part you think appropriate for *me*," said Elizabeth. "I glanced at the book when Edward was reading it. We could never be expected to read the *whole play*. Will you tell us the story, Jane?"

I agreed, and Elizabeth sat down while I gave them a brief overview of the plot, narrating with what I hoped to be theatrical effect. Admittedly, my delivery may have been prejudiced a *tiny* bit in favour of the characters of Hermia and Puck, as these were the roles I hoped my listeners would wish to play. My scheme seemed to work, for when I was finished, the maid was delighted with the story, Elizabeth said she very much wanted to be a fairy, and Fanny said:

"Helena sounds too weak and servile to me. I prefer Hermia. I like that she is the daughter of an Athenian nobleman, and that both young gentlemen are in love with her."

"You would do Hermia justice, I am certain," said I with satisfaction.

There was a gentle knock on the door, and Sophia entered to say good-night. She seemed surprised to find us all assembled.

"Sophia," said Elizabeth, "Jane has just been telling us the story of the play."

"I think you should be Helena," suggested Fanny, under lowered lashes.

"Helena? Oh! I do not know." Sophia blushed. "Helena is a very big and important part; I wonder if I am equal to it."

"Of course you are!" cried I. "Helena suits you, Sophia, for she is a modest young lady, yet she pursues her desires with great fervour."

Sophia admitted that she would be happy to consider the role if my brother and everyone else concurred with the suggestion, but until that was decided, she would not indulge any expectations.

I retired for the night very pleased with my progress, and set to work planning how best to approach my next object: Mr. Cage.

The rain persisted. The Bridges family and their visitors made for a lengthy and colourful procession the next morning as we traversed, beneath our umbrellas, the length of the property along the holly walk en route to church, with the younger children (to their mother's horror) splashing through puddles at the front in the low sections, and Mr. Deedes and Mr. Cage deep in conversation at the back. I managed to elude my own companions by feigning an improperly-tied shoe-lace, and urging them to walk on without me.

When Mr. Deedes and Mr. Cage had caught up to me, my errant lace was miraculously retied, and I fell into step alongside them. We chatted amiably for a few moments about this and that, after which Mr. Deedes said:

"What an excellent idea you had, Miss Jane, to do a home theatrical during this turn in the weather. It will, I believe, afford us much enjoyment."

"I hope so," replied I. "It is gratifying that so many young people wish to participate—nearly everybody in fact."

"Yes, *nearly* everybody." Mr. Deedes gave his

friend a look filled with meaning, and received this reply:

"Why do you continue to press me, Deedes? I have said I do not wish to perform on the stage, and I will not change my mind."

"I press you because I think you are making a great mistake. It is nonsense for you to continue resisting in this stupid manner. Everyone is going to be involved; I imagine that the planning and rehearsing of the play will take up all our waking hours for the coming weeks, and the performance itself will be very amusing. You had much better join us."

"Yes! Do join us," added I, delighted to discover that Mr. Deedes, unprodded, was championing my own cause. Our efforts seemed to be in vain, however, for Mr. Cage replied emphatically:

"I shall not."

"Why not?" said Mr. Deedes. "What will you do to occupy your time while we are busy rehearsing?"

"I shall find something else to do—riding, reading, or walking. I can be a prompter if required. Or, as I have stated repeatedly, I shall be content to watch."

"Come, Cage. This is an opportunity which may never come again, to perform *Shakespeare* in the company of delightful people with moderate expectations. What are you afraid of? That you shall forget your lines?"

"I am afraid of nothing. I have an excellent memory. Had I a wish to memorise and spout the first two acts of the play entire before a roomful of people, I feel confident I could do so; but I have no such desire."

Mr. Deedes sighed and shook his head. "I do not understand it. The love of theatre is, I believe, too strong for *most* people to resist."

"I have as great a love of theatre as you. I make it a point to see as many productions as I can every time I am in town or at Bath. But in one respect, apparently, I differ from you and the others: I have no desire for shew or self-aggrandisement. I prefer to enjoy theatre as a member of the *audience* rather than as a member of the *company*."

"How do you know that is your preference," said I boldly, "if you have only tried one of the alternatives?"

"A valid point!" cried Mr. Deedes.

"What are you implying, Miss Jane? That one *must experience* a thing, before he can tell for certain if he will or will not like it?"

"That is my meaning precisely."

"What if someone dared you to jump off a cliff? Would you be obliged to jump, before making a determination as to whether or not you would *enjoy* taking the plunge?"

I laughed. "Certainly, in *that* instance, I should be able to make up my mind without attempting it. But we are not talking about anything so perilous as leaping off a cliff, Mr. Cage. We are only proposing a bit of harmless entertainment."

"Entertainment for some, but a dire duty for others. Pray, allow me to offer a less dramatic example. What if you were offered a dish at table which was entirely coated in black pepper, and you had an aversion to pepper? Would you try it? Or would you decline, knowing without tasting it, that you should not enjoy it?"

"I should of course decline it." I stepped around a sizeable puddle, then continued, "But Mr. Cage, you forget that the instance you describe involves an experience which you *already* have had; that is, at some point in the past, you must have tasted pepper, in order to recognise your aversion to it. Had you never tried pepper before, and others told you it was delicious, you would have no reason at all to avoid it."

Mr. Cage did not answer.

"I do understand your view, sir," continued I, "that, all life-threatening activities aside, if a person is given sufficient information about a practice from those who *have* experienced it, it is valid for him to make a *choice* as to whether or not to attempt it himself; but to decline can never reflect an accurate examination of a real preference. As my father always says: experience is the best and only true teacher."

Mr. Cage looked thoughtful and glanced away, but continued to remain silent.

This absence of argument seemed to me a promising sign; and, hoping to turn the conversation in an even more productive direction, I said lightly, "Fanny, Elizabeth, and Sophia seem very excited about the play. Last night, we all agreed that Sophia would make the perfect Helena."

"Sophia as Helena?" cried Mr. Deedes. "Yes, yes; I do believe she would play the part to perfection."

"Of course it is not up to *me;* my brother and Edward Taylor must be allowed to share their views, and we will find out later this morning if there are others who covet the same part; but Sophia does seem an excellent choice—and Fanny expressed her desire to play Hermia."

Mr. Cage looked alarmed at this remark, while Mr. Deedes agreed that "Hermia would entirely suit Fanny, and it would be gratifying to see two women, who were grown close by the connection of being sisters, playing characters who were such good friends."

"I should think," said Mr. Cage quietly, "Fanny more suited to the role of Hippolyta."

"She seems to have her heart set on playing Hermia," replied I, adding guardedly: "Perhaps I should not mention it, knowing how absolutely opposed you are to the idea; but I feel certain that she is counting on you, Mr. Cage, to play her fiancé Demetrius."

He hesitated. "Is she? I will be sorry to

disappoint her. Even if I *were* interested in being part of the company, I could not play Demetrius."

"Why not?" asked I.

"I cannot admire him. His infatuation with Hermia caused him to turn his back on Helena, the woman to whom he was once engaged. He is a morally corrupt man."

"What do you care?" cried Mr. Deedes. "It is a character in a play, and one of the heroes of the piece at that! Actors portray scoundrels far more villainous every day; certainly, no one judges the person who is playing a part."

"Very true," said I, "and I beg to differ with your assessment, Mr. Cage. Demetrius is not morally corrupt; he is merely human. His abandonment of Helena is a necessary element to the conflict of the story. We do not begrudge Demetrius his change of heart; it only gives him a direction in which to grow and change, and *us* something to hope for."

Mr. Cage took this in, and appeared to be thinking it over (which I took as a point in my favour); but before he could respond, Mr. Deedes cried eagerly:

"Wait—never mind Demetrius! You ought to play Hermia's lover, Lysander. Really, you must, Cage. It would be a tremendous case of life imitating art."

"Life imitating art?" repeated Mr. Cage. He seemed intrigued.

I was alarmed by this suggestion, for it did not fit with my plans at all. "Lysander is too passionate a character, I think," said I, "to suit Mr. Cage's taste; and his morals are surely even lower than those of Demetrius, for he desires and pursues his friend's fiancée. However, perhaps *you,* Mr. Deedes, would not be offended by the thought of playing Lysander?"

"Me?"

"Lysander is lively, charming, and well-spoken; I believe nothing could suit you better."

"Do you really think so?—That is an excellent part. Well; let us see what the others think. That is—if you are quite sure you do not want it, Cage."

"I should never think of playing *Lysander,*" insisted Mr. Cage.

My heart quickened, for in the way he emphasised the character's name, I thought I detected a certain something, which indicated a lessening of disinclination for playing a part in *general,* but only an aversion to playing Lysander in *particular*.

We had nearly reached the church now, where Fanny and Sophia stood waiting by the portico. As we made our final approach, I said pointedly: "Demetrius is a conscientious gentleman, with only one very relatable flaw; and *he* is the one betrothed to Hermia. If you like the notion of life imitating art, Mr. Cage, you can do no better than that. Only think how pleased Fanny would be, were you to play that part! But if you do not— well, it will be interesting to see who *else,* besides your friend, ends up making love to your fiancée."

Mr. Cage's countenance drained of colour. After a moment's hesitation, he turned from me and joined his waiting lady. Mr. Deedes bowed to Sophia; all closed and shook off their umbrellas, and proceeded into the church.

Watching them go, I felt an immediate pang of conscience. I had no wish to make Mr. Cage *truly* uncomfortable, but only to put into play such steps as might be required to help him recognise and rectify a relationship which I knew to be a terrible mistake.

Had I gone too far? Was he offended, or would my manoeuvrings result in a positive effect?

Only time would tell.

Later that morning, Edward Taylor joined my brother Edward and me at a corner table in the drawing-room (whose furniture remained intact for the moment, the grand removal from the dining-room postponed until the next day), where we shared our views with regard to the casting of the play.

"If there is no objection," said my brother at the start, "I should like to play Oberon."

We all agreed that he would make a very fine King of the Fairies.

"I imagine you as Nick Bottom," I told Edward Taylor. "I realise it is a very great undertaking—I believe he has the most lines—but you said you preferred a comic role, and there is nobody more humorous than Bottom."

"Yes—thank you—why not?" replied Edward Taylor. "Bottom is a very deluded and ridiculous fellow—to play him would prove both a challenge and an amusement."

I struggled to contain my delight. This was going very well, indeed. Now, I had only to put forth my preferred role for myself. "I was thinking I could play Titania."

"Titania? Oh, no," insisted my brother. "You can never be Titania, Jane; *that* part can only be played by Elizabeth."

"Elizabeth?" cried I, dismayed. "But she said she wished to be Puck."

"She told me, only this very morning, that she wished to be Titania; and I could not agree more."

"But—I had my heart set on playing Titania."

"Did you? I am sorry, but a brother and sister cannot play those parts; they are lovers; it would never do. Elizabeth alone must be my Queen of the Fairies."

"You will make a very handsome pair indeed," agreed Edward Taylor, adding, "Jane: you ought to play Puck."

"Puck?" My heart sank. "Puck is a male role."

"*Every* role in Shakespeare is a male role, when

it comes down to it," responded Edward Taylor.

"True! If men could play women in Shakespeare's time, then let *us* be equally as liberal, and allow *women to play men,*" said my brother. "I have heard you read aloud, Jane, and seen you perform; although it was some years ago, you had a great gift for it *then,* and I can only imagine that you have improved since. As such I can only second the motion, that you should be Puck."

I was too devastated to reply. I had lost out on the role which was so important to me, and instead I should be playing a man!

"Do not look so downcast, Jane," added my brother. "Have you forgotten how marvellous and important is the role of Puck?"

"He is, arguably, the leading part in the play," noted Edward Taylor. "It requires someone of a particular talent—which I feel certain you possess."

At length, I forced a smile. If I could not be Titania, then Puck was indeed a most excellent part; I knew I should be flattered and content. "I accept; that is, if you think all the others will agree."

"Let us not leave it up to the others," said my brother. "That will lead only to chaos and confusion. I say, *we* are managing the play, therefore *we* ought to assign the parts. If anyone objects to his own casting, we can listen and reconsider."

I quickly admitted to a similar view, and shewed

them the list I had written out, with all the parts and actors specified. We went over it together, and with only a few exceptions, they thought my ideas to be sound. Their only change was to insist that Marianne ought to play the fairy in Act II Scene 1, for although it was a charming part, it was small enough that it would not tire her beyond her strength; and Charlotte Payler would be the ideal person to play Flute. This development I did not welcome.

"Are you certain Miss Payler is the proper person for that role?" said I. "Again, it is a man's part; and she is so reserved and silent."

"Flute has very few lines until the craftsmen's play," countered Mr. Taylor, "and then *he* plays a young woman—a sweet and lovely young woman. What could be more appropriate?"

My brother agreed with this assessment. I was disconsolate. Mr. Taylor's description was sincere, and conveyed such affection for its object, as to reawaken with sudden force all my feelings of jealousy and insecurity. Now, Charlotte Payler would be in nearly every scene with Edward Taylor—and worse yet, would perform opposite him as Thisbe to his Pyramus! Oh! Was there to be no end to my travails where Charlotte Payler was concerned?

The only thing which concerned my two Edwards was that Mr. Cage had refused to be involved.

"If he does not play Demetrius, I do not know who else should," said Edward Taylor.

Our worries proved to be groundless, for when the entire company assembled an hour later in the same room with copies of the book in hand, Mr. Cage was among them, and said that *if* Fanny was to play Hermia or Helena, then he would be amenable to undertaking the part of Demetrius— should anyone wish it. Mr. Deedes attempted once again to persuade his friend to play Lysander, a role he still considered more suited to him, but Mr. Cage was resolved.

Everybody was pleased with the parts assigned to them except for Brook Edward, Charles, Frederic, and Harry Payler, who wanted first to know how many lines had been given to each, and only after receiving the assurance that their parts were very nearly equal as to length, could be content. At my suggestion we offered the part of Egeus to Sir Brook, who responded with a hearty laugh that he should be "very glad to play the father to his own daughter, but we should be forewarned that he had not been obliged to learn lines by heart since he was at school, and was not certain he retained the facility."

Costumes were discussed, with the conclusion that, as the play was set in ancient Athens, we could simply fashion togas from white bed-sheets, and secure them with a kind of belt.

"The fairies can be similarly attired," proposed

Cassandra, "although *their* dresses might be in colour and more elaborate."

My brother Edward commended this suggestion, and ever the master of delegation, immediately charged Cassandra with the duty of taking charge of costumes, to which she readily acceded. A review was made of the plans for the staging area, and the two Edwards and I agreed to work together to find such furniture and properties as might be required.

Many of the important matters were now settled, and I was pleased; for my casting scheme had, with two exceptions, met with all my hopes; and the task before me—to help shepherd a play into being, while at the same time gently manoeuvring a few of the players into making them aware of their real feelings—was an undertaking which would surely hold all my attention for the coming fortnight, and prove enjoyable.

Chapter the Twenty-second

At the first reading, it became clear that our exercise was to be more challenging than I had anticipated.

Sir Brook joined the rest of us as we squeezed onto chairs and sofas around the room, with the younger boys scattered on the floor, many of us obliged to share books as we read. The two smallest boys, John and George Bridges, as their roles were so minor, were excused. From the first lines spoken I realised to my dismay that Mr. Cage had been quite prescient. I had not truly considered the difficulty of reading with any kind of flair or style when one has little or no experience of acting—much less reading a work entirely in verse, of such verbal complexity as Shakespeare.

The result proved somewhat dreadful. Words were mangled, mispronounced, or missed entirely, often removing all meaning from the speech; great gaps ensued in the dialogue, when people did not notice it was their turn to speak; some talked too low or too rapidly, while others were slow and faltering. In the couples' scenes, the players did not read their lines in such a manner as to render them anything resembling romantic. Sir Brook dozed through most of it, snoring occasionally; Harry Payler complained that he did not have enough to do, and found the whole thing deadly dull; Brook Edward proclaimed it the worst play he had ever heard, and wondered why we had not chosen something else. Fanny was angry to discover, in Act III, that through misapplied magic, the two men who had worshipped Hermia in Act I now hated her and preferred Helena ("You never mentioned *that,* Jane!" cried she). She sulked through many pages until the resolution at last restored Hermia to her "beloved."

There were, however, several high points: Mr. Cage, for all his former insistence that he could not and would not act, proved to have more skill than expected. My brother Edward brought Oberon to life with just the right degree of pompous self-assurance and kingliness. Although I still coveted the role of Titania, I could not deny that Puck was a tremendous part. Sophia was so gentle, funny, and modest in a role which required her to be constantly self-deprecating, that she inspired real sympathy from all.

Charlotte surprised me—and everyone—by reading her lines with a real dramatic flair. When Edward Taylor, astonished and proud, complimented her on her ability, she blushed modestly and only said that she loved Shakespeare and poetry.

Mr. Taylor, even in the simple act of reading lines from a book, proved to be the most accomplished actor among us; everybody said so. He had great confidence and a talent for expression beyond anything I had ever met with, and brought such a depth of humour to the role of Bottom, as had everybody laughing until tears came to our eyes.

His performance reminded me—all of us, I believe—what pleasure a play might give; and gave us all hope that, with great effort, perhaps we *might* be able to accomplish something creditable after all.

• • •

Midsummer's Eve was only twelve days off, and the amount of work to be done in that length of time was acutely felt by everyone. A rehearsal schedule was drawn up on the spot, and we all vowed to devote the evening to studying our lines.

The next morning, the dining-room was once again emptied of most of its furniture, with only a few chairs remaining, while several other pieces were brought in to serve as part of the set. Thenceforward that chamber was referred to, with great enjoyment, as *the theatre;* and many long hours were spent within its four walls over the ensuing days, blocking out and rehearsing the play. Although progress was at first slow, in time the production progressed. I dedicated a great deal of time to copying out scenes for those who did not have books, and to lopping and cropping some of the longer speeches to make them easier to memorise.

An immense roll of green baize was delivered, and Sophia, assisted by several of the maids, took over the duty of making it into a curtain. Sir Brook hired a carpenter as promised to form posts and a frame; and Lady Bridges, after much discussion, approved the rest of the furniture and potted plants requested to dress the scenes. My mother offered to help my sister with costumes, and after a great many bed-sheets were found or furnished from three different households, fashioned them into togas for most of the members of the company.

A quantity of emerald silk and brown satin was discovered in the attic, which Lady Bridges had once thought to have made into gowns; these were dispositioned for the fairies. "The colours are ideal," enthused Cassandra, "as they reflect nature and the earth; and we shall adorn the fairies' costumes with flowers fashioned from colourful fabric, and real flower wreaths for their heads." The fairies were to also have wings made of silk and wire.

The enthusiasm of the company rapidly became evident, as pairs or small groups began to coordinate rehearsals of their own in various rooms all over the house. My brother Edward and Elizabeth were indefatigable rehearsers; he and I spent long hours independently working on Oberon and Puck. I had a great many lines to learn, and applied myself to the task. I was secretly elated to discover, on several occasions, Cassandra and Thomas Payler working together in the billiard room (now the green-room), Fanny meeting with Mr. Deedes in the library, and Sophia and Mr. Cage exchanging lines on the back lawn.

Not everything went according to plan. The youngest children were so full of energy as to be a handful, but Marianne and Cassandra, whose parts were relatively small, took charge of keeping them occupied and out of trouble. Christopher Payler, although adept as Quince, never appeared on time, and his brother Harry could not remember when or where he was to move on the stage. Frederic Fielding, despite having only sixteen lines (and brief ones at that), still could not get through a single one without help. Everyone became disgusted with him except his mother, who (upon observing a rehearsal one morning) applauded his every word with eagerness, and regretted that his part was not more considerable.

By the end of the first week, though, many had learned their lines, and most were more at ease with the text. Elizabeth played the fairy queen as self-centred, passionate, and slightly wanton, an accomplishment which I considered less wonderful in that it required her only to give a performance true to her own nature. Sir Brook brought vigour and dignity to the role of Egeus, and we were grateful to have an elder presence in that role. Charles and Brook Edward began to sense the excitement in what we were putting together, and to find pride in both the play itself, and in being a part of it.

Fanny read her part with real enjoyment, spirit, and abandon, proving that her own opinion of her abilities was not without merit. On several occasions, both on the stage and off, I observed her flirting rather outrageously with Mr. Deedes, and laughing and whispering in his ear, behaviour which always made him blush. Although in their love scenes, *he* was at first reticent (when he and Hermia expressed their love and made a pact to run away together, he kept directing cautious looks at the watching Mr. Cage), in time he performed with more tenderness of expression, so as to emulate a true and mutual attachment between them. To *me,* this progress was elating!

Sophia and Mr. Cage, however, looked on with uncomfortable expressions, prompting Cassandra to say to me: "It must be difficult for Mr. Cage to witness his best friend being so intimate with his fiancée. Sophia is very sympathetic, and seems to feel all his discomfort."

"It is only acting," replied I playfully—secretly hoping that it would, in time, prove to be *more.* Shakespeare's line, *the play's the thing,* had never been more true or more important.

Everything did indeed appear to be moving in the desired direction; for one morning, I happened upon Mr. Deedes alone in the central hall, where were displayed the four works which had won the painting and sketching contest. He was secretly gazing at Fanny's painting.

"It is an excellent rendering, is it not, sir?" said I.

"It is indeed, Miss Jane. How skilled she is! She depicts the windmill with such vivid detail, one can almost feel the force of the wind, and imagine the blades to be spinning." His expression as he spoke left no doubt in my mind, that he not only admired the work, but the person who had painted it!

Just then Fanny entered the hall. I took advantage of the opportunity to say,

"Mr. Deedes was just admiring your painting, Fanny."

"Was he?" Flattered, she came forward.

Mr. Deedes coloured and paused; finally he said, "You are a consummate artist, Miss Bridges, and very deserving of the prize you won."

"Thank you, sir."

After a small hesitation, they fell into a conversation about their love of art in general; filled with delight, I slipped away, leaving them to their own devices.

Later that same morning, I came upon Mr. Cage reading *Gulliver's Travels* in the library, and recognising it as an opportunity, mentioned in an offhand manner that Sophia had expressed a fondness for that particular book.

"Did she indeed?" said he.

"Oh yes; Sophia greatly admires Mr. Swift's work. I have noticed her frequenting the drawing-room every morning before rehearsal to practise the pianoforte. Perhaps she would enjoy discussing it with you some time?"

I said no more, but as I turned from the room, I

noted an intrigued expression on Mr. Cage's countenance.

As I exited the door, I encountered Cassandra in the hall.

"Jane, what are you doing?"

"I am on my way upstairs to work on my lines."

"No; I mean just now. I was walking by and overheard you propose a literary discussion between Mr. Cage and Sophia."

I shrugged and responded innocently, "It just occurred to me that they both enjoy reading."

She studied me, a wary look on her face. "Is that the only reason you suggested it?"

"Yes—of course—what other motive could I have?"

"That is what puzzles me. I have noticed you watching them both of late with rather fixed attention—and Fanny and Mr. Deedes as well."

My cheeks grew warm, but I tossed my head, and said emphatically, "I am the assistant director of our play, Cassandra. It is my duty to observe them, and to monitor their progress."

"I am not talking only of the play, dearest; you watch them when they are off the stage as well. I know you do not like Fanny, and think her and Mr. Cage ill-suited for each other; but you are not qualified to make such a judgement, dearest. It is not a simple matter, to read the depths of the human heart. If you are hoping or expecting that something might come between those two—that would be very wrong indeed."

"I hope for no such thing!" lied I. "You are letting your imagination run away with you, Cassandra."

We said no more on the subject. It was distressing, however, to learn how transparent were my thoughts and motives to my sister. I only hoped that no one else could read me as readily.

Early the next morning as I passed the library, I observed Mr. Cage and Sophia deep in a discussion of the very book in question! My heart sang. It was all progressing precisely as I wished! Despite Cassandra's admonition, I knew that I was doing the right thing. With only a few other subtle promptings, I felt certain that nature would take its course.

To see the play moving forward was delightful to me; to know that all this bustle had been occasioned by *my* idea, was very pleasing; that the planning, rehearsing, and execution required me to see Edward Taylor on a daily basis, *should* have been the most exciting aspect of all. However, to my regret, I could not spend much actual time with him; for not only were we in very few scenes together (and never exchanged any dialogue), but his ease in delivering the lines of Shakespeare (unmatched by anybody else) caused many members of the cast to request his services as a dialogue guide—a service he was happy to provide, and which occupied nearly every moment of the day and evening when he was not absolutely required on the stage.

I say *nearly* because, with the rain continuing incessantly, making it impossible to go without, he could at times be found sitting in a corner playing cards with the Payler boys, and sometimes rolling dice, with real money being wagered. When Lady Bridges and my mother discovered them so engaged one morning, there was a great outcry; but when they applied to Sir Brook in horror, insisting that such activity desist at once, he laughed and said:

"Ladies! It is raining, and boys will be boys." He then moved the game to a table in the billiard room, and with pleasure joined in.

On some days, my only contact with Edward Taylor were our brief meetings with my brother, when we went over a variety of details regarding the production. To my dismay, the play, which had been my own idea, was taking time away from the one thing—the one *person*—with whom I most wished to associate. Although I had reconciled myself to the loss of playing Titania opposite Edward Taylor, I could not observe his daily rehearsals with Charlotte and all the craftsmen without discomfort, for their teasing laughter and jocularity fairly echoed throughout the house.

To make matters worse, the promise which Miss Payler showed at the first reading only blossomed. Although she was still very reserved generally, on the stage she came alive and seemed to be an entirely different person. She and Mr. Taylor performed Pyramus and Thisbe with such a mixture of romantic verve, pathos, and comedic timing, as to instill in me pangs of deep envy. *He* seemed to enjoy every rehearsal as much as she. Oh! Was it not enough that Charlotte Payler was beautiful, perfectly behaved, sweet-natured, soft-spoken, and proficient at art? Did she have to be an excellent actress as well? How I disliked her!

My feelings on this matter soon underwent a very great change.

On Thursday morning just after breakfast, I was studying my lines in the empty theatre before anyone else arrived (a time and place I had found ideally suited to such a solitary endeavour), when Miss Payler entered. Crossing deliberately to me, she said softly,

"Miss Jane, I hoped I might find you here. Pray forgive me for disturbing you, but may I have a word?"

So surprised was I to be approached by her, that I was at a loss. "Of course you may, Miss Payler."

Sitting down in a chair beside me, she said very quietly, "There is something which I have long been wishing to say to you."

"Oh?" I looked at her, puzzled, truly having no idea what to expect.

"Do you remember the day we met, when my mother spoke to you about—about a particular subject—a particular *gentleman*—and her future hopes for me in that regard?" Her face coloured slightly as she looked at me.

"Yes, I remember."

"I was very embarrassed. Mamma talked on and on about my cousin. She fairly forced him to pick strawberries with me, just as she urged him to dance with me at the ball. I can only imagine what you must think of her, and of me."

My mind raced, as I processed this information: that Edward Taylor had, according to her, felt *obliged* to do all those things—that it was her mother's doing. I heard myself say: "Oh! You need not feel embarrassed, Miss Payler. My mother does the same thing. At times, she says things that mortify me."

"Does she? But your mother is a truly lovely woman."

"Do you think so? Well, so is yours."

"Perhaps," replied Charlotte thoughtfully, "as daughters, we are overly sensitive to the way our mothers treat us, and the way they behave. We love them so dearly, that we expect too much from them."

It was an idea I had never considered. "Perhaps that is so." This was the longest conversation I had ever held with Charlotte Payler; indeed, we had never exchanged more than a few words before. It was disconcerting to find her so amiable—more than amiable—so congenial and utterly sincere. "Your mother dearly loves you, Miss Payler, I can tell you that. Everything she said that morning—she was only expressing her hopes for your future happiness."

"Yes, but—if she would only keep her hopes to herself, I would be far more content."

Cautiously, I said: "Why? Do not you—share those same hopes, Miss Payler?"

She blushed and folded her hands in her lap, lowering her gaze before she spoke. "You mean: am I in love with my cousin Edward?"

I nodded, afraid to breathe.

"I am," admitted she softly, "and have been for a long while. My heart is entirely his; to marry him would be my dearest dream. But I cannot be sure he returns my feelings." She raised her eyes to mine, and with gentle honesty said: "I envy you, you know."

"You envy *me?*"

"You are everything that I am not, Miss Jane. I am too quiet, whereas you are so lively. I am cautious by nature, and you are impulsive, like *he* is—he told me about the time you walked the wall. He talks about you all the time. He says you are so intelligent and well-read—you have studied all the subjects which interest Edward, subjects I have barely even heard about." She shook her head with a little, self-deprecating sigh. Lowering her voice to a whisper, she leaned forward, adding, "I do believe that he is half in love with you."

Just then, several members of our acting company entered the room, and Charlotte, smiling softly, retreated to a corner to study her copy of the play. For some long minutes I sat in my chair as the room began to fill, unable to move, hardly daring to believe what she had said.

He talks about you all the time. I do believe that he is half in love with you.

Could it be true? To think that the sentiment had been spoken by the very young lady I considered my rival! It was incredible to think that all this time, I had envied Charlotte Payler, while she had envied me! How very noble and gracious of her to reveal her heart to me in this way, considering what her own feelings were! I had regarded her with such dislike; I saw now that those thoughts and feelings had been uncharitable. All my former animosity melted away. I should think of Charlotte Payler very differently in future.

It was difficult to concentrate all the rest of the day; when I saw Edward Taylor across the room or watched him perform in a scene, my heart alternately caught in my throat or did a little dance. Was Charlotte Payler's assessment of his feelings for me accurate, or merely a reflection of her own deep desires? I had no way of knowing.

That evening, we were treated to a welcome brightening of the skies. Everybody cheered; having spent so many days cooped up inside, we looked forward to a chance to get out of doors.

As we all sat down to dinner, I was thrilled when Edward Taylor took the seat immediately beside me. He whispered in my ear, "It seems ages since you and I have had a real conversation, about anything not related to the play."

I nodded in mutual frustration, encouraged by the warmth in his gaze.

"I aim to change that." Turning to my brother, he announced emphatically, "We have rehearsed every day since Sunday, Austen, and made excellent progress with the play. We still have a week before the performance. I think we have earned a day off."

"I have no objection to taking a respite from rehearsals tomorrow or Saturday," replied my brother, "if everyone wishes it."

This idea met with enthusiastic approval. The Payler boys and Frederic Fielding immediately said they should like to go home for a day.

Mr. Deedes expressed his desire to visit Bifrons. "Sir Brook has been telling me about the improvements your father made to your house," said he to Edward Taylor. "It sounds quite remarkable."

"It is!" cried Sir Brook. "Anyone who knew that house five-and-twenty years ago would not recognise the place today. I never saw a place so altered in my life!"

"So people tell me," replied Edward Taylor with a shrug. "The improvements were begun before I was born, and finished when I was very young. My only reference of what it *used* to look like is an old painting which hangs in the great hall—and I must admit, I liked it better *before*."

"Before?" cried Sir Brook. "Oh, no, no; it was very old-fashioned before, an immense red-brick building from Elizabeth's time. Your father did it up right, Edward, with an entirely new front in the modern style, and all new windows, gables, roof, chimneys, a lovely glass conservatory, and the grounds laid out in the newest style—you can be proud of it, for it is quite a sight to see."

"I suppose I should be proud," admitted Edward Taylor, "and I might better appreciate the result, had my father not impoverished himself in the act of building it." This remark was met with a brief, uncomfortable silence, which the speaker put an end to by smiling and adding lightly, "Of course, I cannot begrudge my father's action, for I have had the benefit of it. It obliged us to emigrate, thus granting me the pleasure of an incomparable childhood travelling the Continent."

"Frederic cannot begrudge it either, I think,"

remarked I, "for he and his family have all the benefit of living in the house, without having had to go to any of the trouble or expense in its improvements."

Everyone laughed; even my mother seemed to appreciate the levity in my remark, and with good humour restored in the room, I added:

"I should love to see Bifrons, and to view all these improvements for myself. On our way here, I was only able to catch the merest glimpse of the house, hidden beyond the trees."

"Would you really like to see it?" said Edward Taylor.

"I would—and might have been there already, had not Mrs. Fielding's concert been cancelled."

Cassandra and Charles admitted that they should be most interested in visiting the place as well, an opinion echoed by Mr. Cage.

"I would be very happy to take you there," said Edward Taylor, "if the Admiral and Mrs. Fielding are amenable to such a visit. Perhaps we could apply to them, and ask."

"Even if they do agree to such a plan," remarked Mr. Cage, "Bifrons is five miles distant. After so many days of rain, the roads will be too muddy for a carriage."

"We can go on horseback," suggested Mr. Deedes. "Most of us have our own mounts. As for the Austens—" (to Sir Brook) "If you have any horses to spare, sir, and could see your way clear to lending them a pair of docile animals for the day—"

Sir Brook graciously replied that his stable was at his guests' disposal.

This idea gave me a moment of concern. I knew Charles to be proficient on horseback, but my sister and I were not expert riders by any means. I gave her a silent look which signified, *Do we dare attempt such a ride?* Cassandra squeezed my hand under the table and whispered,

"I feel certain we can do it."

Fanny, who had been listening to this conversation with indifference, on perceiving the interest of the others, said: "It has been a long while since I was at Bifrons. Why should only *a few* of us go? We should make a party of it!"

Sophia and Charlotte admitted that, if a party was being formed, they should also like to go, the former adding:

"If the weather remains clear, as we hope it shall, we could all return in time for a late dinner here, or stay longer and dine at Bifrons; for as I recall, the full moon is tomorrow."

After further discussion, it was agreed that Frederic would ride home the following morning and present the idea to his mother and father. If they said yes, he would send an invitation for a visit on Saturday; if they were not so inclined, he would return himself, and rehearsals could proceed as usual the next morning.

The weather cooperated. At three o'clock on Friday, a note was delivered from Mrs. Fielding expressing her delight in the proposed excursion, and an invitation to anybody who wished to come, to do so on the following day.

The visit to Bifrons was a settled thing. Thomas Payler added himself to the party at the last minute; and the affectionate looks he gave my sister when he thought nobody was looking made me smile; I knew where *his* inclinations lay, and although my sister, in her usual reserved style, remained quiet on the subject, I could only hope that she felt the same. The other Payler boys were happy to take advantage of the break in rehearsals, to return home to Ileden for a day and night.

Before we retired that evening, Edward Taylor stopped me in the passage and said how much he looked forward to our day off. My night was suffused with pleasant dreams of the delightful time which I anticipated we would spend together.

Chapter the Twenty-third

Saturday was thankfully fine; and soon after breakfast, the horses were brought round from the stables. Those who had elected to make the journey were happy and animated with chatter. I was eager to see Bifrons, for all that it represented as the family home of Edward Taylor; at the same time, I could not help but think of the day ahead without some calculation.

"Fanny," said I, when that young lady appeared, looking very fine in her riding clothes, "as the ride to Bifrons is substantial, ought we to make use of the time by rehearsing our lines along the way with our scene partners?"

Fanny deemed this to be an excellent idea, and had no sooner mounted, than she repeated it to Mr. Deedes.

He, astride his horse and engaged in smiling conversation with Sophia, was reluctant: "Of course he had no objection to riding with Fanny, but he had thought it was to be a day off from rehearsing, &c." But Fanny was insistent, and Mr. Deedes acquiesced.

Sophia momentarily looked troubled, which I suspected was due to a concern for her sister's avid solicitation as a riding partner, of a gentleman other than the one to whom she was betrothed. I was considering how best to smooth this over, when I was saved from such action by Mr. Cage riding up to Sophia and inviting her to ride alongside *him,* so that they might go over their lines in a similar manner. She gracefully accepted.

I silently congratulated myself on the effortless manner in which these pairings had been accomplished. It was shaping up to be a truly marvellous day! I had now only to pair myself with the young man whom I preferred.

As I mounted the animal which had been provided for me (the groom assuring me that she was a gentle creature), Edward Taylor rode over to me with a smile. My pulse leapt; I was all anticipation. His raised eyebrows and the look in his eyes signalled an invitation. He wished to be my riding partner! He was on the point of speaking when Charles trotted up and paused beside me, saying:

"Jane! Will you ride with me?"

I hesitated, truly dismayed, but not wanting my brother to know it. The idea of riding with Charles had not even occurred to me; indeed, since our arrival at Goodnestone, we had both been so busy, we had seen very little of each other. Although I wanted very much to ride with Mr. Taylor, Charles was one of the dearest people in the world to me; I had no wish to hurt him or let him down. Edward Taylor caught my gaze and we silently communicated our mutual disappointment and all the awkwardness of the moment; he then nodded in understanding, and turned his horse away.

I made every effort to shew my brother the affection and delight in the circumstance which he deserved. "I would be happy to ride with you, Charles. It has been some time since *we* had an opportunity to be alone together."

"It certainly has," agreed Charles.

Charlotte, who had been waiting quietly at the road-side, naturally fell in beside Edward Taylor as the twosome rode to the top of the line. Glancing back, he inquired as to whether all were ready; upon receiving an affirmative reply, the ten of us moved forward in the pairs formed, with Charles and I the last in line.

Our road was through a pleasant country, which I had only traversed once before in the opposite direction. This approach opened up new vistas which I was pleased to observe and admire. The roads were very dirty, and for the first few miles, we plodded along at a tranquil tempo. Discovering the groom's description of my mare to be true, I was soon reasonably at ease in the saddle.

Fragments of Shakespearean verse drifted back to me from Fanny and Mr. Cage, and from Sophia and Mr. Deedes. Thomas and Cassandra were talking too quietly for me to guess the content of their dialogue, but both appeared to be in good humour. It did my heart good to see all three couples so properly aligned! Even the sight of Edward Taylor and Charlotte riding side by side could not dismay me. He had *wished* to ride with me; that was all that mattered.

As Charles and I did not share any scenes in the play, we could not use the time to practise our lines, so we talked of other things: of Goodnestone, the people we had met there, what we had enjoyed most (and least), and our expectations for the weeks ahead. Before long, the conversation took a different and more serious bent. I was honoured to find Charles confiding in me, in an open manner, and from the depths of his heart, with all the gravity of a boy not quite twelve, all his hopes and fears for the new life which lay ahead of him, as he prepared to enter the navy. The time was drawing very near; a week after we returned to Steventon, he was to go to Portsmouth to be entered at the Naval Academy.

"I hope to do well," said he, "both at the academy and afterwards, on board ship. I do not want to let my mother and father down."

"I am sure you will distinguish yourself, Charles," replied I sincerely.

"I know the profession is filled with hardships and dangers, and that I could die at sea, but I do not like to think of it."

"Then do *not* think of it, for that is highly unlikely to occur. Think only of the good things which you will experience and accomplish. You will see the world! I am envious. It is something I can never hope to do."

"I *do* look forward to the travelling. It will be exciting to be at sea. But I will miss you and Cassandra and my mother and father terribly. I hate to think of being so far away from you and from Steventon, perhaps for many long years."

I was deeply affected by this discourse.

Naturally, I felt every one of my brother's fears; although selfishly, I saw that I had only considered them from my *own* perspective, and had not really thought what *he* must be feeling. I said all I could think of to allay his dread, while attempting to soften the blow which must eventually come when we would be truly parted.

"Let us make the most of every moment we have together *now,*" said I, "so that we might create a pleasant memory to look back on in future."

These words cheered us both somewhat, and we resolved to be as happy as we could in the weeks which remained to us; but I could not help feeling, as we rode, how very *little* my brother seemed, and how hard it was for a boy to be expected to leave home forever, and enter such a dangerous profession at such a young age.

It suddenly struck me that his birthday, the day he was to turn twelve, was only five days hence, on 23 June—Midsummer's Eve—the very day that we were to perform our theatrical. I silently chastised myself that, in the excitement of preparing for the play, those members of his family who *should* have been thinking of Charles, and the importance which the day must hold for him, had made no plans whatsoever for his birthday! I determined, then and there, to do something about it, the moment we returned to Goodnestone.

My thoughts were interrupted when Edward Taylor called over his shoulder:

"The road is drier here. Let us pick up the pace a bit."

So saying, he and Charlotte took off at a run, and the Bridges sisters and their riding companions immediately followed suit. Cassandra expressed a reluctance to ride too fast, but Thomas Payler assured her that they should keep it to a slow trot; and exchanging a word with Charles, who revealed his fear of being left behind, we urged our horses on to a swifter speed.

Moving so quickly over the rough road proved to be less than comfortable, and at three separate intervals I was truly afraid I might fall off; but I persevered, and we did our best to keep up with the others. The six experienced riders at the head of the line were clearly enjoying the ride, with no concern as to the ability or safety of those left behind; and they moved out of sight at times, which was even more disquieting.

"Do not worry if they should disappear," said Thomas Payler. "I know the way perfectly well."

As we neared our destination, we found the party ahead resting their horses and waiting for us. There was a fine burst of country, and we moved slowly together again as we traversed a bridge over a narrow stream; but when we passed a sturdy and respectable house, where Edward

Taylor said the steward lived, he urged us to ride more quickly, saying:

"Mr. Forrester is not happy with me. I tried to explain about the play, but he says I have been spending far too much time at Goodnestone of late, and neglecting that instruction here at Bifrons which my father deems so necessary."

We soon came to the lodge gates. My eyes eagerly took in everything we passed during the remaining half-mile through the park, for there was some very fine timber, and the coolness of the woods was delightful. The lane was wide enough here that we could ride four abreast; soon the trees opened up and gave way to an immense lawn, from whence we had our first full view of the manor house.

It was truly magnificent. An enormous building with a white stone façade and two elegant wings, Bifrons was configured with every modern improvement. A central, half-domed entry porch was flanked by three tall, gabled windows on each side, and a long row of perfectly symmetrical windows on the floor above. A multitude of gabled attic windows made up the top floor and adorned the roof, above which stood a great many chimneys.

"Oh!" cried Charles. "It is every bit as grand as Sir Brook described!"

All expressed their avid admiration for the house.

"It was certainly the most significant house in the area when it was *originally* built, in 1634," admitted Edward Taylor indifferently.

I wondered at his attitude, which indicated a lack of real interest in or affection for the property. Perhaps, I thought, he is *affecting* indifference, because it feels strange to be at his own house as a *visitor,* while it is occupied by others. But then, recalling what he had told me regarding his feelings for the aristocracy, I wondered if there might be a very different reason.

"Why is the house called Bifrons?" asked Mr. Cage.

"It means 'two fronts,' " replied Edward Taylor, "and refers to the two large wings on either side."

We rode up to the front sweep, where we were met by a flurry of grooms and Frederic Fielding at the door. Our party was welcomed and ushered into the drawing-room, where the Admiral and Mrs. Fielding were happy to receive us. I marvelled at the space, for it was beautifully appointed and embellished by high ceilings, carved plasterwork, fine draperies, and a large and elegantly carved mantel.

The business of arriving took some minutes, after which we were admitted to the dining-parlour, where an abundant collation was served and enjoyed by all. The admiral then excused himself, in his quiet and officious manner, and repaired to his study. The next object of the day was now discussed, as all of us shared our eagerness to see the rest of the house and grounds.

Mrs. Fielding, conscious of having Edward Taylor as a visitor, asked very thoughtfully if *he* might like to shew the place. "The admiral and I, and our Frederic, are very pleased with the house; it is very comfortable, and we are delighted and proud to live here; but it does not really belong to *us*. I cannot take credit even for the furnishings, for Frederic and I used to live in a much smaller place, and when the admiral retired, we leased the house with everything in it. It would be more appropriate, I think, if the true owner of the house—the *future* owner, I should say—were to shew you all around."

Edward Taylor bowed but graciously declined. "I am happy to let you do the honours, Mrs. Fielding. It is your house as long as you occupy it. Today I am merely a visitor, and am content to follow along with the others."

This declaration was warmly received. The whole party rose, and under Mrs. Fielding's guidance, we were shewn through a great many rooms on both the ground floor and the floor above, all of them lofty and handsomely furnished. We reached a picture gallery hung with innumerable family portraits, several of which dated back to Elizabethan times, which meant nothing to the Fieldings. Here we relied on Edward Taylor for an explanation of the family history, which he was able to relate with some knowledge.

"I am told that my ancestor, John Taylor, purchased Bifrons and other estates in Kent in 1694. I am of the sixth generation of Taylors here."

"Does not *our* family's connection with *yours* go back even further than that?" inquired Sophia.

"It does. My family were originally from Whitchurch, in Shropshire; in the 1500s they spelt *Taylour* with an *o-u*. Nathaniel Taylour, Esquire—who I understand represented the county Bedford in Parliament, and was also recorder of Colchester in Essex during the usurpation of Cromwell—*he* married the daughter of Colonel Bridges, of Wallingford, in Essex— ancestor of *your* father; that is how far back the relationship goes. They had eighteen children, and his eldest son, John Taylor, is the one who purchased Bifrons."

Sophia smiled and acknowledged that, no matter how distantly they were related, Edward Taylor should always be a cousin to her, a sentiment he warmly returned.

We now came upon the painting of Bifrons which had been done in 1700, a large and beautifully rendered effort, in a gilded frame as tall as myself. Edward Taylor gave a brief explanation of the work, and we all studied it with pleasure. The painting featured a hunting party in the foreground, who from a hill top, overlooked a prospect of the house and property as it had been nearly a hundred years before, in all its red-brick, Elizabethan grandeur. The building was fronted by a large, walled, cultivated garden, surrounded by fields, and backed by abundant woods.

"It is extraordinary, to think that this is the same house!" cried Mr. Deedes. "Although I recognise the setting in a general sense, the building and approach are so vastly different, that if you did not tell me it was Bifrons, I should not know where I was."

"Your father is truly a visionary," said Cassandra to Edward Taylor, "for he has worked wonders here."

"It *is* a beautiful house," agreed I with feeling. "To think that you shall be master of this place some day!"

He did not reply, but merely glanced away with a slight frown. Again, his manner and expression were very puzzling. How could anyone be anything but enthusiastic about this house? Bifrons was a positively extraordinary property!

I observed a silent, conscious look pass between himself and both Charlotte and Thomas Payler, and knew they must be privy to whatever Edward Taylor was thinking and feeling on the subject. I was determined to find out what lay behind it.

Chapter the Twenty-fourth

We returned downstairs, where Mrs. Fielding said she wished to sit down, but as it was still fine out, we young people might enjoy a turn about the grounds on our own—a suggestion which was met with eager interest. An outward door was thrown open, and all walked out and down the flight of steps which led immediately onto a manicured lawn and all the delights of the pleasure-grounds.

Our party naturally dispersed across the wide green turf, admiring the plants, and making our way towards a long terrace walk. Small groups were formed, but with a sigh, I noticed they were *not* the associations to which I aspired; for Mr. Cage had reclaimed Fanny, and Mr. Deedes was now chatting with Sophia. Thomas Payler had been appropriated by Frederic, who must take him to see the den of foxes he had recently discovered in the adjoining wilderness; Charles went with them.

This left a party of four: myself, my sister, Edward Taylor, and Charlotte. As we traversed the first planted area together, he exclaimed his delight in the joy of liberty, in being out of doors on such a fine day. All concurred and remarked on the beauty of the setting. It was indeed lovely. I had greatly looked forward to this excursion, and was particularly happy to be in the company of Edward Taylor in a setting removed from Goodnestone, and all the cares and worries about the play. However, for some reason *he* did not appear to feel so carefree.

"Bifrons is everything I could have imagined it to be, Mr. Taylor, and more. I should think anyone would be thrilled to know that all this will be his one day; yet—correct me if I am wrong—you seem to have little affection for it."

He looked conscious, but made no immediate reply.

"You have found him out, Miss Jane," said Charlotte softly, shaking her head. "My cousin is rather ridiculous on this subject, I am afraid; but he must tell you himself."

Still, he glanced away and said nothing.

"Do you not care for this place," persisted I, "because of what it represents? Because such a holding designates you irrefutably as a member of the upper class?"

Edward Taylor sighed, considered, and at last said, "No; that is not it at all. I have great respect for my ancestors, and for the property they built; and I am not such an idiot as to wish away a fortune, for the sake of principle alone. My uncertainty stems from a very different source. I do *wish* I felt more; but try as I might, I cannot feel any connection to Bifrons."

"Why not?" said I.

"I think—part of the problem at least—is that I have not lived here enough. It is true that I passed the earliest years of my life here, but we moved way when I was five years old, so I do not have any particular memories of it. The only time of any substance which I have spent here recently was two years ago, when we returned from Germany for an interval of eleven months. Up until that time, we lived in a series of smaller, quaint, European apartments; in contrast, this house feels too large and cold to me. Many of its rooms seem to have no purpose other than to give work to housemaids and contribute to the window-tax. I suppose I have got used to a transitory existence. I have learned to appreciate the freedom that comes with a leased property, which offers the ability to move on, to see new vistas and experience new places, whenever the mood should strike. The idea of being tied down to one location for life does not really appeal to me."

"Oh," responded I. "Your explanation makes sense, now that you put it that way. But surely, owning a property such as this should not tie you down, if you do not wish it to?"

"It has not kept your father from travelling the world and taking his family with him," pointed out Cassandra.

"Precisely what I have been telling him," said

Charlotte. "But he has not told you all. There is another reason, a much bigger reason, why Edward is not enamoured of being heir to Bifrons." She sighed. "He explained it to *me* only last week."

Cassandra and I turned to Edward Taylor, all attention. He very calmly said:

"I am aware of the privilege bestowed on me as the eldest son. I do not wish to appear ungrateful, but—it is not the future I foresee for myself."

"What future *do* you see?" asked I.

"I wish to go into the army."

"The army!" cried my sister and I in unison.

He nodded. "Were I allowed to follow the bent of my own mind, I would choose no other occupation than active military service."

Shocked, I exclaimed: "A first son can never go into the *army!* That is an occupation for second and third sons!"

"That is the traditional thinking, yes. But a man cannot choose his birth order, any more than he can mindlessly accept, with any reasonable chance of happiness or success, whatever personal or professional fate has been decreed for him. My family's position in society guarantees that I would advance to a very great degree in the army. Every nobleman of rank I know who is thus employed, chooses to use his military title rather than his aristocratic title; do you know why?"

"Because," answered I, "to be an army officer is the most prestigious of all professions."

"Yes!" Passionately, he continued: "I cannot envision myself as master of this vast estate, worrying every day about money and the farm, employing dozens of servants, and being responsible for so many tenants. I have no faith in my ability to handle the financial aspect of it. I would let my family down, I feel certain of it. If only I could step aside and give the estate to my brother Herbert—" Here he sighed deeply and corrected himself. "No, that would never do; for Herbert is as resolved to entering military service as am I; it is something we have talked about together since we were very little, and first removed to Brussels. We inhabited there a house near the governor, General Ferraris, who commanded the garrison; we used to walk by and talk to the sentry placed at his door, and in his uniform, he seemed to embody all that manliness, honour, and valour could hope to represent. In Heidelberg, we occupied part of the house with a major of the Elector Palatine Dragoons, who told us stories of his experience in the military, which excited our imagination and furthered our ambitions. Ever since, I have read every book I could find about history and the military; they continue to be the favourite objects of my attention."

It was charming to think of Edward as a little boy, falling under the spells of a colourful uniform and valiant tales from the battlefield— but his ambition troubled me. "Certainly," said I, "the profession, either navy or army, has much in its favour: heroism, action, courage, even fashion. Nobody can wonder that a young man *without property* should choose to distinguish himself as a soldier or a sailor. But I cannot understand how you could conceive of trading the advantages which *you* have been given—and an estate which has been in your family for *six generations*—for a life of danger, hardship, and privation!"

"And yet I would, in an instant. What you call danger and hardship are to me excitement and adventure; I would prefer, infinitely prefer, to experience these *privations* on a daily basis, than to be trapped in the quiet, agrarian life of a gentleman, doing the same dull things day after day, with nothing new to look forward to. I have tried to explain all this to my father, but in vain. I have twin brothers, Brook and William, either one of whom could very well take over the responsibilities which he feels must devolve on me; *they* have heads for this sort of thing, and I feel certain would not only greatly enjoy the legacy, but be thrilled and honoured by it. To expect it of *me* is like forcing a square peg into a round hole. It would be a very bad fit. But my father is intractable on the subject. He insists that, according to law, the property *must* go to the eldest son; it is my privilege and my duty; there is nothing to be done; &c. It is not fair. My brother Bridges is currently at sea, a midshipman on the

Acquilon, and father has no scruples about *that;* but he will not hear a word about the army, even for my brother Herbert; he intends him for a clerkship in the Foreign Office."

"Perhaps your father cannot bear the thought of his two eldest sons entering professions so fraught with peril," said Cassandra.

"That is part of it," admitted he. "He has frequently stated that he fears Herbert's spirit might lead him into dangers."

"If Herbert is anything like *you,* I cannot wonder at it!" My remark elicited a quiet laugh from Mr. Taylor, but then he said:

"If he feels we are men of spirit, that is precisely why he *ought* to let us go. If England is truly to be at war with France soon, as I suppose, we will need every good man we can find to serve and protect our shores. Instead, I am to go to *Oxford*." He invested the name of that institution with disgust.

"You do not wish to go to Oxford?" repeated I, shocked. "I would give anything to go there!"

"I wish I could send you in my place, Miss Jane. I have already studied so long and so hard with the best masters in Europe; I cannot conceive what my father expects me to gain from a university education. If I am obliged to sit in a schoolroom and read the classics again while our nation is at war, I shall go truly mad. And later— if I must sit here, idle, for all the rest of my days—" He broke off, sighing. "It is all a sad twist of fate that has put me in this position. My father only inherited Bifrons because his older brother died and had no children. Had my uncle lived, I would be free to follow the profession of my choice. I will of course do my duty if required, but I would rather *not* be required, for I fear I will do it badly."

He spoke with such feeling as to evoke my deepest sympathies. "I am so sorry, Mr. Taylor. My heart *does* go out to you; but—I can envision no solution to your dilemma, if your father is as intractable on the subject as you say."

"I had never before considered that the blessings of property and fortune might be a burden to some men, as to *you,* they are," added Cassandra.

Charlotte said, "Even knowing how you feel, cousin, I cannot share your wish. I should not like you to go into the army; for if you did, then every day I should be worried for your safety. I prefer to think of you at Oxford, or just a few miles away, living quietly at Bifrons."

"Quietly? If I *do* live here, Charlotte, it will not be quietly; I promise you that." He paused; then, shaking his head, he added with a self-deprecating smile: "Forgive me, ladies. I have been selfish. We have talked of nothing but me and *my* problems, aims, and desires since we got here. It is too beautiful a day to spend on the negative. Let us move on to brighter, more hopeful subjects: let us hear what *you* aspire to. What do you see in *your* futures?"

"*Our* futures?" I laughed. "That promises to be a very brief discussion, Mr. Taylor. We are women. We do not have many choices."

"All *I* have dreamt about since I was a child," said Charlotte Payler, with a certain consciousness, and a slight blush, "is that I should love the man I marry, raise a family, and have a comfortable home."

"My aspirations are identical to yours, Miss Payler," admitted my sister.

"I think anyone of sense, regardless of gender," concurred Edward Taylor, as we continued along the gravel path through the shrubbery, "hopes to have a comfortable place to live, and to share their life with a person they can love and respect." He darted a sidelong glance at me as he spoke, continuing, "But apart from marriage and home: is not there anything else you ladies aspire to? Some noble goal or ambition? Some worthy yet difficult accomplishment you wish to attain? Some exotic place in the world you wish to visit?"

Charlotte shook her head, colouring more deeply as she said, "I do not need to see the world. Marriage, to the right person, will be enough for me."

My sister again echoed the sentiment.

"What about you, Miss Jane?" said Edward Taylor. "What do you dream about?"

"If I may speak to the *immediate* future: I should like to eat ice for dinner, and drink a very good wine."

Everyone laughed.

"And after that?" said Edward Taylor.

"This summer has given me a real taste for the society of new and interesting people—and I wish more than anything that I could be out sooner than seventeen."

"Entirely understandable," agreed he. "But what of the *distant* future?"

I shrugged. "I suppose—I share the same hopes as have just been expressed—which are common to every woman."

"I detect a hesitation in your voice." He looked at me. "There is something else which you are not telling us."

Reluctantly, I admitted: "Well. I do have other ambitions, but—"

"Such as?"

I glanced away. In truth, I wished for a life with *him,* just as I knew Charlotte did; but I could never voice *that* aloud. Neither could I reveal that other, deeper ambition which I held close to my heart. Instead, I said the first thing that popped into my head. "I should like to perfect my satin stitch."

"A worthy goal," praised he, laughing again.

"I should like to make a quilt some day," added I. "I should like to live in the country and plant a syringa near my door, and have an apricot tree along my garden wall that bears excellent fruit."

"Very pleasant. Anything else?"

So many ideas now began to tumble into my head, that I struggled to keep up with them. "I should like to learn Italian and improve my French. I should like to walk for days in the Lake District, spend a fortnight in London, see a dozen plays and concerts, and attend a service in Westminster Abbey."

"Now we are getting somewhere!" cried he. "Now you truly have my attention! And?"

My enthusiasm rose with each statement as I continued: "I should like to see my brothers flourish in the navy and reach the rank of admiral. I should like to play the pianoforte with more dexterity, and have a hundred songs at my disposal. I should like to read every book in my father's library. I should like to have a writing-desk of my very own, and a bound note-book in which to write my stories!"

The last sentiment burst forth from my lips unintentionally.

Edward Taylor said in surprise, "You write stories?"

Warmth took over my face. I regretted my slip of the tongue, for I had never shown my tales to anyone outside my immediate family and closest friends, and to talk about them could only mortify me. "Oh! It is nothing; please forget I said it."

"The desire to write is an interesting and commendable goal."

Cassandra smiled. "For several years now, Jane has been delighting our family with stories which she makes up out of her own head. If too many days go by when she has not written *something,* she grows very irritable."

"I cannot imagine actually thinking up and writing down a story." Charlotte stared at me with a wondering expression.

"I have never been any good at writing myself, but it is a skill I admire," said Edward Taylor. "What kinds of stories do you write?"

"Only silly nonsense—and hardly worth discussing. My brothers James and Henry are the true geniuses in the family; they wrote and edited a weekly periodical at Oxford full of interesting essays, which James had bound into two volumes and published."

"Jane contributed a letter to the editor on one occasion," said Cassandra proudly, "penned by a 'Sophia Sentiment.'"

"Ah!" laughed Edward Taylor. "Then you have had the pleasure of seeing your words in print."

"I fear it will constitute my one and only experience of publishing."

To my relief, the topic was ended by circumstance. We had reached the far side of the property, where it bordered on a stately grove; at the same moment, we caught sight of all the disparate members of our party approaching in our direction: Fanny and Mr. Cage (arguing) came along a path to the left; Sophia and Mr. Deedes (smiling) came from the right; and Charles, Thomas, and Frederic (frowning) were just emerging from the wilderness beyond.

"Here we are, *tout assemblé*!" cried Edward Taylor. "Did you find your foxes?"

As we all converged, the trio explained that their errand had been in vain. Frederic had forgotten where he saw the den.

"I was certain it was dug into the brush to the north of a very tall tree, but then I thought, perhaps it was to the *south* of the tree."

"We have looked in every direction," said Charles, "and can find no sign of it."

"Let us see if a few more pairs of eyes can help," offered Edward Taylor.

We all moved together into the woods, to the spot which Frederic *thought* might be the place; but after searching for some little time in the underbrush, and finding no sign of a fox den anywhere, Frederic said with regret that he must have got the tree wrong, and we ought to waste no more time on it. We were about to turn back when Edward Taylor, glancing up at the tree towering above us, cried:

"I say, this is a very grand tree. I think it is the

same one I climbed when I was here two years ago."

"You *climbed* this tree?" said Frederic, shocked.

"I did. Let me see if I can scale it again."

"Cousin!" cried Charlotte. "It is too tall!"

Edward Taylor paid her no heed. With dexterity and grace, he caught hold of a lower limb, propelled himself up and over it, and began to make his way upwards amongst the branches.

My heart seemed to stop beating. Tree-climbing had been a popular pursuit with my brothers and the schoolboys at Steventon Rectory. While I had on occasion found it exciting to watch them climb, I had never been able to view the activity without deep apprehension and a very real concern for their safety. I was never comfortable until they had descended unharmed, and I had never witnessed *anyone* climb a tree as high as this one.

It was one thing, I thought, when Edward Taylor had walked the wall at Goodnestone—*that* had only been somewhat precarious; to climb this immense tree was pure madness!

"Taylor!" cried Mr. Cage. "Come down. It is far too dangerous."

"Danger is in my blood!" returned he, flashing us a smile from above.

Sophia shook her head. "He is insane."

Everyone stood staring up with grave concern, but Edward Taylor climbed with confidence and determination, briefly hesitating only now and then to test a limb's strength before moving higher. Mr. Deedes and Thomas soon began to whistle and call out encouragements, whilst the cautious wonder and concern of all the young ladies was exhibited by gasps and intermittent cries of warning.

"Higher! Higher!" cried Thomas Payler.

"That is high enough!" warned Mr. Cage.

"Oh!" exclaimed Fanny. "Is not he very brave!"

Edward now reached what seemed to be the highest possible limb which could support his weight. He stopped and turned to face his onlookers, clinging to the branches around him as he let go a great war-cry of victory, and shouted:

"The view is magnificent from up here! I dare say I can see all the way to Dover on this side, and Canterbury on the other! Who will climb up and join me?"

Nervous laughter spread through the crowd.

"It is not difficult. Cousin Thomas! Come up. I dare you!"

Thomas shook his head.

"We are not all so mad as you, Mr. Taylor," cried Mr. Cage, "to risk our lives for the sake of a view."

"Are you afraid, Cage?"

"Yes," replied Mr. Cage honestly, "but more than that: I am sensible and cautious."

"Fie on sense and caution! Is not there an ounce

of spirit and adventure among the lot of you? I tell you, the view is worth the effort."

"I will make the climb!" exclaimed an eager voice.

I gasped in alarm. The words were spoken by my brother Charles, and no sooner had he uttered them, than he raced to the base of the tree and urged Thomas Payler to give him a boost up to the first limb.

"Charles! Do not be an idiot!" exclaimed Cassandra.

"I can do it," cried Charles.

"No, Charles!" warned I. "Edward Taylor is five years older than you, more than a foot taller, and a good deal stronger."

My words fell on deaf ears; the boost was given; and Charles began to climb.

"Dear God." Cassandra clutched my arm, her countenance growing very pale.

I shared her anxiety. All eyes were now directed at Charles as he made his way upwards in the leafy depths of the tree. Since a young age he had proved himself to be a skilled climber, and being still small, he moved like a monkey as he progressed from one limb to the next. Nevertheless, I knew it to be a very risky enterprise, and I felt too ill to speak.

Edward Taylor sat down casually on the limb high above, smiling as he watched Charles's progress. Several of the others, observing with what dexterity Charles ascended, began to whistle, cheer, and issue verbal encouragements. All was going well; it seemed as if my brother might well reach his goal with impunity—but when he had climbed about two-thirds of the way up, disaster struck. Charles reached too quickly for a limb, before he was secure; one foot slipped out from under him; suddenly he was dangling forty feet above the ground, his hands clinging to a branch above, and his feet flailing in the air.

A paroxysm of terror stabbed through me. I screamed; a chorus of anxious cries rang out from my companions. High above, Charles struggled, trying to regain purchase, but failing. If he fell, he would surely die!

Chapter the Twenty-fifth

From the corner of my eye, I saw a flash of movement above; I discerned that Edward Taylor was rapidly propelling himself downwards, branch by branch.

"Hold on, Charles! I am coming down to you."

The ensuing moments passed as though marking an eternity. I could scarcely breathe as I watched Charles's struggle to hang on—(how long before his strength would fail him?)—and Edward Taylor's downward progress. At last, Edward arrived at the appointed spot, where he positioned himself in such a way as to grab Charles and secure him, a moment met with cheers from below. Yet the drama was not over; tension reigned, as Edward Taylor directed Charles to climb upon his back, and take hold round his neck; then he began to climb steadily down the rest of the way. We all watched in absolute silence until both rescuer and his charge were safely delivered to the ground. Applause erupted, accompanied by many sighs of relief, none of them deeper or louder than my own.

Everyone gathered round, the young men clapping Edward Taylor on the back and expressing their admiration for his feat, while his cousins Sophia, Fanny, and Charlotte embraced him. Cassandra and I claimed Charles, taking turns drawing him into our arms.

"You worried us half to death," said Cassandra, tears streaking her cheeks.

"What were you thinking, attempting something so dangerous?" I was crying now myself.

"I wanted to see the view," replied he simply.

"And did you see it?"

"I did!" He squirmed with embarrassment in my embrace. "I did not reach the very top; but it was just as Mr. Taylor said. The view was magnificent. I shall never forget it."

"I am glad." I hugged and kissed him, and let him go. Charles ran off to accept the admiration of the group, where I observed Edward Taylor lay a hand on his shoulder and lean down to speak earnestly in his ear. To whatever was said, Charles beamed in response.

"I do believe," said I slowly, "that Edward Taylor just saved our brother's life."

Cassandra nodded. "So he did."

I found, however, that I could not smile. Although my anxiety was gone, overtaken by relief, another, darker emotion rippled through me—for I knew that the rescue would not have been required, had not Edward Taylor provoked Charles into climbing the tree in the first place.

Dinner at Bifrons was an animated affair, with everyone going over the most exciting event of the day from every possible angle, for the benefit of the Admiral and Mrs. Fielding. Heroes were made out of Charles for attempting the climb, and of Edward Taylor for saving him.

I could not view the event with such a sanguine attitude. The terrible idea of what had *almost* happened to my brother so consumed my thoughts, and filled me with such conflicting feelings— ranging from gratitude to Edward Taylor to anger for his own culpability in the event—that I could not enjoy the meal, nor add anything meaningful to the discourse at the table. Although my sister and I had no opportunity to indulge in private conversation, I deduced from her expression that she felt the same way. It was the first time I had possessed a negative feeling of any kind with regard to Edward Taylor, and it was both troubling and confusing.

Tea and coffee quickly followed dinner, for a five-mile ride home did not allow for any wasted hours; and it was not long before we had proclaimed our thanks to the Fieldings for their hospitality, and were reunited with the horses who had brought us thither. Frederic was happy to sleep in his own bed one more night, and Thomas and Charlotte had elected to ride home to Ileden for similar reasons; they would join us for rehearsal the following morning after church. Everyone else would return to Goodnestone that evening.

So preoccupied was I, that I could spare no thought for any manoeuvrings with regard to the groupings making up our ride, as I had on the way thither. Before I knew it, the same two couples who had walked about the grounds of Bifrons were already saddled and making their way forward at a trot, and I discovered myself mounted and travelling alongside my sister, with Edward Taylor and Charles chatting amiably on horseback some ways ahead of us.

It was a mild June evening. The sun hung low in the sky, with a good two hours or so before it would be dark; a slight breeze stirred the scattered trees bordering the road, filling the air with the pleasant scents of moist earth and grass. Cassandra and I rode in silence for a little while, both of us lost in thought. I heard my sister sigh and observed her cast a withering look at Edward Taylor's back. At last she said:

"I cannot stop thinking how close we came to losing our brother today."

"Neither can I." Those three words seemed to break the dam which had held me back from speaking, and my ire rushed forth. Careful to speak in a tone low enough so as not to meet the ears of those riding ahead of us, I continued: "I am deeply thankful to Edward Taylor for saving Charles, but at the same time, I am so annoyed with both of them!"

"As am I!" returned she.

"It was very wrong of Charles to attempt to climb that tree; but—"

"—he should never have thought of it, had not Edward Taylor encouraged him!"

"He thinks nothing of danger to himself."

"But worse, far worse, is his tendency to goad others into mirroring his own wild and careless behaviour," said Cassandra. "This lack of judgement and concern for others is also reflected in his selfish ideas concerning his family and his property."

"Not to mention his views regarding a university education! No matter how many books he has read, it cannot compare to the experience of Oxford. He seems determined to look down his nose at every privilege afforded him!"

Edward Taylor seemed to sense that we were talking about him, for he glanced back at us with a serious and concerned expression. He said something to Charles, who nodded and rode on alone; then Edward turned his horse and trotted back towards us.

Cassandra and I exchanged a look; we both blushed, embarrassed that we might have been overheard; yet her flashing eyes told me that she was just as perturbed as I.

The object of our irritation approached, turned, and fell in beside me, so that I rode between him and my sister. The look on his face was mildly contrite and infused with charm. "I suspect the Austen sisters are angry with me."

We did not reply. He began again:

"I am so sorry about your brother's mis-adventure—"

"Misadventure!" cried I warmly. "How dare you call it so, when he could have died!"

"Forgive me if I employed the improper word to describe the episode; I had no thought for anyone but Thomas to follow me up that tree."

"That is the trouble," said I. "You do not *think* about anyone but yourself." The words escaped before I could prevent them; they were harsh, and I winced inwardly at having pronounced them aloud—but I knew them to be the truth.

He coloured slightly but did not respond.

"You saved our brother's life," I rushed on. "For

that we can never be grateful enough, Mr. Taylor; but at the same time, your daring rescue, which everybody made so much of, would not have been required, had not you acted so recklessly."

Now he looked annoyed. "I was not reckless. My brothers and I dare each other to do such things all the time, and have never had a dreadful result."

"Is your father aware of your behaviour?" asked I.

He hesitated. "On those occasions when he has found out, we were reprimanded."

"Well then, you must know it is wrong!" cried I.

"That helps explain, I think, his reluctance to have you and your brother go into the army," said my sister.

"What do you mean?"

"How he must worry about you, Mr. Taylor!" said Cassandra. "Have you considered the anxiety you cause, the pain and suffering you inflict on those who love you, by continually putting *yourselves* in harm's way?"

"Whether it was Thomas or Charles who climbed the tree does not make you any less accountable," added I. "By issuing the challenge as you did, you were dooming *somebody* to follow your lead, and thus imperil his own life."

"I was dooming *no one,*" answered he defensively. "A challenge is simply that: a challenge— a call or summons to engage in an activity that might test one's skill or strength. Nobody is *obligated* to participate; if they do, it is a personal choice. *You* do not object to the *idea* of a challenge, Miss Jane: as I recall, you recently volunteered to climb a high wall entirely of your own free will."

My cheeks grew warm at this reminder; how could I refute it? Yet it did nothing to ease my ire.

"I never expected Charles to take me up on my dare today," continued he, "but the very fact that he was brave enough to try it, and the talent he exhibited in its pursuit, shews what a stalwart young lad he is. Did you observe with what dexterity he scaled that tree?"

"What are you saying?" cried I. "That his courage and physical fitness absolve you of any blame?"

"I am saying, he proved today how very *fit* he is for the navy! Cannot you see him climbing the rigging of some great ship in similar fashion, with the sun and sea behind him, and the wind in his hair?"

Having delivered this speech, he urged his horse forward and rode off down the road. I watched him go, my ire rising with every beat of the animal's hooves.

The next morning, I was still so angry with Edward Taylor that I did not speak to him at breakfast or after church, and I avoided him whenever I saw him during our play rehearsals throughout the day. I went over our conversation many times in my mind, and although I could not really find fault with any of his arguments, it yet irked me that he had so vociferously defended his actions, and seemed unable to admit to any real culpability in the affair.

"Is it possible," said I to my sister, "to be very, very angry with someone, yet love them at the same time?"

"Of course," replied she. "I believe we both feel that way about our mother every single day."

About an hour before dinner, I was pacing on my own in the privacy of the central walled garden, practising my lines aloud to the shrubbery and the flowers in the warmth of a calm summer afternoon, when Edward Taylor suddenly appeared. He crossed to where I stood, carrying something wrapped in brown paper, which I thought might be a very thin book.

"Miss Jane."

I stopped and glanced up at him, not entirely thrilled to see him; but there was a look of genuine apology in his dark eyes.

"I wanted you to know that I feel bad about what happened yesterday."

"Do you?"

"Yes. I have been thinking about it. You called me reckless—"

"And so you were," snapped I.

"And so I was," admitted he. "I could not bring myself to say so at the time. But you were right. And you were equally perceptive in your suspicion that my father does not approve of such behaviour. It is the reason I am here in England."

"Oh?" said I, surprised.

"Few people know this, but earlier this spring he caught me challenging my brothers to do something he considered reckless, and it so angered him—that, combined with my gambling debts, which had increased to such a level—let us just say that my father was fed up with me. He sent me home to 'remove my brothers from my bad influence,' as he put it, and to force me to 'confront and think about my future.'"

I paused upon hearing this, somewhat troubled. I was not blind—I knew that Mr. Taylor had a propensity to speculate—but I had never considered that it might have ever proved to be a serious problem. "Thank you for sharing that. It helps explain your antipathy towards your father, which I wondered at—but it in no way excuses it. And as for gambling—"

"I am not perfect, Miss Jane, but I try to learn from my mistakes. I have mended my ways: I now indulge in nothing more than the occasional, impulsive wager—" (colouring slightly) "as you have witnessed—or a friendly card or dice game, with stakes so low as to impoverish nobody."

"I am glad to hear it."

"In all other respects, I aim to be a better man in future. I can only say that I am very sorry I ended up endangering your brother's well-being yesterday, and I hope and pray that you will find it in your heart to forgive me."

The sincerity and contrition in his gaze was so appealing, as to begin wearing away at the core of my anger. "Well. I will try."

"I would like to say one thing, however, in my defense."

"What is that, pray tell?"

"There are three instances, I believe, when it is acceptable to be reckless and daring; nay, not just acceptable, but imperative: one, when one's life or the life of one we love is in danger; two, when one's own reputation is in danger; and three, when following one's passion. In the first two, such action is worth any risk; in the latter, the fastest or safest route does not always lead to happiness, nor rarely to achievement."

I considered his comment, but found that I could make no rebuttal.

"Pray allow me to add," continued he, "where passion and achievement are concerned, I could not stop thinking about what *you* said yesterday. You said you like to write."

This unexpected transition to a topic concerning myself took me off guard. "I *am* fond of writing, Mr. Taylor. You might say I am addicted to it. But—"

"According to your sister, you are also very good at it."

"*She* cannot be impartial."

"Perhaps not; but she claimed that your family is entertained when you read from your work. I am predisposed to believe her. I have engaged in enough conversations with you to appreciate your intellect and wit. Having heard you perform Puck, I can attest to your skills as an actress; you have a talent for achieving just the right pitch, tone, and nuance, to carry a point to its most humorous conclusion. I imagine that anything you write would be equally as entertaining on the page. With that in mind—(and after yesterday, at the very real risk of offending you)—I thought I would dare to offer *you* a challenge of sorts, which I promise is not remotely life-threatening."

"A challenge, Mr. Taylor? Forgive me; I do not have the pleasure of understanding you."

"I requisitioned this from Sir Brook; but suspecting that you would prefer to keep the matter private, I promise you I did not breathe a word about its purpose."

He offered me the object in his hands. I took it; immediately I understood what it contained. "A packet of writing-paper?"

He nodded. "I challenge you to write a story— and I sincerely hope that you will let me read it."

"Oh! No—never!" My face turned scarlet. "I

told you, what I write is of no real interest or value; it is only silly, romantic nonsense."

"Silly, romantic nonsense is very popular. Witness: *A Midsummer Night's Dream*. No sillier, more hilarious bit of fluff and nonsense has ever been penned by human hand, yet it is considered a classic work by a brilliant artist, and endlessly performed."

"I am hardly Shakespeare, Mr. Taylor—as my own mother continually reminds me! What I write can never be considered brilliant or a classic, no matter how enthusiastically my sister might promote it." I tried to return the packet of paper to him, but he refused to take it. "You have read the works of all the greatest writers in history! I would die of shame to think of you reading anything I have written. It is not worthy."

"Then write something new and different," insisted he emphatically, as he turned to go, "something which you think *is* worthy."

All through dinner my thoughts were full of Edward Taylor, and they ran in two divergent channels.

One: I found I could not remain angry with him any longer. He was so very, very charming; he had such a way with words; he had proved himself to be so genuinely sorry for what he had done, that both my heart and mind had already exonerated him. All those feelings which had built up since we met were now restored to their former glory: I could not hate Edward Taylor; no, never; I could only admire and love him.

Two: he had issued me a new, personal challenge which I could not ignore.

I had written nothing since leaving Steventon other than letters to Martha, my father, and my brothers; nor had I expected to. Since arriving at Goodnestone, I had had very little private time; over the past week in particular, since rehearsals for our play had begun, I had been so occupied every minute, that I had not given pleasure-writing a thought. However, at that moment, I could think of little else. Edward Taylor's praise was enough to make anyone blush; I knew I did not have so much potential as *he* seemed to suggest; yet, he had been so very encouraging!

I had, in the past, always written because I felt compelled to do so, even though I could not quite explain why. Perhaps my love of writing was influenced by my deep love of reading; when stories came unbidden to my mind, I could not prevent myself from writing them down. Or perhaps I should blame my predilection on my family. My work made them laugh! The very notion that the ideas, characters, and scenes which had originated in my own mind could be communicated to them through chosen words, particularly arranged, and transmitted either aloud or on paper, was such a joyful, infectious, and powerful enterprise, that it remained unmatched in my experience by any other endeavour.

I was, of a sudden, filled with a kind of quiet but hesitant confidence, which rekindled my desire to write.

It had been a long and active day. We were now seeing the result of the play rehearsals which had, for more than a week, been taking place all over the house; for the acts were being run through together in sequence. I knew I *ought* to be very tired and predisposed to retire early; but now, my strong inclination to go upstairs and sequester myself had a very different purpose in mind. I felt the urgent *need* to pick up a pen and to let my ideas and thoughts flow forth, whatever those thoughts might be!

This craving could not be assuaged with any immediacy, for there was dinner to get through; and after we ladies removed to the library, I did not wish to be rude and leave before the men arrived. As we all sat at our needlework (making fabric leaves and flowers for the fairy costumes), I could pay little heed to anything the ladies were saying; the sea of faces around me were but a blur, my thoughts consumed with some unseen force which was compelling me to *write, write, write!*

What should I write, however? It was a matter of some concern. At times, I wrote because an amusing notion occurred to me; at other times, I had no idea what I should compose until the moment I sat down, sharpened my nib, and allowed my fancy to take me wherever it might wander. I was in the latter position now, with no particular subject in mind—only an overwhelming compulsion to satisfy.

I was brought out of my reverie upon perceiving the following conversation between Fanny and her two eldest sisters, who sat close by:

"I declare, I will not marry him! He can never make me happy."

"Perhaps not, but his fortune, his name, and his house will."

"Elizabeth! Be serious!"

"I am being serious. I am only repeating what *you* have said to *me* any number of times."

"You were happy enough at the thought of marrying Mr. Cage a fortnight ago," said Sophia gently. "What is your complaint? What is different now?"

"*He* is different. He has been in a bad temper all week."

"Mr. Cage is a serious man, but a good man," answered Sophia. "I never considered him to be ill-tempered."

"But he is; or he *has* been, ever since we started practising the play. Mr. Deedes has been *ever* so much nicer to me. He, too, has a very big house— three houses in fact! I am sure *he* will bestow on his wife just as many gowns and jewels as Mr.

Cage has promised, and no doubt a new carriage as well. How can I live with a man who is always complaining and finding fault with everything I say and do? *I* should certainly never behave so to anyone *myself.*"

"I am sure you would not do so intentionally," said Sophia, shaking her head.

"Regarding Mr. Cage's display of temper," commented Elizabeth, "have you considered that it may have been brought on by the anxiety of acting, as well as his concern for *your* performance in such an open display? I have heard him say numerous times that he did not wish to be involved in our theatrical."

"And yet, look with what relish he has thrown himself into his part!"

"I admit that I feel a bit—awkward—acting with Mr. Cage," said Sophia, blushing deeply, "knowing him to be *your* intended. It cannot be easy for *him* to see you acting in romantic scenes with Mr. Deedes."

"Why should that bother Mr. Cage? It is only acting," replied Fanny indifferently; but a puzzled expression took over her face, and she added slowly, "At least, it is acting on *my* part—I *presume* it is so for him, as well."

At this interesting juncture, Lady Bridges joined her daughters and asked of what they were speaking.

"We are talking about Mr. Cage," said Sophia.

"Fanny wonders if she can be truly happy with him." Elizabeth sighed.

Lady Bridges also sighed and sat down. "Are we to go over this yet again? I declare, Fanny, I do not understand you. You accepted him. It is all settled. I like Mr. Cage, and have commended your choice from the start."

"Perhaps I made the choice too quickly," said Fanny petulantly.

"Perhaps you did." Elizabeth pursed her lips. "We all know why you took him with such expediency, Fanny."

"What do you mean?" cried Fanny.

"You barely knew him a month; yet a week after *my* engagement was announced, you were announcing yours. You could not stand the idea of my being wed before you."

Fanny coloured. "That is not true!"

"Yes it is! If you now regret your choice, you have no one to blame but yourself!"

"Girls!" cried Lady Bridges in a serious, subdued tone. "Lower your voices. Do not argue. It matters not how long Fanny knew Mr. Cage before she accepted him. Some of the best and happiest unions have been decided in a far shorter time than theirs; a long engagement is the key."

"I am sure you *will* be very happy," insisted Sophia. "Mr. Cage is a kind man, and warm of heart."

"*Mr. Deedes* is kind and warm of heart," said

Fanny. "I *thought* Mr. Cage was; but I have seen little evidence of it of late."

"He is open; he is frank," insisted Sophia.

"Too frank at times," replied Fanny.

"He dresses well and has a genteel figure," commented Elizabeth.

"Mr. Deedes is similar in that respect."

"Why are we talking of Mr. Deedes?" cried Lady Bridges. "Let us consider only his friend!"

"Mr. Cage is generous," said Sophia.

"Generous! Mr. Cage is stingy. He will not give me a new carriage when we are wed."

"He already has two carriages," said Lady Bridges, "both elegant and very new. Choose your battles, my dearest Fanny. Save your negotiations for the pin-money. His income is good: much can be done on three thousand a year."

"What is three thousand a year? I have met men with more."

"Fanny: I am determined that Mr. Cage will go no farther than our own family for a wife. If *you* will not have him, then *Sophia* must; he has always been kind to her, and I think he could like her."

Sophia's countenance went scarlet.

Lady Bridges patted Fanny on the knee, and smiling slyly, added: "If Sophia will not have him, then perhaps he will think of Marianne." She ended the conversation by abruptly standing and walking away, leaving Elizabeth laughing, and

Sophia and Fanny looking very uncomfortable.

As for myself, I was experiencing a very different kind of emotion than either of the three sisters. While listening to this discussion, a shiver had begun to dance up my spine; and I now found myself filled with excitement for two reasons. Firstly: it appeared that my scheme was working: Fanny was beginning to like Mr. Deedes—and Sophia clearly liked Mr. Cage! If all continued to go in this vein, then the couples who I had predicted as so ideally suited to each other, could very well be connected by the end of the week! Secondly: the dilemma which had been weighing on my mind all evening, had just been resolved in the most expedient manner. All at once, I knew *exactly* what I wanted to write about!

With delight I leapt to my feet, nearly dropping my needlework, and alarming all those seated within my proximity. I suppose the look on my countenance must have been very odd, as four ladies in unison, including my sister, inquired as to whether I was ill.

"No—I am only fatigued," replied I.

I bid all the ladies a hasty good-night, explaining that I wished to retire. Taking a candle, I hurried up the grand staircase, a dozen thoughts buzzing inside my brain.

The opinions and attitudes which the Bridges sisters and their mother had just expressed were so very interesting; I knew they could be fodder for a droll and comical story! It would be a story, I decided, about three sisters, one of whom was extremely materialistic and undecided about her matrimonial prospects. I could write it in my favourite style—as a series of letters from the sisters to one of their friends. All my prior stories to date were mainly comic, but this one, I decided, would combine humour *and* reality; it would emphasize the ridiculous, without being *entirely* absurd.

Already, ideas were forming themselves into complete sentences in my brain. I could hardly wait to set them down in ink.

Once in the privacy of my chamber, I took out the paper Edward Taylor had given me, folded it to my preferred size, assembled my writing materials, sat down at the little desk, and with enthusiasm began to write:

The Three Sisters
A NOVEL

Letter 1st

MISS STANHOPE TO MRS.—
MY DEAR FANNY
I am the happiest creature in the World, for I have received an offer of marriage from Mr. Watts . . .

Chapter the Twenty-sixth

I was still writing an hour later when Cassandra joined me.

"Jane: I thought you were going to bed."

"Forgive me for misleading you; I only said I wished to *retire*. In truth, I had an idea for a story."

Cassandra smiled. "So I see."

Cassandra knew better than to talk to me while I was writing, and she undressed in silence. I kept working, although my mind soon began to grow a bit cloudy, and I could not prevent a yawn. In my eagerness to compose my next sentence, I pressed the nib too hard, splashing a great blot of ink across the page.

"Oh bother!"

A gentle hand descended on my shoulder.

"Dearest, I can see how engrossed you are; but we are both tired. Will you come to bed?"

Reluctantly I nodded, yawning again as I cleaned my pen and my fingers. But even though I was exhausted, long after I had climbed beneath the counterpane and blown out the candle, the characters in my story continued to carry on conversations in my mind, both tantalizing me and frustrating me, as I struggled to fall asleep.

• • •

I awoke just as dawn was creeping through the shutters. On a typical morning at home, I might roll over and enjoy another hour or two of slumber; I would then rise, dress, practice an hour at the pianoforte, take a walk if the weather was fine, or sit by the fire and write until the rest of the household was awake and ready for breakfast. Today, however, there was no possibility of falling back to sleep, for the moment I opened my eyes, I recalled the story I had in progress, and the characters to which I was eager to return.

In short order I was back at work. Two hours flew by in an instant. I was so immersed in my tale that I did not even notice that Cassandra had got up until she was standing beside me, looking on silently but quizzically.

"Oh! Cassandra, I am having such fun. I am not yet finished, but—" I sighed, adding reluctantly: "I suppose I must put down my pen for the day."

"Yes, you ought to, dearest. But it looks as though you have been very productive. What prompted this sudden burst of creativity?"

"It was Edward Taylor's doing."

"Edward Taylor?"

"Yes. I think he was trying to make amends for his part in Charles's brush with death the other day. He gave me a packet of writing-paper and challenged me to write a new story. If I was tired of writing silly nonsense, he said, I should write something else—something I deemed more worthy. *This* is my attempt to do precisely that."

"What is it about?"

"When it is completed, I will let you read it and discover for yourself."

A busy day followed. Midsummer's Eve was only three days distant, and we were mounting our first full rehearsal. It was exciting to see the entire play coming together, and the endeavour took over my every thought. With a cast of two dozen active young people, there was constant activity and commotion. My mother had found a new way to keep the youngest children and the Payler boys out of trouble—by recruiting them, along with all the ladies in the production and several housemaids, to help with the costumes. I was not exempted from this duty, either.

"Your sister and I have been slaving away till we can hardly see straight, Jane," complained my mother. "I appreciate the leaves and flowers which you have been helping us construct, but they require a great deal of time to apply. And the wings! Who ever decided that fairies must have wings? How difficult they are to fashion! If we are to be ready for Wednesday's performance, I will need more help from everyone, including you."

Edward Taylor and I were supposed to sit in the audience with my brother Edward whenever we could, to observe the progress of those scenes which did not include us; but as we were all three also playing leading roles, we could not watch as much as we would like. Puck took all my powers of concentration. After leaving the stage, I often retreated to a corner of the green-room to go over my lines; but as nearly all the other actors were doing exactly the same, along with all the wing-makers and flower-sewers gathered around the room, there was hardly a space unoccupied.

What little I was able to observe of the play brought me satisfaction, however, particularly where the real-life lovers were concerned, whose fates were of such interest to me.

When Lysander (Mr. Deedes) declares his love to Hermia (Fanny), and requests to sleep beside her in the wood—

O, take the sense, sweet, of my innocence!
Love takes the meaning in love's conference.
 I mean, that my heart unto yours is knit
 So that but one heart we can make of it;
 Two bosoms interchained with an oath;
 So then two bosoms and a single troth.
 Then by your side no bed-room me deny;
 For lying so, Hermia, I do not lie.

—I rejoiced to see Mr. Deedes infuse his part with such emotion, and Fanny receive his attentions with such warmth. Their performance seemed to me to presage the future, when they should be lovers in real life.

Mr. Cage, who had watched earlier incarnations of that scene with little expression, now set his jaw and looked away. It must have prompted him to rise to new heights where acting was concerned; for in the third act, when Demetrius awakens under the effects of Puck's love potion, and declares his love for Helena (Sophia)—

To what, my love, shall I compare thine eyne?
Crystal is muddy. O, how ripe in show
Thy lips, those kissing cherries, tempting grow!
. . . O, let me kiss
This princess of pure white, this seal of bliss!

—Mr. Cage proclaimed the words with such passion, as to bring a deep blush to Sophia's cheeks. Indeed, she appeared to bloom before my eyes! I smiled, for it was lovely to see him speaking with such romantic verve to a young lady so *deserving* of his affections. Cassandra and Thomas Payler, in their scenes as Hippolyta and Theseus, were also sweetly demonstrative. Everything seemed to be proceeding according to my hopes and plans!

At the dinner table that evening, the play was all anyone could talk about. A few were certain that the production was not ready, and that we should embarrass ourselves; others were sure that it was an excellent work, and we should all triumph.

One end of the table, where sat Fanny, Mr.

Deedes, Mr. Cage, and Sophia, was peculiarly withdrawn and quiet. All four seemed to be in an introspective mood; why, I could not fathom. All four were remarkable in their parts; soon, all would make their theatrical debuts in one of the world's greatest plays before an audience of family and friends, from whom I knew they would receive great approbation and acclaim. Why, then, were their faces so grim? Why were they so short when speaking to each other?

I gave no more thought to the matter, for now that the rehearsal was over, my mind had drifted to that other matter which was of such interest to me: my story, which was only half-written, and awaited my attention upstairs. The interval following dinner was given over to the frantic sewing of costumes, and the final coordination of the potted greenery meant to portray the forest of Arden. When, at last, the preponderance of the work was in order, and everyone began to say their good-nights, I hastened upstairs and returned to my writing.

I wrote in a fever until I could no longer keep my eyes open, and again rose early to continue my labours. When Cassandra awoke, I put down my pen, gathered my pages, and handed them to her.

"Here, Cassandra. My story—if not *absolutely* finished—has at least reached a *sort* of con-clusion. You may read it now. It is meant to be funny, but—I hope also it expresses my feelings and attitudes on a certain subject." With a happy laugh, I added, "I think you will know at once *who* and what inspired it."

As I dressed, Cassandra sat by the window and read my story. While perusing it, she cried out "Oh! Jane!" in a slightly shocked tone, shook her head more than once, and I heard her chuckle several times. When she had finished, she turned to me with a look of amusement tempered by concern. "Jane: you are very clever, but I think rather wicked."

"Am I?"

"Of course I know exactly who this is about. It is about Fanny and her interminable quandary about Mr. Cage."

"Do you think it humorous?"

"I do; and I am certain *our* family would find it so—but I fear the Bridgeses will *not*. I share your frustration regarding Fanny's indecision, and her attitude towards her fiancé does not seem to *me* all that it should be; but she is never *quite* as disagreeable as you have presented her here."

"Do you really think so? Well; were I not to heighten her weaknesses, the story would not be *funny*. Oh! Cassandra, I could not listen to Fanny's moaning and relentless criticisms of Mr. Cage for another moment. Putting her, or this *version* of her, down on paper was so very satisfying!"

Cassandra laughed. "I admit, having listened to Fanny's complaints for a fortnight, it was very satisfying to *read*. But—Fanny might be offended."

"Only if she recognises herself, which I think extremely unlikely. People, I have come to observe, are rarely aware of their own flaws."

"Lady Bridges might see the resemblance to her daughter."

"Only if she reads it—and I have no intention of shewing it to her, or to anyone else in the house, except—" My voice broke off, my stomach tightening with apprehension as I thought about the one other person whose opinion I truly *did* wish to have. Edward Taylor had specifically asked to read whatever I might write, but did I have the nerve to shew it to him?

I had determined—very nearly determined—that *if* the opportunity should arise, if a quiet moment presented itself where Edward Taylor and I were out of the reach of others' ears, I should *mention* my story to him, and inquire as to whether he was still interested in reading it. In a house so filled with people, I thought, such a chance might never occur at all.

However, shortly after Cassandra and I sat down at breakfast and poured our tea (the chamber was deserted except for Sir Brook, who was reading the newspaper, and Charles, Harriot, and Brook

Edward, who were noisily conversing), Edward Taylor walked into the room.

I gathered my nerves, strove to even my respiration, and forced myself to raise my eyes until I was looking right at him; our gazes caught; he smiled and crossed to sit down beside me. *At that,* my heart felt as if it were truly in my stomach, and it was all I could do to return his friendly "Good morning."

He asked if my sister and I wanted toast, and at my nod, presented us the plate. I concentrated on buttering my slice, drumming up the courage to speak what was on my mind, for I knew that time was short; at any moment, someone else might walk in, and the chance would be lost. After glancing up to be certain the children were otherwise occupied, I turned to Edward Taylor, and said in a low voice,

"I have done it."

"I beg your pardon?"

"I have written a new story."

He stared at me in astonishment. "Already?"

I shrugged, adding covertly, "That packet of paper was staring at me. I had to put it to use."

Laughing, he picked up the tea-pot and poured himself a cup, and matching my confidential tone said, "When on earth did you find the time? We only spoke of this the other evening."

"I stayed up late and rose early."

"Clearly, you were inspired."

"I was."

"I hope you will let me read it?"

I flushed with anxiety. "If you are certain you wish to."

"Please!"

"I would prefer however that you did not shew it, nor speak of it, to anybody else. It is for your eyes only."

"Absolutely. Mum's the word."

I was honoured by his interest and immediacy. At the same time, I was terrified. What if he hated the story? What if he thought my writing to be insipid? Would he be honest and tell me so? And *if* so, how could I live? It was hard to believe that only two days before, I had been almost too angry with Edward Taylor to speak to him! Now, to have his approval meant more to me than anything in the world.

Immediately after we finished eating, I met him in the first-floor passage and gave him my pages. As this was my only copy of the story, he promised to take good care of it.

"I will read it as soon as I am able, and let you know what I think."

The day was equally as full of activity as the one which had preceded it. The rehearsal ran very long, and many scenes had to be run twice; but according to my brother Edward, it went well, and he proclaimed himself proud of us.

"Our final rehearsal tomorrow will be in full

dress," announced he to the cast before we broke for dinner. "I hope you will all spend your free time working on your lines. I would rather not have to prompt anybody during the actual performance!"

At dinner, I was delighted when Edward Taylor took a seat beside me. In *sotto voce*, he said,

"I read it through—twice."

My heart began to race. I glanced around the table to ensure that no one else was listening, and whispered: "And?"

To my dismay, further discourse was impossible, as Sir Brook began to talk to the assembly at large, and the food was subsequently served. An opportunity to continue our conversation did not arise for many hours, for there was still a great deal of work to do regarding the play. When darkness fell, most of the household dispersed or retired, leaving my sister and me alone in the library, working on the fairies' costumes. Edward Taylor entered and, finding us thus engaged, sank down onto a chair opposite us with a smile, and said:

"Alone at last."

I laughed nervously, renewed anxiety knotting my stomach as I awaited his verdict. He glanced cautiously at Cassandra, as if unsure whether or not it was prudent to speak.

"My sister has already read my story, Mr. Taylor, and given me her opinion; she is the only other person I felt comfortable entrusting it to."

"Ah. Very good." From his coat pocket, he retrieved my pages.

Continuing my sewing, and trying not to betray the intensity of my interest, I said, "Pray tell me. What did you think?"

"I think you have a way with words, Jane. It is a very funny story."

I felt such relief as can scarcely be described. "Funny in a *good* way, I hope?"

"Yes indeed. I must have laughed out loud a dozen times. You had so many amusing lines—" (glancing through the pages) "—such as this part here, when Mr. Watts comments on the sizeable settlements he is offering Mary as part of their marriage agreement, and she mumbles out: 'What's the use of a great jointure, if men live forever?' "

"I had a good laugh at that, too," remarked Cassandra, chuckling.

"I loved it when her mother negotiated the pin-money, as if she were selling a mare at market! But best of all is Mary's long list of expectations—what was it? Ah yes, here: Horses, fine clothes, jewels, servants, a theatre to act plays in, a blue carriage spotted with silver (hilarious!), and the mathematically impossible task of spending all four seasons in different places, and *the rest of the year at home* giving balls. Ha!"

I set down my needlework, thrilled by his

enthusiasm. "I do enjoy poking fun at people's foibles and exposing their weaknesses."

"That you did, and quite brilliantly I think."

"Thank you. I *hoped* to be amusing, Mr. Taylor; but I admit, I also hoped to do more than that—to inject the silliness with some *significance*—to present characters who we can recognise and sympathise with."

"And so you did. Without naming names—we both know people who behave and sound very much like Mary Stanhope and her mother." He glanced at me slyly, and we both laughed. Hesitantly, he added: "Would you be offended, however, if I made one small criticism of the work?"

"Not at all; please go ahead."

"There is one sentence which I believe did not fit in."

"One sentence? Is that all?" I laughed. "What sentence is that?"

"Here, when Mary describes the jewels she expects. She asks for 'pearls as large as those of the Princess Badroulbadour in the fourth volume of the *Arabian Nights*, and Rubies, Emeralds, Toppazes, Sapphires, Amythists, Turkey stones, Agate, Beads, Bugles, and Garnets.'—you go on and on. It adds an element of buffoonery which is absent in the rest of the story, and should be truncated, I believe."

"Oh! Thank you for pointing that out. I was

falling back into my old ways with *that* line."

"I agree, that line is a bit too silly for this story," interjected Cassandra, who was still dutifully stitching away, "because your characters feel so real here; but that being said, Jane, I cannot help but think that you are very harsh on poor Mary."

"Poor Mary?" cried Edward Taylor. "Do not tell me you feel sorry for her? She is very weak, and her motives for marrying are all wrong."

"True," answered Cassandra, "and yet still I sympathise with her. Marriage is, for most women, the only possible way to avoid poverty—to have a house and carriage of our own, and spending money of our own. It is not pleasant to think of negotiating for such things, but I can understand why *some* women might feel it necessary to do so."

His eyes narrowed in contemplation. "I never gave the subject a single thought before, but now that you mention it—was that your point, Miss Jane? To call attention to this very dilemma?"

"It was. In Mary's efforts to secure a future for herself, she takes everything to an extreme—"

"And becomes ridiculous in the process."

"Yes! Exaggeration, in my opinion, is the very definition of parody."

"Brilliant. You have found a clever way to deliver a message, while being thoroughly entertaining." Edward Taylor quietly applauded.

I could not remember when I had ever felt so happy.

"It is wonderful," continued he, "when one's truest passion is not something which has been forced upon you by your family, but something unique and particular which you discover for yourself." A little silence ensued, and I knew he was thinking about his own thwarted desires and passions. At length, he added, "I hope you will continue to write."

"I intend to; but I am aware that I am but a fledgling at this art. I long to write an actual novel! But usually when I begin such an enterprise, I lose my way and cannot think how to complete it."

"You will learn how in time," said Cassandra.

"Indeed you will, Miss Jane. You must learn by study and by doing."

"By study and by doing?" repeated I.

"It is the way I learned to play the violin. Under my masters' tutelage, I studied the music of the great composers, then listened to that music played by the world's best violinists at concerts across Germany and Italy. I developed my own skills by beginning with short pieces, eventually moving my way up to longer and more difficult ones. I would imagine it is the same with writing. You have already made an excellent beginning, Miss Jane. You read; you write short works. This is your school. I say: read all you can, and then write, write, write!"

His advice excited me. For the first time, I felt that I had a direction: a path or plan which might lead to me improving my skills as a writer. I determined from that moment forth to follow it.

Chapter the Twenty-seventh

I awoke on the 23rd of June full of hope, excitement, and nervous anticipation. It was Midsummer's Eve, the day of our performance, and also Charles's twelfth birthday. At breakfast, we paid tribute to him with his favourite lemon cake. My mother gave Charles a very smart blue coat which she had remade from my brother Frank's, and Cassandra and I presented him with a set of handkerchiefs embroidered with his initials. To my surprise, Edward Taylor also gave him a gift: his small silver folding knife, which Charles had seen and admired on a previous occasion. Charles was pleased to no end.

Mr. and Mrs. Knight returned to Goodnestone that morning, happy and anxious to see our production. The remainder of the morning was a beehive of activity, as we endeavoured to get everything ready for the start time of two o'clock. The two Edwards oversaw the final placement of the chairs for the audience, which Lady Bridges made them rearrange twice. As it was to be a day-time performance, no candles were needed; the drapes and shutters on the tall windows were left open, flooding the room with summer light. I went over lines with those harried members who felt the need for such attention, and Edward Taylor calmed those who exhibited a sudden case of nerves.

"If you forget a line," Edward Taylor reassured them, "do not worry: simply take a deep breath and clear your mind. The words will come to you."

Cassandra and my mother made the final adjustments to everyone's clothing. The house-maids gathered armfuls of fresh flowers, leaves, and vines from the garden, and with help from the cast, a good three hours were spent dutifully attaching the garden's bounty to all the fairies' head-dresses.

I was particularly fond of my own costume, for my mother and sister had fashioned it from Lady Bridges's emerald-green silk, and covered it over with fabric leaves and real bird feathers in many colours. I braided my long hair and pinned it up around my head, and once adorned by my wreath of fresh leaves, I considered myself to be a very fine Puck indeed. Now, I could only hope that my acting should live up to the weight of the role itself!

At half-past one, the actors, attired in all their finery (and looking truly splendid) gathered in the green-room, most of them chattering excitedly. The child fairies and attendants chased each other around the chamber until my brother Edward gently encouraged them to stop. Not everybody shared the same enthusiasm: Thomas looked as pale as death with anxiety, and Frederic likewise appeared so nervous, I worried that he might be sick at any moment. Four other members of the company—Fanny, Mr. Cage, Mr. Deedes, and Sophia—sat silently apart in the four separate corners of the room, distracted and preoccupied. I took this to be a sound thing, for their roles were substantial; I would also have preferred, before the performance, to remain quietly on my own, to go over my lines in my head.

A few crises were aborted: little Sidney Payler's wings required reattaching at the shoulder; Elizabeth insisted that several withered flowers in her head-dress be replaced with fresh ones; and most alarming of all, Edward Taylor's donkey ears had mysteriously gone missing; a frantic search ensued, and the missing article was thankfully discovered intact behind a sofa.

I soon heard the arrival of carriages without, and a few minutes more brought the sound of activity to the theatre beyond. Unable to restrain myself, I slipped into the central hall, partially opened a connecting door, and peeked through, to observe Lady Bridges talking animatedly as she ushered in Mr. and Mrs. Payler, and Admiral and

Mrs. Fielding, who took seats alongside Mr. and Mrs. Knight. My mother, finished with her costuming duties, now excused herself to join the spectators. Our cast was so large, I had worried that we should surely outnumber the audience; but moments later all the servants began to arrive, and as all excitedly took their seats, the room began to look quite full.

My brother Edward urged everyone in the green-room to be quiet, and a solemn silence followed, causing the tension in the chamber to rise yet higher. I was wild with excitement. We had all worked very hard to usher this play into being over the past twelve days. The occupation had been one of the greatest and most fulfilling pleasures I had ever known. Now, at last, we were to perform before an audience!

At two o'clock exactly, Sir Brook welcomed everyone; and then the curtain parted.

The play opened inauspiciously. Thomas Payler faltered badly through his first three speeches, and as I overheard this slow and awkward beginning from my position behind the scenes, my cheeks warmed with embarrassment; but Edward Taylor whispered in my ear,

"Do not distress yourself, Miss Jane. It will get better. And it is only family and friends out there—and servants who have probably never seen a play. They will be thrilled with whatever we do."

I gave him a grateful look and felt more composed. The scene *did* soon improve, for Hermia, Lysander, and Helena were quite marvellous; and as the performance continued, the key performers were everything I had hoped they would be. The first craftsmen's scene was amusing, with Edward Taylor squeezing every laugh out of the audience which the playwright had intended. Frederic, true to form, mangled his only line in the scene; what should have been, "Have you the lion's part written? pray you, if it be, give it me, for I am slow of study," was delivered as follows:

Have you. The—the part.
The lion's part! Written?
I pray! Give it. Me. I am slow. Thank you.

I smiled to myself, realising that this mutilation of the Bard's words did not matter in the least, for the meaning was clear enough, and the performance was perfectly in character—for Snug was, after all, "slow of study."

Suddenly, it was Act II—and time for my entrance. My heart was pounding so loudly in my ears, I thought I should not be able to hear my own speech. Cassandra gave my hand a squeeze, and Edward Taylor winked at me encouragingly; then I was striding onto the stage from one side, while Marianne entered at another, and uttering my first line:

How now, spirit! whither wander you?

To my mortification, my voice broke on the third word, and I was obliged to clear my throat to pronounce the remainder. Marianne sweetly made her speech, and I crossed to her as we had rehearsed; but I felt wooden and awkward. In all my previous experience of theatre at Steventon, my parts had been small, the audience even smaller. It had been one thing to rehearse *here* with no one except the other players watching; I was now very conscious of the presence of the audience—I could not help glancing out at them. Marianne ended her first speech:

Farewell, thou lob of spirits; I'll be gone.
Our Queen and all her elves come here anon.

I knew I was obliged to respond with *my* first real speech; but the sea of countenances before me was so disconcerting, that I could not remember my line! I froze, in a panic. A brief and horrible silence succeeded. My gaze landed on my mother, who was staring at me with a worried expression. *Her* condemnation I could not take; very quickly, I repeated to myself the verbal antidote which Edward Taylor had given the others to calm their nerves: *take a deep breath. Clear your mind. The words will come to you.*
To my relief, they did:

> The King doth keep his revels here to-night;
> Take heed the Queen come not
> within his sight . . .

The rest of my speech flowed forth, perfect and unhurried; I invested my delivery the way I had rehearsed it, with all the verve, animation, and good humour I could muster.

When Oberon and Titania entered with their train of fairy attendants, the audience *ooohed* and *aaahed* at the lovely costumes, and appeared thrilled as the action unfolded. I particularly enjoyed my moments acting opposite my brother Edward, for he was the personification of the King of the Fairies, and I had begun to feel truly Puckish.

Although some lines were dropped, some entrances were late, and some changes of scenery were executed awkwardly (a chair from the duke's palace unnecessarily found itself in the forest on one occasion), I do not think the audience noticed. Sir Brook had so little to do, that he sat out in the audience (in full costume) for the bulk of the performance, and would have missed his only other cue, had I not managed to overtly signal his attention.

At one point, Mr. Deedes, generally of such a sunny disposition, left the stage frowning and shaking his head with agitation, which I deduced to be dissatisfaction with his own performance;

and during another scene, in which Lysander avows his love for Helena, I heard a gasp of irritation from Fanny, who was watching in the wings, and thought I might have seen a tear in her eye. It proved to me what an accomplished actress Fanny was, for so invested was she in the role of Hermia, that even off the stage, she felt all the emotion of the character she was inhabiting. And with what deep emotion and fierce anger did she invest her challenge to Helena to a fight! Fanny's fit of anguish and jealousy was so keenly executed, as to be worthy of the London stage.

Everyone rose to the occasion. Cassandra was a fine Hippolyta, Elizabeth was a beautiful and seductive Titania, and the craftsmen were just as bumbling as one would wish. Thomas warmed to his part and got through it with a certain aplomb, and even Frederic eventually managed to do himself credit with a minimum of prompting, his very slowness adding to the humour of the character (his each and every line met with applause from his delighted mother).

Edward Taylor was (as expected) hilarious, and indisputably the star of the show. Charlotte played a truly lovely Thisbe to his Pyramus, investing her death scene with such an element of woe, as to raise it above comedy and bring a tear to many a watching eye. I was rewarded for my own efforts with laughter from the audience at the appropriate, key moments. I had never had such a part, had never *been* a part of such an exciting performance before!

All too soon, the play ended. The audience rose to its feet and applauded. As we all took our bows, the feeling in the air was electric; I looked out at the delighted expressions of our admirers, and knew I was experiencing something very special, which for the rest of my life I should never forget.

Afterwards, the spectators mingled with the cast, exchanging hugs and kisses and laudatory remarks all around. Mrs. Fielding was beside herself with joy at the accomplishment of her son. Everybody remarked with astonishment on Charlotte's performance: what a wonder was she! Who could have guessed that Charlotte, normally so quiet and reserved, was such a capable actress! Mrs. Watkinson Payler behaved as proudly as though she were the queen of England, reminding everyone that "the play could not have been done without the *Paylers'* involvement; and were not they all fine actors, every last one of them?"

Praise was heaped upon my brother Edward for his directing efforts, which he accepted modestly, quick to point out the many contributions which I and Edward Taylor had made. My mother and Cassandra were pleased to accept acclaim for designing the costumes, but admitted that the entire cast had helped with their construction. Lady Bridges made so many self-congratulatory statements, as to seemingly take credit for the entire production herself.

A half-hour passed in such a manner, before I happened to notice that Fanny and Mr. Cage were not amongst the company. It occurred to me, that in all this happy display of feeling, I did not recall observing them anywhere. When had they left? Where had they gone? Why had they not remained to accept the congratulations that were their due? I made inquiries, but no one seemed to have any idea what had become of them. At last, when I applied to the youngest children, Harriot said:

"Fanny walked out of the room as soon as the play was over. She had a very dark look on her face."

"Did she?" replied I. "And what of Mr. Cage? Did you see where he went?"

"I saw him," answered little George Bridges. "He left right after Fanny."

Nothing more had been seen nor heard of the pair. I thought it strange that they should vanish at the very moment of our triumph, and wondered what it might mean; but I had little time to consider the matter, as I became immediately embroiled in the business which always attends the end of a theatrical production. A hundred details required our immediate attention: there were the costumes and properties to be gathered up, clothing to be changed, and furniture to be cleared away; and all must be accomplished before the Midsummer's Eve celebratory dinner, after which, all were invited to stay for the bonfire, to be held after dark.

Our company of players were all exhausted when we at last sat down to dine. Fanny and Mr. Cage had still not made an appearance—and now, inexplicably, Sophia was also among the missing. Lady Bridges insisted that there was nothing to worry about; the lovers no doubt desired some private time after all the hubbub of the performance, and Mr. Cage, being a very proper gentleman, must have requisitioned Sophia as their chaperone. This seemed to be a reasonable assessment of the situation; however, I overheard her ladyship quietly ask one of the footmen to see if he could discover what had become of the absent parties. He returned some ten minutes later, and from his apologetic look, and the frown on Lady Bridges's countenance which met his whispered answer, I deduced that his inquiries had not met with success.

The table cloth had just been removed, and the dessert served, when a hurried footfall was heard in the passage, and Sophia burst into the room, her eyes filled with tears. Mr. Deedes leapt to his feet and pulled out the empty chair beside him, but Sophia moved directly to her father's side and stopped there distractedly, seemingly too overcome to speak.

"Sophia," said Sir Brook with deep concern, "what is the matter?"

"Oh, Papa!" responded she softly and brokenly. "It is too horrible for words. I was worried about Fanny and went looking for her. I found her walking in the park, weeping. She—" Leaning down, she whispered something quietly in his ear.

Sir Brook froze in consternation. "Dear God! You cannot mean it!"

"What is it?" cried Lady Bridges.

"It seems that Fanny has just broken off her engagement to Mr. Cage." Sir Brook's reply, despite an attempt to be discreet, was heard by all.

An astonished buzz went round the table. My heart leapt with surprise. Lady Bridges gasped in horror and disappointment. Marianne, sincerely affected, cried:

"Oh no! What happened?"

"Fanny would not tell me," responded Sophia tearfully. "She ran away before I could say a word. As I returned to the house, I ran into Mr. Cage—he appeared very angry and distressed. He sent me back with a message, for you, sir." Struggling to compose herself, Sophia addressed Mr. Deedes: "He is packing his things, and intends to leave the house this very night for Canterbury. He requests an audience with you, sir, at the earliest possible moment."

Mr. Deedes went pale, his visage troubled.

"Thank you, Miss Sophia." Rising, he bowed to her and then to our hosts, adding graciously, "Pray forgive me, Sir Brook, Lady Bridges. I must go to my friend; and if he is leaving, I must go with him." Turning, he quit the room.

Sophia burst into tears.

A tumult erupted at the table, as whispered theories and conflicting observations were passed back and forth, many of which reached my ears: "Such a shame—all for the best—the perfect couple—not suited to each other at all—lovely girl—she is too proud—the best of men—too quiet and stern—deserves better—I like him!— her eye fell upon another gentleman—I think we both know who—a double wedding—so looking forward—timing is very ill—and the play such a triumph!—both were very good—poor Fanny!— to leave on Midsummer's Eve!—to miss the bonfire!—such a shame!"

I listened to the clamour around me with mixed emotions. As this turn of events was the very outcome which I had, for some time, been wishing for, I presumed I should feel a glimmer of satisfaction; yet inexplicably I did not. That Fanny and Mr. Cage were mismatched, I still ardently believed; that my plan had apparently worked—that a slight nudge had averted the disaster of an unhappy marriage—was a source of some little satisfaction; but I had imagined it would all come about amicably, through the discovery of the truth of their affections, and a discussion marked by calm understanding and mutual consent. To happen *this way!* To learn that Fanny and Mr. Cage were both angry and distressed! Worse yet, that both Mr. Cage and Mr. Deedes were to leave Goodnestone that very night—on Midsummer's Eve itself! With that leaving, no fresh admissions of feeling could be made, no new couples could be formed. It was the ruination of all my plans, the end of everything I had been hoping for. It was too, too terrible!

My brother Edward pushed back his chair, stood, and said:

"I will speak to Mr. Cage. Perhaps I can persuade him not to leave." Edward Taylor offered to join him; my brother gave Elizabeth's hand a reassuring squeeze, and the two gentlemen took their leave.

"I do not understand," wailed Lady Bridges, as Mrs. Fielding attempted to comfort her. "*Why* has Fanny broken off with Mr. Cage?"

It was an excellent question: *why?* If Fanny ended her engagement because she preferred Mr. Deedes (which I hoped was the case), then why was she weeping? Why was Mr. Cage angry and distressed, and leaving with such dispatch? If he had feelings for Sophia, would not he stay to court *her,* in the wake of Fanny's defection?

It was all a muddle; and I could not avoid one overriding idea: that something was very wrong, and that somehow, it might all be my fault. I put down my fork, my appetite gone.

Standing up, I called out to Sir Brook: "I beg your forgiveness, sir, but I must find Fanny. May I please be excused?" Without waiting for a response, I dashed from the chamber.

Chapter the Twenty-eighth

I crossed the open park at the front of the house, past flocks of grazing sheep and the area where servants were unloading carts laden with tree branches and twigs, and setting up the bonfire to be lit later that evening. The air was filled with the sweet aroma of sun-warmed grass, and the summer sun was still high enough in the sky as to warm my back and shoulders.

I gazed in all directions, and finally spied a distant female figure quite a long ways from the house, on the edge of the wilderness. As I approached, I discerned that it was indeed Fanny. She still wore her costume from the play, her countenance was flushed, and her eyes were red. Upon observing me, she frowned and quickly wiped away a tear. No words were exchanged for a few moments as I walked beside her. After a while, she said quietly:

"I suppose everyone knows about me and Mr. Cage by now?"

I nodded with an apologetic glance.

"How is my mother? Is she very angry?"

"Not angry; only sad and bewildered."

"Well; if you have come to try to make me change my mind, do not bother."

"I have come with no such purpose."

"No? Why *have* you come?"

I hardly knew how to reply, so I blurted the first thing that came to mind, the statement which seemed obligatory under the circumstances: "I have come to say how very sorry I am that you have broken off your engagement." As I uttered the words, a glance at Fanny's anguished face brought a renewal of that pang of guilt which had assailed me upon hearing the news—a feeling I was determined to get rid of with dispatch. "But," I rushed on, "my father always says that change is difficult but necessary; that often, people must endure through difficult times in order to discover their true destiny, and a higher good."

"I do not see how *any* good can come from *this* change."

"But it will! I understand that it must have been very sad to end your alliance with Mr. Cage, but it was the right thing to do, if you find that you prefer Mr. Deedes."

Fanny looked at me in astonishment. "Mr. Deedes? *Me* prefer Mr. Deedes? Good heaven! Whatever gave you that idea?"

"Why—why—you did! Just the other night, you

said you had made your choice of husband too quickly, and you made all sorts of complimentary remarks about Mr. Deedes!"

"Oh! You must not listen to anything I say!"

"For the past fortnight, you have been flirting openly with him!"

Fanny coloured. "Why on earth have you been paying so much attention to my doings, Jane? I should have thought you would have had more important things to occupy your mind."

"Well—" I could not go on.

"I admit, I did flirt with Mr. Deedes a *little,* and I enjoyed his attentions in return; I suppose that was very wrong of me." She sighed. "But Mr. Deedes is not a man I should *ever* think of for myself. Even were he not the friend of my fiancé—my *former* fiancé—" (her voice breaking) "—I do not regard Mr. Deedes in any capacity other than friendship, and never could."

Upon hearing this, I was overpowered by such a succession of unpleasant sensations, as to be incapable of speech. All my scheming, it seemed, had been to no good purpose. How grievously had I misunderstood Fanny's behaviour! "But—I do not understand. If you do not like Mr. Deedes, why did you flirt with him?"

Fanny glanced at me, as if trying to decide whether or not to share a confidence. Around us, the air was filled with the sounds of bleating sheep and the twittering of the birds in the nearby trees. At last she said, "Jane: has anyone—my mother or sister, perhaps—told you about Lord Rampling?"

"Lord Rampling?" This remark was most unexpected. I shook my head. "They have not."

"It is no great secret. You might as well know." Fanny sighed again before continuing. "When I was sixteen, after I came out, we spent the season in London. I attended too many balls and soirees to count, and I danced with dozens and dozens of young men. My sisters were all green with envy, for of course they were too young to go. Halfway through the season, I was introduced to an extraordinary young man. He was handsome, he was charming, and he was the eldest son of an earl. I could hardly believe it, but over the ensuing weeks of dances and parties, Lord Rampling always sought me out. I had never met anyone like him before, and he seemed equally charmed by me. I—*we*—fell madly in love!"

"Oh!" cried I, both surprised and distressed by this narration, for I began to suspect where it must lead.

"Mamma was beside herself with joy at the idea of me marrying a future earl, and I thought I should die of happiness. But then one night, he deliberately avoided me, he was absent from the next few parties, and I heard nothing of him until a fortnight later, when I saw him at a ball in the company of a pretty young lady—the daughter of a duke. Jane: he never spoke a word to me again. I later heard that they had married. Perhaps his father forced the break—I never could find out—or perhaps he simply recognised his mistake in paying attention to someone so low as the daughter of a baronet."

Hearing this story aroused in me a kind of sympathy for Fanny, which I had never before felt. "I am so sorry, Fanny. How painful that must have been!"

"I went home with a broken heart. Mamma insisted that I attend the assemblies in Canterbury. She said that Lord Rampling was not the only fish in the sea, and that I should fall in love again, and soon. But I did not. Many young men courted me. I compared them all to Lord Rampling, and the frenzy of emotion we had shared, and I found them wanting. I could feel nothing for anybody else, nothing at all. Marriage, I now realised, was for most people a matter of business or social promotion; personal feelings could never enter into it."

"Never is a strong word, Fanny. Elizabeth and my brother appear to be very much in love."

"Theirs is a rare case, I think." She shrugged her shoulders. "I knew that I must marry, so I came to a decision: I should not expect to find love. I should simply look for a decent man with as much money and property as possible, and in this I would find my happiness. I turned down several offers, while waiting for something better—and then Elizabeth announced her engagement. I could not let my younger sister get married before me! It was out of the question! So I accepted Mr. Cage. He was not the handsome youth I had imagined for myself, but he was rich, and he loved *me*. As time wore on I began to feel a bit trapped, and wondered if I had been too hasty. There were certain aspects of being single—and of the courtship process—which I enjoyed. Was I truly to give all that up, to be Mr. Cage's wife? I felt so secure of *his love* that, when the theatrical rehearsals began, I told myself it was perfectly fine to indulge in a little, harmless flirtation before resigning myself forever to wearing a cap and performing all the duties of a married woman."

"Oh!" gasped I again, dismayed.

"You are right to look troubled; my conduct was appalling, I know it now. Looking back, I think I flirted with Mr. Deedes for yet another reason: to make Mr. Cage jealous, so that he would want me all the more. This seemed to have the reverse effect, however; for Mr. Cage, perhaps in retaliation, started flirting with Sophia—and what began as flirtation for *him,* soon turned into something more." Tears started again in Fanny's eyes. "You had it the wrong way around, Jane. It is not *me* who prefers someone else; it is Mr. Cage. He may have loved me once, but now he is in love with my sister Sophia—and *she* is in love with him."

A tremor of guilt shot through me, for that very outcome had been my object. "Are you certain?"

"I am. It does not take a genius to read the signs. He has been so attentive to her. Perhaps, I told myself at first, he is just being kind because she is my sister. But they sat for hours discussing a book in a way that I never could. Sophia is so much smarter than I am; it is not wonderful that he should prefer her. At Tuesday's rehearsal, the truth dawned on me; in today's performance, I could no longer avoid it. Did not you hear with what passion Mr. Cage addressed Sophia, as he remarked on her beauty? Did not you see the expression on his countenance, as he begged her to kiss him? Mr. Cage has never spoken to me in such a manner; nor has Sophia ever reacted with such obvious affection to any gentleman before."

I was now very uncomfortable. I had seen and heard those same things, and had, with wishful thinking, hoped they signified exactly what she suspected; but considering how badly I had misread Fanny's conduct and intentions, perhaps I had been in error. "Fanny: we have all been performers in a play. You made love to Lysander on the stage in a very credible manner; is not it conceivable that Mr. Cage and Sophia, too, were merely acting? He was simply Demetrius, and she Helena."

"I have tried to convince myself of that; but my sister is generally quiet and reserved, and Mr. Cage has never acted in his life before. No; what I saw was no performance; it was an expression of their real feelings! It is so wrong, so unfair, that my own sister should steal away my fiancé—how I hate her! I shall never speak to her again!"

Alarmed, I said: "Fanny: did Sophia admit that she loves Mr. Cage? Did Mr. Cage tell you that *his* affections are placed elsewhere?"

"I would not lower myself to ask. They would both just deny it. After the performance, when Mr. Cage found me, I said a great many hateful things to him which I now regret. I told him it was over, that he was free, and I hoped he would be happy. He was too angry to speak! Jane! I am so wretched! What have I done? I have just cast off the only man I ever loved!"

I stared at her in confusion. "Fanny: you said very emphatically, and on occasions too numerous to count, that you do not love Mr. Cage."

"Oh! I was such a fool, Jane. I think I have always loved Mr. Cage, from the moment of our first acquaintance. He has so many commendable qualities."

"But—"

"Our age difference is nothing. He is very good-looking. He is kind and generous and bright. Yet I looked only to find fault. I am so ashamed of the way I behaved!"

"And—you truly love him?"

Miserable, she nodded. "I do love him, with all my heart! But now it is too late. Oh! How sorry I am that we were both persuaded to be in that stupid, stupid play. How I wish that you had never thought of it!"

Fanny burst into fresh tears, and, signalling in a despairing manner that she did not wish to be followed, ran away into the woods.

I stood at the edge of the grove for many long minutes after Fanny had gone, my mind all in a tumult.

I had been so certain that Fanny did not love Mr. Cage. It had been the very basis of my theorem, the guiding light of my belief that they were ill suited to each other, and should be better off parted. To discover *now* that she truly loved him after all! There was no room for doubt: Fanny had, just now, been so fully aware of Mr. Cage's genuinely good qualities, so filled with remorse for her past behaviour, and so sincere in her assertions of affection, that I felt certain she truly did love him—perhaps, as she maintained, *had* loved him from the first moment of their acquaintance. To see and hear how miserable she was—to know that *I* had (however secretly) deliberately attempted to master-mind the very proceedings which had led to this dissolution—brought pain and humiliation. It had been my full intention to try to part Fanny and Mr. Cage—and I had succeeded only too well.

How misguided had I been! How right Fanny was! Had I not proposed the play, then she and Mr. Cage would still be engaged—they would have married as planned—in time, she would no doubt have discovered her true feelings for him, and they would have been happy.

This breach, which I took to be entirely my fault, was not the only thing for which I felt remorse; for in my scheming, I had tried to manipulate Mr. Deedes into falling in love with Fanny (and I sensed I had succeeded there, as well). As for Mr. Cage and Sophia—if they truly were in love, as Fanny guessed—should they ever profess their feelings for each other and marry, things being what they were, what a cost should be incurred! It would cause a breach between the sisters such as might never be repaired.

I made my way back to the house, miserable, wherein I encountered my brother Edward, Edward Taylor, and Cassandra rushing down the stone steps to the parterre, with worried expressions on their countenances.

"There she is!" cried Cassandra.

"Did you speak to Mr. Cage?" exclaimed I, hurrying to meet them.

"We did," returned my brother, frowning, "but barely for a moment. He is confused, hurt, and angry."

408

"Did you find Fanny?" asked Edward Taylor. "Did you learn anything?"

"I did. She is equally as miserable. She loves Mr. Cage, but ended their engagement because she believes that he and Sophia are in love."

"Mr. Cage in love with Sophia?" My brother looked dumbfounded. "That is ridiculous!"

"Is it?" said I.

"It is preposterous! Only yesterday evening, the poor fellow was pouring out his heart to me about how much he loves *Fanny*. He is entirely devoted to her, and always has been."

"Oh!" cried I.

"He has no idea why Fanny broke off with him," said Edward Taylor. "I declare, I have never in all my life seen a man more heart-broken."

"What ever made Fanny think that Mr. Cage and her sister are in love?" asked Cassandra.

A heat rose to my face. "It—it seems that their performance in the play was too authentic."

"They were only acting!" cried my brother.

"*She* read it very differently."

"Acting can be a very dangerous game." Edward Taylor shook his head.

"Mr. Cage *was* very sweet to Sophia, apart from the play," insisted I, "and she seemed to respond to his attentions."

"Why should they not be sweet to each other?" replied Cassandra. "They were to be brother and sister. I assure you, Sophia has no feelings whatsoever for Mr. Cage. She never has."

"How do you know?"

"I have just spoken with her. She is overcome with grief. Although Mr. Cage's recent overtures were offered and received only in friendship, she believes his attentions inflamed her sister's jealousy. *Her* affections have long been placed in another quarter. In truth, she is in love with Mr. Deedes."

"With Mr. Deedes!" I was astonished.

"Sophia admitted that she has felt an attachment to Mr. Deedes since they first met many months ago. She has secretly cherished a hope that he might return her feelings, and declare himself this very fortnight, while at Goodnestone."

"Mr. Deedes *does* return her feelings," said my brother. "He told me so himself. He was on the point of speaking, when the play was proposed—and events took such a turn from there, that the opportunity never again arose."

"Dear God!" cried I.

"This is a wretched business," said Cassandra.

"We must go to Mr. Cage and Mr. Deedes directly," exclaimed I, "and tell them how Fanny and Sophia really feel."

"It is a bit late for that, I am afraid," said Edward Taylor, "for the two gentlemen left for Canterbury an hour ago."

Chapter the Twenty-ninth

I paced back and forth before the window of my chamber, entirely distraught. Below, the early stages of the migration had begun, from the house to that section of the park where the bonfire had been set up. Although the news of Fanny's break with Mr. Cage, and the sudden departure of that gentleman and his friend, was very distressing indeed, Lady Bridges had decreed that the Midsummer's Eve festivities should go ahead as planned.

"It would be a shame," said she, "to allow the disappointments of a few to become the disappointments of the many; for the bonfire is an event which our family and friends look forward to all year, and it is particularly meaningful to the servants." The Midsummer's Eve bonfire, she explained, was one of the few affairs at Goodnestone other than the Christmas party in which the staff was also included.

I had looked forward to this evening's merriment these many weeks; but now, I was in no mood to celebrate. Fanny refused to speak to Sophia or anyone else. Both had shut themselves in their rooms and refused to answer their doors. Cassandra, perceiving my distressed state of mind, had informed the others that I needed to rest before the bonfire, and she had stayed to listen to me in my despair.

I had just admitted everything to her with regard to my machinations for the four lovers, from the moment the idea was conceived, to Fanny's tearful admission that evening. Cassandra, shocked and distressed, was shaking her head.

"I suspected that you were up to something, Jane, but in my wildest imaginings, it was never this."

"How could I have been so blind and stupid?" cried I. "I took up an idea and made myself believe in it implicitly; yet it was all founded on the shakiest of premises. To know, now, that Fanny is in love with Mr. Cage after all, and that his affections for *her* have never wavered! To understand that Mr. Deedes is just as in love with Sophia as she is with him—and I had no inkling! To learn that he was about to speak, when *I* intervened and kept throwing him at Fanny! Last week, I saw him admiring the pictures which had won the contest, and thought his praise was all for Fanny; now I see that he was not admiring *her* work that day, but rather Sophia's! It was not Mr. Cage's appearance that had caused Sophia to blush, the evening when both gentlemen first arrived; it was *Mr. Deedes's*. It had always been Mr. Deedes! During the Snapdragon game, Mr. Deedes and Sophia were the most eager players—both inspired, I surmise, by the tradition that the winner would marry their true love within a year. Oh! Had I not suggested the play, Fanny and Mr. Cage would still be betrothed, and Mr. Deedes and Sophia might have been engaged by now!"

"That is entirely possible." Cassandra sighed. "Sadly, Mr. Deedes cannot discover her true feelings for a long while yet, if ever; for he has gone to Canterbury, and next week leaves for Scotland with the Knights—and the day after tomorrow, when we depart, the Bridges family all go to Bath."

"How sage is Shakespeare's line, *What fools these mortals be!* How ironic that *I* was obliged to speak those words on this very day, for he may as well have written it specifically about me. Like Puck, I have mistakenly misaligned everybody! I feel like such an idiot." I sank down onto a chair and covered my face with my hands, too mortified to look at her. "My romantic schemes did not end with those four people, Cassandra. There is yet one other couple whom I hoped would form a connection during our stay at Goodnestone."

"Oh? Who is that?" Cassandra replied, an odd tone in her voice.

Flushing, I peeked at her from between my fingers. "You and Thomas Payler."

"Me and Thomas?" She smiled. "Jane: I may not have understood your intentions regarding the others, but did you truly think I did not notice what you were up to on my behalf?"

My hands dropped to my lap. "You knew?"

"Of course I knew. How many times did you ask what I thought of Mr. Payler? How often did you mention his many attributes to me? It was obvious you were promoting the match."

A ray of hope darted through me. Perhaps not everything I had done was in vain! "He is perfect for you, Cassandra. He is a sensible, kind, good-looking young man from an excellent family, with whom you share common interests."

"So you have said many times; and while that may be true, Jane, I am not interested in Thomas Payler in *that* way. I could never love him."

"Why not?"

"Because I am in love with someone else."

I was so astonished, I could hardly formulate a reply. "In love with someone else?"

She nodded, blushing.

"But—with whom?"

"Tom Fowle."

Tom Fowle was one of our father's former students—a young man who had lately become a clergyman. I had barely given him a thought since the day he left our household many years before. "How long have you been in love with him?" cried I, astounded.

"Ever since I was a little girl, I think, and he came to live with us."

"All these years, you have had such feelings, and you never said a word?"

"It has taken all this time to truly know Tom, to understand and appreciate his many good qualities, and to feel certain that we are right for each other. When I *did* know that I loved him, I did not have the nerve to voice my feelings aloud, even to you, dearest; for Tom is so much older than I. I never dared to hope he would notice me; but on his last visit, he gave me reason to believe that my feelings are returned."

I thought back to the time of Mr. Fowle's last visit as well as I could, but I had only the vaguest memory of it; I had been very engrossed, as I recalled, in writing a story at the time, and had paid him little attention.

"Tom is still struggling to establish himself," added Cassandra softly, her colour heightening even further, "but one day, when the time is right, I think it likely—I *hope*—that he will declare himself."

I was surprised, confounded—stupefied. I, who prided myself on my powers of observation, had lived side by side with my sister since childhood, sharing every thought and confidence—yet I had never had a clue that she harboured such deep feelings for another.

"How mortifying it is, Cassandra, to discover that I have so little understanding of others." I crossed to the window again, greatly vexed with myself. Below, I observed Elizabeth and my brother Edward emerge from the house, intimately conversing; she carried a basket of roses on her arm. Behind them came Edward Taylor with Thomas and Charlotte. I sighed, adding:

"There is someone else whom I misjudged for a long while as well: Charlotte Payler. I disliked her unjustly when we first met. Considering how she feels about Edward Taylor, it would be only natural for her to feel threatened by his regard for me; yet she has been very sweet to me."

"I always thought Charlotte a good and amiable young lady."

"Oh! How could I have been so grievously in error about *everybody?* My first impressions were all completely wrong!"

"I *tried* to warn you, dearest, particularly where the others were concerned, but you would not listen."

"I am so ashamed. What a treacherous effect my schemes produced! I attempted to employ a home theatrical, an otherwise innocent activity, for a less than respectable purpose—to manipulate the feelings of others—and what a dangerous intimacy was created! Now Sophia and Fanny are utterly wretched, as are the men who love them. Two sisters who once were close may never speak to each other again—and it is all my fault!"

"The heart cannot be easily deciphered, nor can it be directed or managed; in matters of love and matrimony, people must be left to their own devices."

"I know that now. Oh! I have made so many blunders. If only Papa were here, I should ask him what to do; he always has such excellent advice."

"I think I know what Papa would say, if he were here."

"Do you?"

"Do you remember many years ago, when an elderly friend of Mamma's came to call, whose face had been ravaged by the pox?"

"No; when was this?"

"You were very young, seven or eight perhaps. We laughed at the old woman behind her back, and called her pox-face, and said any number of unkind things, believing she could not hear us. Before she left, she shook our hands graciously, but I saw the hurt in her eyes; she said that she had once been as young and pretty as we were, and that we should take care not to fall ill, or we should meet her fate and both be called pox-face one day."

"Oh!" My cheeks burned now as a fragment of the memory came back to me. "Papa found out what happened, and as I recall, he sat us down and gave us a very stern speech—but I have forgotten what he said."

"He said he was going to share one of the essential truths he had learned in life: that happiness and well-being ultimately depend on *character*—the way we treat other people on a day-to-day basis. He made us walk three miles to her house the next day to apologise."

The entire incident came back to me then, along with the rush of guilty feelings it had engendered; no wonder I had done my best to forget it. "To further demonstrate our good intentions, we worked in her garden all afternoon pulling weeds." At my sister's confirming nod, I sighed grimly. "I understand your implication, dearest. I must apologise for this mess I have made, and find a way to rectify it; but I fear, when I admit to Fanny and Sophia what I have done, they will never forgive me."

My first order of business, in addition to an apology, was to get Fanny and Sophia to speak to each other again, so that the rift between them should be mended. However, despite our most valiant efforts—Cassandra and I knocked on their respective chamber doors several times, begging them to let us in—our appeals were rebuffed. "They did not wish to speak to anyone; they had no wish to attend the bonfire; they preferred to be alone."

"What shall we do?" said I, greatly disappointed, as my sister and I gave up the attempt and started down the passage towards our room. "How shall I mend what I have done, if they will not even hear me? And that is only the first step. Somehow, I must let Mr. Cage and Mr. Deedes know that

Fanny and Sophia truly love them—but how? I cannot write to them, nor can I ride to Canterbury to visit two single gentlemen—and the information must reach their ears by tomorrow at the latest."

"Why tomorrow?"

"Because according to Edward, tomorrow is the only day Mr. Cage will be in Canterbury, and within our reach; the next morning he is to travel on to his own house, some eight-and-thirty miles distant. The day after *that,* we return to Godmersham, the Bridgeses leave for Bath, and Mr. Deedes will be preparing for his tour to Scotland. The opportunity to reunite the lovers will be lost."

As my sister and I pondered this dilemma, two housemaids emerged into the passage from the upper stairs, each carrying a small basket over her arm. I recognised one of them as the maid who had styled and powdered my hair for the ball.

"A lovely evenin' for a bonfire, i'nt it?" said Sally as they both dropped a curtsey before us.

"It is indeed," replied Cassandra.

"So kind o' Lady Bridges to invite us," said the second maid, a fair-haired girl, smiling, "and to let us cut her roses."

"Roses? What do you need roses for?"

"Why, they're to wish on," replied Sally. The two girls exchanged a look, and burst into giggles.

"To wish on?" repeated I, mystified.

"Don't tell me you never made a wish on Midsummer's Eve?" said the second maid.

"I never have," said I.

"Nor I," added Cassandra. "Some of our neighbours in Hampshire have bonfires, but I have heard nothing about roses or wishing."

"Perhaps it i'nt common in your part of the country, miss, but it's a tradition hereabouts; roses are ever so important. It's said that any rose picked on Midsummer's Eve or Midsummer's Day will keep fresh until Christmas."

Sally, with a toss of her dark curls, said, "That's a load of twaddle, Nancy, and well you know it. Howsoever, the legend about wishing at midnight *is* real."

"Tell us about the legend," insisted I.

"It's said," replied Sally solemnly, "that at midnight on Midsummer's Eve, if young girls scatter the petals of roses before them and repeat the ancient saying, the next day their true love will visit them."

"Indeed?" My curiosity was now truly piqued.

"My mother sprinkled petals of roses for my father on Midsummer's Eve, and he come to her next morning, not knowing a thing about it! They've been married now seven-and-twenty years! My young man and I've been courting since Christmas, and I keep hoping he'll pop the question. If I repeat the saying loud enough, maybe he'll do so tomorrow!"

"My own grandmamma swears she married my grandfather because of a Midsummer's Eve wish, and they are very happy," said the fair-haired maid. "*I'm* going to say it above a dozen times, and scatter every single petal in my basket; and if my John should come calling tomorrow, I'll know he's my one true love, and the one I am to marry!" Giggling, the two girls started to dash off.

"Wait!" cried I. "What is the old saying that one should repeat?"

Pausing, the two maids recited to us in unison: " 'Rose leaves, rose leaves, rose leaves I strew; he that will love me, come after me now.' " They ran off down the stairs.

I watched them go, my thoughts in a whirl. An idea began bubbling up in my brain, and at length took hold. "Cassandra: I know what we must do, to help the couples I have misaligned!"

I revealed my plan to my sister in its entirety. She concurred that while the first half was fanciful, the second half was sensible, and therefore worth a try. However, to work as a whole, it required the complicity of my brother Edward, as well as Fanny and Sophia. "Edward has already gone down to the bonfire," she reminded me.

"I will speak to him there."

"How will you get Fanny and Sophia to listen, if neither will open her door to us?"

"There are many different methods to deliver a message," responded I.

We returned to our chamber, wherein I immediately sat down and wrote two notes. The first read:

My Dearest Sophia,

I know of the pain which you are presently enduring, and I am writing to offer my deepest apologies—and to admit, to my everlasting shame, that I have had a hand in everything which has caused your grief. This may surprise you, but it is true. Pray, allow me to explain. For some weeks now, I have been under the impression that Fanny did not love Mr. Cage (a presumption which turned out to be entirely false). In my naïveté, I had a strong wish for him to pay attention to you, believing you to be a better match; at the same time, I hoped Mr. Deedes would look in Fanny's direction. When I could, I gently nudged you all in that direction, and I cast the play with these pairings in mind, believing that the intimacies of the theatre might help you discover your true affections. Only now do I know the real truth, and how wrong I was!

I am so sorry for the rift I have caused. All this ill will must be mended, and without delay. Fanny believes that you stole her fiancé; you must tell her how you really feel! With regard to Mr. Deedes: do not give up all hope. I have an idea of how to bring him back—but you must act to-night. Please, please, do me the honour of coming out and speaking to me—now. I await in my chamber with bated breath, a mortified heart, the greatest respect, and—

All best wishes,
Jane Austen

The second note I addressed to Fanny, expressing similar sentiments, and revealing the truth not only of Mr. Cage's feelings for her, but of Sophia's feelings with respect to Mr. Cage and Mr. Deedes.

I folded both notes, knocked to announce my delivery, and quickly slipped them under each young lady's door; I then returned to my room to wait with Cassandra. Not five minutes passed before two chamber doors were heard opening down the hall, followed by Fanny's and Sophia's tearful voices. Their tender exclamations echoed in the passage; after an interval engaged in conversation, both burst into our room, holding hands, red-eyed, and exchanging loving looks.

"Well, Jane!" cried Fanny. "I suppose I should thank you; you have given me my sister back. But I am very, very angry with you!"

"So you should be," replied I, rising, my cheeks burning with shame.

"I forgive you," said Sophia, wiping her eyes. "I cannot count how many times Fanny has insisted that she did not love Mr. Cage. It is not wonderful that you took her at her word."

"All that is in the past," insisted Fanny crossly. "What matters is what we do *now*. You said that Mr. Cage truly loves me?"

"He does; he told my brother so," replied Cassandra.

A smile lit Fanny's countenance and she heaved a great, relieved sigh. "That is the best news I have ever heard. What is your idea, Jane? How do you propose that we get our gentlemen back?"

Before I could reply, Sophia shook her head, and said:

"There is nothing you can do for me. It is too late. You were affianced to Mr. Cage, Fanny; he might return, and your relationship might well be mended. But Mr. Deedes has no reason to return to this part of the country."

"Then we must give him a reason." The second part of my plan I thought best not to reveal until I had spoken with my brother, lest I falsely raise any hopes; so I only said: "Are you familiar with the old legend regarding the strewing of rose petals on Midsummer's Eve?"

Sophia nodded. "Of course."

"We tried it once, when we were girls; we

scattered petals at midnight, and repeated the saying." Fanny shrugged with a faint smile. "Sadly, no robust young lads came looking for us the next morning."

"Perhaps," said I, with a knowing look, "that was because you had not yet met your one true love."

Sophia and Fanny exchanged a glance; then the former cried, "What are you saying, Jane? You think the legend might work for us to-night?"

"It has worked for other couples. It is certainly worth a try."

The sun had long since set, but its last dusky rays and the brightness of the moon illuminated our way as Sophia, Fanny, my sister, and I stopped in the walled rose garden. The Bridges sisters had quickly changed into the new gowns which had been made for them expressly for the occasion, and together we sought out the oldest-looking roses we could find, sweeping the loosened petals from the stems into our baskets until they were brim-full.

I was not sure I could trust in old legends—I depended on my *other* part of the plan to be the real means of bringing Fanny's and Sophia's wishes to fruition—but I had read and heard enough tales to believe in the *possibility* of magic, and fully intended to scatter rose petals *myself* to-night, with a certain young gentleman in mind.

Cassandra was going to strew rose petals as well. "It might be impossible for Tom Fowle to visit me *tomorrow*," said she, smiling, "but he might *think* of me, and come to call after we return home."

We made our way to the park at the front of the house, where the evening air was filled with the sounds of music performed by a trio of hired musicians, and the lively chatter of the sizeable group assembled on the lawn.

An assortment of dry brush, tree branches, and twigs had been formed into a pile as wide as a horse-cart and nearly as tall as myself. Thankfully, the last few days of sun had so warmed the grass as to make it dry enough to sit upon. The servants reclined on blankets on one side; the family were convened on the other, where chairs had been set up for the senior members of the party. Lady Bridges was engaged in conversation with Mrs. Fielding, Mrs. Payler, and my mother; upon noticing Fanny, a troubled look crossed the former's countenance, but she glanced away.

My eyes sought and found Edward Taylor; he was chatting congenially with his cousin Thomas. My heart ached to be with him; but first, I had important business to attend: I must speak with my brother Edward. I observed that Charlotte, seated not too far off, had her own basket of rose petals. I knew what—or should I say *who—she* would wish for at midnight. If the legend were true—suddenly, I wanted more than anything to believe that it *was*—then only one of us could prevail. *Which* one would it be?

Chapter the Thirtieth

Our presence was immediately detected by Elizabeth and my brother Edward, who, hurrying to our side, expressed their pleasure at seeing us all amongst the company.

"You must sit with us," insisted Elizabeth to her sisters with real sympathy. "Fanny, do sit over here by me; and Sophia, here." Such a kind display on Elizabeth's part, particularly in the manner in which she addressed Fanny, with whom she had up till now been on such unfriendly terms, was both surprising and commendable. Fanny and Sophia obliged, laying their blankets beside her, and a tête-à-tête immediately began.

Cassandra and I sat down next to my brother, to whom I said quietly: "Might I have a word with you, Edward?"

"Certainly; but can it wait until later?" For at that very moment the bonfire was being lit.

A torch was brought to the bed of dry leaves at the base of the immense bonfire pile, the lower sticks and branches caught fire, and within minutes it began to spread. I joined in with the crowd as we cheered our approval. Before long an immense bonfire was raging, the orange and red flames leaping up towards the inky sky, emitting a heat that warmed my face and lit the smiling countenances gathered around its circumference. We all sat admiring the conflagration, talking amongst ourselves and listening to the music.

During this interval, I could not prevent myself from glancing at Edward Taylor from time to time; once or twice, his dark eyes caught mine, and he smiled—a look which, as always, caused a thrill to run through me. I could not help but think about the rose petals; if I scattered them at midnight and made a wish, would he come to me the next day? If so, what might he say? My imagination rapidly went to work on this idea, but my musings were interrupted by my mother, who, having returned to the house to fetch her cloak, paused en route to her chair and said to me and Cassandra:

"The night air here is much cooler than we are accustomed to at home. You girls ought to have brought more than just those thin shawls; here are warmer ones." She handed us two woollen shawls.

"Thank you, Mamma," replied I, "that was very thoughtful of you; but sitting by the fire, I am quite warm."

"I do not care how warm you *think* you feel; the damp grass will surely seep through that blanket and you could catch your death of cold. Do wrap yourself up without delay."

"Yes, Mamma," responded Cassandra. Although, from the look on my sister's face, and the perspiration on her brow, I knew that she was equally as warm as me, we both obeyed my mother's command.

"What do you think, girls? Ought we to have a bonfire at Steventon next year on Midsummer's Eve?" remarked my mother, looking round with a contented smile. "It is very pleasant."

"That would be a fine idea," responded Cassandra.

"We shall have to ask your father what he thinks. Oh! How I miss him! We have been gone far too long, it feels like a year at least! We have had a delightful visit here, and I am happy we came, but how glad I am that we return to Godmersham two days hence, and soon after leave for home!" So saying, my mother moved on, resuming her seat beside Mrs. Payler by the fire.

Her words struck me, reminding me that my remaining time in Kent was very short indeed. In two days, I should be gone, with no idea when, or *if,* I should ever return. The thought of leaving my new friends saddened me—but more particularly, the melancholy realisation that I might never see Edward Taylor again caused moisture to gather in my eyes. I wiped away a tear; moments later, to my surprise, the young gentleman himself dropped onto the blanket beside me.

"Hello," said he, his voice low and deep. "You have been very scarce this evening, and now you look unaccountably sad. What is the matter?"

His nearness caused my heart, as always, to beat more rapidly. Having no wish to tell him what was *really* on my mind, I replied: "I am sad about—what transpired earlier this afternoon."

"This afternoon?" He thought, then added: "Oh! You mean the romantic problems of Fanny and Mr. Cage?"

"Yes; and also of Sophia and Mr. Deedes."

"What happened is very distressing of course; but why should you take it so to heart, Miss Jane? They are grown people who can take care of themselves, and it was not your doing."

"Oh! But it was," replied I in some anguish. Since I had already told all to Fanny and Sophia, I knew that word would get out sooner or later— and so very quietly, in as succinct a manner as possible, I explained what I had done and why. To my relief, he did not appear to judge me, and when I was finished, said (quoting the Bard) with great seriousness:

"*The course of true love never did run smooth.* I had no idea all this was going on. I thought we were just doing a play! But I must point out: not everything that happened was your fault."

I shook my head. "It was."

"I beg to differ. You may have set the stage, so to speak, and made a few subtle suggestions here and there, but it was up to the players themselves to enact their parts, and they did so of their own free will. It was Fanny's *choice* to flirt with Mr. Deedes; the manner in which Mr. Cage responded was *his* choice as well. Furthermore, not everything you did was detrimental. I believe our play had one very beneficial effect where Fanny is concerned."

"What is that?"

"It seems to have awakened romantic feeling in her at last; for—from what you tell me—it was only when Fanny observed Mr. Cage making love to her sister on the stage, that she came to realise the strength of her *own* affections for *him*. For *that,* you should be congratulated."

I laughed. "Thank you for your kind vote of support on my behalf, but that result was entirely unanticipated—indeed, it was the reverse of what I intended—and I can take no credit for it. I still feel responsible, for I indulged in machinations which were very wrong—but I have a plan to fix everything."

"What is your plan?"

"First, we shall try a little magic at midnight." I sifted through the petals in my basket, then glanced meaningfully at Fanny and Sophia, whose hands were idly engaged in the same activity.

His eyebrow lifted. "The old legend? Well, it *is* said that magic is at the height of its power on Midsummer's Eve, and a good time to look into the future, particularly for young maidens seeking suitors." He looked at me intently, and the expression in his dark eyes seemed to hint at something as yet unspoken.

I blushed and groped for words. "It is a whimsical notion; but I do not rely on magic alone." I then revealed to him the rest of my plan: "I intend to ask my brother Edward to ride to Canterbury the first thing tomorrow morning, to speak to Mr. Cage and Mr. Deedes. If Edward tells them the truth of the young ladies' affections, I believe—I *hope*—it will persuade both gentlemen to return to Goodnestone at once, to declare *their* feelings."

"An excellent strategy. I wish I could assist with this mission of yours, or take it on myself, but tomorrow my aunt Payler is holding a birthday party for me at Ileden, so I really cannot leave—I hope you are coming?"

"Of course! I would not miss it for the world."

He seemed pleased. His gaze was now drawn to my own basket, and he added, smiling, "Are *you* going to strew rose petals yourself?"

A blush took over my face; I grew so warm that I was obliged to remove my shawl from my shoulders. "If everyone else is doing so, I would not wish to be the only one left out."

"Oh! Certainly not. It is as good a ritual as any, I am sure. Did you know that in some countries—in the kingdoms of Scandinavia in particular—Midsummer's Eve is the most celebrated holiday apart from Christmas?"

"Is it really?"

"There, it is said that if an unmarried woman collects seven different flowers and places them under her pillow, she will dream of her future husband."

"I had not heard of that."

Our private interview was interrupted as Sophia leaned over, and inquired: "What did you say, Edward, about flowers under a pillow?"

He repeated his remark, which caught the attention of several others. Sophia laughed and said to Fanny, "Perhaps we ought to try that as well."

"All this fuss about petals and flowers!" cried Elizabeth. "It is amusing but very silly. Why do we even celebrate Midsummer's Eve? Does any-one know?"

"I do," responded Edward Taylor. "Because Midsummer's Day is my birthday, I have read up on it. From ancient times, it has been a festival of the summer solstice—the longest day of the year. The exact dates vary between different cultures, but because St. John the Baptist was born on 24 June, the Christian Church designated that as his feast-day, with the observance beginning the evening before. Some people believe that golden-flowered midsummer plants, such as St. John's-wort and calendula, have miraculous healing powers if picked on this night. Just about every European country celebrates with the lighting of bonfires to protect against evil spirits, which were believed to roam freely when the sun was turning southward again."

The conversation had reached the ears of our elders now. Lady Bridges, with a pinched look on her countenance, said:

"I am sure we do not care what they do in *other countries,* Mr. Taylor. *English* traditions are the only thing of concern *here.*"

"I disagree," remarked Admiral Fielding. "I find this all quite fascinating. What other rituals have you heard about, son—other than this rose petal thing?"

Lady Bridges frowned and lapsed into silence, as Edward Taylor continued:

"Well, witches were thought to meet with other powerful beings on Midsummer's Eve. The bigger the fire, it is said, the farther the mischievous spirits stay away."

"Thank God we have a big fire, then!" cried my brother Edward, his comment meeting with laughter from the crowd, whose attention was all focused on Edward Taylor now. The servants, too, appeared to be riveted by his story-telling.

"There is usually feasting and merry-making of

course," Edward Taylor went on. "In Bulgaria, it is thought that anyone seeing the sunrise will be healthy throughout the year. They have another curious tradition as well: they dance barefoot on smouldering embers."

A chorus of voices cried out in horror at this prospect.

"I should like to see a demonstration of *that,*" cried one of the footmen, smiling.

"So should I," agreed Christopher Payler. "Cousin Edward: will you dance barefoot on smouldering embers for us?"

Everyone laughed. Edward Taylor shook his head. "Thank you, Christopher; that is an interesting challenge, but one I think I shall decline."

"Sensible boy," commented Mr. Payler.

I was just thinking how commendable it was that Edward Taylor had declined such an awful dare (reflecting, I believed, a positive step in his personal growth), when he continued:

"It is a far more widespread tradition to jump over the flames."

"Jump over the flames?" cried my mother. "Dear God! That sounds very dangerous."

"You wait until it is safe, of course. The practice occurs in too many countries to count—Germany, Russia, Croatia, Spain, Greece—to jump over the flames on Midsummer's Eve is seen as a way of guaranteeing prosperity and avoiding bad luck. In Spain, it is done three times while crying '*meigas fora*,' which means 'witches off!' "

"Jump over the flames for *us,* Cousin Edward!" urged Thomas Payler.

The group laughed again.

"We will have no such ridiculous displays here!" cried Lady Bridges. "Jumping over flames! I declare, I have never heard the like of it."

Charlotte turned to her brother in dismay. "Why do you persist in challenging each other in this infantile manner, Thomas?"

Edward Taylor regarded his cousin from where he sat. "Are you daring me to jump over the flames, sir?"

"I am. A pound note says you cannot clear the fire without scorching yourself or your clothing."

A great gasp went up at this.

Edward Taylor thought for a moment, and said: "I will do it for nothing—I will jump *three times*—if you will make the jump *once* yourself."

I sighed and shook my head, dismayed. Did Edward Taylor learn nothing when Charles nearly fell from the tree? Did his apology following that debacle mean nothing? Here he was, debating another reckless challenge without a second thought!

Thomas hesitated. The two young men eyed each other, the gauntlet thrown. A tense silence reigned for a long moment.

One of the servants, his eyes wide, exclaimed: "This will be interesting."

"Do it!" cried Brook Edward. "Do it, the both of you! Jump over the flames!"

A chant began, of youthful male voices repeating the challenge. I did not like the direction in which this was going. Although the fire had burned much lower now, it was yet hot and wide, the flames reaching perhaps two feet in height; to attempt to jump over it would be dangerous indeed. I agreed with Charlotte; it was childish, the way these two cousins baited each other. I was annoyed with Edward Taylor in particular. Why did he feel obliged to behave in such a manner? What was he trying to prove? Would Thomas rise to the challenge? I hoped not; if he said no, the matter would end there and then.

Thomas stood, and said quietly: "I will do it, if you go first."

"Done!" replied Edward Taylor, rising with a smile.

I groaned inwardly, also leaping to my feet. "Mr. Taylor, we have spoken of such things before. It is reckless!"

He paused and shrugged slightly. "This marks one of those instances when reckless behaviour is called for: my reputation is at stake." To the general assembly he cried, "Give me a moment to make ready."

I sighed again, my heart hammering in my

chest, as Edward Taylor traversed slowly all the way around the bonfire, studying it, as if taking a measure of its height and circumference in his mind. He then walked some little distance away, where he stretched his arms and legs, presumably in preparation for his exertion.

The crowd all stood in anticipation, the young ladies exclaiming alternately with worry and delight, the matrons shaking their heads, the older men made youthful by their excitement, the young gentlemen clapping their hands and shouting:

"Jump! Jump! Jump!"

Charlotte looked very worried. Cassandra grasped my hand and held it tightly. All eyes were on Edward Taylor. He leaned forward now, legs bent, his attention fixed on the conflagration before him; then he broke out into a run, made a mighty leap, and flew over the bonfire, easily clearing the flames as he cried gleefully, *"meigas fora!"* When he landed neatly on the grass on the other side, a cheer erupted; but he was not yet done. He still had two more attempts to make—both of which he completed with equal success. I felt relief course through me as I joined in the general applause.

It was now Thomas's turn. He had grown pale, his expression suggesting that he regretted making the bet.

"Thomas," cried his mother, "your cousin is

lucky but very foolish. You need not follow in his footsteps. We have all been entertained quite enough for one evening."

"Indeed we have!" exclaimed Lady Bridges, frowning with disapproval at Edward Taylor.

"A bet is a bet!" cried Edward Taylor—and all the men began chanting their agreement, followed in short order by most of the young ladies.

I was alarmed by this foolhardy behaviour, yet at the same time, I could not help but feel a dash of excitement. Nearly all the young people and all the men, a very sizeable group, were clapping and calling out their encouragement, and the mood was infectious.

Thomas's mouth set with determination. Without further hesitation, he repeated the steps his cousin had taken, and then boldly ran and made his own leap. His feet seemed to just miss the uppermost edges of the flames, and his landing appeared rough, but he reached the other side with impunity. I again felt relief as another roar went through the applauding crowd. The two young men were clapped on the back by their admirers.

One of the strapping young footmen now exclaimed, "I want to have a go!"

Before I knew it, he had made his own jump. Additional voices cried out that they wanted to get in on the fun. The air seemed thick with excitement as, one by one, more young men followed suit, with those who had gone before sharing their counsel as to how to accomplish the hurdle. My brother Edward took a turn, as did Christopher Payler and two more of the male servants. To everyone's astonishment, even Frederic insisted on trying it, an endeavour which so terrified his mother that she could not stop shrieking (until I thought she might faint), and whose cries took on an entirely new tone upon his safe landing, reflecting pride and joy at his accomplishment, and the insistence that she had always known he could do it.

With so many young men successfully jumping over the fire, the aspect of danger rapidly faded. What had seemed to me a reckless enterprise now appeared very differently. I could no longer accuse Edward Taylor of poor judgement, for what a merry time we were all having, with everyone laughing and cheering! How much more cheerful had the evening become, as a result of his bold ideas and daring nature!

All at once, an unseen force took hold of me, which I could neither explain nor ignore. I felt an absolute need to prove to the group that I was not a quaking, pathetic girl; that I could be as brave as any man. Without a word, I strode to the point from which everyone else had begun their run, and assumed the runner's stance.

A small gasp went through the assemblage. I felt all eyes turn to me in unison.

Edward Taylor let out a cheer. "Good for you, Jane!"

Cassandra was aghast. "Jane, no!"

"What do you think you are doing, Jane?" cried my mother. "Stop this nonsense at once!"

I ignored their protests. I had seen many others make the leap. I felt equal to the task. I was not afraid; pure excitement coursed through me. I drew together the folds of my skirts in one hand and raised them above my ankles.

I took a deep breath.

I ran.

Chapter the Thirty-first

I flung myself up and over the hot, golden mass, my eyes on the dark stretch of grass on the other side.

To my relief, I landed a foot beyond the edge of the fire. I was safe! However, I landed very hard, and a sharp pain coursed up through my right foot and ankle, causing me to stumble and pitch forward head first onto the ground, where I lay for an instant, dazed and mortified. To further my confusion, a male body hurtled to the ground immediately beside me, and quickly removing his coat, used it to bat forcefully at my skirts.

"Your gown has caught fire!" It was Edward Taylor.

To my horror, from my prone position, I glimpsed sparks and flames in the region of my hem. There was some bustle as Edward Taylor continued to strike at my skirts until the flames went out; then he turned and loomed above me, his hands on either side of my waist, his face inches from my own.

"Are you injured, Miss Jane?" said he with concern.

My heart was racing so speedily, I thought it might jump from my chest. For a brief, thrilling interval, I found myself staring into his beautiful dark eyes, unable to utter a word. At last I responded: "I am fine—I think."

"Thank God."

"Jane!" It was my mother's voice. The moment was over as she, my sister, and a dozen others rushed up to stare at me with worry.

Edward Taylor helped me to rise, and he gave my hands a slight squeeze before letting go. As my right foot touched down, I again felt a sharp pain stab through it, but was determined not to shew any sign that I was injured. People were all around us now, and when they ascertained that I was upright and apparently undamaged, they broke into applause and a round of cheers and compliments in celebration of my achievement. Sophia embraced me with relief; my brother Edward shook my hand. But not *all* were as pleased with me.

"Well!" cried my mother, frowning furiously. "I hope you are proud of yourself, Jane! What a ridiculous display! Jumping over the fire, indeed! You are fortunate you did not break your arm or your leg! Look what you have done to your gown—the hem is all in tatters! I dare say it is forever ruined!"

"I am relieved to see you alive and standing," whispered Cassandra, eyeing me with a stern look of censure.

I was spared from responding to either of my relations, for at that precise moment, Elizabeth announced:

"Good heaven! It is three minutes before midnight!"

"Oh!" cried Sophia, Fanny, and Charlotte at the same instant. They, and a bevy of other young ladies, with cries of excitement, ran to fetch their baskets of rose petals. Cassandra held out her hand to me. "Come, Jane. Let us go make our wishes."

I darted a glance at Edward Taylor, but he was engaged in conversation with others now; and I allowed my sister to lead me away.

"Are you limping, Jane?" said Cassandra with concern, after we had retrieved our baskets and shawls.

"No," lied I; but I could not hide my injury from my perceptive sister, any more than I could help favouring my left foot.

"You *are* limping! Well, I am sorry that you hurt yourself, but glad that it is no worse."

Further reproach, I suspected, would come later; but I could not regret my leap, for it had landed me in Edward Taylor's arms.

As Cassandra and I moved slowly across the grass, my ankle smarted with every step. Although it was dark, the night sky was bright with stars, and the waning moon cast a glow luminous enough to light the entire area, and to see each other's features. We stopped at a point some ways off from the bonfire, apart from the other young ladies, who had dispersed across the lawn. I saw them flinging petals into the air, and heard their cheerful murmurs as they recited the old Midsummer's Eve saying, calling their loves to them.

"Shall we?" said Cassandra eagerly.

I nodded, scooping a handful of rose petals from my basket. We were about to begin when, behind us, I heard male laughter, and turning, became aware of an assemblage of young gentlemen standing around the edge of the bonfire, gazing in our direction and chattering with great mirth. Was Edward Taylor among them? I could not tell; but I felt my cheeks grow warm with embarrassment.

"Do you feel silly doing this?" I asked my sister.

"A bit," admitted she, "but you promoted it with such enthusiasm to Fanny and Sophia, that I fear it would be rude were we not to participate.

And—as we *both* have young men we should like to call to us—*if* it is true that magic is strongest at this very hour on Midsummer's Eve, then we would be foolish not to try it."

"You are right. Let us not delay another moment!" In unison, we pronounced the ancient words as we scattered handfuls of rose petals into the night air:

Rose leaves, rose leaves, rose leaves I strew;
He that will love me, come after me now!

We repeated the saying until no petals remained in our baskets. When the rite had been completed, the joy, exhilaration, and absurdity of the moment caught up to us, and we both burst out laughing. The other young ladies were returning to the bonfire; Cassandra, shivering, proposed that we do the same. Not wanting to admit how much my ankle hurt, and hoping I might escape notice if I walked back on my own, I said:

"It is such a beautiful night, I think I shall stand here a few minutes longer, to contemplate the moon."

My sister warned me not to stay away from the fire too long, and she left me to my reflections.

It had been a long and eventful day; when I looked back on it, I could scarcely believe that we had performed a Shakespearean play that very afternoon, and that the ensuing, dire consequences

(Mr. Cage's and Mr. Deedes's departure, Fanny's and Sophia's broken hearts, and my first overtures to remedy the evils) had also occurred during the same period. I had yet to organise the final step of my plan with regard to those events—I needed desperately to speak to my brother Edward—and I was mentally preparing the speech I intended to make to him, when I heard a sudden foot-fall, and a deep male voice:

"It is a lovely night." Edward Taylor stopped not two feet from my side, eyeing the sky with a smile.

I was alone, and distant from any other people; he could have come thither with only one purpose in mind: to speak to me. My heart drummed; I was thrilled and flattered. Around us, crickets chirped, and a light breeze rustled the leaves in the distant trees, as he continued to glance upwards. I struggled for something to say, at length returning my gaze to the heavens and uttering:

"There is Boötes, the bear driver, and Arcturus."

"You know the stars and constellations?"

"I often look at them at home."

"I believe that Boötes is the most ancient constellation in the sky. Homer wrote of it in *The Odyssey.* There is the Little Bear, my favourite."

"Mine too. And how bright Polaris is to-night! When I look up at a night sky such as this, I feel as if there can never be any sorrow nor evil in the world—that such a sublime canopy can only shelter harmony and repose."

"I quite agree. It leaves all painting and music and prose behind; even poetry cannot hope to accurately describe it." We shared a smile. Unexpectedly, he added, "That was brave, what you did earlier."

"What? Jumping over the fire?" returned I carelessly. "You did it. So did many others."

"Yes, but we are men; as it turns out, it is not a recommended activity for a lady." Observing my indignant expression, he added hastily, "*Not* by virtue of her sex; I mean only with regard to her *attire*. Clearly you had the prowess to complete the exercise as well as any man—but leaping over flames, it seems, is injurious to the health of a lady's gown."

I laughed as I glanced down at my ruined hem. "I hope I can repair it with a border of lace or other fabric; otherwise, I fear I shall never hear the end of it from my mother."

"I hope she will not judge you too harshly. I admired your spirit."

"I admired *yours*. Although I admit, at the first, I thought it foolhardy."

"Sometimes one must let go of fear, and take a leap of faith—as *you* did to-night."

The look in his eyes was so admiring, it made me shiver. My thoughts scattered on the breeze. Again, I searched for something to say. It occurred to me that it was now Midsummer's Day. "Happy birthday."

"Thank you." Frowning, he added, "Are you really leaving in two days?"

"We are."

"I will be sorry to see you go."

"I will be sorry to leave."

"Do you have any idea when you might return to the neighbourhood?"

"No. Perhaps in a year or two? We will have good reason to visit, as my brother and his wife live here—and I look forward to becoming an aunt."

"If you return next year, or soon after—if my father comes home from Italy as planned—then we will all be living at Bifrons again. *I* look forward to welcoming you there, and to introducing you to my whole family."

"I should love to meet them!"

"Pray, come back again in summer, or I may be away at Oxford."

"You do intend to go to Oxford, then?"

"I doubt I shall have a choice, unless my father has a sudden, miraculous change of heart, and allows me to enter the military—but I do not foresee that happening."

"And after Oxford? What will you do?"

"After Oxford? I shall return to Bifrons under my father's rule, and—one day, I suppose, I shall marry."

It was the first time he had ever mentioned

marriage, and my breath caught in my throat. "Who shall you marry, Mr. Taylor?"

He smiled. "That remains to be seen. But I assure you: on *that* subject—the most important of all subjects—I will never be swayed by anyone else's wishes, but must be free to follow my own heart." As he spoke, he seemed to glance at me with meaning.

My heart turned over, and my pulse raced. Was it truly possible that he would one day consider me as his bride? Yet I could not prevent myself from saying, my words slow and measured, "Surely, though, a gentleman like yourself will be obliged to marry a young lady of wealth and property."

"If being the eldest son affords a man any benefit at all," countered he, "it is the freedom to marry for love, and not be dependent on an income from his wife."

"That is a fine sentiment," persisted I, "in *theory*—but what if said eldest son found and wished to marry a respectable gentleman's daughter, who had no dowry nor any property? Would not his family object?"

"His family might indeed object, and *he* might find it difficult to be reconciled to such a match as well; but," added he, his dark gaze dancing, "if the woman in question were intelligent, lively, spirited, good, and in possession of a pair of very fine eyes—if she made him forget every other woman he had ever met—I think it entirely possible that he would fall in love with her, and highly likely that he would marry her."

The affection in his eyes nearly made my heart stop. I drank in his words, feeling all the power and promise of them. I wanted to freeze the moment in time; I wanted to tell him what was in *my* heart. I wanted to say, *I love you, Edward Taylor*. If I had the nerve to say the words aloud, would he say them back to me?

But our conversation went no further, for at that moment Thomas Payler's voice came to us out of the darkness as he dashed across the lawn: "Edward! We are leaving!"

The bubble around us burst. I became aware of much bustle at the bonfire site: the musicians were packing up their instruments, and all were gathering up their things. Thomas stopped before us, announcing breathlessly: "Mamma is cold and tired. Father has ordered the coaches to be brought round; we are to return to Ileden immediately. You are to come, now."

"Thank you."

Thomas ran back to join his family. Disappointment tore through me. "You have to go."

"I promised to go home with the Paylers to-night. They want me there in the morning for some kind of birthday surprise—I have no idea what—but I will see you at my party later in the day?"

"Yes, you will."

Our eyes met and held in the moonlight. "I wish we could stay up until sunrise, like the Bulgarians. I feel that I could talk to you all night."

"I feel the same."

What happened next took me by surprise. He leaned in close—very close—and said softly: "We proved the ancient Midsummer's Eve legend to-night, did we not, Miss Jane?"

His nearness took my breath away; I could barely speak. "What do you mean?"

"Did not you toss the rose petals and recite the saying?"

I nodded.

"Was it *me* you hoped would come after you?"

A blush warmed my cheeks, silently admitting to the truth of his observations. He smiled.

"Well: it is Midsummer's Day, and here I am, answering your call." So saying, he gently kissed my cheek. Drawing back slightly, he paused for a long moment, looking at me. Then he turned and strode away across the grass.

I hardly know how I returned to the fire; I was in too dazed and blissful a state to notice the pain in my ankle, or to be aware of anything except the memory of Edward Taylor's lips brushing against my skin.

Cassandra, carrying our folded blanket, came

up to me with a concerned look. "Jane? I have been waiting for you. Was that Edward Taylor with whom I saw you conversing?"

"Yes."

"What is that smile about?"

"Nothing," replied I; but I thought I might die of happiness.

As we began walking slowly back to the house along with the crowd, I would have been content to not say a word for hours. I was to be granted no time for private musings, however, for my brother Edward walked up to me deliberately, and noticing my limp, said,

"Jane: did you hurt yourself when you jumped over the fire?"

"Slightly. I took a bad step on my landing—as you no doubt saw."

"I am sorry. Allow me to assist you." He offered his arm, and after I took it, continued, "I am sorry I did not have time to speak with you earlier. What was it you wanted to tell me?"

I was instantly reminded of my obligation to the lovers whose lives I had driven askew. I had been so engrossed in other things, that it took me a moment to reorganise my thoughts; I managed however to find the presence of mind to explain what needed to be explained, and to make my request of him. My brother listened with some dismay to my story, shaking his head at intervals, and finally said, with some perturbation:

"Jane, you little devil; you have truly been up to no good. Let me see if I understand you. You have ruined the hopes and prospects of two couples, discovered the error of your ways, feel very bad about what you did, and now want me to fix everything for you?"

I blushed with shame. "I am sorry to be obliged to involve you, Edward, but I see no alternative. I must get word to Mr. Cage and Mr. Deedes tomorrow."

"Tomorrow is Edward Taylor's birthday party at Ileden. We are all expected to attend; yet you wish me to miss it?"

"I do not *wish* it; but I thought—I *hoped*—that if you ride to Canterbury early in the morning, you could ride back to Ileden in the afternoon, and arrive in time for the party."

"And return afterwards to Goodnestone? That is a great deal of travelling in one day, Jane."

"It is; it is hardly convenient, I know, and again I am sorry. But you are great friends with Mr. Deedes! He told you himself how much he loves Sophia. Do not you *want* to help reunite them?"

"I do. But I do not see this as my responsibility, Jane; it is yours."

"I agree; but what can *I* do?"

"You have already apologised to Fanny and Sophia; that is commendable. Now, you ought to apologise to the other two parties involved. I will borrow a carriage and take you to Canterbury tomorrow, but you must speak to Mr. Cage and Mr. Deedes yourself."

"Myself! Oh! But—I thought it best that they hear such things from *you*. You are a man, and their friend and colleague; they will listen to you, not me."

"I disagree. I already tried to reason with both of them, and failed. No, Jane; *you* are the one who is privy to Fanny's and Sophia's hearts; this information must come from you."

"What information has to come from Jane?" cried my mother, falling in with us as we progressed towards the house, and frowning with irritation at the evidence of my injured foot.

My brother concisely acquainted my mother with the essential details of our conversation. She looked aghast upon hearing of my involvement in the lovers' woes, and with anger and asperity, began the following harangue:

"Well; this is beyond anything I could have supposed. You leave me speechless, Jane! I hardly know what to say! Only that I ought to have kept far tighter reins on *your* activities over the past fortnight! Profligate as I knew you to be, I was not prepared for such a revelation! This is beyond anything you ever did before; beyond anything I ever heard of in my life! And this is my reward for all the cares I have taken in raising you. Oh! Jane, you are an abandoned creature, and I do not know what will become of you. To understand that all this misery is your fault! Well! Your brother is entirely correct; you *must* put things to rights, and at once! But I will not hear of the two of you driving all the way to Canterbury and back. No; *that* would be a complete waste of time, for Canterbury is halfway to Godmersham, and our whole family is due to depart for *that* residence the very next day. No; that will not do. You must either delay going to Canterbury for another day, when we will already be on the road, for we will be passing right through that town on our way to Godmersham, and can easily break our journey there; or—*if* Mr. and Mrs. Knight are agreeable— we must all leave tomorrow, or should I say, *today,* for it is already morning. It would mean leaving a day earlier than planned, but I am anxious to get away in any case. Edward, I know you do not like to be parted from Elizabeth, but *you* would not be opposed to going home to Godmersham a day early, would you?"

"I should be happy to oblige you, Mother, if that is your wish."

"It is not only *my* wish, but apparently Jane's— and as depraved as has been her behaviour, we must allow her the opportunity to *try* to set things to rights. I do hope the Knights will approve, and the Bridgeses will not mind, for God knows, we have tarried at Goodnestone long enough. Godmersham is just that much closer to Steventon and your father; and oh! I do so long to go home!"

I stared at my mother, dismayed. We could not wait another day to go to Canterbury! It was important that we see both gentlemen at once, or Mr. Cage would be away and gone. Besides, Fanny and Sophia were counting on their lovers coming back on *Midsummer's Day*. However, leaving early, as my mother proposed, would have a very calamitous result.

"Mamma, today is Edward Taylor's birthday. If we go to Canterbury and thence to Godmersham and do not return, I shall miss his birthday party!" *And,* I added silently, I would have no opportunity to say good-bye to him.

"Why should you mind?" cried my mother. "It is yet one more party with all the same people! I dare say you have been to enough parties over the past fortnight to last you ten years! But, however, I leave the decision up to you, Jane. *You* made this mess; it is up to you to get out of it. Which shall it be? Shall we depart according to our original plan? Or shall we get a few hours of sleep, and leave later this very morning?"

I did not take long to consider. The decision brought a pang to my heart and tears to my eyes. With deep regret I said quietly: "We should leave this very morning."

Chapter the Thirty-second

My mother immediately found and explained everything to Mr. and Mrs. Knight, who were both amenable to an early departure, as were Sir Brook and Lady Bridges.

"Oh! Do not worry about *our* feelings in the matter," stated her ladyship, "it is quite all right if you wish to leave today, for *we* have long intended to depart for Bath the next day, and have a great deal yet to do if we are to make ready for our own journey—all of which has been complicated extremely by the Paylers' idea of giving Edward Taylor a birthday party this morning, an event which is very ill-timed. I am sending the girls to the affair and staying home to pack."

Cassandra and I returned to our chamber and quickly packed our own things, then fell into bed; but I could not sleep. The past few weeks had been the most delightful of my life, but they were over now. Very soon, I should be home at Steventon, hundreds of miles away from Edward Taylor, with no notion of when or if I should ever see him again. I knew that going to Canterbury without delay was the right thing to do, but what a dreadful price I was obliged to pay!

Somehow, I determined, I must find a way to see Edward Taylor before I left. An idea occurred to me; I knew it was slightly scandalous, for being of no relation to Edward Taylor, it was most improper for me to write to him; yet I could see no alternative. I slipped out of bed, lit a candle, and wrote a short note.

Goodnestone Park
24 June, 1791

My dearest Mr. Taylor,
It is with the deepest regret that I write to inform you that I am unable to attend your birthday party today. I am obliged to return to Godmersham with my family this very morning via Canterbury, where I have particular business to attend, of a timely nature—I believe you can guess to what it relates. I cannot tell you how disappointed I am, that we had no opportunity to say good-bye; however, we shall be at Godmersham to-night, and will most likely stay one day more, before returning to Steventon. I realise it is a long way to Godmersham, but if it were within your power to come thither before my departure, even for the shortest of visits, I know you should be very welcome. May I close in saying, I wish you the very happiest of birthdays.

With all best wishes,
Jane Austen

On this idea, I pinned all my hopes.

The next morning, as we said our farewells to the Bridges family, I asked Sophia, Fanny, and Elizabeth to give my best regards to Edward Taylor. Surreptitiously, I gave Sophia the folded note, and implored her with an emotional whisper:

"Pray, Sophia, will you give this to Edward Taylor?"

I saw sympathy in Sophia's eyes, and she nodded silently as she hid the note in the folds of her skirts. After many thanks and embraces, in particular from Fanny and Sophia with regard to my purpose in going to Canterbury, we all tearfully said our good-byes, promising faithfully to write.

As my mother, Charles, and the Knights had no business in Canterbury, they drove on to Godmersham ahead of the rest of us. Cassandra and I took the chaise, and my brother Edward rode alongside. We were both tired from a night of very little sleep, but I was too anxious to be lulled by the motion of the carriage. When we arrived at Mr. Deedes's residence in Canterbury, we were received with surprise and pleasure by him and Mr. Cage.

My brother explained the purpose of our visit, and then turned the matter over to me. I told them everything, beginning with my false impressions, leaving out no detail of my complicity, and ending with the true status of Fanny's and Sophia's sentiments, as well as their hopes, based on the Midsummer's Eve rose-petal ritual.

The two gentlemen listened with avid attention, and in due course, after displaying a great range of emotions, and shedding a few tears, both said they forgave me, expressed their gratitude that we had come to see them, and announced their intention to return to Goodnestone that very day to see their ladies.

"Thank you, Miss Jane," said Mr. Deedes with warmth and a renewed sparkle in his eyes, kissing my hand as we rose to take our leave. "You have given me hope; more than hope, you have given me back my life."

Mr. Cage bowed and also graciously expressed his most sincere thanks, which I received with more than a little embarrassment and humility.

I wished them both well, and very soon my sister and I were back in the carriage on our way to Godmersham. I sighed with relief. I had done all I could to undo the mischief I had caused; it was now up to the lovers to decide their fate. Cassandra again fell asleep, and I spent the entire journey to Godmersham thinking of Edward Taylor, wondering what might be his reaction to my note, and praying that he would come to see me before I left for home.

He did not come that night; nor did I really expect him to, presuming him to be fully occupied all day and evening with his birthday festivities. The next day, however, I awoke full of hope. I was afraid to stray too far from the house, lest Edward Taylor arrive and find me missing, and so declined the long walk which Cassandra proposed in the pretty country-side, and stayed inside by the front window, while all the rest of the household went boating on the river. All morning long, I tried in vain to concentrate on a book I had chosen from the library, as I listened expectantly for the sounds of an approaching horse or carriage, which would signal the arrival of a visitor.

No such visitor appeared.

I retired that night gravely disappointed. Why had Edward Taylor not come? Perhaps I had somehow misread his feelings, and our association meant less to *him* than it had to me. This idea was very distressing, and I shed bitter tears.

The next morning, my mother, sister, Charles, and I left very early. We were to travel post. When the coach and four arrived, Mr. and Mrs. Knight and my brother Edward affectionately embraced us, as we repeated our thanks for their hospitality, and our hopes that the next time we saw each other would not be too distant.

Dejectedly, I sank into the seat beside Cassandra. The coach pulled away and with a rattle, proceeded down the long drive. When we turned onto the main road, as I glanced out the window despondently, I thought I detected a rise of dust in the distance behind us. I looked harder, trying to make out the cause of the slight disturbance, and realised that a horseman was approaching.

Was it possible?

"Someone is riding after us!" cried I.

"What?" said my mother. "Why on earth should someone be riding after us?"

"It might be Edward Taylor," replied I.

"Truly?" With excitement, Charles craned his neck to look without.

I, too, kept my eyes glued to the window, but the rider was yet too far away to determine who it was. "Please, Mamma, tell the coachman to stop!"

"I will do no such thing," cried my mother. "We have a long journey ahead of us, Jane, and are paying good money to get there. We have no idea who is on that horse, it could be anybody."

Frantically, I knocked on the front of the carriage, hoping to attract the driver's attention, as Cassandra, with a compassionate look, assisted in the endeavour. I then opened the window and called out; but at that very moment another vehicle passed us in the opposite direction, raising a cloud of dust which made me choke, and the loud rattle of both conveyances, combined with the beating of the horses' hooves and the jingle of their harnesses, combined to create such a clatter as to obscure my efforts, and the coachman did not respond.

To my infinite distress, when I looked back, the

lone rider had halted in his progress and was now turning round, as our coach and four speedily took us away down the road.

"Oh!" cried Charles. "He has given up!"

"Do not look so dejected," said my mother. "I am sure it was not he; what would Edward Taylor be doing so far from Ileden or Bifrons?"

"Perhaps he wished to say good-bye," replied I brokenly.

"Well, never mind, no one ever died from not saying good-bye. Lord knows you spent time enough with *that* young man these past three weeks, Jane, and look to where it led! With you embarrassing us by your shocking behaviour at the ball, and jumping over fires, and twisting your ankle, and sticking your nose in where it wasn't wanted with your romantic nonsense! I knew it was wrong to bring you here in the first place, and allow you to participate in so many social functions before you are properly *out,* and I promise you, I have learned from my mistake, and will not repeat it again! Mark my words: you will not attend a ball, young lady, nor any other event of consequence, until the day you turn seventeen, and not a minute sooner!"

If I had been dejected before, now I was truly wretched. I burst into tears. For the next half-hour, my tears flowed steadily. My mother, disgusted, closed her eyes and promptly fell asleep, and my brother soon followed suit.

With both of our relations now slumbering, Cassandra took my hand in hers and said very quietly, "There, there, Jane. Do not cry." Her expression told me that she understood all that was within my heart. "You will see him again some day."

"When? Years from now? Even if I do, it will not be the same." My voice caught as I wiped at my tears. "Time and distance are great separators. I would rather spend five minutes with him than a lifetime with any other young man I have ever met— yet we cannot even correspond. It is so unfair!"

"I agree." Cassandra's eyes grew misty, and I guessed she was thinking of Tom Fowle, with whom she no doubt would have also liked to correspond.

"I love him, Cassandra."

"I know you do. But Jane: consider. Apart from Edward Taylor's wealth and property, which puts him in a different class—"

"Such issues hold no weight with him!" replied I stubbornly. "He told me so himself."

"Even if that is true, you are both very young. He is the first young man for whom you have had such feelings. It does not mean he is right for you, or the man with whom you are meant to spend the rest of your life."

"Tom Fowle is the first young man with whom *you* fell in love, and you are determined to marry *him!*"

"Yes; but that is different. I have known Tom Fowle for many years, since I was but a girl. You and Edward Taylor only met a few weeks past. Your relationship is still very new. It takes time to determine if you are truly suited to each other—and Jane, you two are different in so many ways."

"We are the *same* in so many ways! We share sympathies and a multitude of interests. We hold a great many ideals in common. I admire him, and I think he feels the same way about me."

"All that is important, I agree; but true love is, I believe, based on more than that. You must respect each other as well, and both be *worthy* of that respect. Jane: there is hardly an obligation stronger than the exercise of self-control, yet Edward Taylor tends to be careless of the comfort of others. We saw this on numerous occasions."

"He apologised to me for his reckless behaviour."

"Yet he remains essentially unchanged. I fear that Edward Taylor will always be jumping over fires, Jane."

We reached Steventon without incident. I was overjoyed to see my father, whom I had missed very much, and although my heart ached for Edward Taylor, I could not deny that it was good to be home again, in the comfort of my own familiar surroundings.

A letter soon arrived from Sophia.

Camden-Place, Bath
3 July, 1791

Dearest Jane,

We have been at Bath nearly a week now, and I could not wait a moment longer to share with you some very good news. On Midsummer's Day, some hours after you left, Mr. Cage and Mr. Deedes both came to us at Goodnestone. It was just as you predicted, Jane—the rose petals were a resounding success! (Of course I know that you had a hand in the arrangements, and I thank you with all my heart; yet it is still enchanting to think that the legend might be true.)

Fanny is engaged once more to Mr. Cage, and I declare, they are happier now, and more in love, than I have ever yet seen them. As for me—oh Jane! Mr. Deedes was so attentive to me that day! We were both dismayed by the fact that I was leaving the very next morning for Bath; but he promised, before he went with the Knights and your brother to the Scottish Highlands, that he should visit us in this city. He made good on that promise, and we have passed the most delightful time in each other's company. Yesterday, he proposed! He loves me, Jane, and asked me to be his wife! Of course, I said yes. I am so happy I feel as if my heart might burst.

We think to be married in December, at the same time as my sisters. Who would have thought that three of the Bridges sisters should fall in love and become engaged at the very same time? It is too wonderful to believe! As you can imagine, my mother is beside herself with joy.

Mr. Deedes admitted that he might never have had the courage to reveal his feelings for me, had not you gone to see him at Canterbury. Who can say how things might have turned out, had you never come to Kent this summer? I shall be forever grateful that you did! I send love and thanks from Fanny as well, and Marianne asks me to extend her best wishes. Please give my best love to your mother, Cassandra, and Charles.

Yours affectionately,
Sophia Bridges

"Well, Jane," said my mother after I read her the missive, "it seems that in spite of your scheming interference this summer, everything has turned out all right."

Not everything, thought I. I was happy indeed to learn that I had done no lasting harm where Fanny's and Sophia's futures were concerned, but my own romantic hopes had not ended as auspiciously. I thought of Edward Taylor often and with deep longing. Was it he who had appeared on the road that morning? Did he ever think of me? When I wrote to Sophia, I was too proud and embarrassed to inquire about him.

The second week of July found us saying good-bye to Charles, who left for Portsmouth to enter the Naval Academy. I was very sad to see him go, but Charles was excited. "I am a true navy man," insisted he, "and very fit to be a sailor. Edward Taylor told me so!"

In September, we learned that Sir Brook Bridges had taken ill with a fever and suddenly died. We mourned his loss, and knew his family would miss him dearly.

"How awful!" cried Cassandra upon hearing the news. "He was such a good man."

"I liked him very much," agreed I, "and grieve to think that he did not live to see his daughters married."

"At least he lived to see them *engaged,*" said my mother with a heavy sigh, "which I believe made him very happy; and his last summer on earth was a very full and eventful one. How his widow shall get on without him, I cannot imagine—with so many children yet at home! But at least *they* may remain in their own house. *They* will not be booted out, as *we* will from this rectory, should anything happen to your father."

December came, and with it three weddings: Fanny Bridges married Mr. Lewis Cage on 14 December, and two weeks later, on 27 December, Elizabeth and my brother Edward were married in a double wedding ceremony with Sophia and Mr. William Deedes. I rejoiced at the news, and was only sorry that I could not attend the celebrations.

December also brought another mile-stone: my sixteenth birthday. I was happy to achieve this age, which put me ever closer to womanhood, and one year closer to coming out. Curiously, however, I did not find the restrictions which my mother had imposed on me to be as oppressive as anticipated.

"I am sorry you cannot come with me," said Cassandra one wintry evening, as I helped her dress for the assembly at Basingstoke. "I know how much you love a ball."

"I have no wish to dance with anyone other than Edward Taylor," admitted I, "and as he cannot be there, I had rather not dance at all."

"This is a new attitude," remarked she in surprise.

I shrugged as I buttoned up the back of her gown. "I enjoyed a taste of the future last summer, Cassandra. For several weeks, I experienced what it will be like to be out in society—but although it was exhilarating, it opened me up to making a great many blunders. Another year before coming out, I think, will be a very good thing."

Chapter the Thirty-third

Three years passed.
Edward Taylor's predictions of war proved true. The revolutionary government of France executed Louis XVI and his queen, revolts and invasions took place across Europe, and the French and British fleets clashed at sea.

On a happier note, in those three years, I was delighted to become an aunt, for my brother Edward and Elizabeth welcomed two children, a daughter Fanny and a son (of course) called Edward. My brother Henry took a lieutenant's commission in the Oxfordshire Militia; Frank, restless for advancement, continued aboard the sloop HMS *Lark* in home waters; and Charles was soon to leave the Naval Academy to take his first commission as a midshipman aboard HMS *Daedalus*.

Cassandra had recently become engaged to the Reverend Tom Fowle, and they both eagerly awaited the day when he would be settled with a living sufficient to support them.

During those three years, I never stopped thinking, dreaming, and wondering about Edward Taylor. I lamented that I had never heard him play the violin. I kept replaying our many conversations in my mind, filled with longing and regret over the way we had parted. I heard about him now and again: Sophia mentioned in a letter that his family had returned from abroad and now resided at Bifrons, and Elizabeth later wrote that he had gone off to Oxford. But all that time, I had no way to obtain the information I yearned for—the inner workings of his mind and heart.

At last, the silence was broken: for in the summer of 1794, Cassandra and I were so fortunate as to return to Kent to see my brother and Elizabeth at Rowling—the first time we had returned to that country since our initial visit. I was thrilled to discover that Edward Taylor was home from Oxford for the summer and residing at Bifrons.

One warm summer evening, we were invited to dine at Bifrons along with a few other neighbours. The night before I barely slept, counting the minutes until our dinner engagement. I knew his father and sisters would be there as well, and greatly looked forward to meeting them.

I approached our meeting with a fluttering heart. After so many years apart, I was filled with excitement at the idea of seeing him again at last. Would it feel strange, I wondered, to be in his company again? Was he looking forward to my visit? Had he ever thought of me?

When I entered the drawing-room, my pulse was pounding. I was at first distracted by the spectacle of three lovely young ladies who were all elegantly dressed, and bore a resemblance to the young gentleman I knew: clearly they were the sisters about whom I had heard him speak. Then I saw Edward Taylor across the room. After all these years of thinking and dreaming about him, I could hardly believe I was once again standing in the same room as he!

He was twenty years old. He had filled out a bit in form and face, and looked taller than I remembered, but he was every bit as handsome. His dark eyes lit up when he caught sight of me; immediately he came forward and bowed.

"Hello, Miss Jane."

"Mr. Taylor."

His expression approved my looks and told me how glad he was to see me; at the same time, there was something about him which seemed changed, as if the intervening years had worn him down a little.

He introduced me to his father, a serious, intelligent, well-spoken man, and his sisters Charlotte, Mary-Elizabeth, and Margaret, who ranged in age from sixteen to thirteen, and were just as charming as promised. The young ladies, not at all shy, immediately engrossed me in conversation; as they were all intelligent and accomplished, this discourse occupied me for some little time. All the while, I kept glancing at Edward Taylor, who was conversing with another group, as I waited for an opening to speak to him.

At last I caught his eye; he excused himself

from his party and crossed towards me; I broke away at the same time, and we met in the centre of the room. I felt a bit self-conscious, and sensed that he did, too.

"How have you been?" said he.

"I am well. And you?"

"The same." He smiled. "You have grown taller I think."

"So have you."

"I believe I grew three inches after the summer we met. That was quite a time we had, was it not—that month of endless festivities? I often think of it."

"Do you?" I could scarcely breathe.

"Who could forget that momentous evening when you walked the wall in the Bridgeses' garden? I knew, then, that you were a most uncommon young lady. And the ball where we debated the merits of powdered hair, and scandalously danced together more often than we ought? That lives on in my memory as one of the most pleasant nights of my life."

"Mine too." To know that he remembered it all, as vividly, and with as much pleasure, as did I! It was too wonderful to believe.

"Have you participated in any more home theatricals?"

"Lamentably, I have not. Our production of *A Midsummer Night's Dream* remains the pinnacle of my dramatic achievement."

"It was mine as well. I believe I shall never forget it." He paused, as if trying to determine the best way to approach another subject, and then finally said, "There is something which I have long wished to tell you. I received the note you sent me on your last day at Goodnestone."

"You did? Oh!" I could not go on.

"Unfortunately, it was lost for a crucial period. Sophia gave me the note in the midst of my birthday celebration, and explained to me the reason for your early departure. I had no opportunity to look at the note until after everyone had gone home, and by then it was nowhere to be found. I did not locate it until the next night. Imagine my chagrin when I read what you had written, and presumed you to be waiting for me all that time! I rose at dawn and rode like the wind, but I arrived too late—I saw your coach and four pulling away, and even if I could have overtaken it, I knew it was not the seemly thing to do."

"So it *was* you I saw from the coach window! I was never certain."

"I was very sorry to have missed you."

"I cried for days." After all the years of wondering, it was somehow a relief, and very flattering, to know that he had tried.

"I regretted that we could not correspond. Whoever decided that men and women of no relation may not write to each other ought to be shot."

We both laughed. Any trace of self-consciousness had evaporated. I could not help asking: "Speaking of relations: how does your cousin Charlotte?"

"She is well."

"She was quite enamoured of you at the time."

He coloured slightly. "I think her parents intend her for me. She is a lovely young lady, but although my father insists it is a promising match, I have no thoughts of marriage at present, nor at any time in the near future." The brief, conscious look he gave me seemed to indicate that he recalled the conversation *we* had shared on that topic the last time we spoke. He quickly changed the subject. "I wish my whole family could have been here to greet you to-night, but all of my brothers are elsewhere."

"All? Where are they?"

"Bridges is still at sea. Brook and William now serve in the Foreign Office, and Herbert—he is the next eldest, after me—is a lieutenant in the 2nd Dragoon Guards."

I paused, suspecting what he must be feeling. "Your father changed his mind, then, with regard to his anxieties concerning Herbert's military employment?"

"It took a great deal of persuasion from Lord Grenville to bring it about, but at last, very reluctantly, my father relented—at least where

Herbert is concerned. *I* am still consigned to Oxford."

The manner in which he uttered the university's name suggested his antipathy for the place. Hoping I had misread him, I said: "How do you like it there?"

"I feel stifled and restless."

"I am sorry to hear it. I was hoping that the university life would grow on you."

"Not at all. I have nothing in common with the other students. The masters are good enough in their way, but even if there were no war, I prefer to learn through private reading and study. Herbert saw action last spring in France and Belgium, while I am bound to a schoolroom."

"You still wish to join the army, then?"

"More than ever—but my father will not discuss it. My only hope is that Herbert, in his new position, can convince someone of influence to offer me a post and help to champion my cause."

"What about Bifrons?"

"What about it?" He shrugged. "It is my father's house. I do not want it."

I glanced about me at the beauty and splendour of the mansion house in which we stood, saddened to think that his feelings for the place had not changed over the years. I admired his wish to serve in the military, and had only the highest respect for those who did, for it was a very noble profession; but at the same time, I thought it most unfortunate that the heir to Bifrons, upon whom all his sisters might one day depend—the keeper of a property which had been in his family for generations and was the birthright of his descendants—despised the life it represented—the life *I* loved—and his only thought was to get away.

"Well; since you wish it so dearly, Mr. Taylor, I hope that you are successful."

"Thank you. Which reminds me of a wish of your own. Have you done any more writing?"

"I have. I continue to read like a madwoman, and over the past few years I have written several works of a greater length than any I attempted before."

"Wonderful! I hope you are happy with them?"

"I doubt that any would merit a second look, but it is as you predicted: I am learning by doing, and I believe each effort is an improvement over the last."

"You can hope to do no better."

We shared a smile.

Our conversation continued over dinner, and I basked in the glow of admiration which still existed in his beautiful dark eyes, still feeling all the same regard and affection which *I* had harboured for *him* over the years—but at the same time, something real and true began to dawn on me, which I had never before allowed myself to acknowledge:

As much as Edward Taylor and I had in common, we were interested in different things. It seemed likely that he would, indeed, always be jumping over fires. He was a remarkable young man. I loved him—perhaps would always love him—but as Cassandra had said, we were not—never really had been—*right* for each other. This recognition gave rise to threatening tears, which I struggled with difficulty throughout the rest of that evening to contain. Any future connection between us had been no more than a lovely dream. I understood now that our romance was a sweet, first love that was never meant to be.

I saw Edward Taylor a few times more during that visit to Kent. We engaged in several interesting conversations, indulged in fond memories, and enjoyed each other's company. On the eve of my departure, we affectionately wished each other well and parted as friends.

As I write these final lines, I am sitting at my desk by the front window at 4 Sydney Place, overlooking the gardens just beyond. I am more than a dozen years older than I was when the preponderance of this narrative took place, yet my memories remain as vibrant as if I were still fifteen, and my feelings as deep and poignant.

Edward Taylor did achieve his dream, if only briefly: he left Oxford in 1795 to join the army and served with distinction for three years, employed in Ireland as aide-de-camp to Marquis Cornwallis in 1798. The Reverend Edward Taylor died at Bifrons on 8 December of that same year, and his son and heir, at age four-and-twenty, succeeded to the estate and was obliged to give up his military aspirations.

I heard that Edward Taylor is married now. I hope he is happy. Sadly, we have fallen out of touch, as my visits to Kent of late have only taken me as far as Godmersham, where my brother Edward and his family have long since resided. I like to think that Edward Taylor has, or will in time, overcome his reservations with regard to his inheritance; I believe that a man of his intelligence and accomplishments must surely learn to appreciate all that he has been given, that he will embrace his responsibilities, and do his family proud.

I have, as of yet, formed no other lasting romantic attachments; nor has Cassandra, who swore to never love again after Tom died. If one of my mother's and father's hopes in leaving Steventon and removing to Bath was that we should find husbands, they must be very disappointed. Nevertheless, I count myself fortunate, for I enjoy a loving connection with a sister who is the sun of my life, and the keeper of my every thought, hope, joy, and sorrow; I have a large and happy family, and enough nieces and nephews to occupy my time and fill my heart.

After three years in the white glare of this vaporous city, I dearly miss the country, and am desirous of a change. We think to take another tour of the Devon and Dorset coast this summer, and I look forward to it. I dream that one day we will settle in a comfortable house of our own, in the peace and quiet of the country-side that I love.

Cassandra once said of Edward Taylor, "I cannot help but feel that you behave very differently when in his company"—implying that I was not entirely myself when I was with him. I think now that this is true, but not in the negative way that she intended. I may not have been the *self* I was *formerly,* before I met him—but I think he encouraged a new side to my self that never existed before. He challenged me to try things which I might never otherwise have attempted, helped me to view the world a bit differently, and taught me the importance of thinking for and believing in myself.

Whenever I think of Edward Taylor, my heart aches a little. I am deeply grateful for the time we shared. I believe I am a stronger, more confident person for having known him. I learned so much that summer, from him as well as all the others: about the human mind and heart—about what motivates people to marry—about what really matters when two people are falling in love.

I learned one other valuable lesson as well.

As I told Cassandra, shortly after our return from Kent that memorable summer:

"I have done with match-making. Never again will I try to arrange the lives and romantic interests of real people; it is far too volatile and dangerous. From here on out, I shall restrict all such endeavours to the page."

"To the page?" repeated my sister.

I nodded. "Yes. I shall devote myself—as I have been doing of late—to merely *writing* stories about love and courtship. It is a far safer occupation."

Finis
July 1804

Author's Afterword

"We went by Bifrons and I contemplated with a melancholy pleasure the abode of Him, on whom I once fondly doated."

So wrote Jane Austen in a letter to her sister Cassandra in 1796. That tantalizing sentence has long intrigued me. Every Austen scholar concludes that Jane, as a young woman, was enamored of Edward Taylor, the heir to Bifrons, a grand manor house and estate in Kent—but the details of their relationship were never known. Who was Edward Taylor? What did he mean to Jane Austen? Did he return her affections? How did they meet?

Fascinated by the implications of this connection, I was determined to learn as much as I could about it. Unfortunately, Austen biographers presented very little information about Edward Taylor, simply repeating the same brief, generic reference: that Jane met him while visiting her brother Edward in Kent.

I began extensively researching Edward Taylor's life. Luckily, he was a member of the landed gentry, and later in life served as a Member of Parliament; as such, after much digging, I was able to uncover many facts about him, such as the details of his education, career, and marriage. I quickly discovered that many Austen biographers had gotten Edward Taylor's age wrong, citing him as being a year younger than Jane, when in fact he was a year and a half older.

From other sources, I found a great deal of information about the history of the Taylors' ancestral house, Bifrons. Further probing led to the incredible discovery of an obscure memoir written by Herbert Taylor, Edward Taylor's younger brother, which provided a wealth of knowledge about the family and their unusual and well-traveled childhood.

The more I learned about Edward Taylor, the more extraordinary he seemed to me; he was truly the sort of young man with whom Jane Austen would have fallen in love! That he was a real person, and that I had in my possession so many little-known facts about his life, was very exciting. A picture began to form in my mind as to how and when Edward Taylor and Jane Austen might have met as teenagers, and what their relationship might have been.

At the same time, I was intrigued by another Austen fact: in 1791, the year Jane's brother Edward Austen became engaged to Elizabeth Bridges of Goodnestone, Jane wrote a comedic short story, *The Three Sisters*, featuring characters named Fanny and Sophia. It seemed very likely to me that Jane visited Kent that summer, where she not only met the young ladies who inspired that story, but also met and became enamored of Edward Taylor—and that her experiences there greatly shaped her views forever after regarding love and marriage.

That is the story I chose to write: the tale of Jane Austen's first love, inspired by the facts of her life and his, presented as a memoir in Austen's own words. I endeavored, to the best of my ability, to be true to Austen's writing style. However, although I employed the British spellings of many words, I did not re-create Jane's charming idiosyncrasies with regard to capitalization or spelling (rarely did she follow the "i before e" rule!), believing that might distract from the narrative itself.

The locations in this narrative are all real, and their histories based on fact. Godmersham Park currently serves as an opticians college, and Goodnestone Park is prized for its beautiful gardens, which are open to visitors. Sadly, Bifrons was demolished in 1948.

The characters in this narrative are almost all real people, and their personal histories have been thoroughly researched. The only figments of my imagination are the servants and the Fieldings. I was obliged to make up the names of some of the younger Payler children, although they did have seven sons in addition to their daughter, Charlotte.

The story is inspired by actual events. Fanny

and Elizabeth Bridges did indeed announce their engagements in March 1791, and the three weddings took place as described that December. Mr. William Deedes really did travel to Bath to propose. The Thomas Watkinson-Paylers really did have their portraits painted by Sir Joshua Reynolds, and Mrs. Watkinson-Payler's is available to view online.

All the details of Edward Taylor's childhood, his many accomplishments, and his unusual upbringing in Europe, are true and derived from his brother Herbert's astonishingly candid memoir. Edward Taylor's father was against his sons entering the military and fought it for a long while, worried that their spirits might "lead them into dangers." Yet Herbert eventually distinguished himself in the military, rose to the rank of lieutenant general, and received a knighthood; and as Jane notes in this narrative, Edward Taylor did briefly achieve his dream of joining the army.

In November 1800, Jane wrote to Cassandra:

> I hope it is true that Edward Taylor is to marry his cousin Charlotte. Those beautiful dark Eyes will then adorn another Generation at least in all their purity.

In 1802 Edward Taylor *did* marry—not his cousin Charlotte, but Louisa Beckingham of Bourne House, Kent. They had eight children. He was the Member of Parliament for Canterbury from 1807 to 1812—but sadly, in 1830, he was obliged to sell Bifrons and emigrated with his family to the Continent.

Mr. Lewis Cage and Fanny had two daughters, whom they named Fanny and Sophia. Mr. William Deedes and Sophia had fifteen children (ten sons and five daughters). Edward Taylor apparently continued his friendship with the Deedes family for the rest of his life. Mr. Deedes's eldest son, William Deedes, Esquire of Sandling Park, Kent, married Edward Taylor's daughter Emily Octavia, on 30 May, 1833. Charlotte Payler married a Mr. William Egerton in 1804; she died a year later.

Jane and Cassandra remained good friends with the Bridgeses, each paying short visits to Lady Bridges at Goodnestone in 1805, and to Mr. and Mrs. William Deedes at their country house at Sandling. Marianne was considered an invalid all her life; she and her sister Louisa never married. Brook Edward Bridges (more generally known as Edward) became a clergyman, and Jane Austen refers to their friendship in her correspondence.

Mr. Thomas Knight died in October 1794, at which time Edward Austen succeeded to his estate and many properties in Hampshire and Kent. Mrs. Catherine Knight gracefully moved into the dower house, giving Godmersham Park to Edward and his growing family. Years later, due to a stipulation in Catherine Knight's will, Edward Austen changed his legal name to Knight. He and Elizabeth had eleven children; Elizabeth died not long after giving birth the last time, in October 1808. A few days later, Edward Austen offered his widowed mother and his sisters (who had been awkwardly shifting between homes for nearly four years since the death of Mr. George Austen) the choice of two of his properties in which to live free of charge; they chose Chawton Cottage. Jane Austen lived at Chawton in great contentment until her death, and there she wrote or rewrote all her famous novels, four of which were published anonymously during her lifetime. One of her most beloved novels, *Emma*, is about a willful and fallible young matchmaker.

Jane wrote a very abridged *History of England* in the autumn of 1791, and soon after dedicated her short story *The Three Sisters* to her brother Edward. In the original manuscript of *The Three Sisters*, Jane deliberately deleted the very passage to which Edward Taylor referred. These two works make up a very small part of her early writings, which include short plays, short stories, a poem, and several novelettes. Her juvenilia is exuberant and reflects, as early as age fourteen or fifteen, her familiarity with plot structure, thematic patterns, and other essential elements of fiction. Austen's juvenilia, which she copied out into three separate notebooks entitled Volume the

First, Volume the Second, and Volume the Third, were not published until the twentieth century.

My biggest embellishment of the truth in this novel is the imaginary meeting of all these people in this particular manner at Goodnestone in the summer of 1791. Was Edward Taylor actually sent home to England a year ahead of his family? Did Jane and her family truly travel to Kent that summer? Did the Bridges family host a month of parties? We do not know; but I like to believe that they did.

Syrie James

Acknowledgements

I am indebted to my dear friend Laurel Ann Nattress, who read an early version of the proposal for this book and said, "You simply *must* write this next!" She spent untold hours discussing every aspect of this novel with me during the creation, writing, and rewriting process, often in marathon phone conversations lasting until well past our bedtimes. Laurel Ann: you are a talented editor and literary advisor. (And your knowledge of and enthusiasm for All Things Austen is the icing on the cake!) Your unflagging interest, dedication, friendship, and support are invaluable to me.

Maria Stefanopolous of Ingenious Travel sent me and Laurel Ann on an unforgettable tour of Jane Austen's England, for which we are both extremely grateful. To the fourteen lovely and lively ladies who accompanied us on the adventure: thank you for signing up! It was a pleasure to travel with you, and your love of Jane continues to inspire me.

A big thank-you to Hugh Whittaker of Pathfinders Tours, who went out of his way to arrange a private house tour of Goodnestone Park for me. Thank you, Lady Fitzwalter, for your kind hospitality during our visit—it was a thrill to meet you, and to see your beautiful home and grounds in person. My deepest appreciation to Francis Plumtree for the personal tour of Goodnestone, both inside and out, for the images you sent me afterwards, and for all the questions you answered. I do hope you feel I did your home justice in its portrayal.

Thank you to Jackie Cantor, my editor, for your interest in this novel, for allowing me to write my vision of it, for your excellent notes, and for shepherding it into reality. Thanks to everyone on the team at Berkley who prepared this novel for publication. You always do such a great job! Thanks to my copyeditor, Bob Schwager, who went over this manuscript with a fine-toothed comb, seeking out every potential anachronism. Your attention to detail is much appreciated.

Thank you, Tamar Rydzinski, my wonderful agent, for the benefit of your advice and counsel, and for overseeing all business matters with such expertise and efficiency. You are one of the best people I know, and I admire you more than I can say.

Thanks to my son, Ryan, for his input on the final draft. And a huge thank-you to my husband, Bill, my best friend, my love, my financial manager, and my partner in everything, for helping in countless ways to make it possible for me to write this novel and to continue in this profession that I love so dearly. Every day I count my blessings for you.

Discussion Questions

1) What challenges does the author face by tackling such a well-known, and well-loved, literary figure? If you are a reader of Austen, how did this rendering of her early life reflect her own fiction?

2) In *Jane Austen's First Love*, we encounter a social sensibility that now appears very gendered and antiquated. What behavior did you observe in the character of Jane Austen that speaks to today's expectations for female independence and autonomy?

3) In what ways did Jane subvert expectations as a young unmarried woman? In what ways was she a typical, or even stereotypical, young woman of her time?

4) Jane and her companions perform Shakespeare's *A Midsummer Night's Dream* in one of the climactic scenes of the book. In what ways does the book resemble a play, and how do each of the characters perform their respective "roles"? Do we see tropes at play: the gallant knight, the wicked witch, et cetera?

5) Jane and Edward Taylor's courtship begins when Jane and her siblings' carriage is mired in mud. How does the physical act of Jane jumping off the carriage into Edward's arms hint at their future relationship? How do perilous physical situations propel their relationship forward?

6) When describing Elizabeth Bridges, Jane says, "That charm did not appear to reach great depths, however; for her soft voice appeared more to convey a discharge of a duty to *appear* welcoming, rather than a sincere reflection of the emotion." When are other characters "duty bound" to "appear" a certain way?

7) When Cassandra describes the Bridges family as all having "interesting" qualities, Jane says that "interesting" is a term "I reserve to describe people or things so dull or ordinary, that I can find no more promising attribution." When and how do we use euphemisms to obscure our true feelings?

8) Why do you think Fanny criticizes her fiancé to others, despite her affection for him? Do you think this episode might sway her to act differently?

9) The book deals with the relationship between art and artifice; for example, the play provided Jane with a guise: her trick of manipulating the two couples. How do art and artifice differ, and where do they intersect?

10) Edward Taylor remarks to Jane that in other cultures, there are different expressions of beauty: from feet binding to lip piercings. What cultural practices of beauty are present in this historical novel, and how do they factor into the plot?

11) Ultimately, Jane realizes that she is not in love with Edward Taylor as an adult, but he has helped her discover a part of herself. How is finding this other facet of self even more rewarding than her finding a romantic partner? Was it rewarding or disappointing as a reader?

12) How does the comedic confusion of the crossed lovers reflect the plays of Shakespeare and *A Midsummer Night's Dream* in particular? How does Shakespeare reflect the frustrations of romantic love?

13) Did your first love change you—for better or worse? How are past relationships of value

to our character despite their limited romantic success?

14) Jane is smitten with Edward Taylor at their first meeting. What makes him special in her eyes? In what ways are Edward Taylor and Jane similar and different?

15) Jane Austen is known for writing strong female characters: Emma, Elizabeth Bennett. How do those heroines reflect the values and traits of the character Jane as depicted in this novel?

Center Point Large Print
600 Brooks Road / PO Box 1
Thorndike, ME 04986-0001 USA

(207) 568-3717

US & Canada:
1 800 929-9108
www.centerpointlargeprint.com